The City of Lies

Also by Michael Russell

The City in Darkness

The City of Strangers

The City of Shadows

The City of Lies

A Stefan Gillespie Novel

Michael Russell

CONSTABLE • LONDON

CONSTABLE

First published in 2017 by Constable

1 3 5 7 9 10 8 6 4 2

A CIP catalogue record for this book is available from the British Library.

Hardback ISBN: 978-1-47212-196-7
Trade Paperback ISBN 978-1-47212-195-0

Typeset in Dante by SX Composing DTP, Rayleigh Essex
Printed and bound in Great Britain by Clays Ltd, St Ives plc

Papers used by Constable are from well-managed forests and other responsible sources.

Constable
An imprint of
Little, Brown Book Group
Carmelite House
50 Victoria Embankment
London EC4Y 0DZ

An Hachette UK Company
www.hachette.co.uk

www.littlebrown.co.uk

Jabu and Sediba

ex Africa semper aliquid novi

Nicht in alten Bahnen
ist Gott.
Du kannst ihn ahnen,
wo die Fahnen
des Glaubens wehn: am Schafott.

You won't find God today
in the old way.
But you'll feel him close by
when our flags of faith fly,
and the scaffolds are high.

'Am 9. November vor der Feldhernnhalle zu München'
Baldur von Schirach

Part One

The Book Of Evidence

There have been no further developments of importance in connection with the Dunlavin murder case. The murdered persons were three members of a family, two brothers and a sister, and their domestic servant, at La Mancha, a house in Gormanstown, Co. Kildare. A squad of the Civic Guard from Naas and a number of detectives from the Detective Division in Dublin have been engaged for several days in making an exhaustive search of the grounds of La Mancha. Every hedge and ditch on the land was closely scrutinised. The garden at the rear of the house and portions of the surrounding lands were dug up to a depth of a couple of feet. It is understood that the search was made with the twofold object of discovering any instruments that were used in the murders and property which, it is thought, may have been taken from the house.

Irish Times

1
Dunlavin

West Wicklow, September 1940

The town of Dunlavin sits at the edge of the great, flat pan of fields and fens that makes up a large part of the middle of Ireland. To the west its hinterland stretches into the rolling pasture of the Curragh of Kildare, but to the east it is still in the shadow of the Wicklow Mountains. Their nearest outlier, Church Mountain, where St Palladius, St Patrick's less successful predecessor, established a long-forgotten church, is only a few miles away, with the Glen of Imaal and the wildness of the high hills rising beyond. Like most of the towns of West Wicklow there is little that is remarkable about Dunlavin, except for its unexpectedly wide main street and the elegant Doric columns of its miniature courthouse. It was an estate town, created and laid out around the turn of the eighteenth century to reflect an image of order that never really existed in Ireland and was contradicted everywhere – here by the dark line of mountains that looked down in the east. Dunlavin's only claim to fame, and its place in Ireland's history, was short and brutal.

At the eastern end of the main street, by the road that eventually leads up into the mountains, is the fair green, where Dunlavin's livestock markets and fairs were held. It was to that green, as the rebellion of the United Irishmen broke out in

1798, that Captain Morley Saunders rode from Baltinglass to hold a parade of West Wicklow's yeomanry. In an atmosphere of confusion and panic, he accused some of his men of supporting the rebels, claiming that he already knew who they were. He didn't, though the political and religious affiliations of the militia men, Catholic and Protestant alike, could hardly have been any secret in such a small community. Whatever information Saunders did have was coloured, inevitably, by petty spite and local bad blood. But when a surprising number of men stepped forward to confess, the sense of panic and confusion only increased. The men were imprisoned overnight in that Doric-columned courthouse, assuming that little more than a flogging awaited them.

The next day Captain Saunders ordered that all the prisoners be executed. Thirty-six men were marched back to Dunlavin Green and shot in batches, by their neighbours, their friends, even by their relations; several more were hanged. Saunders' motives were partly fear over unfounded rumours of a rebel advance on the town, partly panic over the size of the 'enemy within', partly a reckless reprisal for deaths in fighting elsewhere. He may have felt the brutality would close off rebel sympathy. Maybe – probably – he did it because he could.

On a clear September evening in 1940, a short, dark man in his forties, wiry and tanned, wheeling a bicycle, walked along Sparrow Road towards Dunlavin Green, past the Catholic church of St Nicholas of Myra. The sky was clear. There were martins flying overhead, feeding. It was bright and warm still. He could feel the sun on his skin and that troubled him. The bodies had started to stink. The smell had been in his nostrils in the house at Gormanstown that morning. If he had got the smell out of his nose, he had not got it out of his head. And it would be worse now, after another long and hot day. He had to act.

He was shaking slightly, leaning on the bicycle to steady himself. He was sweating, too, but it wasn't the sun; it wasn't even the whiskey and the stout at Mattie Farrell's. He slowed as he passed the church gates. The Angelus bell had started sounding. He halted and crossed himself, mouthing the Hail Mary. He stopped after 'Holy Mary, Mother of God, pray for us sinners'; the words 'now and at the hour of our death' wouldn't come. The dead were too much on his mind to let those words out. They were not the long-dead who lay somewhere under his feet, buried in a pit after the massacre of 1798, or even Mattie Farrell's mother, in a coffin on the kitchen table in the house he had just left. They were the four bodies that had lain for three days in the house that was called La Mancha.

He hadn't wanted to go to Bridie Farrell's wake, but he'd had no choice. Not to go would have looked odd. Mattie was a friend. People would have wondered, even his wife and his children would have asked why. He had to behave as if nothing was wrong. That was the only way. It was why he was off now, to check the horses. That was what he did. That's where he told them he was going. But it was all more time wasted. He had stayed at the wake longer than he meant to, of course. He had drunk more than he meant to, of course. Jesus, no one could blame him for that. Why had he left it so long? Yet that wasn't the question. Why had he done it? For nothing, for sweet fuck all!

As the man walked on across the green to the wide main street, with its shops and pubs and houses, stretching busily down towards the Church of Ireland church at the far end, he could see people. They were enjoying the evening sun, walking, talking, laughing – all the ordinary things his head had no room for. There were people heading towards him too, friends on their way to Bridie Farrell's wake. He would have to stop; he would have to speak, all the long length of Stephen Street. They couldn't know anything; none of them could. But the sense that they would pick up something, would even see inside him, had grown stronger with the whiskey he had drunk. Alcohol had seen him through the wake, but he couldn't face any more. Unsteady as he was, he climbed on to the bicycle and started to ride. He wouldn't have to stop; he wouldn't have to talk. He was picking up speed coming into the town. His head was down. He barely missed Noel Fisher; he didn't even hear him, roaring, laughing.

'Did you give Bridie a good send-off, Henry, you drunken bastard!'

Henry Casey cycled on, faster and faster, his eyes fixed ahead, wanting to empty his mind. Only as he turned right to face the domed courthouse and the flat-fronted Garda barracks just beyond it, did he slow down. The proximity of the two buildings was unavoidable, pushing away the chaos in his mind to tell him what he should have done. He should have gone to the Guards straight away. He had known it all along, from the beginning. The feeling that he could undo what had happened swept over him again, so strongly he almost believed it, in the way, as a child, he had woken in the night, for weeks after his mother's death, still believing that something could undo it all and return her to him.

He turned on to the Kilcullen Road, past the station, out into the high-hedged countryside. He rode slowly. It was a journey he didn't want to complete. He was sober now, very suddenly. That didn't make it any easier.

For the rest of the way he saw no one, and within ten minutes he had reached the gates of the avenue that led to La Mancha. He stopped. The long, straight drive, lined with old beeches, framed the white house that lay at the end. There were rooks overhead, flying to the trees to roost. Their cawing was the only sound. He got off the bicycle and walked. It was another delay; a few more minutes to hold on to. To either side of the drive, behind the beeches, neat post-and-rail fencing skirted the track. It was less than a fortnight since he had creosoted those fences. He could smell the tar in the air, still fresh enough for the heat of the sun to draw it from the wood. He looked to his right, hearing the rumble of hooves. Three horses were running across the field. They were old friends. The chestnut gelding, the silver mare, the black filly with the white star on her forehead. They were racehorses. Not much in the way of these things. There were better at any number of stables around the Curragh. But they had hopes for the black filly. It felt like she was something special. She wouldn't be, of course. They never were at La Mancha. But they were beautiful. He had never stopped thinking that; he thought it even now as they halted, whinnying, then followed him as he continued along the drive. He could see the grass was thin, patched with brown. He should have moved the horses to the new grass by now.

Suddenly there was another sound. A car. He couldn't see it but it was a car by the house. The engine had just started. Someone was poking around. He stood still. His heart was pounding; his stomach churning. He tasted bile in his throat. He turned and pushed the bicycle between the beeches, flung himself and his bicycle down in a shallow dip. The noise of the engine and the tyres on the stones of the drive grew closer. He flattened himself. The car passed. He didn't look up until there was no sound. Then, as he inched himself up, he could see the car in the gateway, where the drive met the road. He knew it. The Jaguar Roadster wasn't an easy car to forget. The white, sleek body, long and low; the black wheel arches. It was the Welshman. Henry Casey couldn't remember his name. He was not a regular visitor to La Mancha. He had been there only three or four times that Casey knew, on his way to Punchestown or the Curragh for race meetings. But he had been there the previous week. There was no knowing what he had seen now. The doors of the house were locked, the curtains were closed. There was no indication anyone was in. But people would come. Henry Casey had to act. He was out of time. He had been since it started.

He did not go straight to the house. He walked to the back of the bright, white, two-storey building, full of windows, and into the stable yard. There was only one horse in the boxes now. The smell of rotting flesh was strong as he passed a box. La Mancha was an old horse. He had been the last good horse at the stables, but that was a long time ago. He had been out to grass for almost ten years. He was frail; he was coming to the end of his life; but he was still a pampered favourite in the yard. Now he was dead, lying in the straw in his box with part of his head blown away by a 20-bore shotgun. It had taken two shots. Casey could hear a faint, regular hum, even through the heavy doors. Flies.

He opened the door to the barn. The two cans of petrol were just inside, where he had left them. He had been mad not to do it sooner. He picked them up and walked quickly back towards the house. He unlocked the back door and went in, following the dark corridor to the kitchen. The smell was there again, stronger. Not rotten yet, not stinking like the horse, just in the air, still sweet and sickly. There were half a dozen flies crawling over Alice's face, where the blood was black and dry. They flew up angrily as he approached. He stood, fighting the gagging in his throat. He took the first can and opened it. He poured petrol over her and out on to the rug she lay on. He splashed it over the chairs and the table, and dribbled it across the floor. He breathed in the fumes that drove away the smell of death. He walked out into the back hall, carrying the jerrycans through to the stairs. He trailed the petrol up the stair carpet behind him and soaked the curtains at the half-landing. Then he carried on to the bedrooms.

He went into three bedrooms, one after another. In each there was a dead body. The smell was there, of course, but now all he had in his nose was petrol. Annie lay on her bed in her nightgown. He drained the first can over her and the bedclothes. In the next room the body of Patrick lay under the blankets, his head high on the pillows. He opened the second can and poured out more petrol, splashing it along the floor to the landing. In the third bedroom the body of Simon lay with his face staring up, blank and calm. His eyes were open. It was hard not to look at. He drained the contents of the second can.

He took the empty cans to the top of the stairs, then went back. He took out a box of matches. He struck one a little way from Simon's bed. He threw it at the body. It went out. He struck another, trembling, and it fell on the floor. He had to move closer. He struck a third match and let it drop. Petrol fumes were in the air now and a sheet of flame shot up. He turned and ran, quickly setting fires in the other two bedrooms. And the fire was taking. As he ran downstairs with the empty cans, the landing carpet was burning. It soon spread to the stairs. When he reached the kitchen he struck a match and dropped it on Alice's body. Nothing happened. He tried again. Nothing happened. And the matches were gone. He needed more petrol, more matches. It would have to do. He walked back to the hall. The staircase was burning. The fire would soon reach the kitchen. When it did she would burn, as they all would. It would do.

Several minutes later he stood at the front of the house, holding his bicycle. Black smoke was rising from the back, and two of the upstairs windows were full of flame where the curtains had burnt away. There was a crack like a small explosion, as the glass in one of the windows burst, and smoke and flame poured out. He had done all he could. Surely it would be enough. He turned away and rode slowly up the drive, away from La Mancha. He didn't look back. As he pedalled faster, heading towards the gate, he saw the three horses trotting beside the post-and-rail fence, keeping pace with him; the chestnut gelding, the silver mare, the black filly.

2

Jasna Góra

Częstochowa, Poland, September 1939

They say an icon is a window, not only a window through which we look into heaven, but a window through which heaven looks at us. Johannes Rilling knelt before the wrought-iron gate that separated the chancel of the Chapel of the Virgin, in the monastery of Jasna Góra, looking at the altar and the dark face of the Black Madonna, Our Lady of Częstochowa. He saw less than he would have liked. The Virgin's eyes looked at him from the red and black and gold of the jewelled picture, as people said they did, but her gaze didn't so much penetrate as pass through him. The eyes of the infant Jesus she cradled in her left arm did not meet his; they were turned away, and though the child's right arm was raised in a blessing, he seemed to look somewhere else, not at Rilling at all.

Hauptmann Rilling had not come in search of benediction. The three days of blitzkrieg that had carried him across Poland with the German Army made that seem presumptuous at best. There might be a time for it when he had finished the job. It was the job he did, a soldier's job; blood and destruction was its nature. He made no apology for that, even here. If it had to be done, it was better that it was done fast, and it certainly had been; that was the most he could offer. Yet he was still in the

Chapel of the Divine Image, on his knees, because he could not pass through the city of Częstochowa and not come. There were other German soldiers in the chapel as he knelt, mostly officers. They stood in line behind him, as he had stood behind others, awkward, slightly shamefaced, silent, not only because it was right to be silent in the presence of the icon, but because they had nothing to say to each other. They knew that what they were doing was very close, for a moment, to opening up the box where they had put away all the things that didn't necessarily sit comfortably with the Germany they served, or with the very personal oath every soldier had taken to its leader.

The prayer Johannes Rilling was trying to pray didn't form easily out of the things that filled his mind, even though he felt no need to question himself. But he did realise that he was looking for a place where a prayer of some kind might be heard. The words wouldn't come. He was conscious of the black of the Virgin's robe and the red of Christ's; the colours of war. He heard soldiers shuffling behind him. With his own prayer still unspoken he muttered a curt Hail Mary and crossed himself. There was no window; there was only a mirror.

Walking out of the chapel, he stopped at a table by the door. On it lay a variety of guns: revolvers, pistols, rifles. The Field Police officer by the table nodded as Hauptmann Rilling picked up his pistol and holster. Rilling walked away, looking up at the wall ahead of him, filled with the votive offerings of centuries of pilgrims. Prominent among them were the crutches and staffs and even the ancient, crumbling bandages of those who believed they had left the chapel whole, when they had entered it broken. He had nothing to leave. The organ had started playing. He looked up, listening as he strapped on the holster. It was Bach. He knew he recognised it, but he couldn't quite place the piece.

'Lord, from my heart I hold you dear.'

He turned. The speaker was a young SS Untersturmführer.

'Of course it is,' said the captain. 'Thank you.'

'Bach's a good choice today. I think they get the message.'

'I'm sure they do,' replied Johannes Rilling.

He walked on out of the chapel, into the courtyard. He could still hear the organ. The SS officer knew his music; he probably didn't know the place that hymn was most often heard was at a funeral. Rilling stopped to light a cigarette.

There were two more SS men outside the chapel. They nodded politely, but they were there to take note of who went in, rank and regiment, at least as far as the officers were concerned. There was nothing to stop a German soldier coming into the monastery – officially, at any rate – either to go to Mass or to look at the portrait of the Black Madonna. The clergy of Jasna Góra pursued their daily course despite what was happening beyond the walls, but the monastery was secured and guarded. For now, the people of Częstochowa were not allowed through the gates. The presence of the Holy Spirit was no threat to anyone, of course, but the spirit of Poland was here, however pale the light; that needed watching. Meanwhile, lists of soldiers who cared to make the pilgrimage to Jasna Góra would find their way to Berlin and the Reich Main Security Office. You had to be very keen on getting on your knees to put your name on those lists, or very bloody-minded. Either way, you were worth watching.

The small town of Żarki lay amongst woods and fields off the road to Kraków, to the south-east of Częstochowa. The town, like Częstochowa itself, had seen little fighting. Within two days of the German invasion the Polish Army of Kraków, like the rest of the Polish forces, was retreating to regroup in the east. A troop of cavalry and an infantry company had passed through the town without stopping. The bodies of some twenty men and a dozen horses lay unburied at the sides of the dirt road where two screeching Stukas had picked them off. Some of the town's citizens, mostly women and children, had been killed when the Stukas moved on to Żarki itself to make their point more clearly. The area was secure, with no evidence of partisan activity, when Hauptmann Rilling and his infantry company arrived. So it was with some surprise that the captain saw smoke rising from the town as his driver emerged from the woods to the north, to negotiate the potholes and the dead horses. He could hear the crack of rifle and pistol fire, too, sporadic and intermittent.

'What the fuck's going on now?'

The driver put his foot down as they moved through the outskirts of the town towards the market square. Rilling took out his pistol. The soldier who sat next to the driver pushed back the bolt on his rifle. There was the sound of gunfire again, and loud voices. It sounded like they were shouting, cheering.

The square was little more than a blunted triangle of beaten earth. The buildings that surrounded it on three sides were mostly single storey, with crumbling plaster and rough thatching. The tower of the church at one end was the only high building. Rilling had already passed Żarki's other substantial building, the synagogue in Moniuski Street; that was what was on fire. The noise in the square came from Hauptmann Rilling's soldiers. They stood in a great ring, shouting, laughing, jeering. Inside the circle something like a hundred people were running, round and round, all with their hands clasped behind their heads. As the captain's car stopped, he knew who they were. Mostly men and boys, with some old men, they were all Jews. Some had beards and sidelocks and wore black, Orthodox clothes; others were indistinguishable from their Catholic neighbours. And their neighbours were there too, standing outside the circle of soldiers, gazing on in silent fear, and crossing themselves.

Rilling's men were too preoccupied to notice him. As he got out of the car he was conscious, oddly, how young they all were, of their light hair and their bright, rosy faces, cheering and shouting as if they were at a football match. Their faces were contorted with a mixture of hatred and uncontrollable hilarity. They were excited; they were having the time of their lives. He saw his men step forward, as Jews fell behind, beating the offenders with pistols or rifle butts. They kicked the ones who stumbled and fell. They fired into the air, screaming for them all to run faster. The faces of the Jews were filled with pain and terror. Hauptmann Rilling pushed his way through the ring of soldiers. He raised his pistol and fired four times.

'Stop this! Now!'

His presence silenced the soldiers. The only noise in the market square was the sound of the feet of the Jews, still running, slowing down now. But some did not slow. They kept running as fast as they could, their hands still behind their heads, until one of the old men ran straight into Johannes Rilling and collapsed at his feet. The captain looked down. He put his pistol away.

'You can stop,' he said quietly. Then he looked up and shouted. 'You can stop running! Go back to your homes! Clear the square! Now!'

The Jews in the centre of the ring of soldiers were breathless, fearful, but they started to go, helping each other up, passing nervously through the stationary troops. The Poles who had watched were melting away too. Hauptmann Rilling turned in a slow circle, looking at his men. It was a look of cold anger. But he had seen enough in a few days in Poland; he had seen enough at home. He had no business being surprised. But he had order to keep.

'Form yourselves into ranks!'

The Hauptfeldwebel, the oldest man in the company, stepped forward and repeated the command.

'Form into ranks! Form into ranks!'

As if a switch had been pressed, the soldiers moved to the centre of the square and formed lines. The junior officers walked towards Rilling in a group.

'How the fuck did you let this happen, Company Sergeant Major?'

'It was not my command, sir.'

'Then whose was it?' The captain looked at his officers. 'Who started this?' He looked at his Oberleutnant. 'Weber?'

'It was just some fun with the Jews, sir.'

'And burning the fucking town?'

'It's only the synagogue,' said the Oberleutnant.

'Take the men and put it out, Sergeant, before it takes the town with it.'

The Hauptfeldwebel moved across to the lines of soldiers and was soon on his way to deal with the fire, glad to be out of range of his captain's anger.

'I asked you how it started. Who was giving the order?'

'The SS officer, sir.'

'Jesus, that's just what we need,' said Rilling. 'We're moving out tomorrow. The Poles have regrouped across the Vistula. Don't imagine they haven't got enough fight left to give you some fun too, gentlemen. Get on with it and get the men in a fit state to fight. You might want to remind them what they are: soldiers. You might want to remind yourselves at the same time.'

Hauptmann Rilling's officers walked away. Their expressions showed their mixed emotions. They were tight-lipped in the face of a reprimand, but there was resentment, too. Things had got out of control. They knew they should have kept order instead of getting drawn into it. At the same time their captain's fury was out of proportion. After all, these weren't people in the ordinary sense of the word, the German sense. The Jews were the scum of the earth and worse; the Poles weren't far behind. It wasn't war in the ordinary sense of war. It was about survival. They all knew that. They had been told that what lay ahead in Poland would require no ordinary bravery, but something else, an unflinching bravery of the soul that, when it was all over, would be unspoken, unrecorded, even unremembered. The sentiments were abstract; their job was to make them concrete. It was the way you dealt with disease. No quarter. The men had not heard those words the way the officers had, but they sensed it. Blood spoke to blood; when it did there were no questions. And Rilling's anger was a question.

Żarki's Stary Rynek was almost empty. Johannes Rilling stood where he had stood for a long ten minutes now, at the centre of the old square. At one corner a group of old Polish men still talked in whispers. Two of Rilling's soldiers walked slowly round the square, but they were smoking and laughing. All was calm, though smoke still rose from the synagogue several streets away, and the shouts of the men trying to put out the fire could be heard. Rilling was uneasy. It was a sign of the times. He had seen enough of those signs, everyone had, but it wasn't his business to interpret them. In so far as he had thought about them it had been to assure himself he could do his job and step round them. But this was only the beginning; he interpreted that much. He knew that in taking back control, in the face of his men running riot, he had taken a step towards losing it.

He looked up at the sound of an engine. He recognised the shape of an open-topped, slope-fronted Kübelwagen jeep, painted in military camouflage. There were four men in it: a driver and a private with a light machine gun in the front, two officers in the back. They all wore army field grey, but he knew they weren't soldiers. The uniforms bore no regimental markings – in fact, no particular markings at all, except for those of rank – but the caps of the two officers had the death's head motif of the SS. They were Einsatzgruppen men, answerable not to the military command but ultimately to Heinrich Himmler and the Reich Main Security Office; they might be any combination of SS, Gestapo, civilian police. Rilling waited as the car stopped. The officer who got out, smiling, had a triangular patch on his right arm with the letters SD; he was Sicherheitsdienst, then, SS Intelligence. He was probably the one his officers thought was a Gestapo man. Fine distinctions were unnecessary in those kinds of jobs.

'Hauptmann Rilling!'

'I am – and you are?'

'Obersturmführer Gottstein.' The man waited a moment, still smiling, as if expecting a response. He shrugged. 'Liaison officer for Einsatzgruppe II.'

'I suppose I have you to thank for my men shooting up the town and setting fire to it? It wasn't exactly what I had in mind when I went to Częstochowa this morning. We move forward again tomorrow. The Polish Army is regrouping in the east. I'd rather they had their minds on that.'

'It was merely a suggestion, Rilling. When we arrived the Jews were being less than forthcoming about food. It was being requisitioned. Your officers seemed keen to give them a lesson in German manners.'

'Some manners are probably not ideally suited to the German Army.'

'You're as pompous as ever, Rilling!' Gottstein spun round and grinned at the other officer in the Kübelwagen. 'I told you he was a pompous ass!' The SD man turned back to Johannes Rilling. 'So, you don't recognise me?'

'Gottstein,' said Rilling. 'I'm sorry, I should have done.'

There was an awkward silence. Gottstein was no longer smiling. There was something between the two men that neither of them was comfortable with.

'A long time.' Hauptmann Rilling attempted a smile.

'Yes, it's been long enough,' said the Obersturmführer. 'I did see your name on the command orders. I wasn't sure it was you, not until I got here.'

'Well, it is.' Rilling shrugged, smiling more successfully.

For another moment they didn't speak. Then whatever it

was that they had both been conscious of in their silence was pushed aside, as if by agreement.

'I assume you didn't call to say hello, Obersturmführer.'

'Prisoners on the Special Prosecution List.' Gottstein turned back to the Kübelwagen and leant over to pick up a sheaf of papers from the back seat.

'We've detained most of the people on the Żarki list,' said Rilling. 'They're at the school now. Presumably that's where you've just been.'

'Yes, I've checked them. Very thorough. You missed the rabbi.'

'He's dead.'

'He has been replaced.'

'It's not my list, Gottstein. It should be a police action, anyway.'

'I've added the new rabbi. Your men took him to the school.'

The Wehrmacht officer nodded. It was no longer his business.

'However, there is a problem, Hauptmann.'

'Well, it's your problem now.'

'Unfortunately the pace of advance has outstripped all our expectations.'

'And I thought you were here to congratulate us, Obersturmführer,' laughed Rilling. 'You'll just have to try and keep up. Tomorrow we continue.'

'Which is why you need to clear up here before you leave, Rilling.'

'And what does that mean?'

'Einsatzgruppe II hasn't got to Częstochowa yet. We should be there some time tomorrow, I hope, but that's going to be a substantial job in itself. Standartenführer Streckenbach is very concerned about the danger of leaving groups of detainees in the smaller towns, once the army moves forward.'

'You've seen our bunch, Gottstein? I've got the school teachers, the librarian, the parish priest, the mayor, the chairman of the Chamber of Commerce, a bank manager, the head of the farmers' cooperative, and somewhere there's a feller who runs the Boy Scouts. And the list goes on. They're frightening the life out my men! You'll cope with the danger, though.'

The SS man smiled at the sarcasm, a look of contempt.

'But I'll leave a platoon here until your people arrive. Will that do?'

'I'm not asking you to guard the bastards, I'm telling you to clean up.'

'I've had these people arrested. Shooting them is your job, not mine.'

'Standartenführer Streckenbach's orders—'

'Are not my orders.'

'You're refusing to deal with this?'

'I'm a soldier, not a policeman.'

'Not a party member either. I think that's right, isn't it, Rilling?'

'Is that significant? I'm here to fight a war.'

'We're all here to do that. Perhaps not all of us know what that war is.'

'Your prisoners will be here. The rest is down to you. That's it.'

He turned to walk away. The SS man walked after him.

'I will report this. You really shouldn't be so confident, Johannes.'

It was the first time either man had used a Christian name.

'Don't bother to threaten me, please. I'm not interested.'

'You should be. I know more about you than you think.'

Rilling stopped. 'We both know things about each other, Emil.'

'That was a very long time ago,' said the Obersturmführer. 'Some of us have left the past behind, some of us haven't. But don't imagine it stops with all that, Johannes. I know more. It's my business to know. I'm rather good at it.'

Gottstein was smiling again. Rilling had already seen the contempt in that smile, but what he saw now was more. It was a kind of hatred. He knew why, but it wasn't what he had expected; it wasn't about what was happening in this small, unimportant Polish town. What he knew about the SS man was something he could not be forgiven for knowing. He pushed that away. It didn't matter. In the chaos of the war there was no reason even to see Gottstein again.

'You can still shoot your own prisoners, Obersturmführer.'

Johannes Rilling turned away for the second time. Emil Gottstein watched him walk across the square, with something like a look of satisfaction.

3

Iveagh House

Dublin, September 1940

There was a casual routine to the walks that Dr Carl-Heinz Petersen, the press attaché at the German Legation, took through Dublin most weekday mornings, and for several weeks Detective Inspector Stefan Gillespie had been following that routine, trailing the representative of the *Deutsche Nachrichtenbüro* from the very English Gothic of the red-brick building in leafy Northumberland Road, which was the German embassy. The surveillance was shared with other Special Branch Guards and sometimes with officers from Military Intelligence, G2. Cooperation between Special Branch and G2 was erratic, however, and there were days when Petersen was followed by both Special Branch officers and G2 men. From time to time there was an agent from British Intelligence, too – at least, Stefan assumed that's what he was. Carrying a copy of the *Irish Independent*, smoking Sweet Afton cigarettes and drinking bottled Guinness in the various hotel bars Petersen called into, the po-faced English insurance salesman advertised himself as Irish with a consistency of visual props no Irishman could have maintained. Stefan had reported on this occasional British interloper, but at Dublin Castle Stefan's boss, Superintendent Gregory, was unconcerned. British agents were G2's business.

Gregory didn't bother to add, 'They know what they're doing'; he assumed they didn't. The game, anyway, was as much about the German knowing he was under surveillance as it was about being invisible. No one expected anything remarkable, and in that respect expectations were fulfilled.

Dr Petersen did know he was being watched. He didn't recognise all the people who kept him under surveillance, but there were some he occasionally greeted with a nod and a wink. The game wasn't unenjoyable, and he had been told in Berlin not to expect the Irish to be very good at it. At forty-two he was a relatively young man by the standards of the Dublin embassy. He smiled a lot and spoke English with a colloquial ease that owed much to Hollywood and American popular music, even if he now recognised the decadence of those influences. His hair was slightly blonder than might have been expected from his complexion, but he was hardly alone in using a bottle to add lustre to his Aryan credentials.

On this particular morning, the attaché had several familiar calls to make but his mind was on other things. He stopped to buy a newspaper and, as he approached Merrion Square, unfolded it to the racing pages. He lit a cigarette and stood scanning them. Standing at the corner of Holles Street, he looked round at nothing very much. There was nothing to see; it was a route he walked almost daily. He took in the trees of the square and looked back towards the Grand Canal. He turned to look up Holles Street; then he folded the newspaper and stuffed it into the briefcase he carried.

So far Stefan Gillespie had not reached the level of intimacy that warranted a knowing grin from the attaché. He believed he was still unspotted, but he wondered, as Petersen looked back in his direction, whether the game was up. The fact that it was a game was as clear to him as it was to the German. The surveillance was inconsistent and irregular. It often stopped in the afternoons, when the attaché was otherwise occupied.

If Petersen didn't want who he met or where he went observed, it wasn't hard to arrange.

The surveillance took its not unfamiliar course. Petersen walked the length of Merrion Square, then turned up towards Leinster House. He walked past the Guard at the entrance with barely a nod. He was well known there. Whether he was delivering a press statement from the embassy or a complaint about how the Irish press was reporting the war, Éamon de Valera, as Taoiseach and Minister of Foreign Affairs, did not go short of material from Petersen's office. The German emerged ten minutes later and walked up to Stephen's Green, where he went into the Shelbourne Hotel.

Stefan Gillespie entered the Shelbourne several minutes later. He had no need to follow Petersen through the hotel to find where he had gone and who he was meeting. A short conversation at the porter's desk was enough. He walked through reception to the back of the hotel and the empty Horseshoe Bar, and sat with the *Irish Times* and a cup of tea. As he passed the hotel lounge he had seen Carl-Heinz Petersen by a sofa at the far end of the room, shaking hands with two men. He only had to wait for the information he needed to arrive. It did so in the form of the head porter.

'So, how's it going, Anto?'

'Could be worse, Mr Gillespie.' The porter sat down in the small, cramped bar. As he did so he glanced at the barman, bottling up behind the bar. The barman walked out, lighting a cigarette, leaving only Stefan and the porter.

'Who's Dr Petersen here to see?'

'A guest.'

'And who would he be?'

'It'll come to me,' said the porter, grinning.

'It will so,' said Stefan. He took a pound note from his pocket.

'Fivers in short supply in the Branch, Mr Gillespie?'

'I was going to ask for ten bob change. Don't push your luck, Anto.'

The head porter took the note and shrugged.

'Mr Jones, Owain Jones. Welsh, an address in Surrey. Something to do with horses. Likes to splash his money around a bit too much. That's about it. Nice Jaguar in the garage. Here for the racing. Off to the Curragh tomorrow.'

'And is Mr Petersen a racing man?'

'I'd say he is. I've heard the German ambassador is so.'

'Herr Hempel likes a flutter, then?'

'I don't think it's a secret, Mr Gillespie.'

'Anything else?'

'Mr Jones drinks a bit and he likes to talk about how Welsh he is.'

Stefan laughed.

'We're all Celts together, he says,' added the porter, grinning.

'And the other man?'

'An old feller, Irish. Something to do with the Turf Club. Maybe a trainer. I've seen him at a few dinners here. Not staying. And no one's got his name.'

'Any idea what they're talking about?'

The head porter looked down at the pound note he was holding.

'If it's the invasion of Ireland, I'll give you another, Anto.'

'I'm out of luck then, Inspector. All the waiter heard was about horses.'

Stefan Gillespie left the Shelbourne Hotel before Dr Petersen. As he passed the lounge he got a clear look at the two men talking to the German: one, presumably the Welshman, was in his forties, short, dark, slight; the other was closer to seventy than sixty, tall, slightly frail, with gaunt, sallow skin. They were poring over open newspapers. The Welshman held a copy of the *Irish Field*. It was racing, not much doubt about that, and no real surprise with the big meeting at the Curragh.

As Stefan walked out to the street, a car was pulling up.

It was a car that was meant to be noticed: a black and white Jaguar Roadster. It was a beautiful thing, even for a man like Stefan, who had no great interest in what cars looked like. The throaty rumble of the engine was the sound of money. Stefan noted the English number plate. The motor cut and a porter got out, clearly pleased with his thirty-second drive from the Shelbourne Garage in Kildare Street. He walked from the driver's door to the Shelbourne steps. He nodded at Stefan, knowing him for what he was, as most of them did.

'Nice work if you can get it,' said Stefan.

'I did get to clean it, Mr Gillespie. Now I'm saving up tips for one.'

'So, is that Mr Jones's?'

The porter barely nodded, then walked into the hotel. Such questions were not idly asked. A nod was enough, and even a nod was a favour to call in.

Ten minutes later the man called Owain Jones left the Shelbourne and drove away in the Jaguar Roadster. Shortly afterwards Stefan saw Carl-Heinz Petersen emerge through the revolving doors with the older man. They shook hands. The older man walked across the road in the direction of the Green, passing close to Stefan, who was walking slowly alongside the park railings. Seeing the older man close-up, he merely registered the face. It was still no one he knew. He then crossed the road the other way and followed the press attaché down Dawson Street and into St Anne's Street. As Petersen reached Grafton Street, Stefan saw that he had stopped to buy flowers from a flower seller; they were roses, a pale cream. The German bought a dozen, then walked on, heading to Trinity and the Liffey.

Petersen passed the college and crossed into Westmoreland Street. He stopped at the entrance to the offices of the *Irish Times*. Stefan Gillespie watched him go in as he crossed the road and walked along on the other side, towards the river.

He stepped into a café that looked out across the street and sat at a table in the window. He smiled as he opened the copy of the *Irish Times* that he had now read twice. The flowers Petersen had bought would certainly not be for the editor of the *Times*, which was quietly, robustly anti-Nazi, despite everything approaching an opinion on the war being edited out of anything in print in Ireland. Everyone knew that most of Carl-Heinz Petersen's complaints about the Irish press's failure to maintain the vigorous neutral stance of its government were directed at the *Irish Times*. Stefan turned the broadsheet's pages to the racing. It was all that was left to read. He ordered a tea he wouldn't drink and read on.

Meanwhile, in the offices of the *Irish Times*, the German press attaché waited to see the editor. It would be a short meeting, as ever. If he could make headway directing the attention of the censors at the most stubborn of Irish newspapers, he could do little about the fact that every press release he posted was ignored in Westmoreland Street. He delivered them nevertheless, often pointedly by hand. He always smiled profusely as he handed them over, and the cheerfully rotund and verbose editor, Bertie Smillie, always smiled as profusely in return, then spoke for several minutes, with considerable enthusiasm, about the weather, whatever the weather was. Petersen only replied with more smiles. Despite his mastery of English, he had never managed to grasp the significance of conversations about the weather. He suspected sarcasm, though he could never quite find out where it was. Both men knew Petersen's propaganda would find its way into a waste-paper bin as soon as he left, but the German was consoled by his belief that the joke would, before very long, be on Smillie. In the lists that were kept in the Reich Main Security Office in Berlin, and in the Northumberland Road embassy, Smillie's name had a very privileged position.

Detective Sergeant Dessie MacMahon was not a great man for paperwork. Since they worked together most of the time, Dessie left that side of things to his inspector, Stefan Gillespie. His talents lay elsewhere. They lay particularly in the accumulation of rumour and gossip from the streets and bars and tenements of Dublin, stored in his head in a seemingly random and chaotic fashion. The connections that sometimes came out of this crowded attic of information could be unexpected and unlikely. No attempt at collation could bear the weight of so much that was truly redundant, trivial, petty and superfluous. Dessie's ability to identify a suspect from little more than a name that was identical, in the way of Irish names, to several dozen people living within a few streets of each other depended on all the things he had picked up somewhere about all the others, who would probably never be suspected of anything. It wasn't knowledge that carried far enough up the city's greasy pole to encompass the suburbs, let alone Dublin's great and good, but if you lived within a mile of the GPO, and Sergeant MacMahon had your name and the street you lived in, it was likely he would know your school, the pubs you drank in, where you went to Mass, who your friends were, where your second cousins lived and what your politics were if you had any; not to mention a selection of mistakes and misdemeanours and unwise connections over the years that you had probably forgotten yourself.

Today, however, Dessie MacMahon's dislike of paperwork was not in evidence. As Stefan Gillespie came into the detectives' room in the Police Yard at Dublin Castle, Dessie's head was down over his desk. He was surrounded by newspapers, and there were pages of closely written notes, full of names and numbers, crossed out and rewritten and crossed out again. The only other person in the room, Detective Jack Daly, was sitting opposite Dessie, smoking a cigarette and gazing up at the ceiling. Through the glass partition at the end of the office Stefan could see Superintendent Terry Gregory, eating a sandwich and reading the *Irish Times*. It was lunchtime. The only work going on was in Dessie MacMahon's head, as he furrowed his brow and stared down at the sheets of paper in front of him. Stefan reached the desk. Dessie didn't look up.

'So how much do we make?' said Stefan, grinning.

'We'll do fine if I'm right about the outsiders.'

'The last time we did a surveillance stint at Punchestown, you came up with a four-horse accumulator that was going to make you ten quid out of five bob. You won a quid on the first race then lost the lot on the next one.'

'This time he's got his system going, Stevie.' Daly winked.

'You can never tell with the sticks. They can fuck up the form. That's the trouble with National Hunt. But on the flat you haven't got the imponderables?'

'The what, Dessie?' Stefan and Daly laughed.

'Just horse and jockey.' Sergeant MacMahon wasn't in a laughing mood.

'We're at the Curragh to do a job tomorrow, Dessie.'

'We'll do it better if we blend in.' Dessie allowed himself a smile.

The door from the superintendent's office opened.

'Angel of Light in the three o'clock,' said Terry Gregory abruptly.

Detective Sergeant MacMahon shook his head.

'Unplaced in three outings. Three o'clock, I'd say Othello for a place.'

'Not over that distance.' The superintendent shook his head. 'Gillespie.'

As Terry Gregory turned back into his office, Stefan followed him.

'I haven't written up my report yet, sir.'

'Close the door, Inspector.'

Stefan stood in front of the desk. Gregory resumed his sandwich.

'Anything?'

'The usual. Taoiseach's office at Leinster House. Ten minutes at the *Irish Times*. He dropped something off at the *Press* and the *Indo* as well. He met two men at the Shelbourne for a cup of coffee. One was a Welshman – a man called Owain Jones, over here for the meeting at the Curragh. I didn't get a name for the other one, but Anto at the Shelbourne said he was something in racing – trainer, Turf Club steward. He had a drink in the bar at the Gresham then went to the flat in Marlborough Street, with a bunch of roses.'

'Which one's that?'

'Sally Phelps.'

'That's the new addition to the stable. She's the actress at the Gate?'

'She was. She's out of work right now.'

'Not a bad job, is it? You wander round town all morning, with nothing to do but pass the time of day, then spend the afternoon screwing one of your mistresses. What do you have to do to get a mistress, Inspector? I suppose it helps if you're not Irish. We don't go in for that much. I'm not sure I'd have the energy so. Well, not three or four times a week. Jesus, you have to say the man puts the work in somewhere. Anyway, you left him there. Is he on to you?'

'I'm not sure. I don't think so.'

'I've had External Affairs on the phone. You need to go to Iveagh House. Someone wants to talk to you. I wasn't told what it's about. In fact, I was given the polite feck-off. I assume it's to do with your trip to Spain.'

Stefan looked surprised. Gregory shrugged.

'They want you now.'

'I was going to Dún Laoghaire, the British diplomatic bag run with Danny—'

'Danny Skehan isn't in either. He's fecked off to the dentist, for God's sake! So Dessie can do it, with Jack Daly. You get over to External Affairs. You can tell me what they don't want to tell me when you get back.' He grinned. 'You know what pisses me off? Not telling people what they want to know is our job. Now every fucker wants in on it!'

On the south side of St Stephen's Green, Iveagh House was a large eighteenth-century house built in white Portland stone that had belonged, until very recently, to the Guinness family. In an act of generosity not unrelated to the cost of maintaining more property in Ireland than they could entirely pay for, the Guinnesses had given Iveagh House to the state. The house was newly occupied by the Ministry of External Affairs. The move was about the shortage of space in and around Leinster House, but it had given a kind of faded grandeur to Irish foreign affairs that had not existed before. The white stone front, with its long run of nine bays and its central pediment, stood out against the flat brick of the Georgian buildings on either side, but it was the inside that was startling – in particular the huge entrance hall, with its high ceiling and its two staircases sweeping up on either side, to meet as a balcony on the first floor. It was in the entrance hall that Stefan Gillespie now stood, waiting to be called upstairs.

He was surprised that the man who wanted to talk to him was Joseph Walshe, the secretary and senior civil servant at the ministry; not everyone knew the power he exercised in government, but it was no secret in Special Branch. Stefan could see no reason why Walshe would want to speak to him. He assumed it had something to do with the job he had done in Spain, months earlier, working with the Irish ambassador to facilitate the secret release of an Irishman who had fought in the Spanish Civil War from the Spanish prison he seemed certain to die in. The release of Frank Ryan involved German Intelligence, and a level of subterfuge that was there to save both the Irish and the Spanish governments diplomatic embarrassment. The freed man was an ex-IRA leader who was not wanted back in Ireland, and part of the charade, for Ireland, had been pretending the Germans were helping a man whose politics they despised, out of the kindness of their hearts. The fact that Ryan's release coincided with the return to Europe of Seán Russell, the IRA's exiled chief of staff, after he was smuggled out of America by German Intelligence, only added to what the government didn't want anyone to know.

What Stefan Gillespie knew about all this had long since been told, yet he could think of no other reason Walshe might want to speak to him. But as the version of the story he had given Military Intelligence in Ireland differed in certain respects from the version he had given his boss Terry Gregory, he found himself unsure what it was he was supposed to know. As all this went through his mind, he was beneath the great staircase, looking at a wooden relief he recognised as a scene from the *Iliad*. Achilles and Priam, king of Troy; on the ground was the body of Hector, Priam's son, killed by Achilles. He looked at it idly. He had to assume Joseph Walshe would know everything.

'An old man begs for the body of his son.'

Stefan turned to see a man in his fifties looking at him quizzically. His eyes were bright, even piercing, set in a pale face topped with tight, wiry, grey hair. He had just come into the building and he wore an overcoat, even though the sun was shining on a warm September day. Stefan had never seen Joseph Walshe, but he instinctively knew that this man was he, and that he was looking at Stefan with a view to making some kind of judgement.

'I'm not quite sure whether Achilles is still sneering or he has recognised that this old man, king or not, should be treated with some decency.'

'Decency follows, at any rate, sir,' said Stefan.

'Yes,' Walshe smiled, 'it does. Let's go upstairs.'

As Stefan Gillespie followed the head of the department up

one side of the great staircase, Walshe continued the conversation. Stefan knew it was an empty conversation – that it was there to bridge the gap between their meeting and whatever it was he was really there to discuss. He thought it was probably a conversation, one-sided as it was, that Walshe kept by for just such occasions.

'It's hard not to see Achilles as a bit of a gobshite – dragging Hector's body round the walls of Troy in the dirt, sulking in his tent with a dead man under his feet, all because Hector did what he was there to do himself: kill the enemy. But it's at the point where he turns around and does the decent thing, and sees an old man's grief for his son for what it is, king or not, hero or not, that Homer ends the *Iliad*. He doesn't finish with what happens next: death, destruction, slaughter, which is, as he well knows, what the real end is.'

They had reached the top of the stairs and walked through an empty office to a small, inner room that overlooked Stephen's Green. Stefan was unsure whether he was meant to join in with the conversation about the *Iliad* or whether, having concluded what felt like a kind of party piece, it was over.

'I always find myself on the Trojan side. The Greeks remind me of the English. They'd take that as a compliment. It isn't. Have a chair, Inspector.'

As Walshe sat at his desk, his back to Stephen's Green, Stefan sat down.

'There is no reason this can't be short. You did us some service in Spain, and you seem to be able to keep your mouth shut. Keeping your mouth shut is most of what's required in what I'd like you to do for me now. Though your German is obviously some advantage. Do you know anything about Foynes?'

Stefan knew the village in Limerick where the flying boats had landed, en route from England to America, until war had stopped them. He had no idea what else there was to know.

'I flew from there last year, to New York.'

'Of course you did.' Walshe opened a file and turned several pages. 'That's useful. You know the place a bit. You won't know that Foynes is about to be declared a prohibited area. The flying boat service has stopped, but it is not impossible it's going to start up again. If it does, we will have to police who goes in and who goes out. That will be a job for Military Intelligence. For the time being the government is looking at who stays and who has to be moved out for the duration of the Emergency. G2 and Special Branch will need to liaise on that. Superintendent Gregory is aware that will be happening. So, in a couple of weeks you will be transferred to Foynes. At least, that's what will be said.'

Stefan simply nodded. It was clear he wasn't expected to speak.

'The journey you will actually be making will be known only to a few people in the department here. There is no reason why the two other interested parties should know, that's to say Special Branch and G2. Neither of them is watertight. So, Superintendent Gregory is among those who will be under the impression you're going to Foynes. He will find out you're not there quite quickly. By then it won't matter. The same goes for Military Intelligence.'

'And where am I going, sir?'

'Berlin,' replied Walshe with a matter-of-fact smile.

'I see,' said Stefan.

'You will, Inspector. Even with Germany and its allies occupying most of Europe now, the journey isn't difficult once you're on the continent. Diplomatic travel is perfectly feasible. You'll take the route you already know, from Lisbon, through Spain, then through the two sectors of France into Germany. Getting you to Lisbon unnoticed is the only problem. You can't go via England, but we have come up with a solution. The role is really no more than courier, but you'll have the details when you go, which will be at very short notice. You will say nothing to anybody, inside or outside Special Branch, including your family. I hope that is all right, Inspector.'

Walshe ended with an expression of routine courtesy that suggested that if it wasn't all right, Stefan might have some say in it. But he knew he didn't.

At that moment both men turned their heads abruptly to the window. The sounds they heard were unmistakable. It was gunfire. It came from across the city, but it wasn't very far away. Walshe got up and went to the window. Stefan followed him. The secretary pushed up the sash window. The crack of guns.

'Pistols or revolvers,' said Stefan. 'It's not far away.'

'No, it's not.'

'I think perhaps, standing in the window, sir—'

'Oh, I'd say it's further away than that, Inspector. Still, I take the point.'

Walshe turned back to the desk and picked up the telephone.

'What the hell is going on?' He turned to Stefan. 'You'd better go.'

Stefan Gillespie ran down the sweeping staircase to the entrance hall. He was unaware why he was running. It was instinct more than anything else. There were still shots. Their echo carried into Iveagh House. A uniformed Guard was locking the double doors to the street. Another Guard appeared through a door carrying two rifles. A third Guard was at the reception desk holding the phone.

'What's happening?' said Stefan.

The Guard at the door shook his head, taking a rifle from his colleague.

'It's over the other side of the green. Won't be far from Leinster House.'

The Guard at the reception desk held the phone away from his ear.

'It's the far end of Merrion Square. By Holles Street.'

'What is it, a bank?' asked Stefan.

'No, it's the car taking the British diplomatic bag to the mail boat.'

'What about the Guards – the escort?' asked Stefan urgently.

The Guard holding the phone shrugged. There were two more shots.

'Give me a gun.'

'I can't do that, Inspector.'

'Give me a fucking gun!'

As the doors were pulled back, one of the Guards took his Webley from its holster. Stefan Gillespie snatched it from his hand, stuffing it into his pocket, and ran out, straight across the road, through the traffic, into Stephen's Green.

Three more shots sounded as Stefan raced through Stephen's Green. People had stopped. They stood in small groups, though there were others who simply carried on walking wherever they were walking. Gunshots were not common in the streets of Dublin, but they were not unknown. As Stefan crossed the bridge over the pond there were people still throwing bread to the ducks and the swans.

Running past the Shelbourne towards Merrion Street, Stefan Gillespie was aware that the guns had stopped firing. What he heard now were the sounds of the bells on police cars, converging on Merrion Square. And when he turned down towards Government Buildings, the road was blocked by a Garda car.

'Inspector Gillespie, Special Branch,' he shouted, running on.

He ran down to Merrion Square, but as he entered the gardens there were Guards walking the other way. A uniformed inspector recognised him.

'It's all over, Stevie!'

He stopped, breathless.

'What happened?'

'IRA. They came out of Holles Street and tried to cut off the car carrying the bag. They made a hames of it and crashed their own car. Then they started shooting. There was no point. If they'd run, the bastards would have got away.'

'What about the Guards? There was a Special Branch car?'

The inspector shook his head.

'One dead, one in a bad way. Hardly a scratch on the IRA fuckers.'

Stefan didn't reply. He walked on slowly. He passed several officers he knew who spoke to him, but he didn't hear them. This was where he should have been. This was where he would have been if it hadn't been for the summons to Iveagh House. Two Special Branch men had been in the car escorting the diplomatic bag. It wasn't easy to stop the hope that came into his head as he walked out of Merrion Square: that the one who was alive was the man who had been his friend for so many years. It wasn't a hope he liked having, but there was no way to stop it. He saw a car up on to the pavement on the corner of Holles Street. He saw the car that had carried the diplomatic bag. He saw the Garda car that had carried Dessie MacMahon and Jack Daly. He saw an ambulance with its back doors open. Armed Gardaí still stood at the approach to the scene and further back people looked on. Almost without realising it he was walking towards the body of a man lying in the road, with no more than a heavy Garda overcoat thrown over him. His instinct was to walk up to the body and pull back the cover. It felt almost indecent, but he needed to know.

'It's Jack Daly,' said the uniformed superintendent in charge.

Stefan nodded. There was a sense of relief he felt that sickened him.

'Jesus.' He had to say something; that was all there was. 'And Dessie?'

'I don't know, but he's maybe not far behind, Stevie. I'm sorry.'

Stefan followed the superintendent's eyes towards the ambulance. A stretcher was being carried into it. He walked forward again. He could see Dessie MacMahon's face. It was covered in blood, already growing black and hard round his forehead and in his hair. He was unconscious, and in the silence that seemed to surround everything suddenly, Stefan could hear his breath, rasping, uneven. Then he was in the ambulance. The doors slammed shut, and Stefan Gillespie watched it drive off, its bell sounding out, shrill and piercing.

4
The Curragh

A dark stone staircase led down from the flagged entrance to the Special Branch offices in Dublin Castle's Police Yard to a narrow, round-ceilinged tunnel that ran almost the length of the building. The walls were painted in peeling green distemper. The last coat of paint had been paid for by the British, though it had been applied a long time before they left. The corridor was lit by dim bulkhead lights and the doors that lined the sides were heavy and black. The holding cells behind these doors rarely contained prisoners for more than a night. The most frequent visitors were IRA men arrested under the Emergency Powers Act, in transit to the internment camp at the Curragh. As there was no need to produce any evidence of their IRA membership, other than the opinion of a Special Branch inspector, these prisoners didn't stay long. But in the two cells at the end of the corridor, where the lights stopped and a black arch led into the coal cellar, there were now two men who were receiving considerable attention. It was the kind of attention that was familiar enough as far as Special Branch interrogation methods went. It had been familiar when the British ran the Castle, and it wasn't only the paint that was still the same. Even then the Irishmen on the wrong end of that considerable attention had received it, by and large, at the hands of other Irishmen. What Stefan Gillespie heard as he walked towards the cells with Terry Gregory, amplified by the tight corridor, said nothing had changed.

At the end of the tunnel, opposite one of the cells, two uniformed Guards stood smoking. The cell door was open, but despite the noises from inside they were engaged in a conversation about something else, and sniggering. What was happening inside the cell was common enough to be ignored. They straightened up and stopped laughing only as they saw Superintendent Gregory approaching.

Gregory turned into the cell, ducking his head. Stefan was behind him.

The cell contained a mattress on the floor and chair. There was no natural light. A man sat on the chair, his hands tied very tightly behind him. Another man stood behind the chair, holding it steady. A third man stood in front, big, thick-set, balding. Despite being in his shirtsleeves, he wore a pair of brown leather gloves. As Superintendent Gregory and Inspector Gillespie entered, one of the gloves, clenched in a fist, smashed into the face of the man in the chair, who let out a cry, just like the ones Stefan had heard echoing along the holding-cell tunnel. The man's face was bruised. His mouth bled. His white shirt was covered in fresh blood. As the man in gloves stood back the bloodied face fell forward.

'What have you got, Danny?' said Gregory, taking out a cigarette.

'You know Johnny Costello, Terry. He's a hard man. He's told me.'

Gregory walked over to the man in the chair and pulled up his head.

'You made a fucking pig's ear of it, Johnny.'

The man shook his head. He coughed and coughed up blood. 'Fuck you!'

'You know what we want. Who's giving the orders now? Who sent you out? Where's your gen coming from? Where were you going to take the bag?'

Chief Inspector Danny Skehan stepped back; he took off his gloves.

'What bag was that, Mr Gregory?' said the man in the chair.

'Is that it? Ah, Johnny, you were caught at the end of Holles Street.'

'It's not the first time I walked down Holles Street.'

'You were in the fucking car.'

Costello shook his head.

'Your man was driving it, the kid. Do you think he hasn't talked?'

Costello shrugged. He knew he had.

'Jesus, Johnny, when you saw you'd botched the bloody thing, why didn't you just run? The lad crashed the fucking car, for God's sake. What the hell was the point in opening fire? You'd have got away – they weren't going to come after you waving the diplomatic bag. What was the fucking point of it?'

The man in the chair closed his eyes, wincing with pain.

'We've picked up your lookout, Davie Carson. Do you know that?'

Costello didn't open his eyes.

'I don't doubt Chief Inspector Skehan's told you there's a man dead.'

'He has, Mr Gregory,' said Costello, looking up again, 'though he's a man of few words, as you know.' He turned towards the man with the gloves.

'You shot Jack Daly, or the boy did,' said Gregory. 'We still don't know if Dessie MacMahon'll make it. You'd know Dessie, I'd say.'

The IRA man nodded.

'One, two – you'll hang anyway.'

Costello looked away. He already had a good idea what this meant.

'You know how it goes, Johnny. Talk and there may be a chance—'

'I don't think that message has got through, Terry,' said Chief Inspector Skehan. 'I think he's under the impression he's got some sort of defence, or we'll just throw him in the Curragh with the rest. Well, he says he's a soldier.'

'I don't like to feel we haven't made an effort, Danny. After all, there's a man's life at stake here. Maybe he's hard of hearing.'

'I'll do what I can,' said Skehan. 'We might as well see how hard he is, since he takes some pride in that.' He started to put his gloves back on. As he did, he turned to Stefan, grinning. 'Unless you want a go yourself, Inspector?'

'It's not my area of expertise, Danny. I might hurt him.'

As Stefan and Terry Gregory left, there was a thud and a gasp. Even though the chair was held, it flew across the cell floor, with the man tied to it.

Superintendent Gregory walked across the corridor and opened the cell door opposite. Stefan followed him in. A man, barely twenty, lay on a mattress on the floor. He tried to sit up as the two Special Branch men entered. His face was lightly bruised; his arm was in a sling, some blood had seeped through.

'James Brennan. He was the driver. He took a bullet, but it only smashed his elbow. I'd say he panicked and started shooting. Costello would have had the sense to run when he saw they'd screwed it up. Once the shooting started . . .'

Stefan took in the frightened, tear-stained face. The smell of faeces. Brennan still lay in his own filth. No one had bothered to do anything about it.

'Any more names, son?' asked Gregory.

'I don't know any names, sir.'

'If you do – if you know anything – you need to say it. And you know why I'm telling you that, don't you?' said Gregory, almost softly. 'So much for the rebel songs. I'm sure you know them all. Did you ever even fire a gun before?'

'I don't have to say anything. I am a soldier in the Irish Republican—'

'Don't waste that on me, you gobshite.'

A scream of pain came from across the corridor, through the open door.

'The more you tell, the better your chances. Or just sing along with the chorus. "A soldier's life is the life for me, A soldier's death and Ireland free!"'

Another cry of pain from outside. Brennan sank back on the mattress.

Stefan and Gregory walked out. They moved quickly along the corridor.

'The fucker won't know enough to help himself, even if he wants to.'

'Will they hang?'

'They'll have to.'

'Have to?'

'You think they shouldn't?'

'I didn't say that, sir.'

'Hard times, Stevie. That decision was made before they fired a shot.'

As inspector and superintendent started up the stairs, Gregory remembered that he had forgotten something he was still curious about.

'What did they want at External Affairs?'

'They're still wondering about where Frank Ryan is. There's a letter from somewhere that says he's in America. They wanted to know what I thought so.'

'And who did you see?'

'Mr Walshe.' It wasn't something Stefan felt he could sensibly lie about.

'Well, it's not every day you'd meet Mr Walshe.'

'No, sir.'

'Still, it's good to know they're on top of things in External Affairs.'

They reached the top of the stairs. Terry Gregory turned and laughed. 'They know fuck all and they wanted you to confirm it.'

'Something like that,' said Stefan.

'You'd think they'd ask someone who knows, like British Intelligence.'

Stefan looked back at Gregory, surprised. It didn't sound like a joke.

'They'd have a good idea, I'd say,' said Gregory with a shrug.

'And they're up for questions?'

'Neutrality doesn't make it an each-way bet, Inspector.'

The superintendent looked at him momentarily, his eyes screwed into the wry, questioning look he kept for letting people know he wasn't entirely convinced by what he had been told but had filed his reservations away for now.

'First things first,' said Gregory, 'you get back to Stephen's Green now, to St Vincent's. I had a call to say Dessie's come round.' Gregory's voice was matter-of-fact. He made no comment on what he had said about Dessie MacMahon only moments earlier in the cells. 'No one's really talked to him yet. Ask him if he saw anyone else he recognised. The Guards say there was at least one other man involved, but he got away and there's not much of a description.'

Superintendent Gregory walked away without another word. When something was over, for better or worse, he wasn't in the habit of wasting time on conversation or reflection, however much it mattered. If he was relieved, as he surely was, he didn't show it, but he still made it his business to send Stefan across to St Vincent's Hospital, to ask some questions he already knew the answers to.

Detective Sergeant Dessie MacMahon lay in a room on his own at the back of the flat-fronted Georgian building that housed St Vincent's Hospital. His throat and part of his face were bandaged, and he was still weak. A bullet had passed straight through his neck, and he was unable to speak. He was propped up on pillows, writing several names on a piece of paper. But they were not names that had anything to do with the ambush on the British diplomatic bag and its escort. Stefan Gillespie, sitting on a chair beside the bed, had already established that Dessie had recognised nobody in the gun battle on the corner of Holles Street and Merrion Square. He had been hit once in the leg as he got out of the car and again in the throat moments later. He fired only three shots before he passed out. The names he was writing now each had a time or the name of a race written beside it. Dessie wouldn't be going to the Curragh the next day, but Stefan would. He handed the piece of paper to Stefan, who read back the names.

'Apocalypse, in the 2.45, is that right?'

Dessie nodded.

'Harvest Feast in the St Leger; King's Caprice in the 4.15, and Nordic in the Anglesey Stakes? A fourfold accumulator! You're still feeling lucky, then?'

Dessie grinned and reached for the scrap of paper. He scribbled more words and handed it back. Below the horses' names he had written: *I'm alive.*

'Each way, then,' said Stefan with a grin.

Dessie shook his head and grimaced; movement wasn't a good idea.

'To win? You're joking.'

Dessie reached over to the table by the bed and took a ten-shilling note from under a glass of water. He handed it to Stefan, who took it and shrugged.

'That's ten bob you can say goodbye to. I suppose I don't tell Mary?'

Dessie put up his thumb. He gestured for the paper again and wrote.

Stefan read back the new words: *Am I right they got Johnny Costello?*

'Costello and a young feller, they were the ones doing the shooting. We picked up another man, a feller called Davie Carson. If there were any others, they got clear. It wasn't well planned. I'd say the young feller blew it, then started firing off. Your man Costello didn't have much choice except join in.'

Dessie's voice barely breathed a question. 'What's the score so?'

Stefan shrugged and drew his finger across his throat.

Dessie shook his head slowly, closing his eyes.

'Would you know Costello?' asked Stefan.

'Jesus! At school.' Dessie rasped the words. 'I knew him at school.' There was a mixture of anger and something more like pain. 'Stupid fucker!'

The next day Inspector Stefan Gillespie and Chief Inspector Danny Skehan drove south-west out of Dublin to the Curragh Racecourse. They followed a stream of cars and buses through Crumlin and the outskirts of the city to Naas and Newbridge, and the wide pan of grass that was the Curragh. It was at Newbridge that the black Ford driven by Stefan met a short convoy of vehicles heading in the same direction, driving more slowly than other traffic. At the back of the convoy was a black Garda patrol car; a policeman on a BSA motorcycle rode beside it. In front of them there was a khaki Bedford lorry, packed with men, clearly visible beneath the tarpaulin that covered the truck, peering out from the tailgate. Then there were two coaches, also full of men. Between the coaches there was a Landswerk armoured car, with a soldier standing in the open turret. At the front, an open-backed Ford Scout Car contained six more soldiers, leaning on their rifles. Two army motorcycles headed the convoy. Stefan's Special Branch car was a few vehicles behind the lorry and coaches as they went through Newbridge, heading for the Curragh.

'Customers for Tin Town,' said Skehan, taking out a cigarette.

'How many this time?' asked Stefan.

'Terry said fifty or so would do.'

'You think we'd be running out.'

'Every time the Boys play up, Éamon de Valera says lock another bunch of them up in the Tin Town Camp. Well, there's no point having a prime minister who doesn't at least look like he's doing something. But God only knows who we're picking up now. The guts of it'll be barroom Republicans who can't keep their mouths shut. They wouldn't know what to do with a Thompson if you shoved one up their arse.'

'Maybe they're the dangerous ones,' said Stefan. 'Like the kid in Holles Street. Someone stuck a gun in his hand. What was he going to do but fire it?'

Skehan sniffed. He opened the window and threw out his cigarette end.

'One way or another, they haven't got much to look forward to in the Curragh. It's shite. Have you been in there?' Stefan shook his head. 'I'd say the job isn't so much to keep the bastards out of the way, as to break them. But you get what you ask for.'

The convoy was approaching the junction at Ballymany, at the eastern edge of the Curragh, where the road would divide: left to the Irish Army's headquarters at the Curragh and right to the racecourse. At the Curragh Camp were the two internment camps: one housing over a thousand IRA men now, and the other a handful of German and British servicemen – mostly aircrew.

Where the road widened, the convoy pulled in to let the stream of traffic behind pass by. The police motorcyclist pulled out into the middle of the road and waved the cars and buses on.

As Stefan drove past the coaches someone was holding a long strip of paper out of one of the windows; on it were scrawled the words, *Dev's Tours Up the IRA*. The men inside were jostling at the windows, calling out to the racegoers. 'Fuck Dev! Free Ireland!' And through Skehan's open window they caught the sound of raucous laughter and singing.

> Where the helmets glisten in the sun,
> Where the bayonets flash, and the rifles crash,
> To the echo of the Thompson gun!

The sounds were gone almost immediately, and they turned up on to the road to the racecourse, with the broad, green span of the Curragh spread before them.

'They won't have much to sing about behind the wire,' said Skehan. He spat out of the window, then slowly wound it up. 'Still, they'll all be waiting for the Jerries to turn up and let them out so.' He laughed. 'Any day now, they say!'

Stefan Gillespie stood among the crowd pressing into the white rail of the track as the five horses entered the last furlongs of the race. His Majesty's Plate was the longest of the afternoon's races, at two miles and four furlongs, and Stefan, three races into Dessie MacMahon's four-horse accumulator, was surprised to find not only that the bet was still in the running, but that it was going to stay in the running for the last race. Dessie's third pick, King's Caprice, was up with the horse that had led nearly all the way, Royal Down, and was looking strong. The shouts of the thousands of spectators were growing into a roar now, and Stefan was roaring too, as the press pushed him up to the rail, and the thud of the hooves, which somehow cut through all the other noise, grew louder and sharper, and the smell of the horses was in the air they pushed behind them as they hurtled towards the finish. And it was done. Stefan was cheering. They were still in, with one more race, and Dessie's ten-shilling note looked very healthy.

It was a bright day, and doing nothing much except register a few idle encounters in the bars and stands of the Curragh wasn't the worst way to spend time. Stefan was out of Dublin, and even with his job to do, the atmosphere of the racecourse was infectious enough. There was clean air and the sound of laughter everywhere. It felt as if half of Dublin and the surrounding countryside were here, and few things could have made the business of war seem further away, even if, in reality, it was almost within sight, across the gently rolling grassland of the Curragh. They would hear the roar of the crowd loudly enough in the internment camps. But that reality was as old as the place itself. Horses had always run here, and armies had pitched their camps. The first record of a race on the Curragh plain was two thousand years old, when the horses pulled chariots. And all that time, between the races, down the centuries, there had been war as well. For now, it wasn't much war; it felt like nothing, and maybe that was something to celebrate. But it was there, out of sight like the internment camps, but close enough to see if you looked.

The press of people had relaxed, and as Stefan moved back towards the betting ring and the stand, he remembered that he should be doing his job. He saw a Guard in uniform watching him. He recognised Lugs Brannigan from Newmarket Garda station, in Dublin's Coombe, and he was surprised to see him there. The Guard walked up to him with a knowing grin.

'You've got a winner then, Inspector.'

'Dessie has. Three in a row.'

'That's good going. Did you see him? I heard he's doing all right.'

'I'd say so, considering. He can't speak—'

'Ah, well, enjoy that while you can,' laughed Garda Brannigan.

'You're a long way from home, Lugs?'

'There's a few of us down to help out. There's something up – I don't know if it's going to come to anything, but the word's out for some sort of rumble. That's what I heard. I seen enough here to think it's still on the cards.'

'Dessie said something about that. Is it trouble?'

'He heard the same on the Northside. And I know too many faces here.'

'Who?'

'It's not people you'd come across. It's the Animal Gangs from the Coombe and the Liberties. Down here in numbers, and with money to drink away that they didn't have when they got here. And it's the same with lads from the Northside. I know some of my fellers were slipped a bit of cash in Dublin, and not to bet on the St Leger.' He looked round, a faint smile on his face. 'I can pick them out. I stopped two of the fuckers in Dolphin's Barn this morning, walking along with blackthorn sticks and waiting for a taxi to collect them. They said they were off to a wedding. They thought it was great craic saying it. Neither of them over seventeen. I sent them packing, but there's dozens more.'

As Stefan looked round himself now, he was aware of more Garda uniforms than he had noticed before, and more than a race meeting demanded.

'Do they know you know?'

'They know.'

'And you hope that's enough.'

'I'm not a betting man,' said the Guard. 'If not, we'll give you a shout.'

Lugs Brannigan grinned and strolled on. Stefan walked back towards the stand to resume the observation that was his reason for being there. His racecourse badge gave him access to the stand and the bars where the great and the good were gathered, and he walked up through the terraces of seats into the bar. There was nothing new to see. The people he was interested in were still there, talking to the same people they had been talking to before. The German ambassador, Herr Hempel, was talking to a senior army officer in uniform. As the officer turned away, Hempel stepped forward to pick up a glass of wine, and found himself next to the British representative in Dublin, Sir John Maffey. They looked at one another for a moment, nodded with a mixture of curtness and politeness, at almost exactly the same instant, and turned their backs on one another. As if obliged to prove their credentials, each made a bee-line for two groups of Irish politicians and started a conversation. Each conversation, as Stefan knew from listening to both men earlier, would pointedly avoid the war, and be entirely about horses and the weather. The German press attaché, Carl-Heinz Petersen, was at a window, looking out at the course. Stefan saw that he was talking to one of the men he had seen him with at the Shelbourne Hotel two days ago: the Welshman, Owain Jones. Their connection had been racing then; it still was.

'So how's Dessie getting on?'

Danny Skehan was walking towards him, holding a pint.

'He's got three winners and the favourite in the next race.'

'What did he put on?'

'Ten bob.'

'Jesus, that's going to be a few quid. Do you get a commission?'

'Maybe a drink.'

Skehan laughed. Stefan looked across the bar again at Petersen.

'Do you know the feller Petersen's talking to at all?'

The chief inspector followed Stefan's gaze.

'No. I don't recognise him.'

'Man called Owain Jones. He's Welsh.'

'He's not in any of my boxes. In fact, not many are. I'd be better sorting out the fellers on the bus. I'm on the wrong side of the Curragh. But it could be worse.' He raised the glass of beer. 'I can tell you which ministers are pissed, though, and one in particular whose wife would not be very happy about a conversation he's been having with one of the barmaids, which is the kind of information Terry wouldn't mind us to bring back. Now that really is useful.'

Chief Inspector Skehan walked away, heading casually in the direction of a man who was indeed a government minister and was, clearly and loudly, on the wrong side of drink. And as Stefan Gillespie looked back to the windows on to the course, Carl-Heinz Petersen was no longer talking to Jones; the Welshman had gone. The press attaché was now with his ambassador, poring over the race card. Stefan moved to the windows himself, looking down on to the course, feeling that the day was coming to a natural conclusion. He had in his head a web of overlapping conversations between Irish politicians of various hues and a variety of diplomats, primarily German and British. He knew enough to recognise the Germanophiles and the Anglophiles in the bar and the stand, in the owners' enclosure and the betting ring. He knew some of the hangers-on who made a claim to peddling information or influence, or simply liked to be part of any whiff of intrigue. It was the nature of his trade, that people who made a point of peddling anything at all in plain sight, even their friendship, were unlikely to be worth watching in the first place. Dr Petersen was the man who mattered, because Petersen was the real Nazi presence in the German embassy, not the ambassador. And Petersen knew perfectly well he was being watched at an event like this. These things were a waste of time, almost all the time, but it was time that had to be wasted. Those were the rules.

The Anglesey Plate was starting as Stefan came out of the bar and walked along at the top of the stand. The race was only five furlongs, and the horses were already into the straight. He could see that one horse was out in front, but he didn't know which one. This was the last of Dessie MacMahon's horses in the fourfold accumulator. A woman beside him was watching through binoculars.

'Who's in front?' asked Stefan.

'Nordic.'

'Yes!'

He walked forward to get a better view as people in the seats rose up. The noise was growing again, in pace as well as volume. The horse was still there, still out in front, with the winning post coming closer. And Dessie had done it.

Stefan was shouting. It was there. All the horse had to do was to stay in front and keep going. But as he called the name, he could hear that around him the names of other horses were being shouted louder, stronger, clearer: Rose Garland, Breadmaker, Carlia! And with the winning post so very close now, the three horses that had been bunched together behind the leader all the way to the last furlong were level, level with Nordic and moving forward. And within seconds they were in front. Nordic was falling back. It was over. Stefan looked down at the betting slip and smiled. Three winners; the fourth not even placed.

'Shite!' Stefan looked back. It was the woman with the binoculars.

'Shite,' he said, nodding. She laughed and turned back towards the bar.

Stefan tore the betting slip into tiny pieces. Dessie would know already; he would be listening on the radio. But he would have enjoyed it. The crowds were moving back to the bars and the betting ring. Stefan stopped. He could see the Welshman again, some way off, and this time he was with the other man who had been at the Shelbourne with Petersen, the elderly Irishman who was something to do with racing. The two men were arguing. It was one of those arguments conducted in harsh whispers. Stefan could tell that it was very one-sided. The older man was dressed in tweeds that must have once fitted him, but now hung loosely on his thin, almost wasted frame. He looked older than he had at the hotel, and frailer. Stefan watched as he turned and tried to walk away. The Welshman grabbed his jacket and almost spun him round. He spoke again, hissing his angry words. There was nothing about any of this that suggested it was any of Stefan Gillespie's business as a policeman, and he turned away as he was jabbed in the ribs himself. He turned to see Chief Inspector Skehan again.

'Do you know what's going on? I saw Ted Cronin with a dozen of his men, on the other side of the stand. All deep in conversation. Is something up?'

'I'd say there could be. I was talking to Lugs Brannigan just now. There's the sniff of some sort of trouble. It's been around for a few days. Dessie got hold of it on the Northside. Lugs reckons there's a couple of gangs here, lads from the Coombe – and someone had them brought down in taxis.'

'What does "someone" mean?'

Stefan shrugged.

The two detectives peered around. The crowds were thinner now. The last race was still to be run, but people were already heading back to Dublin. They were both aware, now that they were looking, that there were young men among the racegoers, strolling about in a slightly circular, aimless way, and seeming not quite part of it all, amidst the groups of men and women and children.

'Yes, I'd recognise a few of those fellers myself,' said Skehan. 'The older ones, anyway. I wouldn't know many on the Northside, but Brannigan's right. There's a few Animal Gang lads from the Coombe. And most of them pissed.'

As they looked it seemed that the groups of young men were walking less aimlessly, and they were drawing together. There was, suddenly, a clear separation between them and the racegoers milling round. There was a kind of lazy tension in the way they were gathering into larger groups. Most had been drinking all afternoon. There was something too self-conscious in all the grinning, laughing, joshing. They all had their eyes fixed in the same direction towards the betting ring, where throngs of people were crowding round the bookmakers for the last race. The noise of the odds being called sounded across the course, over the buzz of conversation. And as Stefan Gillespie and Danny Skehan followed the eyeline of the gang from the Coombe, they saw another group of young men closing together in the same way, watching and laughing too. From time to time both groups glanced at the uniformed Guards watching them, but it was with a kind of sneering unconcern. They were not there for the Guards.

Now more police were moving into the area in front of the stand. They were doing it quietly, in twos and threes still. But they were too few, and it was too late. There was no particular sign or sound that Stefan heard, but suddenly the two gangs launched themselves at each other, pushing aside racegoers; men, women, children. The Gardaí moved forward, faster now, trying to stand between the two sides, but the battle was already joined. The crowds of racegoers scattered for the stand and terraces, some screaming, some falling, some dragged up out of the way.

'Jesus, the buggers mean business,' said Skehan, lighting a cigarette.

As the two phalanxes met, there were bottles flying as well as fists, and there were knives and sticks and chains, and along with the shouting and cursing that filled the area between the betting ring and the stand there were screams of pain.

The Guards were shouting too; police whistles were sounding; more Guards were arriving. They had been pushed out to the fringes of the fight by the force of the conflict, and they were trying to battle their way back in, to pull the opposing sides apart. It was chaos, with gang members fighting each other and the Guards. The police were outnumbered, though more were running from other parts of the racecourse. The crowds, packed into the stands and back across the betting ring and the owners' enclosure, and with distance between them and the battle, looked on with a mixture of shock and fascination.

The two Special Branch men were still close to the edge of the melee.

The chief inspector dropped his cigarette butt and stubbed it out. He grinned.

'It wasn't what I had planned, but you can hear the shite if we don't—'

'You're probably right. It's my best suit too,' replied Stefan.

'You must be getting more overtime, Stevie. It's my only suit.'

They stepped slowly into the fringe of the fight. A boy who was no more than fifteen was about to crack a heavy walking stick over the head of another teenager he had just knocked to the ground. Stefan tapped him on the shoulder. The boy spun round angrily, brandishing the stick, eyes blazing; he was drunk.

'You want some of this too, you cunt!' he screamed.

'You'd need to put that down, son,' said Stefan quietly.

'I will! I'll put it right down, wanker!'

As he raised the stick to hit Stefan, Danny Skehan's fist came at him hard from the side. He hadn't seen it coming. He collapsed beside the boy whose head he had been about to crack open. Skehan held him down with his foot as Stefan picked up the stick and sent it spinning away across the grass.

'You're lucky you didn't use it. Stay where you are, the both of youse.'

Stefan and Danny stepped over the two boys and joined the uniformed Guards, now pulling the Animal Gang members off each other, and working their way in to the centre of the combat. The fighting continued for only another five minutes, and then, as abruptly as it had started, it ceased. Again, there was no sound, no signal, but there was silence. The same silence had fallen on the thousands of spectators in the stands, staring at the battlefield.

A few fighters broke away and ran, but most just stayed where they were, some standing, some held by Gardaí, some on the ground, some gasping for air. All around weapons had been dropped: sticks, bottles, knuckledusters, chains, knives, and a surprising number of potatoes studded with razor blades.

In the long moment of stillness, as everything froze, eyes moved towards a spot where several policemen stood round one of the fallen men. He was covered in blood; beside him lay the butcher's knife another man had plunged into his chest. The Garda superintendent who knelt beside him stood up, shouting.

'Get me a fucking ambulance! This man is dying!'

To a man and boy, the Animal Gangs crossed themselves, though none had abandoned the comradely solidarity they came with. The day had gone well.

The racecourse Tannoy crackled into life: the last race would be delayed.

5

Czarny Kamień

Żarki, Poland, September 1939

In the old market square in Żarki, Hauptmann Johannes Rilling's company was preparing to leave, in pursuit of the Polish Kraków Army, which so far, in the three days since German troops had crossed the border, had done little more than retreat before their advance. Already, in the darkness before dawn, a company of twenty Panzers and a motorised unit had rumbled through the town, heading towards the River Vistula, as the rest of the German 10th Army was, on a broad front through Silesia, moving east of Częstochowa, Katowice and Kraków. A line of Luftwaffe planes had passed over Żarki half an hour earlier, Messerschmitts and Stukas, cheered on by the soldiers preparing to follow in their wake. Even now the sound of explosions could be heard in the distance. The Poles were out there, and the Luftwaffe had found some. The blitzkrieg was continuing; it was war at a speed the world had never seen. The pause Rilling's company had taken in Żarki was barely a breath to allow the supply line and the fuel tankers to catch up. They were on the move before the Poles had even stopped to work out where it was they should be regrouping.

Rilling's men were still loading their trucks and pumping fuel as the sun rose. The townspeople were indoors. But a few had ventured out to drive cattle and pigs into the fields. Some things had to be done, and the soldiers were leaving. Where they were going, and what that meant, was for another day. The soldiers themselves were in a more amiable mood. Today, when the Company Sergeant Major told a farmer to cut the throat of one of his pigs and stick it in the back of a truck, he paid for it. They all wanted to move on. The chase was fast and nothing had challenged them enough to stop it being enjoyable. The sense of confidence they had brought into Poland had turned into a sense of invulnerability. In that respect everything they had been told was true. The Polish Army was running, and it was only a question of catching them. God help them then. It would be like sticking pigs.

Two streets away, in the school behind the church, Johannes Rilling and his commanding officer, Oberstleutnant Karl Laube, bent over a map in the infants' classroom. Rilling's junior officers stood back respectfully, but with the same eagerness to join the chase that filled the soldiers in the square. Around them, on the walls, were pictures drawn by the children who had sat in the classroom two days before. Laube lit a black cheroot and drew in the smoke.

'You move on to Lelów. We'll be coming from Częstochowa so you should be there first. There's no Polish presence until you get some way east of Lelów. At worst you might meet some partisan snipers.'

'Let's hope so, sir. The men are going to want something to do!'

There was a polite round of laughter from Rilling's lieutenants. Laube nodded and smiled. He looked at Rilling for a moment, thoughtfully, rolling the cheroot on his lips. His adjutant collected up the maps as the junior officers moved out of the classroom, talking cheerfully about the day ahead. Rilling rolled up his own maps. The lieutenant colonel took the cheroot from his mouth. It had gone out. He took out a box of matches, glancing at his adjutant.

'Wait in the car, Wasserman.'

Oberstleutnant Laube relit the cheroot carefully. Rilling watched him.

'I had a visit from our Einsatzgruppen liaison officer last night.'

'Gottstein. I suppose he had a complaint to make. About me.'

'He wasn't very happy.'

'I'm sorry to hear that.'

'Yes, I was sorry too, so sorry that I told him to fuck off.'

Rilling laughed.

'Of course, it's not that simple, Hauptmann. I wish it was.'

'I see.'

'I don't know whether you see or not. But you do need to. You know what happened in Częstochowa yesterday? A little bit of a shooting party . . .'

'I heard something. There was some sort of partisan action?'

'I don't know if there was or wasn't. I have it on very good authority that the rifles that went off were ours. And there wasn't a fucking gun in Polish hands anywhere in the city. Not that I intend to say that very loudly to anyone.'

Hauptmann Rilling said nothing.

'You know Uebe?'

'Oberstleutnant Uebe?'

'He always was a panicker. Not helped by his inability to hold more than one idea in his head at a time. Dear old Willi decided there must be some Polish troops in Częstochowa somewhere, and by God he was going to find them. So, he turned out half his battalion. They didn't come across a single weapon, let alone any Polish soldiers. Not a sausage. But they did shoot anyone who was on the street with a razor blade or a penknife in his pocket. And to make the point more clearly, they dragged a thousand people into Magnacki Square, in front of the fucking cathedral, and shot a couple of hundred of the bastards anyway.'

'That doesn't sound too clever, sir,' said Rilling. He didn't know why Oberstleutnant Laube was telling him this, other than that it had irritated him.

'You wouldn't have thought so. I wouldn't have thought so. General von Hase didn't think so. The word was he wanted Uebe back in Berlin and on a charge. But the word changed quite abruptly. The news had reached our dear chum, Reichsführer Himmler, who sent a telegram to Uebe, offering his profuse congratulations. At that point the general decided to shut up. Uebe is still strutting round Częstochowa like a peacock. Do you understand, Hauptmann?'

'Do I want to?'

'Uebe's a fool. He always was. But for once, he's ahead of the game. I don't know why he did what he did. If he believed there were enemy soldiers or partisans firing, a few dead hostages would have made the point. But perhaps we don't all know what the point is. And perhaps he does. Or perhaps he started the thing off, and his men took over, and he let them. Maybe he couldn't stop them. Because they can feel what's happening. They can smell it better than us.'

Johannes Rilling simply nodded. He had almost been there himself.

'You already knew this SD man, Gottstein, Hauptmann?'

'We were at university together, in Leipzig. We weren't friends.'

'He certainly doesn't like you now.'

'I helped him out of a jam.'

'He doesn't seem very grateful.' Laube laughed.

'It's not a jam an SS man would want people to know about.'

'Tell me.'

'It doesn't matter.'

'It may well matter. This man is dangerous. Understand that.'

Rilling was surprised by the urgency in the battalion commander's voice. 'Gottstein was arrested in a police raid. At a brothel.'

'He was with a prostitute? That doesn't seem like a big deal.'

'The prostitute was a man.'

'Ah. You got him out?'

'I knew someone who knew someone. He was never charged.'

'No, he wouldn't thank you for knowing that.'

'No, sir.'

'Is he still at it?'

'At what, sir?'

'You know what, Rilling.' Laube grinned.

'Sir, I haven't seen the man in seven, eight years.'

'Well, he certainly hasn't forgotten the favour he owes you. And old habits, Hauptmann? But what concerns me – what concerns you, more to the point – is that the Sturmbannführer has it in for you, in a number of ways. He didn't arrive here by accident, even if he was doing his job. He interprets that job rather broadly, as any good SS officer must. That's to say he doesn't consider it stops with disposing of a few Polish school teachers and priests. We try to protect one another, Rilling, as officers. In the new dispensation, we do what we can. It's not easy. It's harder if we don't know what we're protecting.'

'I have done nothing that could embarrass the regiment, sir.'

'I'll take that with a pinch of salt, Johannes. In most cases discretion is enough. But this isn't about anything you've done. It's about who you are.'

'I'm not with you, sir.'

'Gottstein says your mother is Jewish.'

'My mother is Catholic. She was born a Catholic.'

'You know better than that. You're a *Mischling*. You have two grandparents who were full-blood, fucking Yids. That makes her Jewish.'

Rilling was silent.

'Jesus, you're a fucking arsehole! You know you'll be lucky to stay in the army at all? Gottstein isn't about to let it go. He's a man with a mission. Right now, you're it. The best you can hope for is being reduced to the ranks. An ex-officer and a Jew too. A fucking embarrassment to everyone. You'll be pushed into the front line every time it looks like you might take a bullet.'

'You'd rather I'd told you, then, sir?'

'No, I'd rather no one knew at all. Who else knows?'

'I don't know. I don't know how Gottstein does.'

'Are you that naïve?'

'I just assumed it wouldn't happen to me.'

Oberstleutnant Laube paced the classroom. He took out another cheroot. He lit it, but as soon as he drew in the smoke he dropped it and stubbed it out.

'You're not alone, Rilling. I told you, your old chum is on a mission. He has other lists besides a few scraggy Poles and Jews who need bumping off before they overwhelm the armies of the Reich. You're not the only one in the Wehrmacht. Jews, half Jews, quarter Jews, Gottstein's found a little niche for himself. I reckon it's his way up the greasy SS pole. But it may be greasier than he thinks. There are still ways to shut these things down, sometimes. But for how much longer, I don't know. Still, at least while there's a war on we can—'

'So, what do I do, sir? Nothing?'

'Not quite nothing, Hauptmann. The last thing you need to do is draw attention to yourself by arguing with the SS. We're here to help each other, after all. So you will help. Where are these fucking prisoners from the SS lists?'

'They're here, at the back of the school. I told Gottstein I'd leave a platoon behind to keep them under lock and key till the Einsatzgruppen arrive.'

'We are involved in what's happening. That's what I meant

when I told you what went on in Częstochowa. And it's not just there. It's everywhere.'

Johannes Rilling nodded. He knew what was coming.

'You take his fucking prisoners out and shoot them. As requested. Someone in Berlin's decided these people are enemies of the Reich. So by the German standards we live and die for, they've had due process. And that's it.'

'Yes, sir.'

'I would recommend that you show due diligence in front of your men. You need to dispose of any sign that there's something wrong with what they're doing. What they are doing is their duty – and yours, too. So when you shoot the bastards, set your men a good example. You shoot too. When it's done, you're the one who walks the line and finishes off any poor sod who hasn't bought it.'

Rilling nodded again.

'There's a saying, isn't there? I'm not sure where it comes from. "Whoever saves a life, it's as if he saved the whole world." Isn't that right?'

'I wouldn't have thought you were familiar with the Talmud, sir.'

Laube looked puzzled, but it didn't hide a quiet smile.

'Is that where it comes from? I must avoid saying that again, then.'

'I will remember it if I find a life to save, sir.'

'Start with your own, Johannes.'

'And the rest of it, Oberstleutnant? Emil Gottstein, I mean.'

'The good Sturmbannführer hasn't made himself very popular. In not much more than a few days he's managed to flash accusations about Jewish blood in the Wehrmacht around all over Silesia. And at higher levels than a mere Hauptmann. He's clearly been at this for some time. He was probably set up to do it. But the battlefield isn't the place to start trying to take down the army. Don't worry about him. All that liaising, driving all over the place when there are partisans in the woods as well as bears . . . sadly a run-in with a sniper . . .'

Rilling's eyes widened. 'When?'

'I'm not sure, Rilling. I'd say it should be some time this afternoon.'

On the road east from Żarki, only a few kilometres from the town, there was a small outcrop of rocks, not much higher than a two-storey house, called Czarny Kamień, the Black Stone, though in most lights the limestone was pale grey, and in bright sunlight, with the highest point just visible from the road, among the hornbeams and the beeches, it could look so white that it almost shone.

The outcrop was a place where children played, lovers met and families took their summer Sunday picnics. It seemed to have nothing much to do with the flat and uninteresting expanse of forest surrounding it. It was as if it had been dropped there by mistake, and that gave it a small magic in an unmagical landscape. But in all that flatness it did, from the top, provide a wide view over the countryside between Żarki and Niegowa. It was for that reason that a platoon of the Polish Army's 27th Infantry Regiment had set up a signal post there. It didn't last long. They began digging trenches among the trees, between the road and the Black Stone, the day after the Germans invaded, to provide cover from the Luftwaffe, but they were overtaken, before they'd even finished, by the retreat eastwards. Not a single signal had been sent and no roaming Stuka had yet passed overhead as they left. Only the half-dug trenches remained.

Johannes Rilling's German infantrymen were leaving Żarki now, their trucks and half-tracks rolling east. As the convoy moved past Czarny Kamień, one of the field-grey Mercedes trucks turned off the road, on to the track that led through the trees to the Black Stone. A half-track carrying a dozen riflemen followed it. The twenty-three men and one woman crammed in the back of that truck were not Polish soldiers, but they would be going no further east either.

Hauptmann Rilling was waiting as the truck and the half-track pulled up. The men who would make up the firing squad were standing in a group, smoking and talking, not about what they would be doing but about what lay ahead on the road to the Vistula. They were quietly cheerful, unfazed by the last job they had to do in Żarki. They stood only a few yards from the Black Stone, which rose like a pale wall behind them. There was little cloud in the sky and the stone was bright and clean in the September sun. The men glanced at the Poles who were being unloaded from the back of the Mercedes. There was nothing to see. They had sought some of them out and arrested them the previous day. They had watched over them while they were locked in a classroom at the school.

There was an air of orderly unreality about what was happening. Johannes Rilling was aware of it. No one said very much. It was all happening quickly, with a strange ease and a sense even of normality. The Poles who were being ushered towards a long, unfinished trench that ran parallel with the rock wall of Czarny Kamień simply walked silently towards it. There were rifles pointed at them, but there seemed no need to push them or prod them. They knew what was going to happen, yet there was no resistance. They walked, neither slowly nor quickly. Resistance would have achieved nothing, but it still surprised Rilling that there was none. As he looked at the prisoners, lining up along the trench, he felt he was the only one who wasn't part of what everyone there, soldiers and prisoners alike, seemed to be treating as oddly ordinary.

Hauptmann Rilling turned the pages of the list he carried from the *Sonderfahndungsbuch Polen*. It was little more than something to occupy his hands and eyes. But he did, for an instant, want the typewritten names he had ticked off the day before to make it feel there was a kind of due process. The information was curt: name, address and usually no more than the word '*Gestapa*' to indicate that somewhere there was a file containing a reason for the name's inclusion. The lists had been drawn up in Berlin and sent out with the army and the Einsatzgruppen that followed. They held the details of thousands of Poles considered dangerous to German interests, and somewhere among the names, conceivably, were people who might have been. But by the time the Sicherheitsdienst's information gathering found its way to the small towns and villages of rural Poland, it had the qualities of lazy arbitrariness that passed for thoroughness in Germany. All that mattered was that these people played a part in the leadership of their communities, however modest. Their names were as likely to have come from telephone and trade directories as real intelligence.

Twenty-three men and one woman had been arrested in Żarki. Rilling read through their names again, as if checking something he had control over. He had made no attempt to relate details on the pages to the individuals awaiting execution. He had spoken briefly to a few: the mayor, the principal of the secondary school, the parish priest. The names were just names. Stanislaus Ambrozuk, the mayor, and a member of the Polish People's Party; Wlodzimirz Bily, the headmaster of the primary school; Anazy Derkacz, who wasn't a member of the Communist Party but had a cousin in Częstochowa who was, which was close enough; Wincenta Dolotowna, the only woman, and Żarki's librarian; Mendel Epsztajn, who wrote a letter to *Gazeta Polska* in 1938, criticising British appeasement in the face of the annexation of the Czech Sudetenland – at the time he had been rather chuffed to see his name in print.

Rilling was interrupted by laughter behind him. The firing squad had lined up in front of the Black Stone, arm in arm; one was taking a photograph.

He turned to his sergeant. 'Let's get it done.'

The Feldwebel snapped an order at the firing squad. Hauptmann Rilling walked towards the trench. The prisoners still stood in a group; the soldiers guarding them barely even watched. There would be no trouble. Rilling felt a slight irritation that the sergeant had not already lined up the prisoners in front of the trench. The quicker it was done, the easier it would be. The numbers irritated him too. They would have to be dispatched in two lots, which meant the second bunch might start to panic. He didn't want it to be messy. He wondered if the firing squad was a mistake. A machine gun would do it in one, though it was less precise; it risked leaving more wounded. That was messy too. He was surprised to find himself making a mental note of that. But then he did know, they all did, that this ordinariness wasn't only for the day that was in it.

The elderly parish priest stood with the prisoners surrounding him. Their heads were bowed. The words Johannes Rilling caught were not loud, but he recognised them, even in Polish. He heard the word '*Maryjo*', Maria. The prayer became louder as the cluster of prisoners began to speak in unison, '*Święta Maryjo, Matko Boża*', Holy Mary, Mother of God. And he was unable to stop himself saying the prayer himself, in his head. It was the second time in twenty-four hours that an encounter with the Virgin's prayer had been less than satisfactory or committed. 'Now and at the hour of our death. Amen.'

The priest muttered a few words more and raised his hand to bless the men and the one woman who stood round him. He turned to a young, bearded, black-gabardined man behind him, who stood apart with one other prisoner, swaying a little, saying his own prayer. The priest and the rabbi shook hands, in a gesture that somehow expressed a kind of grudging respect for the job they both did and the distance between them that even this shared end would not quite bridge. Johannes took all this in. Taking it in was yet another way of putting it off. He turned to the sergeant, whose patient, calm features did not hide the fact that he, at least, could see his commanding officer's doubts.

'Section one, Feldwebel.'

The sergeant nodded at the soldiers surrounding the prisoners. They moved forward and pushed half the prisoners into a line with their rifles. There was some shoving and prodding now, but still, by and large, the Poles went without protest. They stood in a line in front of the trench, faces turned towards it. The sergeant shouted at them to put their hands on top of their heads and to clasp them there. Rilling wondered why. He hadn't asked for this unnecessary piece of choreography. What the hell did it matter how they stood?

The firing squad had lined up opposite the prisoners. The priest was there, the rabbi, the woman who had been the town's librarian. Johannes Rilling nodded stiffly, and at a command from the sergeant the men raised their rifles to their shoulders. Rilling took his pistol from his holster. It was attached to the lanyard that hung from his neck; it was something he wouldn't normally have worn. He didn't know why he had dressed with particular care for this, but he had. His uniform was complete and correct. There was no sound. Some of the prisoners closed their eyes; others kept them open. Some prayed; some didn't. As he nodded once more several of the men shouted. He heard the woman's voice too. 'God Save Poland' mixed momentarily with 'Fuck you, German bastards!' The second group of prisoners watched and didn't watch, in silence.

At the Feldwebel's order the squad of riflemen fired.

The prisoners fell, most rolling forward into the trench in front of them. Only the parish priest was still standing, and the woman. The priest was trembling, sobbing quietly. He had been ready for death, but not ready to watch it. The woman was unmoving. She still looked straight ahead. Then she took her hands off her head and ran the fingers of one hand through her hair. It was a gesture that Rilling felt he understood. It was the last touch of life, the last touch of her body. With his eyes fixed on her, he almost felt the touch of her hair himself. He knew no one had aimed at them, the priest or the woman. There was no sympathy in that; no real awareness of injustice. It was simply that they had all aimed at other targets, assuming someone else would perform the slightly, only very slightly, more distasteful executions of a priest and a young woman.

Rilling walked forward with a measured step. He moved between the firing squad and the bodies that lay in the trench or were slumped on the ground beside it. As he reached the priest he put the pistol to the back of his head and fired. He walked on to the woman. He held the pistol up again, almost touching her hair, and fired. He put his pistol back into its holster, passing the sergeant.

'We'll do the rest. This time a bullet for every prisoner, Feldwebel.'

As the trench full of bodies was being filled in, Hauptmann Johannes Rilling got into the staff car that was waiting for him, and drove back into Żarki to oversee the departure of the rest of his company. He lit a cigarette as the car passed the trucks driving the other way. A cigarette was what he wanted more than anything. A cigarette was something. It was something to enjoy. He found himself concentrating on the taste with a peculiar intensity. He had done nothing like these executions before. He thought he should have had the decency to feel something more than he did; not to feel sick maybe, but to feel something. What he felt was a kind of relief; it was easier than he had expected.

6

La Mancha

Dublin, September 1940

It was almost a week since Stefan Gillespie's afternoon of quiet surveillance at the Curragh Racecourse had turned into the Battle of the Curragh that had occupied Irish newspapers for most of the intervening period, pushing the war from the headlines to the inside pages, even the Battle of Britain that was being fought out over skies across the Irish Sea, sometimes in sight of the Irish coast.

In the end, no one had died in the Battle of the Curragh, though it had been a close-run thing for a bookie's runner and one of the Animal Gang men from the Coombe. The details of what had happened were, for the most part, known now. A group of bookmakers in South Dublin had been on the receiving end of a spate of bet-hedging from a Northside bookie. It had involved not simply spreading a lot of bets around without putting the cash up front, but also a series of big wins from those bets at long odds, by horses that should have been lucky to get a place. It had happened several times over the summer, at different Irish racecourses, and though nothing could be proved there was an unshakable belief in the trade that some quiet nobbling had been going on to give the outsiders the chance of achieving unexpected results. There was too much coincidence. The odds against it were high for men used to judging odds keenly. And the eyes of the Southside bookies who had lost heavily on those results were on a Northside man who, rumour had it, had come out surprisingly well.

Aware of the suspicions of his colleagues, the Northside bookmaker had paid a group of youths from one of what Dublin called the Animal Gangs to come to the Curragh meeting as protection. Just in case. They were mostly teenagers and young men, unemployed and disaffected, adding to whatever income they could scrape together with a bit of thieving and low-level intimidation. The Northside bookie drew his men from the tenement flats of the Corporation Buildings, but when news leaked across the Liffey, the Southside bookies turned to their own gangs in the Coombe and the Liberties. What they had in mind was not so much protection as revenge. It had been a proxy war. As the Animal Gangs fought, the bookmakers who hired them sat in the Curragh bars, or watched from the stands. And since payment on both sides had been in drink, not money, it was unsurprising it got out of hand.

Inspector Gillespie and Chief Inspector Skehan had contributed little to the quelling of the riot, though they still had some of the bruises a week on. And while the fact that they had salvaged the honour of Special Branch had amused everyone else at Dublin Castle, Terry Gregory was unimpressed. There was little more they could have done, on surveillance, to advertise who they were.

As Stefan Gillespie walked into the detectives' room in the Police Yard at eight in the morning, anticipating another day of watching someone, somewhere, Danny Skehan was on his way out, looking ruefully at the packet of Woodbines he was extracting the last cigarette from. He stepped back, grinning.

'That black eye's still shining. Terry wants you. There's a G2 feller in.'

'What's that about?'

'Four dead bodies.'

'Where?'

'Don't you ever read the papers you're hiding behind? La Mancha!'

'The fire, right. They didn't sound much like spies to me.'

'Ah, they're everywhere now! But if they are they're dead ones.'

Skehan shrugged and carried on out of the office.

Stefan walked towards Superintendent Gregory's office. Gregory had already got up from his desk, seeing him. He came to the door and opened it.

'You're wanted, Stevie. Come on in.'

As Stefan entered the superintendent's office he saw Commandant Geróid de Paor get up. The Military Intelligence man was dressed in civvies.

'Stefan, how are you?' De Paor shook his hand. He was looking at Stefan's face, where the vestiges of a black eye were very clearly visible.

'In the absence of a real war to give him, he found his own,' said the superintendent. 'He was mentioned in dispatches at the Battle of the Curragh.'

De Paor laughed and the three men sat down round the desk.

'You know about these killings in Dunlavin?' Gregory asked Stefan.

'I've read about it. A fire at the house, but not an accident.'

'No, not an accident. Four people called McCall. All dead. Everyone who lived in the house. Two brothers and a sister, and a younger woman who worked for them, a cousin. CID in Naas don't have much doubt it's murder, but there are questions. The house was set on fire, but they were probably dead when it started. The State Pathologist has the bodies at the County Hospital in Naas, so we'll know how they died soon enough. But it's your neck of the woods, isn't it? Not far from

Baltinglass. The house is called La Mancha. It's somewhere on the way to Kilcullen. Did you know any of them, the McCalls?'

'I'd know the name, that's all. I can't remember that I ever met any of them. And I'd know where the house is, more or less – near Gormanstown – but that's it. Are they something to do with horses, maybe? A stables or a stud?'

'You'll be going down there,' said Gregory. 'You'll have seen this has knocked the Battle of the Curragh off its post as something to fill up the papers. However, we're not sure too much interest in the McCalls is what we want. That's according to our Military Intelligence friends, isn't that right, Geróid?'

Terry Gregory paused, waiting for a response.

'I wouldn't go as far as that, Superintendent.'

'Then why don't you tell us how far you would go, Commandant?'

'It's simply that we need to know what was going on there, and whether there are any connections between La Mancha and anything that does come under the auspices of G2, or even Special Branch. It could involve you, too.'

'There you are, Stevie,' said Gregory, leaning back in his chair. 'Clear as shite. You have got to admire a man who can tell you all that and say fuck all.'

'A picture is worth a thousand words,' said Commandant de Paor.

He reached down and picked up a briefcase. He took out a folder and opened it on the desk. There was a photograph of a small suitcase. It was blackened and partly burnt, but not badly damaged. The lid was open and it was lined in a check pattern, and inside, taking up most of the case, were two dark, metallic boxes, perforated in places and with a series of knobs and dials on them. Wound behind were coils of wire, which had been fused together by heat.

'It's a radio.'

'I think we can get that far,' said Superintendent Gregory.

'But I'd guess not for listening to Fintan Lalor's Pipe Band of an evening on Radio Éireann?'

'To be more precise, it's a German Abwehr SE 85/14 transmitter – a radio supplied to German agents. In our case, it's a handy size if you're being landed from a submarine or dropped by parachute. We've recovered one of these radios that was being used by the IRA, to broadcast propaganda rather than for contacting Berlin. This one was on the kitchen table at La Mancha.'

Stefan Gillespie took the train from Kingsbridge Station to Naas. At the County Hospital he found Edward Wayland-Smith, the State Pathologist, in the mortuary, filling his pipe and pouring a cup of tea from a thermos flask. It was some time since the two men had met, but for Wayland-Smith all encounters with detectives were about the same thing. The dead were always the business in hand, and it was a business that needed to be conducted with a directness that called for only minimal preliminaries. As Wayland-Smith drained his tea, the green rubber apron he wore was splattered with blood. He was tall, taller than Stefan, and heavier, but he moved with a lightness and precision that reflected his work. He smiled a faint smile, almost of anticipation. He remembered the policemen who listened. There were plenty who didn't, who simply wanted someone to do their work for them. He remembered Inspector Gillespie was a listener. He liked an audience, especially if there were unusual circumstances.

'A curious business, Inspector, and curiouser and curiouser it gets.'

He picked up the thermos and screwed the lid back on. Then he stood for a moment, pressing the tobacco down hard into his pipe before lighting it.

'I shouldn't ask why Gregory's interested in this. You'd only lie.'

'I wouldn't at all, sir, I'd say you're right, you shouldn't ask.'

'However, you're more interested in the living than the dead these days.'

'We're very flexible in Special Branch.'

'Some might say lethally so, on occasions.'

Stefan didn't reply. The reputation Special Branch had for shooting first, when circumstances demanded it, and, in the view of many, when it didn't, wasn't something he relished. He didn't like it because it was true. He didn't like it now, especially, because he knew Wayland-Smith was putting him into a compartment in his head that he didn't want to be in. A dislike for the men in Special Branch was common enough among Gardaí everywhere. Stefan could see that behind the businesslike smile, the State Pathologist shared that dislike.

'You'll want a look at them.'

The State Pathologist gestured across the white-tiled room. Two slabs stood at the centre of the mortuary: shallow porcelain with more white tiles round the pedestals. There was a body on each slab. They were blackened and charred around the head and the extremities, and in places around the torso and the arms, but there were also areas, where the clothing had been cut away, where the flesh was undamaged, just grey from the process of death. The bodies had been cut open from chest cavity to the stomach. On one, burnt skin on the face had been cut away to reveal the muscle on the skull. Looking at the two bodies, it was possible to see one had been a man, the other a woman.

To the left of the mortuary slabs there were two trestle tables, set up to deal with two more bodies. The tables were covered in green rubber sheets, and the bodies were draped in brown oilcloths. Wayland-Smith stepped forward and pulled each of the oilcloths to the floor, revealing another man and another woman. These bodies were still intact, still partly clothed in the unidentifiable clothes they had worn, blackened and fused in places with their burnt skin.

'So, right to left. Mr Simon McCall, sixty-seven years old; Miss Annie McCall, fifty-nine, sister to the aforementioned Simon; Mr Patrick McCall, brother, sixty-four. Two bachelors and a spinster. Last, and probably least, Miss Alice McCall, a cousin, but also La Mancha's cook and housemaid – in short, the skivvy. It seems to have been no great secret in Dunlavin – at any rate in the Garda station – that although she was always referred to as a cousin, Alice McCall was Miss McCall's illegitimate daughter.'

Stefan followed him to the second trestle table.

'The bodies are all damaged and disfigured to a greater or lesser extent by fire. I should say now that there's no question in my mind it was started deliberately. I think that has been confirmed by the Guards and the fire brigade. Petrol was used, and the bodies had been drenched in the stuff. I say drenched, but it was clumsy. Nowhere near the quantities required. Bodies are surprisingly resistant to most methods of disposal, and burning is particularly inefficient. So, we'll deal with Alice first, because she's the simplest. She was found in the kitchen, and although she was quite badly burnt it's very superficial. The cause of death was almost certainly a blow to the head, which you see here. On the left temple. I haven't cut the flesh away, but the skull is fractured underneath. There is another blow to the back of the head. Although the skin isn't in a good condition to offer much evidence, there's enough to say there was a struggle.'

'Was there a weapon?' asked Stefan.

'The Guards came up with this, from a sink in a scullery.' He walked to a bench and held up a heavy iron poker. 'There's blood, which I think will prove to be hers. I don't know about the blow to the temple, but I would be confident this caused the lesion on the back of her head. So, Alice is straightforward, so far.'

'And she was dead before the fire started?'

'They all were. They had been dead for several days before

the fire. Some of the early stages of decomposition had set in. If it wasn't for the lingering scent of smoke and charred flesh, they'd smell riper.'

Stefan nodded. It was an unexpected piece of information.

'That is odd, yes,' said the State Pathologist, reading the thought. 'And it gets odder as we look at the other three, that's to say it gets more complicated.'

They moved slowly towards the bodies on the slabs.

'These three were all in bed, Simon, Annie and Patrick. What remained of the clothing consisted of pyjamas and a nightgown. There was no obvious and immediate cause of death. The damage from fire is not that great as far as internal organs go, but it is enough to dispose of a lot of things that might have pointed us in the right direction. That doesn't mean the onset of decomposition and the effects of the fire haven't compromised matters, but the signs I found myself looking for, which can be slight in themselves, are there.'

'And they're signs of what?' said Stefan, holding back a smile. He knew Wayland-Smith enough to recognise that it was when he expressed himself with a little too much convolution that he was about to reveal a winning hand.

'Asphyxiation,' said the State Pathologist simply.

'But not from smoke?'

'We've disposed of that, Gillespie. Do keep up!'

Wayland-Smith grinned. He walked back to the bend and pointed at a pillow. It was grubby and black from smoke and dirt, but it wasn't burnt at all.

'Look at the middle of this. You'll find blood, very faint, watery.'

Stefan moved closer. He nodded.

'This was on the floor in Miss McCall's bedroom, pushed or kicked, whatever, under the bed, which kept it from catching fire. What you see is a pale ring, slightly pink, slightly yellow. A mixture of blood, not much, and saliva. There could be many reasons for that, but if we look at the body . . .' Wayland-Smith stepped back to the slab. 'She's bitten her tongue. It's swollen.'

He pointed at the blackened face, the tongue protruding from the lips.

'There wasn't a lot in the way of bloodstained fluids in the air passages, but some, along with slight emphysema and oedema of the lungs. I think we'll find the other brother, Patrick, has very congested lungs when I open him up. Again, forget the fire, forget the smoke. I think these two were smothered.'

'Is there any evidence of a struggle?' asked Stefan.

'Nothing I can see, even allowing for fire damage to the skin.'

'You'd expect them to put up a fight, even at their age.'

'Possibly,' replied the State Pathologist.

'Which means you wouldn't, for some reason?'

'Moving on to Mr McCall, senior, we have no evidence of asphyxiation. And no need to search for any. He died of poisoning – arsenic, pure and simple.'

Stefan looked down at the body. That was unexpected.

'A considerable quantity of arsenic, much of which was still in his stomach, so undigested that I can guess it's basic lead arsenate, just by looking. And that, to add complication to variety, brings me back to the brother and the sister. I've tested their urine, and there is evidence of arsenic there too. Not in anything like such a quantity, but there all the same. It's too long after death to be very accurate, and I'll know better when their hair and fingernails have been tested. It's certainly not just sitting in their bellies, and I'm not saying it killed them, but if they were smothered, it could be they weren't in a fit state to resist.'

From Naas, there was only one stop before Dunlavin, at Harristown. It was a familiar journey. Stefan knew its sounds as well as its sights. He would not see the western outliers of the Wicklow Mountains yet. They were only visible beyond Dunlavin, rising up on the left as the Tullow Line went south through Colbinstown and Grangecon to Baltinglass. And it was Baltinglass that was home to Stefan's parents and to his ten-year-old son, Tom, and, though he spent most of his working life in Dublin, to him too. Special Branch had kept him from going home for over three weeks now, and for a time, as he looked out of the window at the fields and woods of Kildare, heading towards West Wicklow, it was the thought of spending a night at the farm below Kilranelagh Hill that occupied him. It was only as the train slowed, on the approach to Dunlavin Station, that his mind returned to the four dead bodies in the mortuary. It was a picture noisy with detail, even before he got to the scene of the crime. Murder didn't often accumulate such a wealth of lethal minutiae. A woman battered to death; a man and woman smothered without resistance, with arsenic in their bodies, yet not dead from it; a man neither battered nor smothered, but with his stomach full of the undigested arsenic that killed him; then all of them clumsily drenched with petrol and set on fire, along with the house they lived in. And alongside that a radio that was the property of German Military Intelligence.

Commandant Geróid de Paor was waiting at Dunlavin Station. Stefan's phone call from the County Hospital had gone through to the Garda barracks in Dunlavin, but as the G2 man was already there, he was the one who came to collect him. As they drove on to Gormanstown and the house called La Mancha, Stefan outlined what he had learnt from the State Pathologist. When de Paor's car turned the bend in the high-ditched road, there was a small patch of grass to the side of the turning to the McCalls' house. A concrete plinth for milk churns stood there, crumbling and overgrown. Two cars were parked beside it, along with a tractor and a motorcycle. Several bicycles leant against it. And on the plinth itself, their bare legs dangling down, half a dozen children of various ages sat watching the gate and now watching the car that was approaching. A dozen people stood at one side of the entrance to La Mancha, talking and watching too. Two uniformed Gardaí blocked the gateway, stepping back to wave in de Paor's car. Stefan recognised one of the bystanders as an *Irish Times* reporter. He moved to pull his hat down over his eyes, then began laughing.

'Jesus, this secret policeman craic is getting to me.'

'What?'

'There's a feller at the gate from the *Irish Times*. And here I am, sinking in the seat, pulling down the brim of the hat, in case he recognises me for a Special Branch man, when we'll likely as not catch up in the pub in Dunlavin. I know the Guards standing at the bloody gate. They've just told him who I am.'

'It doesn't much matter. There's murder enough to keep the papers happy. More than enough from what you've just said. Arsenic, for God's sake!'

As Stefan looked out at the pasture on either side of the drive, he registered that it was bare and patchy, poached by over-grazing. It wasn't an observation that meant anything, but these fields weren't cared for. To the right he saw a man, short and thin, standing beyond the post-and-rail fence, attaching a nosebag to a black horse. Two other horses stood behind him, one of them nudging his back, pushing him, expecting a nosebag too. They would be good horses; they didn't go with such poorly kept fields. The man was laughing as he turned to scold the horse. He looked at the car and waved. It was an oddly ordinary moment, given what had happened in the house at the end of the drive.

'Who's running this?' asked Stefan. 'Someone from Naas?'

'Inspector Harrington. Paul, would it be?'

'I know him,' said Stefan. 'He's sound enough.'

'He's quick enough, and quick enough to avoid the wrong questions. I think he had a good idea what the radio was as soon as he saw it. He had the sense to lock it away. That's information no one wants out in the open. He's made sure no one's been into the house, other than a couple of his detectives and the Guards from Dunlavin, and the State Pathologist. The Guards brought the bodies up to Naas. There were all sorts in and out the day of the fire, from the fire brigade, to the McCalls' stable man, but he's kept it tight since.'

'So, what are we meant to be doing?'

'For now, I'll take the radio back to Dublin. There's no need to advertise G2's interest. What we want to know is how the radio got here, who brought it, who knew it was here. Were there people who came here we'd have an interest in? I don't know if anyone can answer those questions, anyone who isn't dead.'

'But we're not much interested in who killed them?'

'I'm sure your colleagues will find that out.' De Paor smiled. 'First things first.'

'First things first, Inspector.'

'And if the killings are tied up with the radio, and German Intelligence?'

'That would depend how they're tied up, if they're tied up.'

Stefan laughed. 'You don't make it easy, do you? Are we looking for German agents, British agents, the IRA or just any old passing Republican?'

'No idea, Stefan, but I'm struggling with any of them having a reason to bump off a house full of people down a Kildare boreen. And if they did, good God, would any self-respecting assassin make quite such a hames of it? What did you say you've got so far? A poker, pillows, arsenic and old lace, and then the funeral pyres to finish the job, which didn't at all. Talk about belt and braces.'

The car pulled up outside the house. Stefan looked out at the blackened frontage and the broken windows. At one side, part of the roof had gone, where the timbers had burnt. It all still shone from the water that been hosed into the house and over its walls. The smell of smoke hung in the air, acrid and sour.

'Let's be serious for a moment,' said de Paor.

'That's not serious?' Stefan grinned. 'Fuck me, you're a hard man.'

The uniformed Guard at the door was watching them curiously.

'This is what you need to know, for now,' continued Geróid de Paor. 'We've had at least three German agents landed over the last two months – the ones we are aware of, anyway. You'll already know that in Special Branch, since you fellers picked up one who claimed he was here as a circus performer.'

'He was,' laughed Stefan. 'He had been. Wasn't he a strong man?'

'Well, if that's the calibre of men they're sending,' de Paor smiled, 'we may be in with a chance. But there's at least one still out there, parachuted in a couple of weeks ago. No one knows exactly what these agents are doing, and we want to deal with them without a fuss. We're not turning a blind eye to them, but the government doesn't want to start throwing accusations at Germany. Not when they could be on our doorstep tomorrow. The job is to pick them up and shut them down. As for what they're up to, we're all playing the three wise monkeys. It may be about us in the Republic, and finding out what we're doing. It may be about organising sabotage in the North. It may be information gathering. A lot of radio we've picked up is weather reporting. Maybe they are planning landings here, if they invade Britain, whether that's a diversion or a way in through the back door. Maybe it means bugger all, and one half of German Intelligence doesn't know what the other half's doing.'

'Is bugger all the fingers-crossed option?'

'All we know is that these agents are in contact with the IRA, and they're using the IRA to provide shelter and move them about. They're using a network of safe houses all over the country. Some we know, and some you'll have info on too. But there are others they seem to have kept quiet. People you wouldn't normally be looking at. People your average Volunteer would know. The fact there was a radio here makes it look like this was one of them. So, who brought it here? Was our missing German agent here? If he was, where did he go next?'

'Even if he was here, unless he's roaming the countryside murdering the people who put him up for the night, and burning their houses down afterwards, this is a dead end, in every sense. There's no one left to ask, is there, Geróid?'

'There'll be a list of people who came to this house over the last week or so, or came somewhere near it. There'll be statements about the last time the McCalls were seen, and where they were seen, and who they were seen with. You know that better than I do, Stefan. It's not about locals. It's not about suspects. Mostly I'd say you're looking for strangers. Does that make sense?'

'If it does, you'll be the first to know,' Stefan said with a smile. For several seconds he looked through the windscreen at the dirty, mutilated front of La Mancha. There was something pointless about it, just as there was something pointless, almost futile, about the half-burnt bodies of the people who had lived there. He had the feeling he sometimes had, as a policeman looking at the dead, that he was intruding; not only was he intruding, but his intrusion was pointless too. 'There's a smell here that isn't much about sense. I hope I can find you some.'

A tour of the partly burnt-out house added little to what Stefan Gillespie already knew, and nothing at all to what he was actually there to find out. It still stood, despite the damage, though walls had cracked from the heat. The stairs were solid enough to be used with care. The interior of the house was black and putrid with the aftermath of the flames. And fire was not the only scent that lingered. In the shells of the bedrooms, where the McCalls had lain for days after their deaths, the sweet-sick odour of decomposing flesh was strong.

He caught it in the air. Downstairs there was less damage, though most things that were combustible had burnt. Only one room had remained relatively unscathed. The drawing-room door was black and charred, but somehow it had not burnt through, and although the room itself had filled with smoke, almost nothing had caught fire by the time the fire brigade got the worst of the blaze under control. It had been flooded with water, like the rest of the house, where the carpets and curtains and some of the furniture had begun to smoulder, but it was oddly untouched, and the heavy Victorian furniture that filled it was defiantly solid.

It was here that Naas CID's Detective Inspector Harrington finished the tour, and it was here that he had gathered his own notes on a desk by the window. He knew Stefan; he was only a few years older. He was a man of quiet common sense, and he already understood that he would not be party to whatever it was the Special Branch man and the army officer in civvies were here for. He had recognised the peculiarity of the radio in the suitcase as soon as he saw it. It had escaped serious damage in the fire, and he could see immediately that it was military in nature, and that there were several words in German on the dials. The hunt for radio transmitters was not restricted to G2 and Special Branch, but it wasn't a matter for general conversation. Harrington had taken the precaution of locking it out of the sight of Dunlavin's Guards.

'I don't know what you want to do, Stevie,' said Harrington. 'You can read through my notes. If you want to sit in on any interviews, help yourself. But I do already have a good idea where I'm going. Sadly, it's not complicated.'

'It sounds complicated enough to me, Paul. What about the arsenic?'

'I've found where it's made. In the workshop, in the yard.'

'Made?' asked de Paor, surprised.

'A lot of farmers made it years ago,' Harrington continued.

'Some still do. I remember my father doing it. It's simple enough. Lead salts and sodium arsenate. And that's what you'll find in a cupboard under the workbench. There's a big orchard here. They'll use it on the fruit trees, and maybe on the potatoes, for blight. So, there was as much arsenic as anyone cared to make.'

'It definitely came from here, then?' said Stefan.

'Why would you look any further?'

Stefan looked harder at Paul Harrington. It wasn't an idle remark, and it was about more than the arsenic. Stefan smiled. The CID man wasn't saying that he had solved the crime, but he believed he would do. The confidence on his face told Stefan that he wasn't going to be looking for any help from him.

'No one else knows about the arsenic?' asked Stefan.

'Not yet. None of the Guards in Dunlavin, and none of my detectives.'

'Is that it, in terms of what happened?' It was de Paor who asked now.

'It is,' said Harrington. 'The dead all accounted for, except for the horse.'

'A dead horse too?' said the commandant. 'And why not?' He shook his head. The house had affected him more than he had expected. The proximity of the deaths and the strangeness of it all left him uncomfortable and uneasy, as did the feeling of inexplicable violence that somehow hung in the air. This was not his territory, and he found himself wanting to get back to what he knew. Death had an intimacy here that he would be glad to leave to the two policemen.

'Where does a horse come into it?' asked Stefan.

'I don't know if it does. It's a dead horse. One more odd thing, for sure.'

'I've lost this,' laughed de Paor.

'There was a dead horse in the stable yard, well, in a loose box. It had been shot, and when I say shot, I mean put down.

The way you'd normally do. It was an old gelding. It was done a day or so before the McCalls died, maybe even a couple of days. No one had made any attempt to move it. That was something. It had started to stink. Jesus, the whole thing, maggots, flies.'

Stefan was thinking about the McCalls now. He had not tried to place them yet, except in a cursory way. He had never met any of them. He didn't know the family. But they were only a few miles from Baltinglass. He knew people who would have known the McCalls. He knew Simon McCall had worked with racehorses, and that he had some reputation in that business.

'Simon McCall was a trainer, is that right?'

'He was when he was younger. He had a Cheltenham Gold Cup winner twenty years ago. La Mancha. That's why he gave the name to the house. They bought it ten or eleven years ago. He'd already stopped doing much by then. You're only as good as your last win round here. And there were never many. He was a big Turf Club man, but no one thought much of him as a trainer in the end. There were money problems, and he retired years back. What a way to go.'

Stefan was looking at the sideboard. It was not loaded with photographs, but there were a number in old silver and ebony frames. The smoke had left them dusty and the heat had warped them slightly, but that was all. There were a few that must have been the McCall family members he had seen, blackened and disfigured, in the County Hospital, but there were more photographs of horses than people. He stepped closer, looking down at one of the pictures. Something about it caught his attention. It was a photograph of a man standing by a black horse, holding a beribboned silver cup and smiling broadly. He picked it up and turned into the light with it, examining it much more closely.

'Is this Simon McCall?'

Detective Inspector Harrington moved forward.

'It is. In happier days.'

The man was younger, a lot younger, but there was no mistaking him. He was the man Stefan had seen at the Shelbourne Hotel with Carl-Heinz Petersen and Owain Jones, the man he had seen again at the Curragh, arguing with the Welshman. Now it was the unrecognisable man he'd seen on a slab in the mortuary at Naas County Hospital, who kept an Abwehr radio in his kitchen. They were one and the same; Simon McCall, deceased, La Mancha, Dunlavin.

7

Baltinglass

Stefan Gillespie walked through the farmyard at Kilranelagh, up from the road where Detective Inspector Harrington had dropped him. He had not yet told Harrington that he recognised Simon McCall. He didn't know what it meant; he didn't know if it meant anything. It had to have something to do with the German radio, but whether that was anything he should be talking to a rural policeman about he wasn't sure. For now, it simply added to the confusion that surrounded the deaths at La Mancha. He wasn't there to solve a crime, though that's what his instincts told him mattered most. He wasn't even sure he was there for the reasons Terry Gregory and Geróid de Paor had given him. He would do what he could on that; he would find out if there was anything to know about who had been at the McCalls' house, anything that mattered to Special Branch and Military Intelligence. But it wasn't always the case that what mattered at Dublin Castle and McKee Barracks needed to see the light. In that sense his job might be the opposite of the one Harrington was doing. In the Branch it was not unusual to find confusion and then leave it exactly as it was.

For now the familiar smell of the yard shunted aside what he was in West Wicklow for. All that would be back soon enough. He stopped as a small black-and-white dog emerged from the barn, heading at speed, barking. He crouched down slowly and laughed. The dog flattened itself on the cobbles and growled.

'I don't know you, do I? Come on, come on here.'

The dog inched forward uncertainly, still almost flat on the ground.

Stefan looked round to see another dog in the doorway of the barn.

'Ah, Tess, that's more like it. Haven't you put manners on this one yet?'

Tess stepped down to the yard. She walked towards him slowly, wagging her tail. It was barely a month since he had seen her, but he was startled by how thin she was. She wasn't limping, but her legs moved awkwardly, as if she wasn't quite sure she could stand. She looked very old now, when only weeks ago she had looked the same as she had always looked. He got up and met her, and stood rubbing her ears. The young dog, assured by the old dog's response, was running round them, his suspicious growls replaced by yaps of greeting.

The door from the house opened and Tom, Stefan's ten-year-old son, ran across the yard, laughing. Stefan smiled. It was a smile of quiet pleasure before he embraced his son's excitement. They had come a long way together, father and son, since the death of Tom's mother, Maeve, eight years earlier, in what had been thought of as a tragic swimming accident. It was still not long since Stefan had discovered that accident was murder. Now the man who had killed his wife was dead too. It was over, as far as anything like that could be over, and Tom would never know what happened. That was the decision Stefan had made. The past was something you carried with you. In Ireland that had always been a blessing and a burden that touched everything, but the truth of Maeve Gillespie's death was a burden he would carry alone. Time had made it lighter.

The young dog had turned away from Stefan, leaping up at Tom.

'His name was Blackie, but we call him Jumble now.'

'Now why would that be?' laughed Stefan.

'He likes it.' Tom grinned. 'Try him?'

Stefan bent down, petting and scratching the Border collie's head.

'Come on, Jumble, come on then!' Stefan called, still stroking Tess.

The young dog took no notice. He only came closer when Tom did.

'He's seven months now, and he's part trained.'

'Which part would that be?' laughed Stefan.

'He can herd ducks!'

'That's handy.'

'I'm training him with Opa. He's teaching me. He'll be good.'

The words Tom used for his grandfather and grandmother were German. The German roots of the family found little expression in life at Kilranelagh, but they were still there, and still something precious for Stefan's mother, Helena.

'He'd better be good, Tom. He's got a lot to live up to.'

Stefan looked down at Tess fondly.

'She's been ill. Did Opa tell you?' Tom was quieter.

'He did. But I didn't realise—' He smiled. 'Let's go in.'

He scratched Tess's ear once more, and then followed Tom indoors.

The dog watched him until the door closed. She looked round as the young dog barked enthusiastically and raced towards the big horse chestnut tree that spread over the top end of the yard and rose higher than the two-storey house. Three ducks walked from behind the tree, into the yard, and in seconds Jumble had gathered them into a group and was driving them slowly forward. Tess turned, shaky on her legs, and hobbled back into the dark of the barn.

The evening at Kilranelagh was like evenings there always were. The talk was of ordinary things. It was of the farm and the stock, and the neighbours and the prices at the mart, and the school at Talbotstown and Tom's friends, and the winter that was coming. But Stefan found himself looking at his mother and father as they ate and as they sat and talked. It was the shock of seeing how old Tess had become, so suddenly, that he couldn't quite get out of his mind. Because he wasn't there, he didn't see what was happening, slowly, naturally. He saw it abruptly, as he had in the farmyard earlier. Age was one of those things he never thought about, but Helena and David were older, of course they were older, and he felt he could see it today, where he had not seen it before.

It was a thought that passed, as the evening passed, and they talked on after Tom had gone to bed. It was inevitable that the war was there, and the battle that was being fought in the skies over England, and the people they knew in England, and the people they knew in Germany, too, because of the German blood that flowed through Tom and Stefan and his mother, which had flowed through his grandparents, back to Germany. There were bombs in London now, and in Berlin. But the news from London that mattered most to Tom was the book Kate O'Donnell had sent him. *William and the Evacuees* had come after the arrival of the new sheepdog, and Blackie had, inevitably, turned into Jumble. When Tom was in bed, Stefan read a story in which Jumble showed all the characteristics that David Gillespie would never want in his new sheepdog.

'Kate's going to be home from England, Tom.'

'When?'

'It'll only be two nights and she'll be back on the boat to England. It's her godson's confirmation, in Dún Laoghaire. She won't have time to come here.'

'Will you see her?'

'Well, that's up to you.'

'How's it up to me?'

'We're invited to the party, after the confirmation. How would that be?'

'In Dún Laoghaire?' Tom looked slightly unsure.

Stefan smiled. He was slightly unsure himself. He had met Kate O'Donnell less than a year earlier in New York. She was working for the Irish exhibition at the World's Fair; he was bringing a murder suspect back to Ireland to face trial. They had fallen in love in circumstances that had brought them an immediate intimacy, but the business of neutrality and war had not been easy on them since their return to Ireland. Stefan had been pulled into the shabby and all-consuming world of Terry Gregory's Special Branch, and Kate was now working in England, with few opportunities to come home. It meant a lot to them both that they would have this brief time together, but Stefan wasn't enthusiastic about sharing it with other people. It was too precious for that.

'You'll come up and stay, and see Kate. There'll be loads of children.'

'I won't know them,' said Tom, with a look of panic.

'They won't know you,' laughed Stefan. 'God help them, eh?'

The next morning, after Tom had gone to school, Stefan Gillespie waited in the barn as his father finished the milking. They had hardly talked of the killings in Dunlavin the previous night, but a new day had brought them back again. The McCalls were in Stefan's head once more, yet for a moment he stood watching the old sheepdog, Tess, as she slept in her corner of the barn, on a bed of straw.

'She seems better this morning.'

'She's better when she's asleep,' said David, as he milked.

'You didn't tell me she was so bad.'

'It's come on faster now.'

'And what is it?'

'I had the vet look at her when he was up here. Her heart's giving out, and she's got a lot of fluid on her lungs. You can hear it. He's given me something to help her breathing. She won't have long. She's hardly eating.'

'You'll put her down.'

'When the time comes. If you're here, you should do it.' David smiled, looking up. 'She worked for me, but she was always yours. Dogs are like that.'

Stefan nodded. He bent and stroked her. She opened her eyes, but didn't move. She breathed more deeply. He could hear it was hard for her. He stood up and walked across the barn, looking through a cobwebbed window to the yard.

'Did you know the McCalls?' asked Stefan after a while.

'I might have seen your man, Simon McCall, years ago. He trained horses, didn't he? Jesus, you can't get a hold of what happened there. I didn't want to say it in front of Tom. Is it all true?'

'That's only the half of it. I've never seen anything like it.'

'Have you got any idea who did it?'

'I think Inspector Harrington has. He's in Naas.'

'There can't be far to look in Dunlavin.'

'You wouldn't think so.'

As David Gillespie moved the milking stool and bucket to the next cow, he marked the thoughtfulness in his son's words, but he knew better than to ask.

'I never heard anything about them, even when I was in the station here,' continued Stefan. 'I'd only have known the name, and the name of the house.'

'That was his horse that won at Cheltenham, La Mancha.'

Stefan nodded. The dead horse.

'I don't know if that was his one bit of luck,' said David, 'but I wouldn't say anyone had much time for him as a trainer, apart from being cheap. That's the way of it. If you can't produce winners, you're going to be cheap.'

'Is that it?' said Stefan.

'You'd hear more in Dunlavin, but they were people who kept themselves to themselves. That's all anyone was saying yesterday. But they had good reason.'

'Did they?'

'The brother and the sister were as mad as buggery.'

'It was an odd set-up there, I gathered that much,' said Stefan.

'Tony White always called the sister Mad Annie. He reckoned as racing stables went, it was the only one he ever knew that was run like an asylum.'

There was the sound of an engine, and the blast of a car horn.

'That'll be Paul Harrington,' said Stefan. 'You take care, Pa.'

'Poor bastards,' said David, getting to his feet. 'And what for, eh?'

Stefan stood in the workshop at the back of the stable yard at La Mancha, with Inspector Harrington and the State Pathologist. Wayland-Smith was packing several tins and bottles into a wooden box. Through the door, across the yard, Henry Casey was forking hay from the Dutch barn into a trailer hooked to the back of a small tractor. The only sound was his tuneless, rhythmless whistling.

'That'll do it,' said Wayland-Smith, picking up the box. 'I may not match the arsenic in Simon McCall's stomach to what was produced here, but I scarcely need to. A ready supply. That's enough. I don't think you'll have to scour the pharmacies of West Wicklow, Inspector.' He grinned. 'Inspectors!'

'The boots you took?' asked Harrington.

'Well-scrubbed, but definitely blood on the soles.'

'And the trousers?'

'One pair with traces of blood, and stained with petrol.'

'The others?'

'Two pairs match the jackets you gave me. The same cloth

exactly.' Wayland-Smith carried the box outside to the big shooting brake that was parked outside. As a man who shot all sorts of things, the back of the car often carried the carcass of a deer, but it had been known to double as a mortuary van.

Stefan Gillespie and Paul Harrington stood in the yard, while the shooting brake pulled away. They were in front of the loose box where the remains of the dead horse had been found. Above the door a pokerwork sign bore the name: *La Mancha*. The door was shut, but the smell of decay hung over the whole yard.

'I don't think there's any point waiting,' said Harrington.

Stefan nodded. He had most of the information from the Naas detective.

'I'll just sit in, if that's all right, Paul?'

'Ask what you like.' Harrington grinned. 'But if he's a German agent, you'd have to hand it to those fellers. You wouldn't beat them for a disguise.'

As they walked towards Henry Casey, there were no more idle words.

'How's it going?' asked the CID inspector.

'Not so bad, Mr Harrington. We've so little grass, that's the trouble.'

'Yes, I saw that in the paddocks, Henry.'

'And this hay will never last the winter.' Casey shook his head.

'We need a proper talk,' said Harrington. 'At the barracks.'

'You know where I am, Mr Harrington. I have the horses to feed now.'

'I'll have the Guards see to the horses. Mr Wayland-Smith has been looking at the boots I took, and the trousers. I think now is the right time.'

In a small office in the Garda station in Dunlavin, Henry Casey sat across a desk from Detective Inspector Harrington. Stefan sat to one side, and another man in plain clothes sat on the other side taking notes. It was a big desk, and there was little space for anything else. The room was lined with books and files, on shelves and in cabinets. It had stored documents since the building had been taken over from the Royal Irish Constabulary by the Garda Síochána, and since in Dunlavin the sergeant responsible for the records had merely replaced a uniform with a crown and harp for a uniform with a harp unadorned, the records remained in place to be added to through the years of the Free State. No one ever consulted them now, as no one had consulted them before, but they filled the walls of the room and left barely space in the middle for a desk. It was a tight, ill-lit room that smelt of dust and old paper. But it was out of the way, and for the time being Paul Harrington felt that out of the way was the thing.

As Harrington spoke to Henry Casey, Stefan was leafing through a file of statements. They included Casey's own initial statement about the fire, and statements by various people in and around Dunlavin concerning the events at La Mancha and any sightings of, or contact with, the McCalls that people might have had over the previous week. He could see, as he read, that more and more of the questions Harrington had asked were about the man being interviewed.

Henry Casey seemed relaxed. The only sign of tension was the tuneless, half-breathed whistling, hardly audible, that came though his teeth whenever there was silence, and the intermittent tapping of the fingers of his left hand on his knee. He had his story and it didn't occur to him that it wouldn't be enough. He was aware of what he had done, but while he knew he shouldn't have done it he was, after a fashion, telling the truth. It wasn't all the truth, but then as far as the rest of it was concerned, he knew nothing anyway. The fact that he knew 'nothing' considerably earlier than he said he did didn't alter that. He had to tell his story, and keep telling it. He had not considered that it wasn't that simple.

'Let me just go through your statement again, Henry. To get it straight.'

'That's grand, Mr Harrington.'

'We'll start last Thursday. The last time you were at La Mancha, till Sunday, which was the day before the fire. You were there all day Thursday?'

'Yes, sir.'

'And Mr McCall gave you Friday off?'

'He did.'

'Friday and Saturday?'

'He said he wouldn't need me. He'd manage himself.'

'But normally you'd work six days, sometimes seven?'

'We were short of a man. We have been all year.'

'Mr McCall gave no reason for giving you two days off?'

'He's the boss.' Casey shrugged.

'You didn't go to the house on the Friday or the Saturday?'

'I didn't.'

'You have a list of the places you were, each of the days—'

'Far as I recall, Mr Harrington.'

'So, the next time you went to La Mancha was Sunday evening?'

Casey nodded again.

'And you fed the horses?'

'I did. I took them some nuts and a bit of hay.'

'You'd say they hadn't been fed?'

'They had not.'

'And you didn't go to the house and ask Mr McCall about that?'

'I knocked at the back door, but no one came. I got on with it.'

'I see. The door was locked?'

'It was.'

'Was that usual?'

Casey looked puzzled.

'That the door was locked? That no one was there?'

'It would be locked sometimes. You couldn't tell. They wouldn't always answer. They don't like strangers. If one of them was playing up, Annie or Patrick, well – there was difficulties with them, the Guards will tell you that.'

Casey tapped his head several times, at the temple, and grinned.

'So you assumed Simon McCall was out – and what about Alice?'

'I don't know as I thought about it. I was there to see to the horses.'

There was silence for a moment. Stefan looked up.

'And was the horse in the loose box dead? La Mancha?'

Henry Casey looked confused for the first time. Both Stefan and Paul Harrington could feel that his first instinct was to say that he didn't go into the loose box, that he didn't know La Mancha was dead. But he knew he couldn't.

'He was dead, yes,' said Casey.

'Had Mr McCall talked about putting him down?'

'I think he had. He was getting on. He always said it would come.'

'You didn't think it had come very suddenly? You didn't think it was strange that the horse had been put down and left there to rot? You didn't think to ask? La Mancha was a special animal. And very special to Mr McCall.'

'It was a shock, but I couldn't find Mr McCall. He wouldn't have done it without a reason, course not. And you wouldn't get the knacker up till Monday.'

Casey spoke the last words with more confidence. He had an explanation.

'We might return to that, Henry,' said Inspector Harrington. 'But back to Sunday evening. You said you didn't see anyone at the house. No one at all?'

'I thought you meant in the house before. I forgot about the children.'

'Peter and Assumpta Clarke arrived at La Mancha at about six o'clock on the Sunday evening. They were selling tickets for a concert their school was putting on. They knocked at the front door and got no reply. They walked round the back, where they met you coming from the yard. Is that what happened?'

Casey nodded.

'You said, "They are all sick." The children told you Mr McCall had specially asked for the tickets, and you said you'd take three tickets and get them the money. You told them to wait, then you went to the back of the house and came back with three shillings. You took the tickets and the children went.'

'I took the tickets.'

'And where did you go to get the three shilling?'

'I would have had it in my jacket. I left it by the pump.'

'You didn't go into the house?'

'No. It was all locked up, I told you.'

'What did you do with the tickets, Henry?'

'I put them in my pocket. I probably chucked them.'

'Why, if Mr McCall wanted them?'

'I don't know. I don't know what I did with them.'

'Do you know what this is?'

Paul Harrington took a brown envelope from the file in front of him. He took out a charred and blackened piece of paper, only a few inches square. He held it out to Casey, who peered down at it, uncomprehending, and shrugged.

'It was in the kitchen fireplace, with papers that had been burnt. Not burnt in the house fire, but put in the fireplace to burn. Do you see the difference?'

'I'd say burning's burning,' said Casey, with an awkward grin.

'This is a ticket for a concert at St Nicholas' School.'

Casey frowned.

'Do you have any idea how it got into the kitchen?'

'They're selling them all over the town, everywhere.'

'We'll maybe come back to that too, Henry. Let's get to the

fire. Monday afternoon. You were meant to be at work that morning, but you didn't go in.'

'Bridie Farrell passed away Friday night, and it was her wake. I had to go in and see Mattie, and I thought I'd get that done before I went out to Gormanstown. To tell the truth, I was up a bit late myself the day before.'

'That's not surprising, Henry. You spent Sunday night in the West Wicklow House. And drunk enough, I'd say. You'd something to sleep off.'

'There's no crime in that, Mr Harrington.' Casey tried to laugh.

'And you'd your fair share at Mattie Farrell's the next afternoon.'

'I didn't mean to stay as long as I did. But you know yourself—'

'So, at four o'clock on Monday afternoon you cycled to Gormanstown. You went straight to the yard and you filled a barrow with nuts for the horses in the paddock and wheeled it out there. You made no attempt to go in the house?'

'Well, I'd missed half a day's work, I wasn't looking for trouble!'

Henry Casey gave a nervous snort. He felt it was a good answer.

Stefan Gillespie was listening to everything that was going back and forth between Casey and Inspector Harrington, but his attention was as much on the statements he was reading as the interview. He already knew where this was going; there was nowhere else for it to go. He had read enough of Henry Casey's earlier statements to know that they made no sense. They didn't help clarify what had actually happened at La Mancha, but presumably all that would come. As Stefan turned a page in the file he was poring over, he saw another statement by Henry Casey, given to the sergeant in Dunlavin on the day of the fire. These were precisely the events Harrington was now asking about. He skipped quickly through the account of

Bridie Farrell's wake and the bicycle ride to Gormanstown. He read and reread what came next with surprise. He had been sent to Dunlavin to look for connections to things that had no obvious place in the back roads of West Wicklow and Kildare, and he had found them.

'And when you started back towards the house,' continued Harrington, 'that was when you saw smoke. You were at the end of the drive, by the road?'

'I was.'

'And you ran back.'

'I did so.'

'And by the time you got to the house, it was in flames.'

'It was.'

'You tried to get in?'

'I went to the back door, but it was locked. I went and got a spare key from the yard, but when I opened the door the passage was alight inside. It was roaring with flames. I couldn't even get in there.'

'But you tried the front?'

'I did. The fire was even worse. The door was burning through and I tried to push in that way. I was shouting their names. I couldn't get in there either. There was no doing it. I could see the stairs burning. It was the same back as front. I had to get help – the fire brigade. I rode the bike here, to the barracks.'

There was a kind of finality in those words. He believed it was enough.

Harrington was looking at him, knowing it was actually the beginning, puzzled only that the man appeared oblivious to what was happening to him.

Stefan Gillespie cleared his throat. Harrington looked at him and nodded.

'You saw a car, Mr Casey, when you got to the house that afternoon?'

Casey looked bewildered for several seconds; he had forgotten.

'I did. It was coming out when I was going in.'

'You knew the car?'

'Yes.'

'You saw the driver?'

'I knew the man. He'd been to the house.'

Henry Casey looked down, more awkward, his fingers drumming on his knee. He couldn't say he'd hidden from the driver. He didn't know why he'd mentioned the car. The story he was telling wasn't the truth. He could lie easily enough, but the real things, the things that weren't lies and were in there too – that was confusing. He couldn't remember why he'd bothered with the car at all. It didn't matter, and he wondered if he had made a mistake talking about it. He didn't know what the man in the car had seen. They might look for him now.

'A black and white Jaguar Roadster,' said Stefan. 'A nice motor that . . .'

'Yes,' Casey nodded. 'A looker.'

'Were the number plates English?'

'There was a GB plate. So they would have been, I suppose.'

Casey felt easier. He didn't know what these questions were for, but the fact that he wasn't being asked about the fire and the house was a kind of relief.

Paul Harrington watched Stefan; he had no idea what this was for either.

'This man was a friend of Simon McCall's, is that right?'

'Like I said, he visited a few times. He was a racing man.'

'And do you know his name?'

'It was only the last few months.' Casey was struggling to remember. 'He'd come over for a race meeting, and they'd go off together. He never stayed at La Mancha. It was Mr Jones, I'd say. They always called him the Welshman.'

8

Savignyplatz

Berlin, September 1940

Zandra Purcell was waiting outside the Sophie-Charlotte-Platz U-Bahn station at midday. She had been waiting half an hour. Her friend was late. She was in her mid-thirties, an elegant, dark woman, slim, even thin, with a neat bob of hair that belonged in the previous decade. She carried a black case containing the saxophone that was more than the way she scraped a living now; it had long been most of what there was of her identity. She was an Irishwoman who lived in Berlin for reasons that had little to do with her own decisions, at least now, though once her reasons had been something she could relish and enjoy.

She had arrived in Berlin in 1928, when the all-girl band she formed in London, 'Zandra Purcell's Queens of Jazz', was touring Europe. London had taken her out of Ireland, and the Queens of Jazz had taken her out of England. Along the way she had played with Django Reinhardt and Coleman Hawkins, and in clubs and cabarets all over Europe. But her band found its home in Berlin, and for a time the Queens of Jazz – English, Irish, French, German – earned a good living in the last days of the Weimar Republic. Love had been less kind. Affairs that never seemed to last – with women in the band and with men in other people's bands – had meant that what always mattered was the Queens of Jazz. That was her solid ground. Then suddenly, when the Nazis came, the band and the little world apart that stretched between Berlin's Kurfürstendamm and Alexanderplatz were shattered. The bands were gone; the clubs were gone; the music was gone; the people she had known and loved had drifted away. They had all seen it coming, but few had believed it would truly happen. And when it came, Zandra Purcell couldn't leave. She had a son.

Zandra was surprised to see Johannes Rilling walking towards her along Bismarckstrasse, from the direction of the Opera House, not emerging from the entrance to the underground station. She was surprised that he was wearing his army uniform. It was something he didn't make a habit of doing when he was at home. She kissed him on the cheek. As they dodged the traffic, running across the street into Wundtstrasse, she took his hand. It was quieter now, traffic left behind. She was pleased to see him; she knew Andreas would be pleased too.

'Thanks for coming, Johannes.'

'I wanted to.'

'I'm sorry, have you been hanging about?'

'No, I didn't come from Spandau. I was in town. I walked here.'

'You walked all this way – to go for a walk. A glutton for punishment! We could have come out together. I've been at a rehearsal all morning. Jesus!'

In that last word, attached to her good but heavily accented German, was a moment of her Irishness, dismissing everything she had spent the last three hours doing with purposeful, though light-hearted, contempt. She laughed.

'I do get a solo in "You're Driving Me Crazy". Forbidden music! If I shut my ears to the shite they've written in to it, it'll almost be like playing for real.'

He smiled, but she could see something wasn't right.

'I didn't know you were going back so soon?' she said.

He looked puzzled.

'You're in uniform. Does that mean you're off again?'

'I am, yes, but that's not . . . I'll tell you later.'

Holding his hand, she could feel his tension. He was hot, too, sweating, as if the walk out of the centre of Berlin had been done at a fierce pace. But she thought no more about it. They had reached the long, high wall that closed off the building that housed the Convent of the Holy Mother. Zandra pulled the iron rod at the side of the entrance and rang the bell inside. A small grille in the heavy, black door opened, and there was a lined and smiling face looking out.

'I was waiting. I never knew you to be late, Zandra!'

The grille closed and the door opened. Zandra and Johannes went in.

'Herr Hauptmann, it's good to see you.'

'You too, Sister Mary Joseph.'

As they walked along the path into the small garden at the front of the house, a boy of around ten hurtled towards them and flung himself at Zandra.

'Mammy! You're late, you're very late!'

If the rest of the words were German, the first was Irish enough.

'I am hardly late at all, Andreas Purcell!' She closed her arms round him.

He grinned and broke away, looking at Johannes Rilling.

'I didn't know you would be here, Herr Rilling.'

'Should I go, then?'

Andreas laughed. He stretched out his hand with an air of seriousness, and the army captain shook it with an equally serious expression – and winked.

'Will you be out with him long, Zandra?'

Sister Mary Joseph spoke in English. It was not something she did often. Her languages, since joining the Sisters of the Holy Mother forty years ago, had been French and German, and the accent she had taken with her to France from Ireland all that time ago was more French than anything else. She liked the fact that Andreas's mother was a reminder of her own country, a country that, really, she knew almost nothing of now. What she knew of the world outside the small convent was little enough; it featured very sparely in the life of the nuns, even though they were in the middle of a city at the heart of a world war, and a city that had seen the most violent changes in the years Sister Mary Joseph had lived at the convent in Knobelsdorffstrasse. The door and the walls kept a lot of that at bay. There was only prayer, and the children they cared for.

'Just a walk in Charlottenburg. I've got to be back at work quite early.'

'We'll see you later, then. Be good, Andreas!'

'Maybe, maybe not,' the boy said with a grin.

They left the convent and walked on towards Charlottenburg, Andreas in the middle, holding hands with them both. He had the thick-set features and the distinctive round face that went with who he was. He was one of three Down Syndrome children who lived at the convent. He saw his mother every week, but it was a long time since he had seen her friend, Hauptmann Rilling. He was thrilled, seeing him in his Wehrmacht uniform. He walked with pride, wanting everyone to see them together. He was with a German soldier. A German hero.

It was a warm afternoon in the Charlottenburg Gardens, and there were a lot of Berliners enjoying it, even on this ordinary working day. Zandra and Johannes had stopped where the formal garden ended and the park began. The palace was behind them, and Zandra was looking towards the sweep of trees that grew up, thicker and higher as it rose, at the edge of the parkland. Andreas had met a boy with a kite and he was running across the grass now, flying it. Johannes lay on his back, looking up at the sky. He had said nothing for ten minutes.

The energy he had found to entertain Andreas seemed to have disappeared very suddenly.

'Do you want to tell me, Johannes?'

Johannes looked round, still lying flat. He shook his head.

'Not especially, Zandra.' He sounded weary.

'That's fine.' She stretched forward and stroked his head.

'The fuckers!' He sat up. 'It's shit – real, unadorned, shit.'

'So, tell me something new,' said Zandra.

'Someone sent a letter to the Gestapo to say my mother wasn't a *Mischling*, she was a full Jew. She thinks it was her landlord. He's been trying to force her out of her apartment. He says he needs it for his daughter, but he just wants her out. The police have been round. Her identity card taken away—'

'But you can prove she's right?'

'I could. I could once. I had two Jewish grandparents, that's what it said. It's in black and white on the documents we got in 1936. But they reclassified another grandparent as Jewish, last year. I don't even know how. I went to the police station with her this morning, with all the birth certificates and baptism certificates. But I've done it before. It didn't change anything then. I've asked them to look again, to check again. They could help her. Even if it's true, these things get altered. A stroke of the pen would do it. I went in uniform, complete with Iron Cross Second Class. I wanted to remind them her son has the same medal as the Führer. At least it stopped them treating her like shit. But . . .'

'Didn't it work?'

'Well, it embarrassed them.' He shrugged. 'They returned her ID card.'

'You are going back to your regiment?'

'I don't know for how long.' He laughed. 'Roll on England!'

'What do you mean?'

'There's hardly any fighting now. It's all down to the Luftwaffe. We're in Belgium, waiting for the order to start the attack on England. So, someone in Berlin's decided it's time to clear out the *Mischlinge*. A bit of Jewish blood can be tolerated when you're in the firing line, and there's a good chance of dying for the Fatherland, but not now. I'm getting protection, but the best protection's more war. I've seen a lot of officers discharged. A lot of friends. If it comes to it for me, the best I can hope for, as a quarter-Jew – half-Jew now – is being reduced to the ranks.'

'Is a discharge that bad? Maybe you'd be better to leave them to it.'

'You know what I think about that. Look at Berlin, Zandra . . .'

There was silence for a moment. They both looked across the grass at Andreas, running with the kite and laughing. She reached for Johannes' hand.

'Have you done anything about the book?'

'I've asked you to forget that, Zandra. I didn't mean to tell you.'

'Why don't you just get rid of it, Johannes? What's the point?'

'I don't know. I have to do something about it.'

'I don't want to see anything happen to you—'

'I'll be fine.'

'That's bollocks. It's not true at all, is it?'

'Forget about it, Zandra. You don't know anything—'

'No one cares about me. I'm not important. I keep myself to myself.'

He shook his head slowly, then he was silent, frowning.

'I think I'm being followed. I'm not entirely sure. I noticed someone when I left Spandau this morning, and then outside my mother's apartment. It could be about that. Who knows? I'd already been into the police to complain.'

She didn't question him. Being followed, being watched, was not unusual in Berlin. It hadn't been for a very long time. The reasons never mattered much.

'That's why I ended up walking here, after trailing around

the U-Bahn and changing trains three times. If I'm right, at least no one's followed me here.'

'When are you going back to Belgium?'

'Two, three days' time.'

'If you want to stay with me – if you don't want to go home to Spandau . . .'

She opened her bag and took out a key.

'A spare. Use it if you want. I've a bottle of wine that needs drinking!'

He smiled and took it. He leant over and kissed her cheek.

'That sounds like it could be a very good end to a bad day!'

Johannes Rilling left Zandra and Andreas in the Charlottenburg Gardens, and as they headed back to the convent, he left the park at its northern end and took a slow, circuitous walk along the River Spree, north and west, still conscious of what his instincts told him. The two unidentified men he had seen too many times, in too many places, over several days could be explained away, but he felt his instincts could not. They were sharp; they had saved his life in battle. Now it was all a battle. Along the isolated stretches of the river, where he saw no one, he felt reassured that he was alone. It was safe to do what he needed to do.

He came into the Westend Kleingärten colony from the north, where the Spree bent round it at the top end. It was a place of neatness and order and colour, imposed on the hundreds of allotment plots of vegetables and flowers and shrubs, though it was an order that abundance often seemed on the verge of cheerfully bursting apart. But order was always maintained, though the only policing that went on here was with a rake and hoe. Westend was one of the dozens of allotment colonies that surrounded Berlin, and gave it lungs. For a population that lived mostly in gardenless apartment blocks, old and new, large and small, the Kleingärten were more than a place to grow vegetables and flowers. They were a playground for children to escape the city and for their parents and grandparents a place to breathe. Each allotment had a hut, small and compact, but lovingly painted and decorated, inside and out, and although you weren't allowed to live on your allotment permanently, it was a place to stay at weekends and in holidays. And now, as British bombs had fallen on Berlin for the first time, the Kleingärten offered a different kind of refuge and, for those lucky enough to own one, food that was already difficult to find.

Johannes walked along the Spree and turned down into the Westend allotments; he had decided what he had to do. For a time he had been lost in the sweeping victories that crushed France and sent a broken English army scuttling back across the Channel. Now the whole western seaboard of Europe belonged to the Reich, and the whole continent, in one way or another, was in thrall to German triumph. The future was what everyone was talking about, because every prophecy had been fulfilled; the world was changed. Now there was time to stop, to celebrate, to think. Johannes had to face what he had seen of that future.

The allotment that Johannes Rilling arrived at was not his own, though there had been many times he had enjoyed it, in the company of its owner. He had spent many nights in the green and white hut, and once it had been a place he cherished, along with a friendship he had cherished too. But he was not looking for his friend. It was midweek and he assumed he would be at work.

He opened the small white-painted picket gate and stopped, smiling. The approach to the garden was guarded by a row of gnomes, brightly coloured, fat and bearded. There were seven of them, and two of them he had bought for Rudi as a present. They had given the gnomes, quietly, the names of various Nazi Party functionaries. He could remember which was which. But it wasn't a joke Rudi would want to make now, however quietly. That was another time.

Johannes walked past the rows of vegetables and the apple trees full of fruit. Rudi had always been good with the garden; that hadn't changed. He found the key that Rudi kept in the grey plaster boot by the door. He did not go into the hut, but went straight to the shed behind it. He took out a spade, and walked round to the asparagus bed by the hedge. He began to dig.

The metal cash box Johannes Rilling dug up from under the asparagus bed had started to rust. He had to use a pickaxe to smash it open. He placed the contents – the book, the papers, the photographs – in his briefcase. He did not intend to leave any evidence of his visit. The state of the asparagus would leave some unanswered questions, but the hole would be filled in. He could not imagine Rudi getting much further than bewilderment and irritation. Imagination had never been his strong point.

'What the fuck are you doing?'

Johannes had not heard Rudi Trunz approach. He straightened up, smiling wryly. The two men had not seen each other for some time. The closeness they had once shared they shared no longer. Trunz was younger than Rilling, taller, thinner, with more delicate features. Neither was very pleased to see the other.

'Digging,' said Rilling, standing up. 'Well, I'm filling in now. I'm sorry about the asparagus. It'll be all right in the spring. I wasn't expecting you.'

'I'm staying out here.'

'Bombs?' Rilling put his finger to his lips. 'Bombs can't reach Berlin!'

'How are you?' said Trunz. 'I did hear you were back—' As he looked down at the ground he saw the broken metal box. 'What's that?'

'Something I left behind. A place of safety.'

'And what was in it, Johannes?'

'What you don't know won't hurt you. Wise words these days.'

The younger man bent down, tense with anger, shaking slightly. He didn't pick up the box. He reached for the briefcase that lay next to it on the grass. But as he stood up, Johannes Rilling stepped forward and snatched it.

'You never were one to take advice, Rudi. Leave it alone.'

'And why would it hurt me?' said Trunz coldly.

'I'll leave the asparagus to you, sweetheart. You're better with plants.'

'This is the thing you told me about, Johannes. The book.'

'Perhaps it's my life savings. Just forget it. You weren't interested at the time, as I remember. You said you didn't want to know. I don't blame you.'

'You've got a fucking nerve. If they'd found it here—'

'Do me a favour, Rudi. You don't look good on a high horse.'

'What if they'd come looking—'

'Do you know what my reasoning was?' said Rilling. 'If anyone gets hold of the idea that there really is something to look for, apart from what I've got in my head, this is the last place they'd look. And you know exactly why that is.'

Rudi Trunz said nothing. He seemed to have taken a step back.

'So is that it? Is that the only reason you came, Johannes?'

'I didn't think there was anything else. I didn't think you did either.'

'What are you going to do with it?'

'Get it out,' said Rilling, looking down at the case.

'I think they know. You said someone suspected you had it—'

'I had that feeling, yes. But then you'd know more about that.'

The young man bit his lip.

'How, Johannes? If they do know—'

'There's always a way, isn't there? Irish eyes will do the trick.'

Rilling smiled. Rudi Trunz stepped closer.

'I was surprised, that's all, Hannes. You don't need to go.'

He reached out and stroked his palm along Rilling's cheek.
'It's certainly tempting, Rudi. It's been a while.'
'Too long. We should do something about that. Now.'
Johannes pulled the other man closer and kissed him. For some seconds he held him, as their bodies pressed against one another. Then Rilling stepped back.
'How many Judas kisses is that?'
'What?' laughed Trunz. 'You're in an odd mood. Is it what war does?'
'It may be. It makes you see things more clearly. That's if you can be bothered to look. Most of the time it's easier not to. But I've known they owned you for a long time – the Gestapo, the SD, the SS, whoever the fuck. So if you didn't understand before, I'm sure you can now – what better place to hide something than under an informer's bed. In this case, his asparagus bed.'
'You fucking shit,' was as many words as Trunz could find.
'We're all shits now, Rudi, but we're German shits. And you were always a good fuck, sweetheart, so neither of us suffered in that department. Or do I flatter myself? Still, for old times' sake, you might want to take some advice for once. It might not be a great idea to act the indignant queen and tell your Sicherheitsdienst chums you kept such interesting material under your veggies. And didn't even know? Wow! Anyone for Sachsenhausen and a pink triangle?'

At the Villa Concordia, where the Ministry of Propaganda broadcast its programmes in English and other languages to those who were still fighting against the Third Reich and to those neutral countries, like America and Ireland, that needed to hear the truth, Charlie's Swing Orchestra was playing 'You're Driving Me Crazy'. After the first verse, which used the song's original lyrics, Zandra Purcell blew out a tenor-sax solo, with an enthusiasm that the rest of the orchestra enjoyed. There were moments when what they did triumphed over what they were supposed to be doing. It was private pleasure they didn't even communicate to one another.

There weren't many ways to earn a living playing what felt like some version of the music they had all once rejoiced in in the bars and cabarets of Berlin. The jazz and swing they pumped out mechanically for the consumption of Britain and its Empire, and other Allied hangers-on, was banned. No German could listen to it. It represented all that was degenerate about the world the Third Reich had replaced. It was Nigger music, Yid music.

But it could be played here. It even kept the men out of the army. And because the commentators and newsreaders at the Villa Concordia included highly prized foreign nationals fighting Germany's propaganda war, there was a canteen where food was notably better than what was becoming the norm in Berlin. Food had begun to matter a lot. And instrument cases were ideal vehicles for smuggling it out.

For Zandra, who only picked up work with the orchestra now and again, the food was as precious as the money she was paid. But there was also a pleasure in playing. The only other work she could get was the occasional private party, in venues that varied from military messes to the upmarket brothels used by the SS and the Wehrmacht's upper echelons. They didn't mind a little degenerate music when the time was right. For now, as she played her solo, she was somewhere else. It was ten years ago, in a club on Ku'damm. The music in her head, as she played 'You're Driving Me Crazy', was Guy Lombardo's, Al Bowlly's, Louis Armstrong's, Django Reinhardt's, and it was for some of the others, keeping pace, and for a moment somewhere else too.

As she came out of her solo, the vocalist, Karl Schwedler, stepped to the microphone to sing. The orchestra played more quietly, Schwedler winked at Zandra and then pretended to yawn. They were back in the Villa Concordia, on the job.

'Here is Winston Churchill's latest tear-jerker!
Yes, the Germans are driving me crazy!
I thought I had brains
But they shattered my planes,
They built up a front against me,
It's truly amazing,
Clouding the skies with their planes.
The Jews are the friends who are near me to cheer me –
Believe me they do,
But Jews are the kind that now hurt me, desert me,
And laugh at me too!'

When Zandra Purcell left the S-Bahn train at Savignyplatz, she walked the short distance to the house at the far end of Carmerstrasse with a light step. She was glad to be out of the studio, and she hoped that Johannes Rilling would be in the apartment. She had a bottle of wine that she had been given as part-payment for playing at an officers' club in Potsdam at the weekend, and she had not only managed to secrete a piece of cheese and some bratwurst from the canteen at the Villa Concordia, she had two rolls that were real bread in her saxophone case. At the top of the stairs she opened the door into the narrow corridor that divided the apartment into two main rooms: a bedroom and a kitchen. As she turned on the light and walked into the kitchen, her first thought was that she had been robbed. Drawers were pulled open, and the contents had been thrown across the floor; the furniture had been pushed aside and upended. She went quickly back to the corridor and into the bedroom. She didn't register that it was in the same state as the other room. All she saw was her friend, Johannes Rilling. He was propped up by pillows, as he lay on the bed. At the top of his body there was a bloody, blackened mess. It wasn't shock that hit her first, but the awareness that on the left of that mess, half his head was missing.

9

Kiltegan

West Wicklow

The list of people who had visited La Mancha in the two weeks before the deaths of Simon, Patrick, Annie and Alice McCall was very short. There were at least two Henry Casey had seen, or chose to recall. There were no corroborating statements. There were several people Simon McCall had spoken to in Dunlavin, including Father Clinton, the parish priest, and several shopkeepers. Owain Jones, the Welshman, had visited three times when Casey was there. Once he had spent an hour in the house with Simon; once he had arrived in the morning and had taken McCall to the Curragh for the race meeting; once he had called at the house and got no answer, just before the fire.

Stefan Gillespie could add another meeting with the Welshman – a meeting that included the press attaché at the German embassy in Dublin, but he didn't do so. He had also seen an argument between McCall and Jones at the Curragh.

The other man on the list was someone Stefan knew.

Mostyn Trevor lived on the other side of Baltinglass, just outside Kiltegan. He was a landowner, a racehorse owner and a pillar of what was left of Protestant West Wicklow. He was also a Royal Artillery general in the British Army. It came as a surprise to Stefan that the General, as he was universally known in and around Baltinglass, even by those who spat when they said it, was in Ireland at all. But Inspector Harrington had already established that he had just returned from England, and was at home in Kiltegan. He was expecting a Garda visit now, as one of the last people to see the McCalls alive.

'You know the man?' asked Harrington.

'A bit.'

'They were both Turf Club stewards. Casey says it was something to do with that. That's all he heard. Whether anything the man says is true, given the shite he's come up with today, is anybody's guess. I'm assuming when he's not talking about dead bodies and fires, some of it is, but whether I'm right . . .'

'You want me to talk to Mr Trevor?'

'Well, he's one of yours. You might as well do it.'

In other places 'one of yours' might have meant that Stefan knew Baltinglass and Harrington didn't. Here it meant Protestant. Stefan shrugged.

'And British Army generals sound like a Branch job to me.'

'You mean you can't be arsed to drive to Kiltegan?'

'I've got my murderer, Stevie. You're here for the frills. You do it.'

Before he left the Garda station, Stefan called Terry Gregory and established that the Welshman was still at the Shelbourne Hotel. Jones was not being watched and Gregory said he would send someone to the Shelbourne to find out what was happening. For now they would keep the Welshman under surveillance. Stefan was surprised at a certain hesitancy in the superintendent's voice. He said he would pass the information on to Geróid de Paor in G2, since Jones was mainly of interest to Military Intelligence. It was the first Stefan knew of the Welshman being of much interest to anybody, despite his report of the meeting with Carl-Heinz Petersen. Gregory showed no desire to bring Jones in. When Stefan said that should be the next step, he could almost see a shrug.

'We'll see what Commandant de Paor thinks.'

'There's no doubt he was here, sir. And with a house full of bodies.'

'You think he killed them and came back to check they were dead?'

'He was here several times. We don't know what he saw—'

'You're not investigating the murder, Inspector. No one cares.'

The gates into Fort Trevor, General Mostyn Trevor's estate, between Baltinglass and Kiltegan, were guarded by two small crenellated turrets, like the buttresses of a miniature castle. They were picturesque rather than defensive, but they reiterated the point an earlier generation of Trevors had made when they renamed the townland where their house had been built, Fort Trevor. It was a place Stefan Gillespie knew. The Trevors had long been prominent leaders of the Protestant community in Baltinglass and Kiltegan, and though they had left the idea of the Ascendancy behind themselves, its memory still clung to the big, square, stone-fronted house that lay beyond the castellated gates. For Stefan the wide, flat field in front of Fort Trevor belonged to his teenage years and to the long summers on the farm at Kilranelagh. The big field was still called the Cricket Field locally, and he had spent many summer afternoons playing there.

The front door was open when he arrived in the car he had borrowed from Harrington. Mostyn Trevor was expecting him. He walked down the steps from the house to the pebbled drive. He was a big man, red in the face at the best of times, red now from exertion. He reached out and shook Stefan's hand firmly.

'Gillespie. It's a long time. Inspector, is it now?'

'Mr Trevor.'

'How are you?'

'Not so bad?'

'Dublin Castle, I hear?'

'Yes, sir.' Stefan smiled. Trevor knew what that meant.

'Your parents? I did see your father at the market last week.'

'They're grand. Still there or thereabouts.'

'We're all still here, just about,' laughed Trevor.

'But you're in England mostly, sir?'

'Just about, I should probably say again. Well, we got out of France anyway, earlier in the year. Not with much grace. I left half my guns behind. I shouldn't be in Ireland at all, but I'm shutting up the house. The rest of the family's up at Eadestown. My son's in England. The stock's still here, but the house is empty. It won't pay for itself. God knows how long this is going on.'

'People say longer rather than shorter?' said Stefan. It was a question.

'Maybe in Dublin, but not in West Wicklow. Half my neighbours expect Hitler to be in London the week after next – they're already eyeing my cattle!'

'I think we hear less than you do in England.' Stefan's thoughts were with the war suddenly, as they rarely were. This was a man who did know.

'Well, I'm not sure there's a lot to hear, Gillespie. It's all up there.' He pointed up at the sky. 'The rest of us are only watching. And it's a fine calculation. We have to shoot down more of their fighters and pilots than they do ours. If you ignore the fact that it all involves a lot of dead young men, ours and theirs, it's a mathematical calculation. Whoever scores most wins most.'

They walked forward, towards the Cricket Field.

'Though we have finally got some bombs to Berlin.'

'Is that having an effect?'

'It's undoubtedly had the effect of getting them to bomb London.'

'That doesn't sound like much of an achievement, sir.'

'Wrong,' said the general, looking out across the grass to the trees at the demesne's edge. 'We can afford to lose a lot more civilians than fighter pilots.'

'Is that a calculation too?' Stefan asked.

'No one would say so publicly, but I'm sure somewhere in Whitehall, some bugger's done the sums. There we are. But you're here as a policeman.'

'I'm investigating the deaths in Dunlavin, the McCalls at La Mancha.'

'Yes, it's a shocking business. I mean, hard to grasp . . .'

Stefan waited. It had been only days before the McCalls had been killed that Mostyn Trevor had visited La Mancha. He didn't volunteer the information.

'We have to put together everything – events. It's not easy, given—'

'I know. I have heard some of the details.'

'You were at La Mancha last week, to see Mr McCall?'

'I was.'

'I hope you won't mind me asking you about that.'

'I doubt I can help you. I know I can't, Inspector.'

'Were you a friend of Mr McCall's? Simon, I mean.'

'Not really, no. We worked together, in the Turf Club. We were both stewards, on various committees and so on. Colleagues rather than friends. A lot of years ago, I did put a horse with Simon, for training. It wasn't a particularly happy relationship.' He gave a wry smile. 'For me. The horse was La Mancha.'

'The Gold Cup winner? I thought that was his horse?'

'The bloody animal was going nowhere. Simon McCall was a useless trainer and La Mancha was about as bloody useless a gelding as you'd find. There was a parting of the ways, and I settled what I owed Simon by letting him buy the horse cheap. Two years later he won at Cheltenham. I never did know whether it was luck or Simon had codded me. Given his subsequent record, I'd plump for luck.'

Stefan Gillespie thought about the horse again; the horse bothered him.

'It's odd, sir, but the horse was shot, La Mancha, maybe a couple of days before the McCalls died. Did he mention the horse at all when you were there?'

'La Mancha would have been getting on. Comes to us all, Inspector.' The general smiled. 'I've told my children to put me down when the time comes.'

'I'd be right to say Mr McCall cared about the horse?'

'That damned animal was almost all he did care about.'

Stefan took it in. It was what he had already come to believe.

'You wouldn't have been a frequent visitor at La Mancha?'

'You could measure my visits in blue moons. Simon and I didn't have much in common except horses, and since he was such an abysmal trainer, even that had its limits. He was a rabid Republican, as his parents had been rabid Home Rulers and then Irish Nationalists, whatever the nom de guerre of the times. Not that Simon ever did much about it except march past the GPO every Easter Monday. You'll appreciate it wasn't my favourite topic over port and cigars.'

'Can I ask why you went to see Mr McCall?'

'I'm sorry, you can't. Well, you can ask. I won't reply.'

It was an unexpectedly blunt response.

'If it was a personal matter—'

'Gillespie, I'm sure you're one hell of a discreet feller and all that, but there is no connection between what I had to say to Simon and these awful events. It was Turf Club business, that's all I'll tell you. The man's dead, and sadly in circumstances you wouldn't wish on anyone – but he still has his self-respect.'

General Trevor turned away from the Cricket Field. Stefan turned with him, heading back towards the car. It was evident that the conversation was over. He wanted to ask more. It seemed there had been something in Mostyn Trevor's business at La Mancha that asked questions of Simon McCall's self-respect. He knew the general enough to recognise there would be no more, but as they kept pace with each other, across the stones of the drive, he tried again.

'It doesn't sound as if it was a very comfortable conversation, sir.'

'Whatever it was, it's nothing now. And no one killed him for it.'

Stefan Gillespie left Inspector Harrington's car at the Garda barracks in Dunlavin, and travelled back to Dublin on the train in the late morning. Nothing in the La Mancha investigation had changed in the course of the morning, and Harrington had left Henry Casey largely alone. He had not arrested him, but he had called him into the station briefly to answer a few precise questions about times and places. Stefan was aware, as the Naas detective was, that Casey had formed the remarkable view that his explanations were coming to an end, and that he had successfully covered his tracks. It was a reflection of a man whose intelligence was limited, in a way that both police officers had begun to understand, by an inability to see anything through other people's eyes. It wasn't that Henry Casey couldn't think clearly, or that the circumstances he was in didn't make sense, even the danger, but these things only made his sense. There was something in him that meant the most ordinary kind of empathy was not there. If he was convinced by what he said, the idea that someone else might not be was beyond his grasp. He was lying, lying at every turn, but there was something he believed that made him feel that didn't matter. There was an essential truth behind the lies, even if only he knew it. It ought to be enough.

The air of disconnection between Casey and reality troubled Paul Harrington just as it troubled Stefan Gillespie. Increasingly there was nothing left behind Casey's lies, and even people in the town, avoiding him now in the street, knew that, without ever needing to know what had happened in his interviews with the police. Yet Henry Casey believed in himself. You could see it even as he lied. It was as if he believed that whatever else happened, he was an innocent man. That was the last thought that had gone through Stefan Gillespie's mind as Casey had walked out of the Garda station the previous day.

At Kingsbridge Station a black Special Branch Ford was waiting for Stefan, and Chief Inspector Skehan was driving it. They were to go straight to the Shelbourne. The decision had been made to bring Owain Jones in for questioning, though it remained the case that it had nothing to do with the murders in Dunlavin.

'Terry said you'd fill me in,' said Skehan.

'I don't know what there is, except a German radio transmitter and a meeting with the German press attaché. The rest is about racing and four people who were probably killed by a man who worked for them. I don't know what we get out of all that, but Mr Jones is some kind of agent – or a courier, maybe.'

'What about the killings? They have got the feller?'

As they drove along the Quays, Stefan outlined the deaths of the McCalls in Dunlavin. Danny Skehan already knew something about it. In a country in which murder was still a rare commodity, at least outside the political arena, it was bloody enough to provide gossip far beyond West Wicklow. He had heard of Owain Jones in connection with his surveillance of the German press attaché, but the Welshman remained outside Special Branch's list of Republican and pro-Nazi familiars, as did Simon McCall. Had it not been for the presence of the Abwehr radio in the kitchen at La Mancha, it could well have been that the two men's relationship with Carl-Heinz Petersen would have been put down to racing and nothing more. It was only the transmitter that questioned that. But there was more to know now, and as they approached Stephen's Green, it was Skehan's turn to fill Stefan in on new information.

Terry Gregory had reconsidered his apparent indifference to the Welshman, and had spoken that morning to British Special Branch, in Belfast and at Scotland Yard in London. This three-way contact was primarily about sharing information on IRA movements in and out of Northern Ireland and mainland Britain. It was common knowledge in the Gardaí that such cooperation existed, but if it was an open secret, it was still a secret. Nobody talked about it, even in Dublin Castle; few knew how much of it there was. All three police intelligence arms – in Dublin, Belfast and London – had their own informers and their own secrets, and they spent a lot less time deciding what they told each other than what they didn't. But that wasn't all about national jurisdiction and neutrality. Special Branch in Belfast was as unforthcoming to Scotland Yard as Dublin Castle. Suspicion about the English came in all shapes and sizes on the island of Ireland. It didn't stop at the border with the North. But Mr Jones was a wildcard, certainly as far as the Castle was concerned. Scotland Yard knew more. They had an interest in what the Welshman was doing in Ireland. There was a reason to trade information. Whether the Yard would get back everything the Castle found out was unlikely, but as they hadn't given everything they had in the first place, it didn't matter. You kept your best cards.

'He's some sort of Welsh Nationalist.'

'What sort of Welsh Nationalist?' said Stefan, smiling. Welsh Nationalists didn't feature very prominently on anybody's list of threats.

'I don't exactly know what Scotland Yard told Terry, but this is what he told me. Not necessarily the same thing, of course. It's the All-Celts-Together-and-Fuck-the-English plan. There's some Germans over the water winding up a collection of Welsh Nationalists and Scottish Nationalists to do something with the

IRA. Do what, nobody seems to know. Plant a bomb or go to an Eisteddfod? There's probably two of them in the Outer Hebrides and three fellers and a sheepdog somewhere in North Wales. But Mr Jones is to be the sales rep for this bollocks. At least, he's been trying to interest the IRA in it. I can't see the Boys taking it seriously. And the English aren't taking it seriously either, but these fellers could put together a way of smuggling arms, explosives, even fucking spies, across the Irish Sea. And they'd all be unknowns. Off anyone's map. Come a German invasion, even Fred Karno's army could do damage.'

'How does that fit in with a dead racehorse trainer and his family?'

'You're the expert, Stevie. Now you've got a chance to ask him.'

When Stefan Gillespie and Danny Skehan walked into the entrance hall of the Shelbourne Hotel, the first person they saw, sitting in a deep leather armchair, idly reading the *Irish Times*, was Commandant Geróid de Paor of G2. He stood up with a slightly sheepish smile. The head porter nodded at Stefan, and from the frown on his face Stefan could see he had some idea what was going on. There was little the porters missed. But the combination of de Paor's sheepish smile and Anto's frown already made Stefan feel something was wrong.

'A bit of a cock-up, I'm afraid,' said the Intelligence officer.

'What does that mean, Commandant?' replied Skehan.

'Well, to use what has to be the appropriate metaphor, under the circumstances, the horse has bolted from the stable. We've lost the favourite!'

The two detectives stared.

'He wasn't due to leave for another two days, but he left very abruptly this morning. I don't know how abruptly, or why. But he did settle his bill.'

'I thought he was being watched?' said Stefan.

'There was some confusion, between us and you, as to who was doing what, Inspector. Terry and I were still in two minds about whether the man should be brought in straightaway, or whether we should see who he was in contact with. There didn't seem to be any urgency. He'd been here a week, and was in no hurry to leave. We didn't want to spook him. Oh, no, horses again!'

'I thought you wanted to know about this,' said Stefan, irritated.

'Well, we can't bring the man back.'

'And where is he, Commandant, do we know?' asked the chief inspector.

'Liverpool, or on his way somewhere from Liverpool.'

'That's impossible,' said Stefan.

'Unfortunately not. He managed to catch the Aer Lingus flight from Collinstown. His car will be shipped back to England. Some motor, isn't it?'

'Can't he be picked up in England?'

'I doubt that's on, Stefan, but Terry Gregory would know better.'

'He's a witness in a murder investigation, Geróid.'

'I don't think that's why we're interested in him, is it? And I'd say the English a lot less so. If they do get on to his trail, they'll be wanting to know where he goes and who he talks to, especially as he's been waltzing round Ireland talking to various—' De Paor lowered his voice. 'Well, obviously this is not the place to go into detail. His Majesty's Government may not have been too keen on us picking Jones up in the first place. That's only my guess, of course.'

'Perhaps they tipped him off, then,' said Stefan sarcastically.

'Stranger things have happened,' laughed de Paor.

Stefan looked at the G2 man harder. The commandant was a man who was rarely flustered by anything, but he was remarkably unperturbed by this considerable display of incompetence on the part of Irish Intelligence, as well as Special Branch. Stefan found himself wondering if Owain Jones's departure had been as unobserved as the Intelligence officer said. Perhaps it was no accident de Paor was there and no one from the Branch, and that it had all been so easy.

'If he went in a hurry, did he leave anything behind?' said Stefan.

'Nothing important. We've looked. But help yourself. Room 142.'

'We'll have a look, Stevie, come on.' Skehan walked on into the hotel.

'We're also looking at his car,' de Paor went on. 'It's in the garage.'

The commandant shrugged, as if to say none of this mattered, and went out through the revolving doors to Stephen's Green. Stefan followed Skehan.

A Military Intelligence officer was in the Welshman's room, doing nothing except look out at the view over the Green and smoke a cigarette. He took the arrival of Stefan and Danny Skehan as a good opportunity to go for a cup of tea. Before he left he pointed out some toiletries left behind by Owain Jones, along with some dirty laundry, a touring map of Ireland and several Ordnance Survey maps of Leinster and the east coast; a collection of race cards, race badges and betting slips was by the bed, along with a copy of *The Big Sleep*. None of it, as de Paor had said, seemed important. The maps, which might have been, were barely used and entirely unmarked. They would show nothing of where Jones had been that wasn't already known. The two Special Branch men looked round for anything that might have been hidden or lost; there was nothing more.

'That was a fucking waste of time,' said Stefan.

'It was so,' replied Skehan. He took out a cigarette.

'And if there was anything worthwhile left, it won't be here now.'

'I hope you're not suggesting you don't trust G2, Stevie?'

'It was a bloody easy getaway.'

'True. If Terry had got someone down here quicker—'

'I get the impression no one wanted us to talk to him anyway, Danny.'

'You're settling in nicely, Stevie. You're as suspicious as the rest of us!'

Stefan laughed. 'Will we look at this car, then? Might as well.'

'You go. I've an appointment in Farrelly's Bar. This'll do me.'

'So, is that it?' said Stefan.

'Ask Terry. It's his cock-up, isn't it? If that's what he says it is.'

Stefan passed through the Shelbourne, out through the side door into Kildare Street. He crossed over and walked through some scruffy wooden doors, oddly framed by a pair of Greek columns, into a dark, dilapidated building that had once been a house. Below an unexpected Venetian window, full of cracked and cobwebbed panes, was the legend: *Shelbourne Hotel Garage*. There seemed to be no one around, in the gutted interior where walls had been demolished to make space for the vehicles. Half a dozen cars were visible in the cramped space, all parked in ways that made it impossible to move one without moving others. As Stefan moved past them he could hear someone whistling. He turned a corner to find Geróid de Paor and the Welshman's Jaguar Roadster. The doors were open, the bonnet up; the boot was pulled open too. The Intelligence officer was on his knees, feeling under the seats. The sports car had only two. Stefan walked up.

'Nothing important there either, Geróid?'

De Paor backed out of the car and stood up.

'Well, I've found nearly five bob under the seats. Not bad.'

'It was almost worth coming, then,' said Stefan.

'And there is this.'

He walked round to the boot. It was empty. The contents lay on the floor beside it: a small wicker picnic basket, some travel rugs, a gabardine mac, an oilcloth bag full of tools, several torches. There was a piece of shaped, carpet-covered board that made up the floor of the boot. De Paor pointed inside. There was a rectangular metal well. A metal plate had just been unscrewed to reveal it.

'The floor was false. And underneath there's a compartment.'

'Not very big,' said Stefan.

'Depends what you wanted to put in it. It would take a radio.'

'It would,' replied Stefan, 'of a certain kind.'

'It would take a lot of things you might not want anyone to see.'

'It's not that well hidden.'

'Nothing's that well hidden if you're looking for it. If you're not—'

'And you were looking for it?'

'I'm inquisitive, Stefan, that's all.'

'It's a pity you weren't more inquisitive before Mr Jones left.'

'You never know where these things lead, Inspector.' De Paor grinned.

'This one isn't leading anywhere, is it?'

'Everything leads somewhere. Whether it's where you want to go—'

'I don't know if it's because I've spent the last few days in the company of four dead bodies, Geróid, but I couldn't give a fuck about all this. I don't know who's telling the truth about any of this shit, or whether we even know what the truth is. But if you want my guess, to go with yours, I'd take some convincing our Welsh friend left the Shelbourne at ten minutes' notice, and found the only way to get himself out of Dublin and Ireland in an hour flat, unless someone tipped him the wink. There are various candidates, and one of them is you, and whoever else you're playing the game with. God knows why.'

'There could be something in that. There isn't, as it happens.'

'But someone told him he was going to be picked up?'

'All roads lead to Rome.'

'And what the fuck does that mean?'

'It means a job's a job, that's all. And it means watch yourself.'

'Do I need to watch myself?'

'We all do, Stefan.'

Geróid de Paor gave a faint, equivocal smile. It could have meant no more than that he could say nothing, or knew nothing; but it felt like a warning.

That evening, when Stefan Gillespie crossed into Crane Lane and walked down to Farrelly's, the bar was more full of Special Branch men than usual, and at the centre of the throng at the bar was Dessie MacMahon. His face was still bruised and scarred and his neck was bandaged underneath his shirt and jacket, but it was the news that Dessie was back that had brought Stefan to the pub that night.

'Jesus, I thought we were shot of you for a month at least, Dessie!'

'The boss said I needed to come and sort you out, Stevie.'

Dessie's voice was still a rasping whisper.

'But you're quieter, that's something,' said Stefan.

'Still under doctor's orders. Drink plenty, he says.' Dessie drank.

'Terry says you're on light duties. Will you do that in here?'

'I may have to,' said Sergeant MacMahon with a shrug and a frown.

The door from the snug opened, and Terry Gregory's head appeared.

'Gillespie, away in here!'

Stefan took the bottle of Guinness and the glass that had been thrust at him and walked on into the tiny room that blocked off the end of the bar. In the snug, which was the other office Terry Gregory used beside the one in the Police Yard, the superintendent sat at the table with Chief Inspector Skehan. The two men had been drinking for some time, but where the only difference this made to Gregory was a deeper flush on his ruddy face, Skehan spoke with the slow, determined intensity of a man who knows his words are being slurred.

'You'll need to leave all this Dunlavin business with Danny now.'

Stefan sat down. He nodded, not quite sure he was happy with that.

'There's not much to leave, sir.'

'There's enough. That doesn't mean it gets us anywhere. I think we can put a few things together, though. You did see Commandant de Paor earlier?'

'At the Shelbourne.'

Skehan grinned.

'Danny thinks it's funny, that's because he reckons it's my fault.'

'I'd never say that, Terry?'

'Did he ever say that, Stevie?'

'It wouldn't be for me to give a colleague away, sir.'

'He may be right. But I'd say the tight-arses in G2 share the blame.'

'They knew all about Jones, then?'

'What do you think?'

'So, what have you put together? I've put together fuck all,' said Stefan.

'Never mind all the Celtic-fringe stuff. I don't believe any of that, and neither does anyone in the IRA, except when the pubs are throwing out. But that doesn't mean there's nothing going on. The Welshman is a German agent. That's clear enough. De Paor has that from British Intelligence too. There's a connection to Petersen and the German embassy, and we know Herr Petersen has been in contact with at least one German agent who landed in Ireland.'

'The one we lost,' added Skehan.

'That one,' said Terry Gregory. 'We're assuming he's still here, though there is a question about whether they want to get him into England. If that's true, de Paor thinks our Mr Jones could have been arranging it. He ships racehorses back and forth. There's plenty of scope there for getting people across too.'

'Is that where McCall came into it?'

'Possibly. But the best guess is La Mancha was a safe house. Off the IRA map, off every map, including ours. But on the Abwehr's – and on Petersen's.'

'Do we know that?' asked Stefan.

'It's a guess,' said Chief Inspector Skehan.

'My guess,' said Gregory, smiling, 'and De Paor's. Sometimes we agree.'

Danny Skehan stood up, slightly unsteady on his legs.

'I'm going for a piss.'

As the door closed behind him, Terry Gregory looked at Stefan.

'You don't seem happy about Danny taking over. Why's that?'

'Nothing really. I'm just interested. There doesn't seem to be much doubt your man Casey killed the people he worked for, but some things don't fit that.'

'Anything that concerns what you're supposed to be doing?'

'Probably not,' laughed Stefan.

'That's what I thought. You know why you're off it?'

'No, sir.'

'Foynes.'

'Foynes?' It was unexpected, but not a surprise. It was what he had been told would happen. He had almost forgotten the conversation in Iveagh House.

'They want someone in Foynes, to work with Military Intelligence.'

'I see.'

'Do you?' said the superintendent. 'The commissioner told me to send you. No discussion. He'd made up his mind. So, does that come from Geróid?'

'He hasn't talked to me about it.'

'Do you know what's going on in Foynes?'

Stefan shook his head.

'You'll find out.' Gregory smiled again. He was not entirely convinced by Stefan's ignorance, but that was his position on everything. He always assumed that even his own men were as likely to be lying as telling the truth.

'It's secret. Like all our secrets, it's not much of one. But there it is.'

The door opened and Danny Skehan reappeared with a tray of drinks.

'On the house!'

'A bad sign,' said Terry Gregory. 'We're spending too much in here!'

'I'll drink to that,' laughed Skehan.

It was late when Stefan Gillespie and Danny Skehan left Farrelly's and walked down the back alley into Essex Street, where Skehan had parked the Special Branch car. Hanging on to cars was a speciality of Chief Inspector Skehan's, so much so that his neighbours in Dundrum thought he owned one. It was a habit Superintendent Gregory indulged, partly because he couldn't be bothered to do anything about it and partly because Danny Skehan's methods of interrogation were no secret where the IRA was concerned. All Special Branch men were targets to some extent, but Skehan's reputation meant that it did no harm for him to be in a car, rather than sitting on trams and buses on his way to work.

'I'll give you a lift, Stevie.'

'I'd be safer walking,' laughed Stefan.

'I hope you're not suggesting I'm pissed.'

'It's not a suggestion at all, Danny.'

'Get in the fucking car.'

Skehan stopped to take out a Woodbine and light it. He saw the piece of paper under the windscreen wiper at the same time as Stefan Gillespie, walking round to the passenger door. Stefan reached forward and pulled the paper off.

'For me?'

Stefan nodded.

'For you. "The Boys owe you, Danny. We'll be coming for you."'

'Not the first.'

'You'd better tell Terry. They're following you.'

'I'll tell him.'

As they got into the car, Stefan handed Skehan the piece of paper. He folded it up without reading it and put it in his pocket. He opened his jacket and took the Webley from his shoulder holster. He put it up on the dashboard.

'They can try. If they come, there won't be so many going back.'

It was said without bravado, but all the drunkenness seemed to have gone. It was the business they were in. You didn't know when something would happen, yet the truth was it didn't happen often. Even the IRA needed a reason now. The response to killing a Guard made it no idle decision. But the sense of being watched was an unpleasant one. Stefan wasn't well known himself, certainly not to the IRA, but Danny Skehan was. What Superintendent Gregory had told him felt like a kind of release. He knew he would hear from the Department of External Affairs any day. There was no job to do in Foynes; there was the journey to Germany. It would be no easy trip, but the task didn't amount to much. The idea of getting away from what he was doing didn't often occur to him, because he couldn't, but Germany didn't seem a bad option now that it was on offer. As he looked out at the Quays, the unanswerable question that entered his mind from time to time returned: Why the fuck did he do this?

10
Mountjoy

It was a week later that Superintendent Gregory walked into the detectives' room from the Police Yard and stood in the doorway of his office, still in his hat and coat, in an attitude that told his detectives he had something to say. He didn't need to draw anyone's attention to it. They all knew what was coming.

'On Wednesday the military tribunal found John Costello and James Brennan guilty of the murder of Detective Garda Jack Daly. At six o'clock this morning, at Mountjoy, they were executed by firing squad. I have no whispers of a response. Not yet. But if I had an ulcer, it would be playing up now. So, if any of you are not taking a weapon home with you at night, you're to do so.'

He turned away abruptly and went into the office.

There was silence in the room. Nothing like this happened without mixed feelings. There was no sentimentality attached to it. The men in Special Branch had expected it. There was probably no one in the room who didn't believe it was necessary. But necessary and deserved were different things. A lot of the detectives were ex-IRA men. Some of them had known John Costello, and had fought beside him as young men, against the British and even against the Free State in the Civil War. Special Branch was not a place of reflection, but for a moment the shadow of what an Irish state had cost, and still cost, hung over it.

Dessie MacMahon crossed himself, then turned back to his work.

The door to Terry Gregory's office opened again.

'Danny, Gillespie, the feller from Naas – Harrington – is coming up to talk to your man Casey. The Dunlavin business. You might as well get the end of this, Stevie, while you're still with us. He's been charged with murder and remanded in Mountjoy. He wants to change his story. I'm not surprised. You'd better be there, in case he's got anything to say about radios, or he left the Nazi invasion plans under his bed. Meet Inspector Harrington at Kingsbridge at ten.'

Danny Skehan sat back in his chair and looked at Stefan.

'Isn't the Joy a great place altogether, right after an execution?'

When Stefan Gillespie and Danny Skehan picked up Paul Harrington from Kingsbridge, the polite preliminaries were followed by a silence that none of them broke until the car was approaching Mountjoy Prison. Harrington spoke.

'I'm sorry. It wouldn't be my choice to go today either.'

'You know, then?' said Stefan.

'Yes. They don't need to make an announcement.'

'There'll be no announcement,' said Skehan. 'It's a state secret.'

'Well, we knew in Naas by seven.'

'And what do your fellers say?' continued the chief inspector.

'Maybe they had it coming.' Harrington chose his words carefully.

'And maybe they didn't?'

'There's a story about forensic evidence going round.'

'What's that?' asked Skehan, as the car stopped outside the prison.

'There wasn't any.'

'I'd say you're right, Inspector.' Danny Skehan laughed.

'And the bullet that killed Daly was a Garda one,' continued Harrington.

'I heard that too. That's the IRA line. Did you hear that, Stevie?'

'I've heard something like it.'

Skehan got out his cigarettes. They all took one. There wasn't exactly a reluctance to leave the car, but no one was eager. Skehan held out his lighter.

'Doesn't matter who fired the bullet,' said the chief inspector. 'One day the Boys want a war, the next they want justice. Some neck, eh? It's bollocks.'

Inside the echoing corridors of Mountjoy Prison there was a silence that only normally occurred in the earliest hours of morning, and even then the silence would be punctuated from time to time by roars of anger, defiance, pain, and by screams that were about nothing more than the enclosing stone walls and a need to break the oppression of the stillness. Now every man in the gaol was locked in his cell, and would be all day. That was the way of it on any execution day, when the fury that filled the prison – whatever the crime, whatever the guilt – became an act of human solidarity that threatened to spill over into violence. It was much more the case today, when the executed men were Republicans, and the Republic leadership in the prison had a duty to show not only grief, but its refusal to be cowed. The noise of protest that had filled the prison earlier that morning had stopped for now. It would stop and start all day.

In a room off the governor's office, Henry Casey sat at a table in front of Inspector Harrington. Stefan Gillespie and Danny Skehan sat on either side of the Naas detective. It was Harrington's case. They were there for reasons that had nothing to do with the charges against Casey.

"The governor says you want to change your story.'

'Yes, Mr Harrington. I'm sorry for what I did—'

'You're going to tell us what you did?'

'I don't know why I did it, but once it started—'

'I'm listening, Henry. Let's have the truth now, shall we?'

'I didn't kill anyone, though. That's not it. You know that, don't you?'

Harrington sat back with a look of weariness. He didn't know that.

'They owed me something. Mr McCall did. I worked for them for fucking years, you know. And how else was I going to get a job? That's all it was . . .'

He looked at each of the detectives, as if this explained something.

'Try the beginning, Henry. Let's take it from there,' said Harrington.

'Mr McCall gave me the Friday off, and the weekend. So the Thursday was the last time I saw any of them alive, when I finished work—'

'This is the same fucking story, isn't it?'

'It's not, Mr Harrington. I did find them in the house, dead.'

'All right, Thursday. Tell me about the Thursday.'

'I was there the usual time, in the morning, to feed the horses, like every day. Alice called me in for breakfast, same as she usually did. Well, same as usual except there was no one else there. Annie and Patrick were poorly. They had been all week. I'd seen them about a bit, but they'd been in their beds a lot. McCall said it was the flu, the vomiting sort, and they were quare bad with it.'

Harrington waited. Casey looked slightly less nervous.

'I worked in the garden most of the morning. I only saw Mr McCall – Simon – but when I was in the yard his sister came out. She said she was feeling better and would I kill a chicken for the dinner. She said a bit of chicken would do her and Patrick good, as they couldn't keep anything down. She was bad, though, still. When I was killing the chicken, I heard her throw up in the yard.'

Henry Casey stopped, frowning, as if getting things in order.

'Alice brought my dinner out to the workshop. Mr McCall said it was better with the flu in the house. He didn't want me bringing such a bad do home to the kids. He was in the town all afternoon, and when he came back he said I could go early and take a few days off. He said to come to work on Monday.'

'Was that a normal thing?'

'No, but it happened. It did in August, and a fortnight back. He took it into his head a few times lately, that me and Alice would have a few days off.'

There was a moment's silence. Stefan Gillespie could see that Casey felt more confident about his story. His voice was stronger. He nodded as he spoke.

'Do you know why he decided to give you this time off?' asked Stefan.

'No, but I didn't complain. I got paid.' For the first time, Casey smiled.

Inspector Harrington turned to Stefan for more questions.

'That's it, Paul.'

'All right,' said the Naas detective. 'When were you back at La Mancha?'

'I went Sunday night.'

'That's when you saw the children, Assumpta and Peter Clarke?'

Casey nodded. Then he shook his head.

'But I didn't tell the truth about that.'

'And what was the truth?'

'I went on Sunday because he didn't give me my wages. I always got them on a Friday, and on the Thursday he forgot it. We were short at home.'

'You couldn't wait till Monday?'

'I don't get paid so much I have money sitting at home.'

'You were hardly at home that weekend. You were in the pub.''

'It was a bit of a holiday. Nothing wrong with that.'

'So, Sunday evening, Henry. Let's get on with it.'

'When I got there, I saw the horses hadn't been fed. And the house was shut up. All the curtains was drawn, and the doors locked. And it was still light. Well, it wasn't even five o'clock. I knocked and I couldn't get an answer, back or front. So I left off and got on with seeing to the horses. Someone needed to.'

'You'd have noticed one was dead then – La Mancha?'

'I did, when I went to see him. Poor old feller.'

'And what did you make of that?'

'He'd been shot. I thought Mr McCall must have had him put down.'

Stefan leant forward.

'Was there anything wrong with La Mancha on Thursday?'

'Nothing I could see.'

'Mr McCall didn't say anything about putting him down?'

'Not to me.'

Stefan nodded at Paul Harrington. He had finished.

'Carry on, Henry,' said the inspector.

'I still couldn't get an answer at the house. I got the spare key—'

Again Henry Casey looked from policeman to policeman.

'I saw Alice, in the kitchen. Dead, I mean. And all bloody. I went through the house and – and when I got up the stairs, I found them all, Mr McCall and Patrick and Annie, in their beds. Dead as you like. Then there was a knocking at the door – and it was the kids, selling tickets . . .'

'So you came out, bought some tickets, and took them back in.'

'I didn't know what to do, sir.'

'Four dead people and you didn't know what to do?'

'It was the end of my job, I knew that.'

'That's what you were thinking? Not: Jesus, I better call the Guards!'

'I thought . . . I thought I would, but it could . . . it could wait a bit. I was owed something, Mr Harrington, after the years I gave . . . and I was . . . it didn't seem wrong to have something ... I couldn't bring them back. I thought there was something there to . . . I'm not saying it's right – I know it wasn't – but I thought if there was just something, to help me out . . . but there was fuck all. And all that talk about the fucking treasure – it was bollocks – just bollocks!'

The words expressed a strange anger, a kind of resentment.

'I see. You were looking for some treasure?'

'That's what Alice and me called it. It was August – the time we had a weekend off – and when I came back, Mr McCall said he'd a box wanted burying, for safe keeping. He said it was papers, insurance policies – he wanted it safe, but handy – and with his arthritis he couldn't dig – so I helped him dig a hole, behind the Dutch barn. That was it, but me and Alice joked about it being treasure. It had to be money. Who'd want to bury a fucking insurance policy?'

'You thought there was a box full of money?'

'I did.'

'And since they were all dead, you'd have some?'

'I was owed something, Mr Harrington.'

'You've told us. So we have four dead bodies and a box of treasure?'

Danny Skehan snorted. He was trying to stop himself laughing.

'You've seen it. A radio! He buried a fucking radio!'

Stefan glanced at Skehan, who nodded. This had to be true.

'Now we have four dead bodies and a radio. Okay, let's take all this as gospel. You could see Alice McCall had been attacked and killed, even if you believed the other three had died in their beds of the fucking flu. You did nothing.'

'I still thought there'd be something, just to tide me—'

'All right, you searched the place, and you took what – a bit of cash, a couple of watches – and three pairs of trousers. Talk about Treasure Island!'

'I didn't know what to do, Mr Harrington. I knew I should have gone to the barracks. That's when I thought of a fire. If they'd all died in a fire. . . '

Henry Casey shrugged. He had finished. The three detectives all waited for more to come, but he had no more to say. He gave an apologetic half-smile.

'And that's it?' said Inspector Harrington.

'That's it, Mr Harrington. I'm sorry. But now you know what happened.'

As the three detectives walked through the prison yard, the silence that had met them on their arrival had broken. The rhythmic noise began as Henry Casey was being escorted back to his cell. All through the gaol, in every locked cell, prisoners were banging whatever they could find against the bars and the doors and the walls, and as the sound spread it developed a slow, solid stroke that echoed the rhythm of the single word that accompanied every beat now, and came from every prisoner's mouth, louder and louder. It would last a long time, and when it stopped, it would stop for an hour and then start again. It would go on all day, and all through the night, until it finally stopped for good, as a tribute to the two men who had been executed.

'Cunts! Cunts! Cunts! Cunts!'

Stefan Gillespie drove Paul Harrington back to Kingsbridge Station for the train to Naas. Harrington sat beside him and Danny Skehan sat in the back. The journey had not given Harrington what he expected, a confession. It was simply another version of what Henry Casey had already said. On the surface it contained more elements of truth, yet they were presented with more confusion and complexity than before. It changed nothing, even if Casey seemed to think it did. If anything, it made what defence he had weaker. The story of the buried box, which he thought contained money, had now provided his motive.

For the two Special Branch men there was little to take back to Superintendent Gregory, but there was something. The radio had been hidden.

'So the radio really was buried?' said Stefan.

'I'd say so,' replied Harrington. 'There was a wooden box in the kitchen that the suitcase fitted in. The box was burnt, but it showed signs of being in the ground. And there is a fresh hole behind the Dutch barn, where Casey says.'

'He killed them, the lot of them, for that?' Stefan shook his head.

'He thought there was money,' said Harrington, 'a lot of money. I don't know what else. Maybe there's spite, too, some grievance he's not telling us, stupidity? Does he even know himself? He's not far behind Simon McCall's mad brother and sister in terms of what's in his head, not to mention the drink.'

'It wasn't some drunken rage,' said Stefan. 'He had to make up the arsenic. You think he'd been putting it in the food? Annie and Patrick's?'

'He must have been. Just a bit. That was happening slowly.'

'But not Simon, and not Alice.'

'He got it into Simon in the end, somehow,' continued the Naas detective. 'It does make sense, Stefan. I'm going on what Casey says, but that's all there is. When he was working, he ate his breakfast and his dinner in the kitchen, with Patrick and Annie. Simon never ate in the middle of the day, so he wasn't there. He had an ulcer, mostly he got his own food. Alice usually went into Dunlavin to shop once she'd served up the dinner. When the dinner was being eaten, there was only Casey and the brother and sister.'

'So how did he get Simon to take it?'

'I don't know. Maybe he'll tell us.'

'And what about Alice?'

'Her blood is on his boots and clothes. That's the State Pathologist's view. Not much room for doubt. But I don't think she was meant to be there.'

'What do you mean?'

'She had the weekend off too. All that's true. She was going to spend a couple of days in Dublin with a friend. But she came back early. That's what the friend told us, Louise Allen. She was worried about how ill Patrick and Annie were. Well, we know why. Alice wasn't due back at work until Monday.'

'Did McCall always give the two of them days off at the same time?'

'Henry Casey thought there wouldn't be anyone else at La Mancha that weekend. But Alice was worried enough to get the train home on Saturday.'

'And Saturday's when they died?'

'I think we can say that. It's certainly when she died.'

'And the horse?' said Stefan.

In the back, Danny Skehan laughed.

'You've got a soft spot for that horse, Stevie. He worries you.'

'It doesn't fit.' He looked at Harrington. 'When was La Mancha shot?'

'Thursday, maybe Friday morning.'

'And who shot him?'

'Either McCall did have a reason to put him down or Casey did it. If there was a grievance behind it, you wouldn't find a better way to spite Simon McCall than to shoot La Mancha.'

'He shot the horse and then killed the McCalls two days later?'

'Stevie's a stickler, Paul,' said Skehan, 'a fucking stickler!'

'I'm not investigating the horse's death,' said Harrington, irritated now. 'He killed four people. And halfwit or not, that's what he's going to hang for.'

After dropping Detective Inspector Harrington at Kingsbridge, Stefan Gillespie drove back towards Dublin Castle, with Danny Skehan now in the front.

'Drop me at Farrelly's, Stevie.'

'It's a bit early.'

'Even for me?' said the chief inspector, laughing.

Stefan shrugged.

'I could do with getting the taste of the Joy out of my mouth.'

Skehan lit a cigarette.

'Do you believe that, any of it?' he asked Stefan.

'Casey, you mean? I'd say it's worse than his first story. If you're going to say you know nothing, saw nothing, did nothing, keep it fucking simple.'

'There are a few buts, though,' said Skehan quietly.

'There are,' said Stefan. 'Not enough. No one's going to believe it.'

'Not a fucking word, Stevie. But I'll tell you what's odd.'

'What's that?'

'He believes it himself.'

Chief Inspector Skehan spoke with a measure of curiosity that was no more than idle. It stopped almost as he finished speaking. There was nothing there that concerned him. But his last words didn't leave Stefan's mind so quickly. It was what had been in his head all the time Casey was speaking, however bizarre, however convoluted the story became. He couldn't put it any more rationally than Skehan. There was nothing that seriously questioned the view that Casey's story was a hopeless attempt to deny the undeniable. Yet Stefan felt he wanted to find something that did. He was struggling. The horse didn't make sense. It seemed trivial, set against the horrors inside the house, but it needed explaining. He still wondered what it was that General Trevor had come to La Mancha to say, that couldn't be said without speaking ill of the dead. The two things that stuck in his head were almost nothing. He didn't believe they necessarily asked questions of Henry Casey's guilt. But they were loose threads. They were things that didn't fit. Yet things didn't always fit. Murders like that emerged from a kind of chaos. It was what lent them their particular brutality. They were puzzles that always had half the pieces missing.

11

Potsdamer Platz

Berlin

William Warnock arrived at the People's Court in Potsdamer Platz with no real idea of what to expect. He knew the reputation of the *Volksgerichtshof* for harsh sentences, but not much more than that. His mind was less occupied by the nature of the court than by why an Irish woman called Zandra Purcell, who had been accused of murder, was being tried there at all. It was a criminal offence that seemed to have no connection to the little he did know about the *Volksgerichtshof*. The court dealt almost entirely with offences against the state that were defined, in one way or another, as political. In the diplomatic circles Warnock moved in, as the representative of the Irish government in Berlin, the way in which the concept of political offences had spread into almost every area of German life was not a topic of conversation that cropped up frequently. It was everywhere, of course, but it had become so much the business of ordinary life that it was invisible. It was all the more invisible because the diplomatic community, and to some extent even the German Foreign Ministry, existed, as few other areas of life in the Third Reich did any more, slightly outside it.

Warnock was also irritated. The German authorities had

made no attempt to contact him about providing consular assistance for Miss Purcell. He only knew about her arrest because another member of Berlin's small Irish community had contacted him. The charge against Zandra Purcell was a very serious one, but she was an Irish citizen, and he had a responsibility to do what he could to help her. He had no cooperation at all from the Justice Ministry or the police; it had only been by badgering the Foreign Ministry in Wilhelmstrasse that he had, finally, been given the details of an initial court hearing, at the People's Court in Potsdamer Platz. His request to see her at the Moabit Prison had been ignored, and now the only access he was to be allowed would happen moments before the hearing was about to take place.

He knew Potsdamer Platz well enough. It was a busy, noisy junction at the heart of the west of the city, full of traffic and criss-crossing tramlines. He had often, when life in Berlin was easier and more relaxed, visited the cafés and cinemas in the Vaterland Haus that dominated one side of the junction. And he did know the building at Bellevuestrasse 15, which housed the People's Court. Among the circling offices and shops decked with flags, it always bore the biggest swastika banner, falling down from the roof over much of its facade.

The first thing he noticed, on entering the building, was that almost everyone in the foyer was in uniform, whether Nazi or police or military. Even in a city where uniforms were everywhere, the sheer concentration of them here was unusual. It was a loud, even raucous atmosphere too, and already it was not what Warnock expected from a court. He was immediately approached by a man who knew, despite the noise and bustle of the foyer, exactly who he was.

'Herr Ambassador Warnock?'

'It is,' he said amiably, in heavily accented German.

'Please follow me, sir.'

William Warnock was shown into a small, bare room, off a corridor just behind the entrance lobby. A woman in her mid-thirties, in a grey prison smock, stood between two prison guards, a man and a woman. A man in a lawyer's black gown stood beside a table, smoking. He was, perhaps, sixty, and the years showed. He was short and stout, and he walked with a stick. Everyone stood. There were chairs round the table, but no one suggested that they were used.

The man who had accompanied Warnock introduced the lawyer.

'This is Herr Dr Maiwald, the defence lawyer.'

'Herr Ambassador.' Maiwald reached out his hand.

Warnock stood for a moment, unsure what he was supposed to do. No one said anything. Herr Maiwald smiled and reached down to the table to stub his cigarette out in an ashtray. Then he took out a cigarette case and lit another.

'I have no details of the case,' said Warnock. 'I have asked repeatedly—'

'It's murder. We'll find out the rest in court,' said the lawyer.

'It would be good to know more than that, Herr Maiwald.'

The old man smiled again, and gave the barest of shrugs.

The Irishman turned to the woman. No one was about to introduce him to her, even her lawyer. She was watching him with an expression that made him feel she was afraid to speak, afraid to step forward; a quiet shock in her eyes.

'Miss Purcell, I am the Irish chargé d'affaires,' said William Warnock in English. 'I'm sorry we haven't been able to speak. I only heard yesterday.'

'Thank you for coming, Mr Warnock.'

'You'll speak in German please,' said the man who had brought Warnock to the room. He said it in good English, as if to make the point more pointedly.

'I know very little, Fraulein—' Warnock continued in German.

'I am innocent. I killed no one. Johannes, Herr Rilling, was my friend.'

Warnock looked at her hard, not knowing what he should say.

'You do have a lawyer. Of course, I will make sure that any help—'

He was interrupted, as the man who had escorted him stepped forward.

'I'm sorry, Herr Ambassador, but the People's Court will be in session very shortly now, and the presiding judge expects us to start exactly on time.'

The female warder took Zandra Purcell's arm and led her out. Zandra made no protest. She just followed. She made no attempt to say anything more.

'I have hardly spoken to the woman!' said Warnock, now quite angry.

'My apologies, Herr Ambassador,' said the man, and walked out.

William Warnock stared at the door as it shut, leaving him in the room with Zandra Purcell's lawyer, Herr Maiwald, who moved to the door himself.

'I still know nothing,' said Warnock. 'What has she said to you?'

'I'm afraid I haven't spoken to her.'

'Aren't you her lawyer?'

'That's not how it works, Herr Ambassador.'

'You don't speak to your client?'

'I don't even know the charges until I hear them in court.'

'Why is she here at all? Isn't this a political court?'

'The man Fraulein Purcell is supposed to have shot was a German soldier, a Hauptmann Rilling. Killing a German soldier is an act of treason.'

'Treason, Herr Doctor! I don't understand how this court works.'

The lawyer stubbed out a half-smoked cigarette and smiled.

'You've read Lewis Carroll, I presume?' Maiwald spoke in English now. 'This is the court of the Red Queen. As a lawyer, that's really all I can tell you.'

The People's Court was in session. William Warnock had found a seat close to the front, only a few rows back from the dock in which Zandra Purcell now stood. The rows of onlookers who sat around him talked noisily and incessantly; many of them were eating. No one seemed to make any attempt to quieten them, although men in police uniforms, SS uniforms, SA uniforms, stood all round the room. On a dais at the front, under a huge portrait of Adolf Hitler, flanked by swastika banners, sat the presiding official, Judge-President Roland Freisler, reading through the pages of a document. He was a middle-aged man, thin and round-faced, wearing the same black gown as the other lawyers in the court, along with the flat, black cap. He seemed unfazed by the chatter going on around him. Warnock had already heard him speak, and when he did he made no attempt to still the noise from what the Irishman already felt was more of an audience than anything else he recognised. He simply shouted.

After five minutes, Freisler looked up and stared at Zandra Purcell. She had a deceptive aura of calm; her stillness remained a symptom of shock.

The judge-president looked down at a court official, who immediately picked up a piece of paper. He read the charges against the accused, Fraulein Zandra Purcell. They amounted to no more than that she had shot and killed Hauptmann Johannes Rilling, and was charged with his murder. A short summary of the police evidence was read, and Warnock strained to hear it. The conversations all round him continued. The judge-president had stepped down from his seat and was talking to an SS officer. As he returned to it he leant forward and snapped an instruction that halted the summary of evidence.

'I've read the charges. There is no argument about this evidence.'

'No, Herr Judge-President,' said the clerk.

'Put it in the record.'

Freisler stared at Zandra Purcell for almost a minute, then looked across the courtroom to the bench where her lawyer was sitting, in front of Warnock.

Maiwald stood up, leaning on his stick.

'Your client pleads not guilty?' said the judge.

'She does, your honour.'

'On what basis?'

'On the basis that's she's innocent of the charge, Judge-President.'

Roland Freisler gave a sniff of irritation, and turned back to Zandra.

'You are aware of the gravity of the charge against you, Fraulein?'

The Irishwoman said nothing, barely aware he was talking.

'I asked you a question!' shouted the judge-president.

'Yes, sir.'

'You earn your living as a musician, is that right?'

'Yes, sir.'

'The saxophone. So, a musician might be overstating the case?'

There was a ripple of laughter around the court.

Zandra Purcell said nothing.

'That was a question, Fraulein. When I ask a question, you answer.'

'I do play the saxophone, sir.'

'You used to have what you called your own "orchestra", is that right?'

'That was a long time ago, your honour.'

'And what did this "orchestra" play?'

'It was – well, mostly jazz.'

'And all the players were women? A sort of band for freaks, then?'

There was more laughter.

Warnock watched in bewilderment. He was not a naïve man. He had been in Germany a long time. He did know what it was. But this was more, far more.

'And what led you to bring us your peculiar musical gifts, Fraulein?'

'We did play a lot.' Zandra was puzzled, confused. She didn't understand what she was being asked. 'That was when I came to Germany. We were asked to play in Berlin. I had a contract to play – in a lot of clubs. It's why I stayed.'

'Marvellous! You brought us a band of whores to give us Nigger music.'

'We stopped playing, that's all,' she said flatly.

'More accurate to say you were stopped, when that kind of shit was banned. It might have been a good time to leave Germany, Fraulein. Fraulein?'

The defence lawyer took a small step forward.

'Herr Judge-President, Fraulein Purcell has been playing for the Reich Propaganda Ministry. On radio. She does work in the interests of the Reich.'

'I'm sure the Reich can manage without her, Maiwald, unless you're proposing to call Dr Goebbels to tell us her work is indispensable for the war effort. I think he might decline the request. She shot and killed a German officer, a recipient of the Iron Cross. That's what this is about, or am I wrong?'

'Fraulein Purcell asserts her innocence. She did not—'

'The evidence says she did. And so do I! Hauptmann Rilling was in her bed. The only place he could have found anything in common with a woman like this, I'm sure. It is regrettable that he chose so poorly, but our men have needs. We understand that. We understand their sacrifices. But in this case, the captain's whore was not content with a position she should have been grateful for. She wanted more. The police have heard from witnesses who speak of violent arguments between Hauptmann Rilling and this slut. She seemed to expect the rights of a German wife. Or was it money? More likely that. Either way, it appears that the captain wanted rid of her. So, she took his own gun and shot him. Here she is, a whore who wants us to believe what? A man walked into her apartment, got into her bed, and was shot by a passing gangster?'

The laughter was louder and more raucous in the courtroom now.

'Herr Judge-President,' said Maiwald quietly, 'we believe there is evidence of the time of Hauptmann Rilling's death that conflicts with Fraulein Purcell's movements that night. At least one witness reports a sound, possibly a shot, two hours before she returned from the studio at the Villa Concordia.'

'And other witnesses, including a policeman, place the gunshot later.'

'It is also not the case that Fraulein Purcell had a sexual relationship with Hauptmann Rilling. They were only friends. There is, therefore, no motive.'

'Ah, yes, they were friends. That's why he was in her bed.'

He looked round the court, waiting for more laughter.

'I'm sorry, Herr Doctor, but while we might understand why Hauptmann Rilling wanted to fuck this woman, I don't think you're going to convince us they climbed into bed to discuss Goethe, or maybe it was Schubert's Lieder?'

'Herr Judge-President—'

Freisler cut Maiwald off as he turned back to Zandra Purcell.

'You have a son, yes?'

'Yes, sir.'

'Kept at the Convent of the Holy Mother. An imbecile.'

'He has Down Syndrome, it doesn't mean—'

'Are we in the presence of a medical expert? I'll rephrase it. You have a spastic, idiot son. Doubtless born out of the genetic miscegenation you like to set to music. Do you even know who the father was?'

'Of course I know who his father—'

'And where is he?'

'He is in America.'

'Well, he had the sense to run anyway! Was he a Jew or a Nigger?'

Roland Freisler looked down at her with contempt.

'Germany took you in. We didn't ask for you. We didn't want you. But we are a generous people. Our reward? You give us a hideous child-moron and murder a German hero. I think we have all heard enough. The case will go to trial in October, date to be determined. It will be short. If you imagine a foreign passport will save you, it won't. And the guillotine will follow immediately.'

William Warnock was still standing at the back of the court as Zandra Purcell was led out. She didn't look round. She didn't look back. He was almost glad she didn't. Under different circumstances he might have hoped to catch her eye, to let her know he was still there, that there was help of some kind, that she wasn't cut off from the outside world completely; that he would use whatever influence he had, whatever influence the Irish government had. Now he knew his face would have shown only helplessness and shock. There was a lot of Germany he had never seen, en route from the Irish legation to the Foreign Ministry in Wilhelmstrasse. He was by no means blind to what was around him, or to what were sometimes referred to in his reports as the 'excesses' of the regime. He knew them, but he didn't know them as they were lived in the ordinary lives of ordinary people. He told no lies, either to himself or to Dublin, but the truth he saw was the truth he was required to see. For all diplomats, the polite fictions of diplomacy were a reality that fuelled the business they were in, and that reality was where they lived. William Warnock had, for an hour, stepped into another reality. He walked through Berlin's busy streets until he found somewhere calmer, quieter. Passing through the Brandenburg Gate, he turned and went into the Adlon Hotel. The bar was empty. It was still early. He didn't want to speak to anyone. He didn't want to go back to the embassy. Mostly he felt he would simply like to be somewhere else. Home. He didn't leave till several drinks later. They didn't offer him any more hope for Zandra Purcell.

12
Dún Laoghaire

Dublin

Stefan Gillespie had spent Saturday morning at Iveagh House with Joseph Walshe, the head of the Department of External Affairs, and a professor from University College Dublin, who was introduced simply as Dick. He had nothing to do with the department, but a lot to do with codes, making and breaking. Stefan received his instructions for the journey to Berlin in an almost empty Iveagh House. He would leave Dublin on the Monday night and would be driven to Arklow, where he would board an Irish cargo ship for Lisbon. From there he would go, with no show of secrecy, by train through Spain and through Vichy and occupied France, to Paris; from Paris he would go to Berlin. If the trains ran to time there would be almost no break in the journey. He would travel as a diplomatic courier from a neutral state. He had no reason to expect his journey to be interfered with. It would certainly not be in Portugal and Spain, and there was no reason it should be in France or Germany. The assumption was that nothing would be done to embarrass a neutrality that Adolf Hitler himself valued immensely; not because it gave him anything, but because it infuriated the British. In the Reich Chancellery and Wilhelmstrasse, Irish neutrality was as near to hostility to

Britain as made no difference. The eyes of spite, like the eyes of love, saw what they wanted to see. Ireland's position was to be indulged, at least until the conquest of Britain made any indulgence, anywhere, redundant.

As far as Superintendent Gregory was concerned, Stefan was being transferred to the now-defunct flying boat station at Foynes on the River Shannon, west of Limerick. No flying boats flew from Foynes; the last service to America stopped shortly after the outbreak of war. Publicly, nothing was happening in Foynes at all, but you needed a permit to get in there, and the fact that you did could not be discussed or reported anywhere. Terry Gregory knew all that; it wasn't of much interest to his detectives, but they had all heard some story about it. It shouldn't have been odd that one of Gregory's officers was being sent into a closed area to work with Military Intelligence, but Stefan could see he wasn't happy that the decision had been made without his knowledge. That would seem odd, and what was odd was the stuff of life for Superintendent Gregory. For now, no one else at Dublin Castle would be told where Stefan Gillespie was supposed to be going. He would simply be away for a time; Special Branch officers were not unused to unexplained absences. But Stefan didn't imagine the secret that was there to cover another secret would be difficult to crack for his boss, whatever the Department of External Affairs thought. Terry Gregory would not know where he was going, but he would already know it wasn't to Foynes. He would say nothing, but he would know.

None of that mattered much. At some point, when he was back, Superintendent Gregory would find out where he had been. It was likely he would know before then. Gossip from all the departments of government found their way into Special Branch in dribs and drabs and lazy barroom conversations; usually it was idle enough, but there were always useful things to be weeded out and remembered. It wasn't only the remit of

Special Branch to pursue the enemies of the state; there was an eye to be kept on its servants too.

But as the morning turned into the afternoon, Stefan put aside what he was doing and walked along the Quays to Kingsbridge Station, to meet Tom's train from Baltinglass. He was there as Tom got off the train, with all the nervousness of his first journey to Dublin on his own, full of the fear that his father wouldn't be there, or that somehow he would miss him. His train ticket was still attached to the lapel of his jacket, where his grandmother had pinned it as she put him into the carriage. He had been scrubbed and brushed and squeezed into his best clothes, though even an hour on the train had put paid to most of Helena's effort. As he walked slowly, doubtfully, along the platform, surrounded by purposeful adults, he saw his father and ran to meet him. The journey had been a small adventure, and Tom was now pleased with its success.

Sitting on the No 7 tram for the next journey, out to Dún Laoghaire, Tom Gillespie was less pleased with the prospect of a crowd of children he didn't know, who all knew each other, at the confirmation party. He took little comfort in Stefan's poker-faced admission that he felt the same about the crowd of adults he didn't know, who were waiting for him. It was meant to be a joke, but it wasn't that far from the truth. Stefan had not seen Kate in two months. It was not so very long, but the distance between them seemed to be stretching out; him in Dublin, her in London. He wanted the time with her for himself. It would be spent meeting her friends, and then, in a day, she would be away.

Kate O'Donnell met them at the tram stop. She had come from her friend Sally McGowan's house in Dún Laoghaire, and the party for her godson's confirmation. She had been at the confirmation service that morning, and the party had just started. The greetings between Stefan and Kate were short-lived, as Tom immediately monopolised the conversation on the way to the house in Clarinda Park. His knowledge of what was happening in England was largely based on what he heard on the radio and what he had read recently in the copy of *William and the Evacuees* Kate had sent him. He knew about the Battle of Britain and bombs and air-raid shelters; about the blackout and ration books and Air Raid Precautions and German spies, as rooted out of rural English towns by William and the Outlaws. But Kate was the living embodiment of it. He was disappointed she had never witnessed a dogfight between a Spitfire and a Messerschmitt, but her knowledge of bombs and air raids was impressive. She joined in as enthusiastically as she could, but Stefan could see that her very real experience of bombs in London was not something she wanted to talk about. He could tell she was skirting round what she had really seen, and as soon as he could he changed the subject.

'I've already forgotten, Kate. It's Sally McGowan, right?'

'And her husband's Mark. Ryan, their son, is my godson.'

'You were at school together?'

'She lived round the corner, so it's even longer. . . '

'And I get to meet all your old friends.' He winked at Tom. 'Great!'

'I wish you were a bit more presentable, but at least Tom's here.'

'You never really mentioned Sally.'

'I suppose we've drifted apart. That's all. I didn't see her so much lately, which means I've been a terrible godmother. Mostly I've salvaged my conscience by putting ten-shilling notes in birthday cards and Christmas cards.'

'You know, I'd have loved godparents like that!' laughed Stefan.

'I'll introduce you as we go. I don't even know who'll be there. There will be Kieran, that's Mark's brother. He's Ryan's godfather, and my only saving grace as a godparent. He can't even remember when Ryan's birthday is. He's the family's armchair Republican. I'd steer clear of politics with him.'

'I'm an expert at steering clear – of almost everything.' Stefan grinned.

'I know.'

'What's that supposed to mean?'

She laughed and took his arm, leaning up to kiss his cheek.

The McGowans' home in Clarinda Park was a big, three-storey terraced house overlooking a long square of grass and trees. It was a quiet place, barely yards from Dún Laoghaire's busy main street and the port below it. There were two large rooms on the ground floor, joined by doors that had been pushed back for the party. There were French windows at the back, giving on to steps down to a neat garden, and the afternoon was warm enough for them to be open. At the front a bay window looked out to the square. There were a lot of people, and from the start, as Stefan Gillespie shook hands with Kate's friend Sally and her husband Mark, he was easier with the larger numbers than he would have been with smaller. It meant he could be ignored if he wanted to be. It was what he preferred. He was introduced to a dozen people in succession, with barely time to say a few words before Kate saw someone else and moved him on. Tom had met Ryan and his brothers and sisters, and all the other children at the party, as soon as they entered the house, and that, to Stefan's relief, had worked. Within ten minutes he had disappeared, first into the back garden, then across to the square.

Stefan stood at a table in the bay window, where the drinks were being served. A tall, round-faced man with a look of determined cheeriness thrust a glass of beer into his hand. He stood with several other men, all in their thirties and forties, all wearing an air of good-humoured diffidence. Stefan recognised them as the men who always found a corner on these occasions, where they could express their demurral at having to be there and, more importantly, drink.

'Kieran McGowan. I'm Mark's brother.'

'I'm with Kate – Kate O'Donnell.'

'The policeman,' said Kieran with a grin.

'I am,' laughed Stefan. 'I'm sorry!'

'They say someone has to do it.'

'That's what I tell myself.'

Kieran McGowan laughed and raised his glass. Stefan raised his, and as the other man seemed disinclined to continue the conversation, he smiled and walked on, through the two rooms, occasionally stopping and talking, but as often just quietly avoiding talking. The general conversations were ones he didn't really want to join in with. They were about the war, and the Emergency, and the situation in Britain, and the bombing of London, and the threat of invasion in England, and whether de Valera was right or wrong; and when he thought he had found a conversation that touched on something else, it was about the murders in Dunlavin and the way crime was out of control.

Stefan drank little, but as the afternoon went on, the small group of men who stood by the table in the bay window drank more. The whiskey came out, and when food was being served few of the drinkers ate. It was always that way at a big do. There was nothing unpleasant about it, but the men were getting louder, and Stefan recognised the signs of what was happening. Mark McGowan had joined his brother by the table, and seemed to have abandoned his role as host to take up a fixed position there. Stefan saw Sally McGowan, on several occasions, looking with increasing anxiety at her husband and her brother-in-law, and trying to get Mark back to their other guests. She gave up.

Coming back into the house from the square, where Tom was engaged in a raucous game of hide-and-seek, Stefan saw that Kate was standing by the table where the drinkers still held their own, talking to Mark and Kieran. Kate had drunk more than she normally did, for no reason other than that people kept putting drinks into her hand. She was laughing, but Stefan could see that she was irritated.

'Don't be so daft, Kieran! I work a couple of nights a week in the ARP centre in Shepherd's Bush. Why ever not? I'm on the other end of the bombs.'

'I'm sure the uniform suits you, Kate.' Kieran meant it as a put-down.

'Well, they did give me a tin hat. It's not the bloody army.'

'It's the bloody next best bloody thing.' Kieran put on an accent that was meant to be some sort of mock Cockney as he repeated 'bloody' to show that he had noticed that Kate's use of words did bear witness to living in London.

'Very funny, Kieran.'

Mark McGowan thought so, as did several others with drinks in hand.

'Bugger off! I'll think of you next time I've got my tin hat on.'

She grinned and turned away, but Kieran wasn't finished. He reached out and pulled her round. He didn't do it hard, but he did it with temper. And suddenly it was quieter round the table. Several of the men were still grinning, but uneasily; they sensed that this had already gone further than it should have.

'Take it easy, Kieran,' said Mark. 'It doesn't matter.'

'I'd say it does matter,' said Kieran, looking hard at Kate.

'We'll agree to differ, shall we?' said Kate. Her voice was colder now.

'I don't think it's a joke. You're fighting their fucking war. Anyone who helps them is fighting their war. You're just doing a job there. I don't think much of that, as it happens. But if you put on their eejit hat, you're on their side.'

'People are dying, Kieran, every night. It's about warning them.'

'Maybe they're getting a taste of what they did to the rest of the world.'

'Oh, for God's sake, where did you get that bollocks?'

'What Ireland needs is for the Germans to win. Don't you know that?'

'I've heard it, but we've never had a shortage of gobshites, have we?'

Stefan had moved closer, as other people were moving away.

'You are on their side, then?' said Kieran, as if he had proved something.

'Yes, I am. And I have no trouble saying it. Is that loud enough?'

'I was thinking we should maybe get off, Kate . . .' Stefan touched her arm.

She turned, smiling, recognising his words were a warning. She heard it.

'Ah, and here's the Dublin Castle man to the rescue,' said Kieran.

'Don't be an arse as well as an eejit,' said Kate.

Sally was standing by her husband, glaring at him. It was getting out of hand. Mark McGowan put down his glass.

'We don't need this, Kieran. Everyone has an opinion. Forget it.'

'Were you at Mountjoy this week, Stefan?' Kieran asked quietly.

Stefan knew what this was. He put his arm through Kate's.

'I thought maybe we'd take Tom to the pictures—'

'Not just a Guard, are you?' continued Kieran. 'Special Branch.' He looked round at the few people still standing at the table. 'So, watch yourselves, fellers, or you could all end up in the Curragh.'

'Yes, Stefan,' said Kate, 'we should go.'

'Two fellers shot by a firing squad!' Kieran felt he had a platform, and he didn't want to get off. 'You know that man Costello, do you? Well, he was wounded by the English in 1916. He was at the Post Office. Did you know they had him in prison? They didn't shoot him, though. Even the fucking Tans didn't shoot him. But Dev did. And what did your man do? Fight for Ireland. You boys in Dublin Castle must be proud of yourselves. You're fucking murderers so.'

Kate shook off Stefan's arm and walked forward. She slapped Kieran's face; as she did she knocked the glass of whiskey he was holding to the floor.

'You're pissed, Kieran. But then you were always full of shite sober.'

There was silence. Most people had tried to ignore the argument, and there were even a few at the back of the house, by the French windows, who hadn't noticed it was happening. However, there wasn't any ignoring it now.

Kate turned away and smiled at Sally, as if nothing had happened.

'We did promise to take Tom to the pictures. We do have to go.'

For a moment the two women looked at each other. It was a look that said it would be a long time before they saw each other again. Sally nodded.

'I'll get your things, Kate.'

Tom Gillespie was not pleased to leave the party. He had been enjoying himself and felt he had made new friends. He had wanted to stay. None of the children saw the argument, but Tom realised that something wasn't right as they left.

Walking towards Marine Point to get the tram back into Dublin, no one spoke.

'Anyway,' said Stefan very suddenly, 'it was good to meet your friends.'

Kate looked at him. He was poker-faced. Then he grinned, and she began to laugh. She took his hand and they were both laughing, loudly, almost uncontrollably. Tom looked up at them, still irritated and now bewildered.

'*Pinocchio*'s on at the pictures,' said Stefan. 'How about that?'

Tom nodded. He did want to see it, but he was still miffed.

'We'll see it so,' said Kate. 'And then fish and chips from Beshoff's!'

Tom smiled. That sounded better. When they walked on, Stefan took one of his hands; Kate took the other. But he hadn't quite finished with his regrets.

'Why did we have to go?' he said. 'I was having a grand time there!'

Neither Stefan nor Kate answered him, but after a moment they started to snigger. And then they couldn't stop laughing again. But Tom had no idea why.

That night, in the flat over Paddy Geary's tobacconist's, with the fish and chips eaten and the best bits of *Pinocchio* rehearsed and retold along with the half-remembered songs, Tom Gillespie finally went to sleep on the sofa and was carried into the bedroom by his father. For Stefan and Kate, with the day over, and with separation imminent again, it was a time to stop talking. They sat for a while with the curtains open and the lights and sounds of the Quays below them, looking out on the Liffey. Despite all the laughter, Stefan knew that Kate had come away from the Confirmation party uneasy and uncomfortable. She had come home to Dublin and was going to go away again feeling, for the first time in her life, that she didn't quite belong. It wasn't that she had any real sense of belonging in London. It wasn't like that. It was nothing as deep as that. But that was where she was, and it had come to make sense to her, in a way that home didn't right now. When she tried to say that to Stefan, she found the words difficult to put together. She was afraid it would sound like she was separating herself from him, and that wasn't it. She was sure it wasn't. So she said less than she wanted to say. And Stefan, who could feel her awkwardness, but didn't understand it, was content to let the conversation stop. There was distance between them. They were living different lives. And the barriers he had to put up about his own life didn't help at all. He couldn't even talk about what he would be doing in two days' time. He had to pretend he would simply be working in Dublin, doing what he always did, which he couldn't talk about either. He had so little to say about almost everything that Kate was more and more conscious she was doing most of the talking. There were things they both wanted that might have made talking unnecessary, but with Tom in the other room, their one night together would be light on the communication they most needed. Kate leant closer on the sofa. She looked up. He bent his head down and kissed her.

'We can't do much,' she laughed, 'but sure, we can do something . . .'

Part Two

The Book Of Revelations

The Third Reich, as the guardian and energising force of European policy, is inevitably interested in the continuity of the principles of national freedom enunciated in the past by Germany and the other Great European Powers and if, in the prosecution of the present war, German forces land in Ireland, they will land, as they did in 1916, as friends and liberators of the Irish people. Germany desires in Ireland neither territory nor the fruit of economic penetration; her reward for any help she may accord, directly or indirectly, is the freedom of civilised nations from the yoke of Britain and Britain's satellites and the reconstruction of a free and progressive Europe.

IRA War News

13

The *Irish Pine*

When Stefan Gillespie was sitting in Iveagh House again, in the room looking out over Stephen's Green, Joseph Walshe's instructions were spoken. Nothing in writing. Walshe referred to no notes as he spoke. There was no paperwork.

'The *Irish Pine* sails from Arklow on Monday. We'll send a car to pick you up from Wellington Quay. The boat will cross to South Wales, where it will unload a cargo of cattle and take on coal for Portugal. Only James Fortune, the captain, knows he is carrying you as a diplomat. He thinks you work for the department, and he won't ask any questions. As far as the crew goes, you're in Portugal to discuss trade on the Lisbon run. We want to increase it, which is true enough. The vaguer the better, I think. Mostly the boats bring back fertiliser and grain, and you have a background in farming. I'd say you'll pass muster. I'll give you a list of shipping companies and agricultural suppliers in Lisbon. If you can remember half a dozen names, should a conversation arise, it will do.'

'And in Lisbon?' asked Stefan.

'There's a sleeper booked on the *Sud Express*. That's been done through Wagon-Lits, and you'll collect the tickets from their offices in the Rua Carmo. There's nothing secretive about any of that. And you know the train, of course.'

'I took it as far as Burgos.'

'You'll take it as far as Paris. It still runs all the way, in theory, but we don't know what the situation is in France. Crossing from the Vichy French zone to the German zone seems reasonably easy, though. The journey may take longer than it did. Whether you can still get a train all the way through to Paris, we don't know. If not you'll have to change, but the ticket will get you there. Paris to Berlin is more difficult. The trains are mainly used by the military, but as a diplomat you'll qualify for a pass to allow you to get a ticket. We've no ambassador in Paris. Mr Cremin has moved down to Vichy, with what's left of the French government. But Count Gerard O'Kelly, our Honorary Consul, says he can push the paperwork through and get you on a train, without you having to hang around in Paris for very long. Gerry's a good man for pulling strings. And if he does seem a little puffed about that, just smile so.'

Stefan looked puzzled. The first secretary shrugged.

'The Taoiseach dispensed with his services as ambassador some years ago. He finds it amusing he is now all we've got, and likes to make the point.'

'He was on the wrong side, you see.' There was a chuckle from a small, slight man in glasses who had said nothing since he had been introduced as 'Dick, a professor at UCD'. 'He went to school at Clongowes Wood, and Dev was at Blackrock. Some divisions never heal. Now wasn't that the story, Joe?'

'Dick, why don't you deal with your side of things? I wouldn't like to think I'm boring you.' Joseph Walshe was not amused by sarcastic asides.

'Could you ever bore anyone, Joe?'

The man picked up a briefcase and opened it, as Walshe continued: 'You are travelling as a diplomatic courier, Gillespie. You will take one sealed bag containing letters and money orders. But it represents the reason for your journey. It is a diplomatic bag, and you should make a hell of a fuss if anyone wants to inspect it.' Walshe smiled. 'What matters is this Tiomna Nua.'

Dick handed Stefan a small black book with a gold cross on it.

'This a New Testament, obviously, in Irish.'

Stefan took the book and flicked through it, with no idea what he was supposed to do with it. It was small enough to fit in his pocket; it was printed on the thinnest paper. Christ's words were printed in red against the black text.

'You will find some pretty poor Irish in there,' laughed the professor.

'Keep it in your pocket, Gillespie,' said Walshe, 'and if anyone doubts your religious convictions, I'm sure you know how to make a holy show of yourself. You're Irish, after all. But the book is why I'm sending you to Berlin. The code we have used to communicate with our legations is now being read, and being read in both Berlin and London. London doesn't much matter, since anything sensitive can be said face to face, but with Germany it's different. We have to do a lot of reading between the lines to make a guess at what Warnock's telling us some of the time. He has to be circumspect. There is a real possibility of events taking a very serious turn, so it's not helpful that his views and our instructions are read in transit. A new code book is bound into the Tiomna Nua.'

Stefan looked down at the book and flicked though it again.

'It's not that hard to spot the pages,' said the man from UCD. 'But unless you're looking for it, and you have a bit of Irish too, it's hiding in plain sight.'

'You don't need to know anything more than that, Gillespie,' continued Walshe. 'Our chargé d'affaires in Berlin, William Warnock, knows it's coming. You'll also take this. Doubtless the embassy has it, but it must be the right edition.'

Dick handed him a copy of Baedeker's guide to Germany.

'The Baedeker's guide produced for the Olympics, an

unremarkable thing for you to have in your case. You will leave it with Mr Warnock, and tell him that it is to be used, in emergencies, as a substitution cipher. He knows how to use it. But it must be the same edition we have at this end, in every detail.'

'I know how a substitution code works,' said Stefan.

'Good,' said the other man. 'And that's it, Joe. Good luck, Inspector.'

Walshe nodded, and the UCD professor left.

'All these things have a limited life,' said Joseph Walshe. 'Codes are not unbreakable. Dick spends as much time breaking them as he does dreaming them up. That's the game, and everyone is playing it at some level. So, although we have a new code, we can't be sure how long before the Germans break it. If we suspect the code has been compromised, Warnock can fall back on the Baedeker, in an emergency, and use the simple substitution cipher. That's breakable too, but for something so simple it's still hard work. More manpower than anyone might want to spend – when there are far more important targets.'

Stefan said nothing. Walshe stood up and took out a cigarette. As he lit it, he turned and looked out at the trees of Stephen's Green. He turned back.

'Mr Warnock will know what "emergency" means.'

Stefan nodded.

'Not hard to fathom. The invasion of England. Or a German landing here, north or south. Or indeed all that at the same time, God help us. And under those circumstances, we do need to be able to talk to him quickly and secretly.'

'Do you think it's going to happen?' said Stefan quietly.

'I haven't the foggiest, Inspector. Doubtless we will find out. Soon.'

The journey from Ireland to Portugal had been uneventful. The sea was still, even in the Bay of Biscay, and the September weather was blue and clear. Stefan Gillespie was accepted by the uninquisitive crew of the *Irish Pine* for what he was supposed to be – some kind of government emissary, looking to boost agricultural trade with one of the only countries accessible to Irish ships. James Fortune, the captain, knew there was more to it, though he had no interest in what that was, and despite Stefan's best endeavours, he had given up his cabin. It seemed best his passenger could keep out of the way if he wanted to.

They had unloaded cattle in Wales, at Port Talbot, and Stefan's ability to drive some of the more recalcitrant beasts off the boat established him more firmly in the men's mind as a cattle man of some kind. British police and customs showed no special interest in yet another Irish ship unloading beef and picking up Welsh coal for Lisbon; the only person they spoke to was Captain Fortune. The stopover in Wales lasted twelve hours, and then the *Irish Pine* sailed south, round the tip of Cornwall, off Land's End, and out into the Atlantic.

There were risks in the passage from South Wales to Lisbon. Several ships of the tiny Irish merchant marine had been sunk by German U-boats, though the huge tricolour painted on the hulls, and the word 'Eire' were meant to be enough to establish their neutral status. It was usually enough, but some U-boat captains were less fastidious than others, once they had established a boat wasn't German, and although the sinking of an Irish vessel eventually produced a German apology, the unspoken truth was that the occasional 'mistake' was there to remind Ireland that trading with Britain in the middle of a war had to come at some price. At sea, neutrality was a guarantee of nothing.

It was on the second day out of Port Talbot that two RAF Mosquitos flew low over the *Irish Pine*. One circled the boat several times. Stefan was on deck, looking up at the planes with no special interest. The RAF markings were obvious enough. A few crew members waved idly. Then as the Mosquito made one last, low pass, there was a rattle of gunfire; the machine gun spat a dozen shots into the sea ahead of the boat. The plane headed back to the English coast.

'What the fuck was that for?' said Stefan. 'He could see us.'

'Not everyone loves the Irish. Those were Polish planes. I don't know what the Polish is for "Fuck you!", but you'll get the gist of the message so.'

'But they're still RAF.'

Fortune shrugged, turning away, clearly unsurprised by it.

'They take a less charitable view of neutrality than the English. If you look at what the Germans did to Poland, you may even feel they have a point.'

In Lisbon Stefan Gillespie spoke to no one except the customs officials at the port, the clerk at the Wagon-Lits office in the Rua Carmo, where he picked up his tickets, and a few waiters. He had been in the city earlier that year, and he understood its position as another compromised neutral and as one of Europe's only entry and exit points. He knew the routine. Everyone wondered what everyone passing through the city was up to, but there was an etiquette. You never asked. All he had to do was kill time unobtrusively. The *Irish Pine* had docked that morning, so he had no need to spend a night in the city; as darkness fell he was already leaving it, on the night train from the Rossio Station.

The train from Lisbon travelled through the night, through Spain, to the French border. He woke at various stations along the way, and saw the cities he had visited in the spring: Salamanca and Burgos. As he looked out, they were only empty platforms, with a few people straggling away into the darkness. He kept to his compartment and talked to no one, sleeping most of the way, the kind of fitful, unsatisfying sleep that goes with a night train. He crossed into France next morning, walking over the bridge from Irun to Hendaye, for the train north. It was a new

France, Vichy France; the half of the country that the Germans had left the French to govern themselves. The half that didn't matter.

Through southern France the pace was slower, but apart from a long delay of three hours, when the train stopped after crossing from Vichy France into the German zone, it was a through passage. Vichy France was quiet. Looking out through the window, at the countryside and the towns passing by, the idea that there was a war at all, and that one of Europe's greatest nations had been divided in two by a victorious enemy, wasn't easy to take in. There had never been fighting in the south. Stefan felt as if nothing was different even though, somehow, it should be. But there was something about the journey that jarred. Passengers got in and out along the way; a few, like him, had travelled from Spain. Yet though people who knew each other talked amiably enough, he could see that strangers avoided looking at one another. At several stations gendarmes joined the train, and as the guard checked tickets, they checked identity papers. When Stefan's elementary French failed him, and he couldn't answer a question from one of the gendarmes, the policeman spoke to him in German. The fact that he answered fluently didn't go unnoticed, and he was aware that he was watched by the other passengers, who spoke more quietly. The man who had been sitting next to him moved to another seat.

The Deutsche Reichsbahn train had been sitting outside a station for almost two hours. It was two in the morning. Stefan didn't know where they were. The outskirts of a town; somewhere big, though with everything blacked out all he could see from the window of the sleeper were the outlines of the usual industrial buildings and warehouses that sprawl along railway lines into any city. The train had crossed from Belgium into Germany an hour before they stopped. The borders between northern

France, Belgium and Germany didn't matter much now, but at each one customs and police came through the train to check papers. Most of the carriages were overflowing with soldiers, heading home on leave, and there was a noisy, almost festive mood further down the train, away from the sleeping cars and the first-class carriages at the front.

Arriving in Paris on a curtailed version of the *Sud Express* from Lisbon, Stefan had discovered there was no shortage of trains to Germany, but getting a ticket was difficult. The railway system of Europe was being conscripted into Germany's war machine, and access to it was more and more restricted to those whose business was the business of the Reich. He had noticed the change as soon as the train from the Spanish border crossed from the remnant of France the Germans had left the French into the zone that was under military government. Immediately there were more German soldiers; not only on the train but in the stations he passed through. Along the roads he saw from the train, it was never long before a convoy of trucks in field grey appeared. When French gendarmes walked through the train, looking at identity papers, as they did repeatedly, they were with Wehrmacht soldiers or military policemen.

In Paris Stefan Gillespie was met at the Gare d'Orsay by all that was left of an Irish diplomatic presence in the city, the Honorary Consul. Gerry, as he introduced himself, was Count Gerard O'Kelly de Gallagh, and as Joseph Walshe predicted, he found his role ferrying Stefan around on behalf of Éamon de Valera permanently entertaining. However, in the two days Stefan knew him, he saw that this was the count's approach to almost everything. He also saw that it hid a deeper awareness of what was going on than O'Kelly let anyone see. He knew nothing of what Stefan was doing, and made no attempt to find out.

The count lived in an apartment of some size, over his wine emporium in the Place de Vendôme, and for two days

Stefan drank good wine and ate good food. He didn't leave the flat. O'Kelly took the instruction that Stefan should not draw any attention to himself at face value. He spent those days battering the military governor's office with enough relentless charm to procure the necessary pass and ticket, and an almost miraculous sleeping-car berth; all stamped and re-stamped with the required eagles and swastikas. It was no mean feat, but while the count was a man of limitless acquaintance, who had friends everywhere, he was a great believer in going to the top. The contract he had to supply French wines to Reichsmarschall Hermann Göring was not the least influential factor in his charm offensive on the German military governor.

The train that would take Stefan Gillespie to Berlin left the Gare du Nord on the evening of his third day in Paris. The single sleeping car was occupied by a Wehrmacht general, several senior SS and Gestapo officers and a number of German businessmen. Stefan was aware there was some interest in him in the first-class carriages, once he was identified as an Irishman, but it didn't go beyond idle pleasantries. He was only a courier, and the German sense of hierarchy, along with the door of his sleeper, kept curiosity at bay. But he had also discovered that the quality of his German was more of an asset than he had realised. It did more than ease communication. It seemed to go without saying that an Irishman who spoke such good German must have his heart in the German Volk and German success in the war.

After the long stop in the darkness, outside the unidentified German city, the train finally moved forward again, after almost three hours, but only another kilometre. It pulled into a station and stopped. It was a big station, and although Stefan could not quite see the high roof in the darkness, he could feel the train was under a great glass and iron canopy. There were only dim lights on the platform, as required by the blackout. Looking out through the blind at the window, Stefan could see soldiers disembarking. He saw two trolleys on the platform, with urns of coffee. Two women were serving lines of troops.

There was something familiar about the place. He picked up his sealed diplomatic case and walked along the corridor to the open door on to the platform. He was hungry. He had brought no food and there was none on the train. All he had was a bottle of champagne and a bottle of brandy Count O'Kelly had given him to pass the time. He walked to the trolley and stood in line. After a few minutes a woman thrust a cup of coffee and a roll into his hand. He took out a banknote from his pocket, but the woman ignored him and held out a cup and a roll to the soldier behind him. He carried on along the platform slowly, drinking the coffee, which tasted of not much more than hot water and chicory, and eating the roll, which tasted of nothing at all and had the texture of paper. Then he saw the station name on a sign: Hannover.

He had been here before. He tried to count the years. It was his last journey to Germany as a child. He had been almost sixteen. He was with his mother, and his cousins, Lotte and Franz. They had been travelling from Weimar to Celle, to see Helena's great uncle, an almost unimaginably old man in his mid-nineties, who had no idea who any of them were. It had been a futile journey. It had filled the teenagers with the embarrassing awkwardness and idiocy of an old age that, somehow, they felt they would never connect to, but it had upset Stefan's mother. He had only noticed her crying once, and then forgotten all about it. He had a lot more to think about. For three short, burning weeks in that summer, Lotte had been the first woman he loved, though their words for each other were still girl and boy. Standing on the dark platform at Hannover, he wondered where she was. He knew she had married, that she had children, that her husband was in the army; so was Franz. That news had reached Kilranelagh. He smiled, remembering her. A fond memory of someone he knew almost nothing of, who knew nothing of him. It was an odd place to be. The journey had brought him back as well as forward, for a moment at least.

Stefan looked around at the soldiers on the platform, most of them much younger than him, but more than a few about the same age. There was a loud hiss of steam from the engine. The train's whistle let out a long, low wail. They were leaving again. Soldiers rushed back to their carriages. The doors slammed, and the train lurched and then inched forward. Stefan opened the bottle of brandy. He looked out at the platform once more. And then Hannover was gone.

14

Berlin Friedrichstrasse

It was late afternoon when the train from Paris arrived at the Friedrichstrasse station. The journey into the city was like the journey into any city: an untidy sprawl of factories and warehouses and scruffy sidings, and waste ground that seemed unconnected to anything. There were clusters of apartment blocks and roads hemmed by the backs of houses, all thinly spread, then more and more densely packed, until buildings closed the railway lines in on either side, and even the smallest, scruffiest patches of empty space had disappeared. Berlin was a city Stefan Gillespie felt he knew in some way. On childhood visits to Germany, a trip to the city had often been planned, though it had never materialised, but once, five years earlier, he had changed planes at the Tempelhof aerodrome, on his way to the Baltic city of Danzig. He didn't even leave the airport. He felt he knew Berlin in the same way he had always felt he knew London long before he went to England. It existed in his imagination, because it existed in the imaginations of the people around him. Yet the way it existed in his youth, when that knowledge came from his family, was not the way it existed now. Berlin was the city of Adolf Hitler, and as such it had a place in everyone's imagination. For some it had been a city of new hope and light, of glorious parades and joyful patriotism; the city of a shining future, where everything modern and new met ancient values of order and faith, to shape a destiny for a world in chaos; it was a shining city, built on a hill. For others it was the fount of all the darkness spilling out across Europe and the world; not simply the cause of the war that had become what the world was, but the war itself. But as Stefan watched the heart of Berlin grow around him, it was its ordinariness that struck him. From the train, it was any city anywhere.

Stefan was met at the Bahnhof Friedrichstrasse by the Irish embassy's German driver, an oval-faced Bavarian called Otto, who spoke a little English and seemed relieved not to have to use it. He had memorised one phrase in Irish, 'Céad mile fáilte', a hundred thousand welcomes, which he used whenever he could, to advertise the job he did; a badge of identity. They were the words he greeted Stefan with as he left the train, and they were repeated half a dozen times, with a cheerful grin, while they walked to the car. Stefan felt obliged to offer one polite reply in Irish, but left it at that when he realised that whatever he said would provoke Otto to repeat his one Irish phrase over and over again.

As they walked to the car, Stefan saw a gap in the row of buildings on the other side of Friedrichstrasse, only a short distance away. Further back, several floors of two buildings still stood, but had been torn open. Where the buildings had fronted the street, there were only high piles of rubble. A line of men in thin, grey serge were clearing the rubble with shovels, watched over by uniformed policemen. It was bomb damage.

'You have had bombs?' Stefan asked. 'Very many?'

'A few, a very few. Nothing. They will be stopped.'

Otto spoke quietly and looked uncomfortable for the first time, but then he reached the car and held the back door open for Stefan to get in. He grinned.

'Céad mile fáilte!'

It was a short journey from Friedrichstrasse to the Irish legation in Drakestrasse, on the north side of the Tiergarten, but Otto took Stefan along Unter den Linden, Berlin's grandest, widest boulevard, and through the Brandenburg Gate to get there. He kept up a constant, easy chatter about the journey from Ireland, but Stefan caught him glancing into the driving mirror enough times to know that he was meant to show he was impressed by the great buildings that lined Unter den Linden. This was still Imperial Germany in disguise. The chaos of the Weimar Republic had not changed it, and even the order imposed by the Nazis had done little more than add banners and flags and swastikas to the solid Prussian version of classical architecture that defined this part of Berlin. It wasn't the heart of the city, but it was its best face, and Stefan already knew it, in his head, as he had known Whitehall and Trafalgar Square the first time he saw them. And from newsreels and newspapers he knew the rest, too: the red and the black that was everywhere, and the uniforms; though there were more than he expected. Half the people they passed were in some kind of uniform.

Drakestrasse was a small tree-lined street, just across the Landwehr Canal from the Tiergarten, the great open park that gave Berlin its lungs and its sense of space, away from the crowded streets of the centre, just as the Phoenix Park did for Dublin. It was a street of buildings that had once been large family homes. They were grand, but in a modest, almost suburban way. It was a quiet corner of the city. There were no flags, no uniforms. It was a memory of another Berlin that, oddly, the presence of other countries' embassies had left intact.

Stefan Gillespie sat opposite the Irish chargé d'affaires, in his office on the first floor of the house at 3 Drakestrasse. Warnock was a few years younger than Stefan, and he had inherited his position only because there was no real ambassador. The war, and the peculiarities of Irish neutrality, had interrupted the appointment of a new ambassador, since the role still had to be authorised, officially, by the King of England, as King of Ireland. It was part of the constitutional mess that still cluttered the relationship between Britain and Ireland, and since Britain was at war with Germany, nothing could be done. So, doing nothing became the answer, and Warnock, the legation's first secretary, filled the gap as chargé d'affaires, even if he was always called the ambassador.

Warnock turned the pages of the Irish New Testament Stefan Gillespie had carried in his pocket from Dublin, which contained, bound into it, the new codes the embassy was meant to use in communicating with home. Several times Warnock smiled, and then he shut the book and leant back in his chair.

'You'd better give me the Baedeker as well.'

Stefan pushed the small red book across the desk.

'We have that edition, but whether it's the same printing, I don't know. It's possible there are a few discrepancies. It's sod's law I'd pick the one line they changed.' Warnock smiled. 'Did you meet Dick Stevens, the code man?'

'Yes. At Iveagh House.'

'We were at UCD together. Say I appreciate the joke, if you see him.'

Stefan smiled, with no idea what the joke was.

'You didn't see he'd underlined, "In the beginning was the word."'

'I didn't read it, sir,' said Stefan, smiling.

'It's O'Donnell's translation. I don't know if you know—'

'I know who he was.'

'It always amused Dick that the first translation of the Bible into Irish was a Protestant one. He'd also claim it was the best. And he's probably right. So, the joke is he's given me a Protestant translation with an imprimatur from a Catholic bishop. Still, that's a fond memory of home in its own right, isn't it?'

The ambassador looked down at the small book again, quieter.

'I'd like to be out of this shite hole, I tell you.'

Stefan didn't answer.

'I was in a court the other day – and if anything showed me—' Warnock stopped and took a cigarette from a box on the desk. He turned and looked out of the window, at the trees in Drakestrasse, as he lit it. 'There was a feller quoting *Alice in Wonderland* at me there, that's all – and it's stuck.' He turned back to Stefan. 'I keep remembering more bits. It's turning into my Baedeker guide. The Cheshire cat says, "We're all mad here. I'm mad." And Alice says, "How do you know I'm mad?" "You must be, or you wouldn't have come," the cat says back. You can see I've been in Berlin for too long, Gillespie. Beginning to feel I belong here. Not good! Did you see any bomb damage on the way here?'

'In Friedrichstrasse, yes.'

'There's not a lot, but the RAF is getting planes through. We've had them most nights for the last ten days. I don't think it's heavy, but I don't really have anything to compare it with, of course. And no one talks about it. We hear it, we see it, we go down into the air-raid shelters, and I'm sure people must have died somewhere. We pass buildings that have been hit, and mostly we say nothing. It wasn't supposed to happen, you see. That was the story. There would be no bombs on Berlin. It was impossible. Even as they fall, it's still impossible. But you'll want to sort yourself out, Gillespie. I'll leave you to yourself this evening, but perhaps we'll have a meal and I'll sound off on what I'm not supposed to sound off on. It can be liberating to whisper the truth occasionally.'

'I did notice your driver wasn't keen to talk about bombs.'

'Avoid bombs and food. Rationing hasn't hit hard yet, but some things are getting scarce. And the rumours are that there will be more serious rationing as winter comes. It's the kind of thing I can never report to Joe Walshe, because everything's being read. I don't really know how long till they crack these codes, but we'll see. Anyway, the restaurants are still fine, certainly the ones the officers and the SS use. If you see a lot of men in uniform, you'll probably get a good meal. People will be intrigued you're Irish, but generally our neutrality is seen as a poke in the eye for the English, so we're popular.'

'I won't be starting many conversations, sir.'

'Your German is a lot better than mine, says Otto.' Warnock grinned. 'And as a Special Branch man, I'm sure you nod as well in German as English.'

'I'd say I do, sir. Do I go straight back to Ireland?'

'I've booked you into a hotel in Kurfürstendamm, the am Zoo. We're stretched here. It's down to me and one secretary now. And she runs the thing anyway. But we're not up to much on the accommodation front. I have got you a military travel pass, and I'll sort the tickets out tomorrow. To get home you'll take the train to Sassnitz on the Baltic. The train ferry takes you to Malmö. You're in Sweden then, and you can get to Stockholm easily enough. I have the documentation, that's what matters. It's what life revolves around. The right pass and everything is possible! When you reach Stockholm the British embassy will get you on to the BOAC flight to Scotland. They'll be a bit sniffy, but they'll do it. The Germans will know how you're getting to Ireland, but you are travelling as a courier. You won't be carrying anything of any consequence, but make a fuss if anyone wants to search you. We try to keep up appearances.'

William Warnock stubbed out his cigarette and stood up.

'I'll get Otto to drive you to Ku'damm.'

'Thank you, sir.' Stefan got up too.

'I suppose you had a long chat with Otto about the trip?'

'He's quite a chatterer,' smiled Stefan.

'Nothing to hide, but bear in mind he'll take everything to the Gestapo.'

Stefan looked surprised. Warnock laughed.

'If I sacked him the next one would do the same. You get used to it.'

Stefan had little need to nod. The receptionist at the Hotel am Zoo had no desire to discuss the war, nor did the porter, or the barman, or the waiter in the restaurant he ate in, Die drei Bären. Kurfürstendamm was a street he had heard about. When he and his cousins had planned the trips to Berlin that had never happened, it was still a part of what was extraordinary about the city. It was a shabbier place than he imagined. There were shops, but the window displays were drab and uninteresting, and everything was accompanied by flags and posters. There were restaurants and bars, but where they were full, they were full of men in uniform. He saw also, at the kerbside, what went with that: the prostitutes. They stood by the roadside while it was still light, because the nights were no longer full of crowds. The police ignored them. It was not the advertisement for National Socialist Berlin that the authorities demanded, but unless there was a clampdown, Ku'damm was a place where this necessary business was tolerated. Even though the night was young, the streets were emptying quickly. Something simply wasn't there, something that had nothing to do with the blackout and early closing. He thought of London, New York, even Dublin itself. It was a kind of vitality that was missing. Everywhere he saw newspapers, billboards, hoardings, celebrating the famous victories that had given Germany command of the coast of Europe, from the Arctic Circle to the Spanish border, but what was in the air was somehow empty and unenthusiastic. It was a tired city, when it shouldn't be at all. In the Three Bears he had even said something.

'It seems very quiet.'

The waiter looked at him for a moment.

'Where are you from?'

'Ireland.'

The man nodded slowly, as if trying to place it.

'You know Berlin?'

'No. I knew Germany. A while ago.' He laughed. 'When I was young.'

'There was a time Ku'damm never slept.' The waiter grinned. 'Never!'

'I have heard that.'

'But we do wake up now. We wake up when the Führer speaks!'

It was said with an ambiguous smile that could have meant anything, from bitter sarcasm to the expression of profound love for the country's leader. Stefan was looking for the wry humour that every Berliner was supposed to possess, and half expecting a wink; but he couldn't read the impenetrable grin.

The days of interrupted sleep at sea and on trains meant that Stefan Gillespie slept soundly, so soundly that he was woken abruptly by someone knocking on the door of the room the next morning. A sharp rap, a pause, then another sharp rap. Then again. The persistence irritated him. He had asked to be left to sleep. It was still only eight o'clock. He walked to the door and opened it, not looking for a row, but more than inclined to show how pissed off he was. The final rap on the door stopped as he snatched open the door, still in pyjamas.

The two men in the corridor weren't there to clean the room. One was short and thin, the other was tall and thin. They wore dark overcoats and hats that were pulled too far down on their heads to have been comfortable. The short man had to look up to see past the brim of his Homburg. If he didn't know the species, Stefan knew the genus. One of the men held up an oval, brass disc.

'Kripo,' snapped the short one, without elaborating.

Stefan frowned, not making the connection immediately.

'Kriminalpolizei,' said the tall man more slowly, smiling.
'Oh, yes,' replied Stefan, as if this now made sense.
'Kriminalkommissar Vordermaier wants to see you.'
Stefan waited several seconds for an explanation. None came.

15

Alexanderplatz

The centre of any great city is not to be found among its grand edifices and monuments, or in its widest boulevards and most elegant shopping streets, but at some traffic-choked mishmash of intersecting roads and unimpressive buildings that few outsiders would even identify as a place. Alexanderplatz, the centre of Berlin's centre, Mitte, was jammed with buses and trams all day and half the night, and it was a lonely, slightly threatening place in its few hours of quiet, which had extended considerably now that the city was blacked out during the hours of darkness. Two buildings dominated Alexanderplatz: the arched and soaring greenhouse roof of the station on one side and, opposite it, through a jumble of mismatched, down-at-heel offices and shops, Berlin's police headquarters, the Polizeipräsidium, a long, square, red-brick building with domed corner-turrets that resembled, oddly, Harrods department store in London, and was almost as big. It had been remarked that the resemblance said something about the souls of Germany and Britain. Although there was a big department store, Hertie, near the Präsidium, it never contributed much to the area's character; it had offered even less since Aryanisation rescued it from people who knew how to run it, and left it empty of goods and customers. The station and Präsidium – the Alex – defined Alexanderplatz; above all the Alex.

However, the Alex had not been the headquarters of anything for a long time. The orders that mattered came from the Reich Main Security Office in the more elegant Prinz-Albrecht-Strasse, where the Gestapo and the Security Police, the SD, were based. Though the business of the Kripo detectives in Alexanderplatz, the Kriminalpolizei, was still the investigation of what was now called 'ordinary' crime, they had long been absorbed into the political structures of German policing. They were enmeshed in the web of overlapping and often contradictory interests that defined all Nazi structures. In the Alex's offices there were officers who were members of the SS or the SA, as well as being policemen, and while most had now become members of the Nazi Party, there were a few who had not. If that caused confusion, it was meant to. There were hierarchies of loyalty to be negotiated that were never clear. You could never guess, let alone work out, which conflicting instructions to follow. All things were connected, and, depending on the way the wind blew, obeying orders that subsequently changed could be more costly than ignoring them. But if you did emerge from the swamp in one piece, you were working towards the Führer. If not, your Gestapo file grew a bit thicker. Thin Gestapo files were everything.

Kriminalkommissar Diedrich Vordermaier didn't spend a lot of time thinking about these things. The randomness of almost everything meant there was little point. But from time to time it was necessary to take stock. Gestapo files did land on his desk now and then. It was natural enough; at some level all crimes were political, and all branches of the police were ultimately working to defend Germany from its enemies, large or small. But it still surprised him how much detail these files contained, and how trivial, even banal, much of it was. He had never seen his own Gestapo file, of course, but he knew he had one. He had joined the Nazi Party later than advisable, at least among the higher Kripo ranks. He knew that was enough, of itself, to prevent him being promoted any further within the Kriminalpolizei. But he was no longer ambitious. He was good at his job; he always had been; yet that presented problems too. No amount of dedication to the new regime could entirely erase the fact that he had also been a good and faithful servant of the previous one. And now he had made a mistake. It wasn't a big one, but you could never quite tell the consequences.

Vordermaier looked down from his office on the third floor of the Alex. He could see the railway lines running into the glass hall of the Alexanderplatz Station. It was a view he liked – something of Berlin that was the same as it had been the first time he looked out of that window, ten years earlier. He lit one of the tiny Jakob Saemann cigars he smoked. They were another small thing that was the same. They came from Ostdorf, the Swabian town where he grew up. He had not been back there in twenty-five years, but he bought the cigars from the one tobacconist in Berlin who kept them. He was fifty-four now, and he prided himself on his ability to steer a course that kept him either out of the way of trouble or on the right side of it. But he had drawn attention to himself, in a way he could not have expected. He sat down, drawing in smoke, and opened the Gestapo file on Hauptmann Johannes Rilling, deceased, but not yet defunct.

The first mistake was to have pushed the Rilling case too far, instead of following the man and handing the results to the Gestapo. Dremmel and Lamm had fucked that up. The second mistake had been the Irishwoman. He hadn't known she was Irish. Now the fucking Foreign Ministry had the fucking Irish ambassador on their backs. If asked, Kriminalkommissar Vordermaier wouldn't have thought the fucking Irish ambassador counted for much, but it seemed he did. The result was that his bosses at the Alex were getting bollocked by Prinz-Albrecht-Strasse because the Foreign Ministry in Wilhelmstrasse was pissed off over a country that shouldn't matter. And it was his fault. It was his fault and it would end up adding pages to his Gestapo file. What he had to do was bring it back under his control. Never mind the politics; he had to give the Gestapo something they wanted, or at least shift the blame. If he couldn't, he had to take the heat out and shut it down. This unlooked-for Irish policeman could help.

Stefan Gillespie sat in Kriminalkommissar Vordermaier's office as the Kommissar outlined the case of the Irishwoman, Zandra Purcell. Vordermaier explained that the problem was a political one, and shrugged; everything was a political problem. His superiors in the Reich Main Security Office were under pressure from the Foreign Ministry. They were under pressure from the Irish ambassador, and although the murder of Hauptmann Johannes Rilling appeared to be an open-and-shut case, the German government was keen to reassure the Irish government that everything had been done that justice demanded.

The information that the courier who had just arrived from Dublin was a policeman had only reached the Kripo offices the previous night, and it had been felt this was a chance not to be missed, in terms of providing the ambassador with the reassurances he was asking for. There was nothing to hide, and now that could be made very clear, with an Irish detective inspector to cast a professional eye over things. Vordermaier seemed pleased with the way he phrased this. He apologised for the failure in communication between the Reich Main Security and the Foreign Ministry; Herr Warnock had not been informed in time to talk to Stefan but that, as he said, was fucking bureaucracy for you.

As Stefan listened to the details of the murder, Vordermaier flicked back and forward through a file. It was a very thin file. It appeared to contain no more than a couple of photographs and some short statements. He made no attempt to refer to it, or to show it to Stefan. All he talked about was his decision to go back to the day of Rilling's death and talk to a number of people the captain had visited. Fraulein Purcell had been the last of those, but the others were also Irish, or had Irish connections. Some were also people who knew Fraulein Purcell, and that might help explain more about what had happened. Stefan did not ask why the people the dead man had seen and spoken to around the time of his death had not been interviewed already. It should have been done immediately. But since it hadn't been, since no one seemed interested in anything other than events in Zandra Purcell's apartment, as far as evidence went, he couldn't see why it mattered now. There was no sense that any of this would change anything. It already felt as if it was no more than a lot of activity, suggesting something was being done when it wasn't. He could smell a sop to William Warnock. No more. His job was to carry the sop back to the legation. Kriminalkommissar Vordermaier didn't seem bothered about disguising that.

'Can I see the file?' asked Stefan.

Vordermaier shrugged and pushed it across his desk.

It didn't take Stefan long to read it. It contained nothing the Kommissar hadn't said in five minutes. What passed as evidence was all assumption. The assumptions weren't unreasonable. Zandra Purcell was Johannes Rilling's lover. He was shot with his own pistol, in her bed, after an argument that others in the apartment block had heard. Witnesses placed Fraulein Purcell in her flat at the time a shot was heard. The two photographs of Hauptmann Rilling showed the upper body of a man, with part of his head missing, propped up against some pillows in a bed. It was a medium shot; no wide shot and no close-ups of the wound. Little forensic work had been done. The autopsy said only that a shot to the head at close range, from a gun identified as Hauptmann Rilling's service weapon, had been the cause of the trauma that resulted in almost immediate death.

The telephone rang. Diedrich Vordermaier picked it up.

'Yes, put him through.'

Vordermaier stood up as he spoke.

'Kriminalkommissar Vordermaier, Herr Ambassador. Yes, sir, he is.'

Vordermaier held out the telephone.

'Your ambassador, Inspector.'

Stefan took the phone.

'It's Gillespie, sir.'

'Jesus,' said Warnock, 'I've only just heard from the Foreign Ministry.'

'It was something of a surprise to me, sir.'

Stefan glanced at Vordermaier, who was obviously amused.

'You're at the Alex now?' asked Warnock.

'I am.'

'Why the fuck didn't they talk to me first? I had no idea—'

'Well, they have their own ways of doing things. Very much so.'

'Is that code for something, Gillespie?'

'Not as far as picking me up goes. It's how it works, even when they're looking for a favour. Old habits die hard. On the other hand, it may be worth remembering that someone with good English will probably be listening now.'

Stefan looked up and smiled at Vordermaier.

The Kriminalkommissar frowned, as if he had not understood the words, but Stefan knew he spoke enough English. Stefan's next words were in Irish.

'But I doubt they'll have an Irish speaker handy.'

'So what's your end of this?' replied Warnock, in Irish.

'A woman called Zandra Purcell, who's accused of murdering a German officer, who was her lover. The evidence says she is guilty, and if she is, she faces execution. You know something about that already, I assume, sir. But Kriminalkommissar Vordermaier is the man dealing with the case. He's been asked to look at it again, and he wants me to tag along. There seems to be some political pressure to make sure you're happy that everything's above board, and you can report that home. They don't want any friction with Ireland. The Kriminalkommissar seems happy enough with me. Is that what you want, sir?'

'I suppose so.' Warnock laughed. 'I'm surprised I'm getting it, though.'

'But you want me to do this?'

'Yes, I do. I have been making representations to the Foreign Ministry. I've been back and forth to Wilhelmstrasse all week. I still know fuck all about the case, and I certainly didn't get much when Miss Purcell was in court. Is there any chance you can get to talk to her? I got a couple of minutes, that's all.'

'I'll try, sir.'

'I was told the whole case was watertight. She shot the man. It was in her flat. They have the evidence. They have the witnesses. That's it.'

'It seems this man, Rilling, had some connections with the Irish community here. Kriminalkommissar Vordermaier says they are looking at Rilling's movements on the day he died, to make sure that nothing has been missed. He visited several people. And it seems some of them were Irish.'

'Do you know who?' asked Warnock.

Stefan Gillespie leant across the desk and picked up a piece of paper. He smiled amiably at Diedrich Vordermaier, who was leaning against the window, smoking a small cigar, and watching him with an expression of amusement.

'Yes. They're people I know something about. At least I know who they are. Helmut Clissman, who's a German officer, but has strong Irish connections. Francis Stuart. A name I've heard at Dublin Castle. And Mr Charles Bewley.'

'Jesus, Charles!' Warnock was surprised.

'A friend of the dead man's, apparently.'

'You know he was the ambassador—'

'Sacked by Mr de Valera, yes, sir, I do know.'

'They're all people I'd know a bit,' said the ambassador quietly.

'The police are going to talk to them. They do happen to be among the last people who saw Hauptmann Rilling alive. I don't know what I'm supposed to do. Listen, I suppose, and then reassure you that the Kriminalpolizei have turned over every last stone, and there's still no doubt about Miss Purcell's guilt. I don't think anyone's come up with any doubt. That's it. Do I go ahead?'

'Yes,' said Warnock thoughtfully. 'How serious are they, Gillespie?'

'They're still very sure of their ground.'

'If they want to reassure me, make them work for it. Insist you see her.'

Stefan put the phone down and smiled at Vordermaier.

'The ambassador said he's very grateful for all this, very grateful.'

Stefan could read the amiable shrug from the Kommissar: my arse he did!

'You caught me by surprise, Inspector. Was that Irish?'

'We like to use it when we can, Herr Kriminalkommissar.'

'Call me, Diedrich, Stefan. I think you just earned that.'

He reached out his hand. Stefan shook it.

'I want to see Zandra Purcell, Diedrich.'

Vordermaier nodded thoughtfully.

'I think she's said all she has to say, unfortunately.'

'Well, I'd like to hear her say it myself.'

Vordermaier looked harder at Stefan; he smiled.

'Why not?'

He opened a drawer. He took out a Walther PPK pistol.

'You're undressed without it.' Vordermaier grinned. 'If you don't have a uniform, at least you've got to have a gun. Otherwise you're just an arsehole!'

16

Moabit

They did not get far into the Moabit Prison, which was like a great red-brick starfish across the Spree from the Tiergarten. The entrance, in one of the gaol's five spoke-like wings, led them to an office only a few doors along a corridor. They were not really in the prison at all, and it was immediately clear they would go no further. But even without really entering the Moabit, something of its atmosphere seeped through the walls. Even the corridor they had walked along was silent, and it was a silence Stefan could feel, as something solid, all around him. The prison guard who led them to the empty office where they waited for Zandra Purcell spoke to them quietly, though there was no need.

'Three this morning,' said the guard.

Vordermaier nodded.

'That's nine heads off this week. Bastards, eh?'

The guard laughed, though still in a self-consciously hushed voice.

'Executions,' said the Kriminalkommissar to Stefan.

'Heads off?' said Stefan, still not quite understanding.

'The guillotine. Quick and clean. But these are busy days.'

The guard laughed again at Vordermaier's words, holding open the office door.

Stefan wasn't sure what the expression on the Kommissar's face said. There was relish, certainly, in the guard's amusement. Vordermaier's tone was more ambiguous. What Stefan did know now was the precise fate that awaited Zandra Purcell. He also knew something about the silence he sensed around him. This wasn't Mountjoy. There would be no days of furious protest here when people died on the guillotine. There would be barely any sound at all.

There was an almost pathetic gratitude in Zandra Purcell's eyes when she discovered that Stefan Gillespie was Irish. Before she even knew he was a policeman and that the Irish ambassador had asked him to help, it was enough that there was someone to speak to. But as Stefan explained who he was, there was more than gratitude. It was as if the grey pallor of her face changed when he looked at her. It wasn't that she smiled. She didn't smile once. There was a look on her face as if fear had frozen in her muscles. It said something not only about what was happening to her, but about where she was. It was a place without hope, and Stefan saw that in Zandra's eyes. And yet she was not broken. She was an elegant woman, tall and dark, with hair cut short and close to her face. The hair was dank and greasy now, but it framed her face in a way that made her striking. And something lifted in her as she looked at Stefan; however tenuously, something gave a hint of colour to her cheeks. She watched him as if there was something miraculous about him, and even when she left to return to her cell, she would look back at him, frowning, hardly believing he was real.

'When you came back to the flat, he was dead. He was already dead?'

Zandra Purcell nodded. Stefan had asked more questions than anyone had bothered to ask before. But what she said, however often she said it, provided no more evidence, no witnesses. It gave her nothing.

'I didn't kill him, Mr Gillespie. That's all I can say. I wasn't there. I walked into the flat and he was there, in the bed. That was how I found him.'

Diedrich Vordermaier had become bored with the whole thing, and seemed not to care if he showed it. His English wasn't good enough to follow the conversation, but he had no interest in doing so anyway. He knew she had nothing to say. It didn't matter how often she said it. He walked up and down much of the time, smoking one small cigar after another. However useful this Irish detective might be, he was turning out to be a stickler, a pain in the arse.

'I'm going for a piss,' Vordermaier announced. 'The guard's outside.'

'Don't worry,' Stefan smiled, 'I'll be safe enough.'

Vordermaier sniffed. He was the one who did the jokes. He walked out.

'I didn't do it,' said Zandra Purcell again. 'Please help me.'

Stefan nodded, but he didn't say anything. He didn't know if he could help her. The atmosphere of certainty around the case felt hard, impenetrable.

'What happened in the flat? People heard you arguing.'

'They didn't. There was no argument. I wasn't there.'

'Had you argued before?'

'Why would we argue? We were friends, that's all.'

'You were lovers.'

'He was a dear friend, that's all.'

'That's not the police story.'

'It's not a secret. They know. He didn't even like women that way . . .'

Stefan looked at her quizzically.

'They know that!' she said.

'He was a homosexual?'

'Yes!'

Stefan said nothing for a moment. She couldn't make that

sound true in the way she had, unless it was true. He felt he did believe what she had said so far, but he couldn't be certain. All she was saying was that she didn't do it, over and over. But these words had come out of nowhere, and they felt unintended.

'You've never said that anywhere. I've read your statements.'

'It won't help me.'

'I would have thought it helped a lot. It takes away your motive.'

'Johannes is a hero. That's what they keep telling me. The police, in court, here, everywhere. I killed a hero. All I can do is keep trying to prove I wasn't there. That's my only hope. If I turn round and tell them the truth, their hero was queer, what do you think they'll do? You can't say that about a hero!'

'Not even to save your life?' Stefan knew the words were hard.

'I know what this means, Mr Gillespie. But it won't. It won't save me. If there's one small hope, it's that someone will believe me, and believe I wasn't there. It's all I have. If I told the truth about Johannes, I wouldn't have that . . .'

When Stefan walked away from the Moabit Prison he believed Zandra Purcell was telling the truth. He also knew that however compelling the circumstantial evidence against her, no one was interested in whether she was telling the truth or not. No one cared. The police had found their killer and that was it. But there was a smell he recognised too. It wasn't only about bad policing and easy answers. It wasn't simply that no one wanted to look. Things were being hidden. He couldn't know what. He couldn't know why. But even the motive that had been foisted on Zandra was a lie. Johannes Rilling's homosexuality made nonsense of the scorned woman. It even made nonsense of the fact that the dead man was in her bed. If what she said was true, then there were all sorts of lies piling up. It would only take one of those lies being picked apart for the whole thing to collapse. He didn't believe Diedrich Vordermaier would want that. And whatever was happening now, this business of tracing Rilling's last contacts would not be about finding any truth that questioned Zandra's guilt.

But Zandra's last words had not been about Johannes Rilling; they had been about her son. She wanted William Warnock to make sure her son was all right. She didn't add, 'If there's no help for it', but the words were in her eyes.

'There was nothing about a child in the file,' said Stefan to Vordermaier.

'He doesn't live with her. He's in some convent. Looked after by Catholic nuns. You know, the halt and the lame. Some sort of spastic, maybe.'

As the two detectives reached the car, Stefan stopped, looking back at the Moabit. He had no idea what he could do for her. He felt entirely helpless.

'You're right,' said Vordermaier, 'you wouldn't want to be in there.'

'I can smell that, Diedrich, I really can,' replied Stefan, turning round.

'That's why I smoke these,' replied the Kriminalkommissar, drawing on his cigar. 'But I'll tell you what, Stefan, you've fucked her up, Fraulein Purcell.'

'What do you mean?'

'In there, the least valuable commodity is hope. You gave her some.'

17
Schöneberg

Kriminalkommissar Vordermaier drove the black Mercedes-Benz 170 back to Alexanderplatz and picked up the two men who had collected Stefan from the am Zoo that morning, Kriminalsekretär Conrad Dremmel and Kriminalinspektor Edsel Lamm. The tall, thin detective and the short, thin detective were distant but deferential. Stefan wasn't sure whether they said little because in Vordermaier's company it was always the Kriminalkommissar who did the talking, or because they were under instructions to keep their distance. He concluded it was a bit of both.

Vordermaier was affable and talkative as he drove away from the Alex again, heading for the inner suburb of Schöneberg, just south of the centre. He appeared to be a man who worked entirely out of his head. He carried no notes, and he never made any. When the Kommissar flicked through the files in front of him in his office, it was like a nervous tic. He never looked at them. It was a way of working that might have explained the lack of detail in Zandra Purcell's file, but Stefan already felt that such detail was neither desirable nor necessary. After all, detail asked questions.

When Vordermaier's commentary on anything and everything they passed dried up, he ran through the people they were going to interview again, speaking somehow in the same tone he used of Berlin's sights and sounds.

'These three men, who our friend the brave Hauptmann visited in the course of the last afternoon, probably have nothing to do with anything. But he did make a point of visiting them, that's all I can say. They all live in and around Schöneberg, and they're all friends Rilling made in Ireland or through his interest in Ireland. He studied there in 1935 for a short time. He was part of a student exchange scheme organised by Oberleutnant Clissman. He's German, naturally, but he lived in Ireland for some time, and married an Irishwoman. He is in the army now, but he's home on leave. He shares a flat with another Irishman living in Berlin, a Herr Richards. I don't know what he does.'

Stefan did not say he knew who Helmut Clissman was. He didn't say that Clissman had a hefty Special Branch file, as did the next man he spoke about.

'Then there's Herr Stuart, who works for the Ministry of Propaganda. A writer of some sort, for English radio broadcasts. He would know Fraulein Purcell from the Villa Concordia studios. She plays in a band there. Do you know Lord Haw-Haw, Herr Joyce? Isn't that what they call him in England?'

'I have heard him.'

'I think Herr Stuart writes for him sometimes.'

'I've heard of Stuart,' said Stefan. 'I can't say I've read his books.'

'And the third one is Herr Bewley. You know who he is – or was?'

'The Irish ambassador, yes.'

'He also works for the Ministry of Propaganda. A pet Ireland expert.'

Stefan simply nodded. He couldn't help feeling that Diedrich Vordermaier had no more interest in the details of this trawl through Berlin's small Irish community than he had in the sights he pointed out along the way.

Francis Stuart was still in bed when they arrived at his flat in Feurigstrasse. He was ill-tempered in a way that seemed to owe as much to a half-empty bottle of whiskey on the kitchen table as to the late night he had spent writing and rewriting radio propaganda at the Villa Concordia. He knew about the death of Johannes Rilling and the arrest of Zandra Purcell, and he made no bones about saying he didn't believe she had killed him. He didn't say why, except that Zandra Purcell was an amiable, likeable woman and the whole thing was bollocks. But Stefan saw there was something unspoken. Stuart said he knew Johannes Rilling only slightly. He knew Zandra in the same way, but also because she played in the Villa Concordia jazz band. He had no reason to believe they were lovers. Stefan sensed he knew enough to know why not.

The only questions Vordermaier asked were about Rilling's visit to Stuart's apartment the day he died. There seemed to have been no real reason for it. He had been passing and he dropped in for a coffee. The men were not close. There was no particular friendship. But it wasn't that unusual. Real coffee was scarce in Berlin by now, and the Ministry of Propaganda's foreign staff got access to certain things most Berliners could no longer buy. Sometimes a little real coffee. As they spoke Dremmel and Lamm stood in the background. They made no contribution. They were there as intimidation. Francis Stuart was not intimidated. If anything made him uneasy, it was Stefan Gillespie's presence. He was polite, even friendly, in an Irishman-to-Irishman sort of way, but Stefan felt he disliked him being there far more than he did the Kripo men.

'Johannes said he was going back to his regiment.'

'What did he talk about?' asked the Kriminalkommissar.

'Nothing much. Ireland – he loved the Burren – he was there in—'

Vordermaier wasn't interested in Irish scenery.

'Yes. Anything else?'

'He'd read a book of mine. Well, I say that. I don't think he'd read it at all. If he did, he certainly didn't like it much. I don't suppose he understood it.'

Stefan smiled. Rilling might be dead; he was still owed some petulance.

'Was he in contact with people in Ireland? People you know, perhaps?'

'If he was, he didn't say so. Contact isn't exactly easy, is it?'

'Parcels and letters do get through,' said Vordermaier.

'If you're very lucky.' Stuart shrugged.

'Did he mention Fraulein Purcell?' continued Vordermaier.

'No.'

'Anyone else?'

'Anyone else, what?'

'He was having a bit of an Irish reunion that afternoon, that's all. I just wondered if there was anyone else he was going to call in on, mutual friends?'

'I don't know anyone Irish who might have shot him,' laughed Stuart.

'It would be good to know what was in his mind, that's all.'

Stefan looked at Vordermaier. There wasn't much about Johannes Rilling the Kommissar had shown real interest in, other than the fact that he was dead. He certainly had no interest in his homosexuality, even though that asked some very serious questions about his relationship with Zandra Purcell. Vordermaier's interest in what happened in the course of Rilling's last day on earth was oddly specific.

'You know, it's a funny thing, Herr Kriminalkommissar . . .' Francis Stuart smiled as he spoke, as if something had suddenly clicked.

'What's that, Herr Stuart?'

'I'd swear someone was in my apartment last night, when I was at the Villa Concordia. I wasn't entirely sure, but the more I think about it, I am now.'

'I hope nothing was taken?' said Vordermaier.

'I don't think so. But I'm bloody certain the place was searched.'

'I can't believe that. But if you're concerned, you should report it.'

'I don't know if there'd be any point.'

'Why not?'

'The police might already know. What do you think?'

'Perhaps it was someone looking for coffee,' said the Kommissar blandly.

Stuart shrugged and laughed.

'Do you have any questions, Inspector?' asked Vordermaier.

'Nothing I can think of, Diedrich.'

'Are you going back to Ireland, Mr Gillespie?' said Stuart.

'In a few days.'

'Well, kiss the ould sod for me when you touch land.'

Stefan smiled, but he read the expression on Stuart's face without any difficulty. It said, *What the hell are you doing here? Who the fuck sent you?*

'She didn't do it,' said Stuart, looking back to Kriminalkommissar Vordermaier. 'Whatever happened, Zandra Purcell didn't do it. She couldn't.'

The next call was to Oberleutnant Helmut Clissman's apartment in an old house in Katzbachstrasse. It took up the whole top floor of a mansion that had been converted into flats. It was a bare, uninviting place, sparsely furnished. Clissman had been working in Denmark for almost six months, and his real home was there. There was no discussion of what Clissman did, except that he was in the army. Stefan knew, however, that he was a soldier in the Abwehr's Brandenburger regiment. He was an Intelligence officer. He doubted that Diedrich Vordermaier didn't know either. Stefan could still not understand the point of what was happening. All he could see was that the Kripo man was trying to make a judgement about the men he was talking to. He was looking for responses to his questions about Johannes Rilling, not answers, not facts.

Clissman was genuinely pleased to see an Irishman, in a way that Francis Stuart had definitely not been. The Oberleutnant's love of Ireland was all-embracing, and for almost ten minutes the conversation was entirely about that. Clissman had lived and worked there for years. He had married into a well-known Republican family, the Mulcahys, and as Dremmel and Lamm stood in the doorway, and Vordermaier lit one of his cigars, it was Ireland that occupied Helmut Clissman and Stefan Gillespie. The Abwehr man seemed barely concerned about why three detectives from the Kriminalpolizei were in his flat. He had the rank and connections to ignore them, and he did so. And when he turned to Vordermaier, he was giving permission for questions to be asked.

The questions were the same. When did Rilling arrive? Why did he come? What did he say? Did he mention anyone else he was going to see? Did he talk about friends or connections in Ireland at all, or about the Irish community in Berlin? The answers were the same too. He had dropped in for no special reason. He had talked about Ireland. He had mentioned some mutual friends. He had talked about going back to his regiment. Helmut Clissman did not seem to know Zandra Purcell. He thought he might have met her once at a party. But it was evident, when the Kriminalkommissar trotted out the details of Johannes Rilling's death at the hands of his Irish lover, that Clissman's eyebrows were raised. He didn't know her, but he didn't believe a word of it.

'The Irishman who shares this apartment – Herr Richards – was he here?'

'No. I don't think he'd ever met Johannes, anyway. Ask him . . .'

As the Oberleutnant looked towards the door to the landing,

a thin, slight man, with short, almost cropped hair was walking in. His clothes seemed two sizes too big for him. A thin, rolled cigarette was sticking to his bottom lip. Stefan knew him immediately as Frank Ryan, ex-IRA leader, ex-brigadier in the International Brigades in Spain's civil war, ex-prisoner of Generalissimo Francisco Franco in the Prisión Central in Burgos. A man Stefan Gillespie had helped escape from Spain only a few months earlier, with the aid of the Irish ambassador to Spain and German Military Intelligence. It had been unclear, when he last saw him, on the Spanish coast near Santander, in the company of the IRA's exiled chief of staff Seán Russell, where Ryan would go. They had talked about France or America, but Stefan had always assumed the Abwehr had not sprung Frank Ryan from gaol to take him anywhere other than Berlin.

'Herr Richards?' said Vordermaier.

Frank Ryan nodded, but he was looking at Stefan.

'You've heard about the murder of Hauptmann Johannes Rilling?'

'Helmut told me. He was a friend of Helmut's . . .'

Ryan's German was slow, awkward.

'This is Kriminalkommissar Vordermaier,' said Clissman.

'You didn't see him the day he came here?'

'I never met him, no.'

Ryan looked at Vordermaier and shrugged. He spoke in English.

'My German's shite, so even if I've got something to say I find it's best to keep my mouth shut. Very firmly shut. I wouldn't have known the feller.'

While Frank Ryan was speaking, he smiled a tight, wry smile, looking from the Kripo man to Stefan, and back, three or four times. Stefan had no doubt that the words about keeping your mouth shut were directed at him.

When Stefan Gillespie left the apartment, walking out last after Dremmel, Lamm and Vordermaier, he exchanged one long moment of eye contact with Frank Ryan. He knew he was meant to say nothing. He also knew that Ryan wanted to talk to him, and it was the pain behind his eyes that said it. But although it was Ryan who most occupied Stefan's mind as they filed down the wide staircase, there was one other thought that stuck there too. It had stayed in his head when Vordermaier so casually dismissed Francis Stuart's suspicion that his apartment had been searched. Another flat, another round of questions that appeared to have no real purpose, except to put the Kriminalkommissar face to face with someone who interested him, for no apparent reason. He found himself wondering if the flat Clissman and Ryan shared had been searched too.

'Herr Bewley next,' said Vordermaier laconically.

'Herr Bewley it is.'

'Not Herr Warnock's favourite Irishman,' continued the Kommissar.

'I wouldn't know.'

'You'd know enough, I'm sure, Stefan.'

They got back into the Mercedes.

'The thing to remember is that although he hangs on the coat-tails of a few nobodies who work for Reichsminister Goebbels, Herr Bewley is a man of no importance. It says so in his Gestapo file.' Vordermaier shifted into English. 'A friend of my brother's worked in Ireland for a time. He was with Siemens, I think. He taught me a word for Herr Bewley. I hope I have it right. Gobshite.'

For a man who, not very long ago, had been the accredited ambassador of Ireland to the Third Reich, Charles Bewley's two rooms at the back of an apartment block overlooking the Friedenau S-Bahn station left something to be desired, although it was oddly well furnished for its size and location. Bewley sat at a heavy walnut table, far too big for the room, while Stefan Gillespie and Diedrich Vordermaier sat opposite him. Kriminalsekretär Dremmel and Kriminalinspektor Lamm had attempted to stand on either side of the doorway, in their usual position, but Herr Bewley was having none of it. He insisted they wait in the next room. He was in no mood to be intimidated, and repeatedly threatened Vordermaier with his superiors at the Ministry of Propaganda, including Goebbels himself. He said it often, and just as often Vordermaier ignored it, and carried on with the questions. Bewley was indignant he was being questioned. And he was extremely unhappy about Stefan's presence. He wasn't merely suspicious, as Stuart had been; he assumed Stefan was there to spy on him. Vordermaier sat back, pushing out the same questions as before, and even less interested in the answers. The Kripo man found Bewley funny in some way. It was as if he had wound him up and was enjoying watching him scurry around.

'You've no right questioning me without permission.'

'We're simply tying up loose ends, Herr Bewley. These things have to be done. Isn't that how you say it in English: dotting i's, crossing t's? We have to trace the movements of Hauptmann Rilling. And that does bring us here.'

'I don't know what the hell the man wanted. I hardly knew him.'

'He had an interest in Ireland, of course,' said the Kommissar.

'I had met him when I was ambassador. I can't say I liked the man.'

'Did he talk about Ireland, friends here, friends there?'

'I doubt we had friends in common, Herr Vordermaier, here or there.'

Stefan felt not just the sneer, but an element of bitterness.

'I see. And what did Hauptmann Rilling talk about, Herr Bewley?'

'Fuck all, as I remember. He brought back a couple of books I'd lent him, years ago. I don't know why. Rather pointless really. He wasn't here that long.'

'Did you know Fraulein Purcell, his mistress?'

Bewley gave a snort of derisive laughter.

Stefan watched him. It was the first genuine reaction.

'You're not much of a detective, Herr Vordermaier. Jesus wept!'

'You didn't know her, then.'

'As a matter of fact, I did know her. Well, know isn't the right word. She was a very persistent irritant when I was at the Irish legation. She has a child, I remember, some vaguely idiot specimen, that she keeps locked up somewhere.' Charles Bewley shook his head with a shudder of distaste. 'She spent a year trying to get one thing, an Irish birth certificate, so that she could get out of Germany and take the brat to Ireland. My arse, was I going to give her that! I think we've enough problems, without collecting up other countries' bastards. She was never off my doorstep, like the bloody Jews looking for visas, who thought they'd some sort of link to Ireland, or a job we'd want them to do, for God's sake. So, I did know the Fraulein. Not, as you might imagine, socially.'

Stefan had stood up while Bewley almost spat these words across the table. He was looking at the mahogany sideboard. It was full of photographs in tasteful, delicate silver frames. There were groups of men, or single shots of men. They were all very young men. They were all very good-looking men.

'You don't seem to have much to say, Inspector Gillespie.'

As Vordermaier watched Bewley, smiling, Bewley watched Stefan.

'I'm only really here at the ambassador's request, sir.'

'Warnock's not actually an ambassador.'

'Well, I'm no diplomat, sir.'

'I suppose Warnock thinks he's going to get something out of sending you here, does he? Or are you here to report back to Joe Walshe, or Dev? If you are, you might pass on my position with Dr Goebbels. You might want to suggest Warnock does the same. You might both point out that I'm probably the only Irishman in Berlin with the ear of senior men in the Party. I think it's all you need to say. And with what's on the horizon, they'll know what I mean.'

Stefan Gillespie smiled an amiable, noncommittal smile.

Vordermaier stood up.

'You've been very helpful, Herr Bewley. Thank you.'

Charles Bewley frowned. He was slightly put out now. He had more to say. Not about anything that concerned Vordermaier's investigation, or his questions, or Rilling's murder, or Zandra Purcell. He just had more to say, more to complain about and more opinions to give. It was his business to end the conversation. It wasn't down to a Kripo man and some half-arsed Irish Guard.

That evening Diedrich Vordermaier drove Stefan Gillespie back to the Hotel am Zoo, in Kurfürstendamm. Dremmel and Lamm, who had stood in various rooms and doorways, saying and doing nothing, were at their desks writing reports, although it was hard to see what they would be about. Vordermaier was not really satisfied with the day's work. It had generated paperwork, and the paperwork should be enough to shut people up. It would have to do for the Foreign Ministry and the Irish ambassador. The rest had been unproductive; the important part. He had probably been naïve to think that following Johannes Rilling's trail round Berlin would give him anything, but there was still something odd about it. The man had been under surveillance. He had been lost several times, picked up several times, but all those visits must have meant something. 'Irish eyes will do the trick.' Those had been the words Vordermaier got out of Rudi Trunz. There was an Irish connection. That was how the book the Gestapo wanted would leave Germany. That's all he could read into it.

Yet if that had been Rilling's plan, it was leading nowhere.

That afternoon, having retrieved the book he had hidden at Trunz's allotment, the captain had visited three men who were either Irish or had Irish connections. Stuart was a maverick, according to the Gestapo. No one could tell what he might do. Bewley was a pompous fool, but he had his secrets; he was open to pressure, blackmail. And Clissman was unreliable. He might be an Abwehr officer, but his Gestapo file was thicker than it ought to be. He wasn't a true Nazi believer. None of the Abwehr were. They could never be trusted by Himmler's men.

Those were the thoughts going through Vordermaier's head as he drove through Berlin, with the radio playing low in the background. There was a roar of applause and shouting that went on for minutes, and then the voice of Adolf Hitler, speaking at a rally. The Kriminalkommissar wasn't listening, neither was his passenger in the car. He had almost forgotten about the Irish detective next to him. That part was almost over. There would be a shrug, and Herr Warnock would receive his reassurances. Work had been done; questions had been asked. But there were no more leads. There was nowhere else to go.

'So, what was all that about, Diedrich?' said Stefan Gillespie.

'Sorry, miles away. Not a great day. I didn't expect anything, but . . .'

Stefan let the silence drift, behind the noise from the radio.

'So what were you looking for, Diedrich?'

'What?'

'You were curious, I know that. It wasn't random. Whatever you were sniffing around for had nothing to do with Hauptmann Rilling's death, not in the sense I'm supposed to take back to Herr Warnock. You didn't get it, though.'

'I didn't get what?'

'You were looking for a lead, but not to who killed Rilling.'

'Is that right?'

'It's as right as I can make it, unless it was all a waste of time.'

'I can't produce evidence that isn't there, Stefan. We did our best.'

The bland platitude didn't come as easily as the Kommissar meant it to.

'Do you think anyone else's flat was searched? Besides Stuart's, I mean. I bet your Reichsmarks against my pounds that all three of them were.'

'You tell a good story, Inspector.'

'Sometimes I do, Diedrich. We're famous for it in Ireland.'

The car pulled up outside the Hotel am Zoo.

'I don't need to tell you Johannes Rilling was a poof, do I?'

'You think so?' said Vordermaier.

'I think so. Fraulein Purcell knows it, Herr Stuart knows it, Oberleutnant Clissman knows it, and I reckon Charles Bewley knows it better than any of them, because he's probably been up his arse, or vice versa. You've got Bewley's file on your desk. It's a Vice Squad file, and it's thick enough.'

'You could be right, Stefan. These things happen, even if they're not supposed to in the Führer's Germany. There are men who like their bread buttered on both sides. There are women who don't like that in their lovers.'

'I don't expect you to tell me what's going on, Diedrich, but you'll need to do better at hiding the shit if you want to shut the Foreign Ministry up, and give them a chance to shut the Irish ambassador up. I know Ireland doesn't matter a lot, but it matters enough. It's politics, and that doesn't have to make much sense anywhere, let alone here. It's not going to work. I'm going to tell Herr Warnock that Fraulein Purcell is going to lose her head for something she didn't do. Worse than that, something you know very well she didn't do.'

The Kriminalkommissar lit the cigar he had been playing with.

'There's something in what you say, Stefan. I'm out of the habit of having to explain anything. We don't bother with all that crap these days.'

'Let me do it for you. You're not looking for who shot Hauptmann Rilling, but you do want to know where he went that day, who he talked to. And for some reason, the people he talked to were Irish, or had something to do with Ireland. You know he was in Ireland before the war. He was supposed to be going back to his regiment, so a fond farewell, who knows? Or maybe he wasn't so sure he'd ever get back to his regiment, so an even fonder farewell?'

'You think he knew someone wanted to kill him?' said Vordermaier blandly.

'You know what went on. You're not going to tell me. I don't much care. I do know Rilling wasn't fond of them all. Bewley hated his guts. And I think we could hazard a guess about that, wouldn't you? Lovers' tiffs – or maybe there was a boyfriend along the way who changed his allegiances? Is that it?'

'You can draw your own conclusions,' said the Kommissar.

'I can, Diedrich. You're looking for something. There's something this man Rilling had that you want. You had to find out if any of these people he went to see know anything about it – maybe he left it with one of them? That's why I'd guess that everywhere we went today had already been searched. Dremmel and Lamm? Dragging me around was killing two birds with one stone. All this flurry of activity was going to send me back to the ambassador to say, "Jesus, those Kripo fellers worked their arses off to get to the bottom of this. Got them nowhere. She must have done it!" Or did you think I might help? Did you think a bit of old Ireland would get one of those fellers opening up about what Rilling did or didn't do with whatever it was you . . . Well, I get the drift. You need to be better informed on Ireland, if that's where you are. Francis Stuart's a Republican who thinks I'm not much better than the British, when it comes to murdering IRA men. As for Herr Bewley, I'd say hating the Irish government is about all he's got to keep him sane. But I use the word loosely.'

Vordermaier nodded, and for a moment he didn't reply. On the radio, still low, was the sound of Hitler's voice, sharp, insistent, but indistinct.

'There's a limit to how important a disgruntled Irish ambassador is,' said the Kriminalkommissar. 'There are things you can't put back in the bottle.'

'She's going to die, for fuck's sake. Would it change anything if you found what you were looking for? For Zandra? Would it make any difference?'

'Say you're right. And say we haven't found it, whatever it is. I say whatever, because I don't know. That's the truth. I'm looking for something, but what it's about, who cares? It's not anything to do with Kripo, except for passing it on to the Gestapo. But no fucker knows where it is. Make sense?'

'After a fashion. But why does that have to involve Zandra Purcell?'

'As far as I'm concerned, she shot Hauptmann Rilling.' Vordermaier was back on track. For a few moments he had said something true. It was a mistake.

'If you have to tell your ambassador you're dissatisfied with our investigation, the fact remains that we have given you access to it. That's all the Foreign Ministry asked for. It may not satisfy Herr Warnock, but there will be a lot of paperwork. I'll make sure there is. In my experience, if there's enough, complaints run out of steam. I don't imagine it's any different in diplomacy.'

'That's it, then?'

'That's it.'

As if to close the conversation, Diedrich Vordermaier turned up the radio. The strident tones of Adolf Hitler filled the car. Behind him the crowd roared.

'Now France has fallen. And what rationale did the Allies find for that? What plan was that? When Norway was finally cleansed of the Allies, they declared: "Ah, this was precisely what we wanted. This was a victory, an unequalled victory for us." And after France had been knocked to the ground for good, they declared: "Now England, for the first time, can concentrate its forces. We have reached the strategic position we longed for. We are rid of the burden of France. And it only cost us what? Only precious British blood. Now we are in a position to confront the Germans properly." Right at the beginning of the war, the English prophesied about its length. They said: "The war will last three years. Britain will prepare for three years." I was more careful, I saw further, and I said to Reichsmarschall Göring, prepare everything for five years! Not because I believe the war will last five years, it won't at all, because come what may, England will break! That's the only deadline I work towards! For that I will prepare everything prudently and cautiously. You understand me. You know it. And when the people of England today ask, loudly, noisily, fearfully: "Why isn't he coming?" I say, "Calm yourselves: he is coming! He is coming! He is coming!"'

Diedrich Vordermaier switched off the radio.

'You've heard him before?'

'Only on the radio, in newsreels, snatches.'

'You have to be there.' He laughed. 'You have to be there.'

Stefan Gillespie walked into the Hotel am Zoo and went straight to the bar. He drank two whiskeys in quick succession. He had pushed Zandra Purcell's face out of his mind for most of the day. Now she was there again. Her dark hair, her dark eyes; the look of fear and hopelessness. Then the look that was something else. A light; the smallest light. And he had given her that light. Diedrich Vordermaier was right. He had done her no favours. And whatever he said to William Warnock, however much the ambassador believed him, Vordermaier was right about that, too. The gesture had been made, in all its sterile emptiness. The sop wasn't trailing around with the

Kripo detectives to listen to a series of questions that were about something else altogether. He was the sop, in person. He had been given access to Vordermaier's investigation. He had watched the Kriminalkommissar make one last effort to look into the events surrounding Johannes Rilling's death. He could tell Warnock it was all bollocks, and Warnock would believe him, but by the time a few more diplomatic expressions of concern had circulated between Iveagh House, the embassy in Berlin and the Wilhelmstrasse, Zandra Purcell would be dead, guillotined in the Moabit Prison.

In his head now was the file he had looked at, one more time, as he waited in Vordermaier's office, just before he left the Präsidium, only half an hour earlier. The photograph of Johannes Rilling, sitting up in Zandra Purcell's bed, with only half a head. The black-and-white photograph was not close enough to show much detail. But it struck Stefan, quite suddenly, that there was no detail anyway. It wouldn't have mattered if there had been a halfway decent close-up. There was a pale bedhead and an even paler wall above it. And there was nothing there. Nothing dark, nothing spreading, nothing staining the bedhead or the wall. There was no blood, none whatsoever. In a file that contained no evidence at all, there was evidence of one simple thing. Wherever Johannes Rilling had been shot and killed, it wasn't in Zandra Purcell's bed.

18
Bahnhof Zoo

From the outside, Zandra Purcell's apartment block in Carmerstrasse was an elegant building, even if the paint was peeling. There were big double doors and arched windows above them, and there was an entrance at the side to a back yard. The façade was stuccoed and the front windows had balconies. Over the doorway there was an oval relief of cherubs drinking from a Roman amphora. But it was many years since a wealthy family had lived here; the house had long ago been divided up into flats. And as Stefan Gillespie walked in from the street, the hall was dark and cold. The glass of the front doors and the windows above them let in no light; it had been painted over for the blackout. There was one bare bulb hanging from the high ceiling. There was a smell of disinfectant and rubbish. A line of bins sat in the stairwell. The wide stairs rose up to a landing that was darker than the hall, and almost invisible. Beside the stairs was a cage-like elevator. Its folding iron gate was studded with small brass discs, each one contoured into a swirl of feminine hair, a meticulous art nouveau detail that still spoke of the better days the building had seen. A short, elderly man was polishing the brass and the iron gate, though it was padlocked and a sign hung on it saying, *Out of Order*. The sign had been there a long time. The sharp tang of the metal polish cut through the stench from the bins. Stefan's footsteps had announced his arrival all the way along the hall, but the old man didn't look round. It was only as Stefan stood behind him that he decided, irritably, to take any notice. He turned round with a dismissive sniff, and an expression that announced he was too busy working to be interrupted.

'Kripo, from the Alex.'

Stefan spoke in the tone he knew no ordinary German would question.

'You are?' he snapped.

'Blenker, sir.'

'Kriminalkommissar Vordermaier wants something from the flat.'

It needed no more explanation. To explain was to be unconvincing.

The caretaker, now standing very straight, unclipped a ring full of keys from his belt and fumbled slightly as he found the right one. He took it off.

'Do you want me to come up, Herr—'

'Just give me the key.'

'Is she – have they . . . ?' The caretaker looked down for a moment.

'Not yet,' said Stefan. He turned and started up the stairs.

The caretaker watched him disappear into the darkness of the landing above. He looked down at the floor and shook his head. He didn't know whether it was advisable to show the sadness he felt, in front of a policeman, let alone that he liked the Irishwoman. He resumed polishing the elevator gate.

Apart from locking the door of Zandra Purcell's flat, no attempt had been made to preserve the scene of the crime. No one had been there since the day after Zandra had discovered the body. She had been arrested that morning. The photographs Stefan had seen in the file on Vordermaier's desk had been taken. A report had been written. Statements had been made. No examination of the flat had been made that could have been described, even loosely, as forensic.

Everything was as it had been when Zandra walked in that night. It was, as far as Stefan could see, as the photographs had recorded it. But the disruption he had seen there didn't reflect the reality. The place had been ransacked. He had no doubt someone had been searching for something, with no regard at all for damage done. The nearest anyone had come up with by way of an explanation for the mess was that the row between Zandra Purcell and Johannes Rilling had turned into a physical brawl. He knew it wasn't that.

In the bedroom, all the bedding had been stripped and taken away. The only sign of blood was on the headboard. He pictured Rilling as he was in the photographs, propped up against the pillows. His head would have touched the headboard, but the brown stain on the wood was barely anything against the state of the dead man's head. Not just the headboard, but the wall behind it should have been covered in blood. And if the bullet had been fired at close range, as the mess indicated, it should have come out of the back of the shattered skull and embedded itself in the wall. No bullet had ever been there.

As he walked towards the door to the bathroom, Stefan saw immediately that the lock was broken. The wood was splintered. It looked as if it had been kicked in. He pushed it open. There was a swathe of brown staining on the yellow wall behind the toilet. It was blood. A lot of blood. There was blood on the floor too. The bathroom had been cleaned; he could smell the bleach. But no one had been bothered about the bloodstains. He imagined it was only the solid matter they had worried about: the skin and brains and the fragments of bone.

Examining the wall below the frosted window, he found what he was looking for. A piece of plaster had been chipped out. At its centre was a narrow, slightly irregular hole, pushing in deeper than the cracked plaster and brick around it. It seemed unlikely a bullet had not been dug out of the wall. This was where Johannes Rilling died, before he was put into Zandra Purcell's bed.

Stefan stopped and spun round. There was a noise. It wasn't loud, but it came from the kitchen. It was a short thud, like feet landing from a short jump. He heard the creak of a floorboard. Someone was moving in the next room.

He took the Walther PPK from his pocket and moved out into the corridor. The door to the kitchen was on the right. He heard movement again as he reached it. The door was slightly open, but he could see nothing. He listened again, trying to gauge where the intruder was in the room. Then he stepped back. He kicked the door open hard and stepped into the kitchen, pointing the pistol.

A man stood in front of the now open window, holding a tin and a tin opener. He was dressed in shabby overalls. He was dirty and unshaven. He was not a young man. He must have been in his sixties. He stared at Stefan, terrified.

'Who the fuck are you?' said Stefan.

The man didn't reply. He sank to his knees, still holding the tin.

'I was only looking for food.'

'You always come up the fire escape and in the window?'

'Fraulein Purcell always gave me something . . .'

The man was struggling to breathe now. He was sobbing, but almost silently. He let the tin and the tin opener fall to the ground. He crossed himself, and bowed his head. Stefan realised he was expecting to be shot there and then.

'I'm not the police. Get up.'

The man got to his feet slowly. He leant against the table, shaking.

'She always helped me . . .'

'Now you're helping yourself.'

'She always helped . . .'

'You've told me. I get it.' Stefan put the gun away. He walked closer, looking at the man's face. His accent was strong; his German wasn't good; even in the simple words he had said. 'You're not German. Where are you from?'

'I am Polish.'

'What are you doing here?'

The man looked at Stefan, not understanding the question.

'I'm a Polish worker, sir.' He said it as if it was self-explanatory. 'From the Gatow camp. This is where I clean the streets. But people help – people—'

'I'm not German,' said Stefan. He felt it would help. 'I am only here . . . I'm trying to help Fraulein Purcell. I want to find out what really happened.'

'Are you Irish?'

'Yes.'

'My German isn't so good.' The man smiled for the first time, speaking English. 'I learnt it at school, but I never used it till they brought us here. I speak English, though. I hope not so badly.' There was a look of pride in his face. 'I would come and talk to Fraulein Purcell sometimes – just to speak—'

He shook his head, then suddenly the fear returned. 'You won't tell the police.'

'No, I won't tell them.'

'We go back to the camp every night. We have to. But sometimes you get some extra work. Here, I clean the stairs and the hall, and I bring out the rubbish. People give me a bit of food, a few pfennigs. Herr Blenker lets me sleep in the bin room. They turn a blind eye at the camp, if there's no trouble.'

'You speak better English than German.' Stefan smiled.

'I was a teacher in Kraków. But they need workers, with the war. So they brought us. We live in the camps – we come in every day – we go back every night – but if you want to eat – if you want to keep going – you take a risk . . .'

Stefan understood. He had passed the men, and a few women, in overalls, thin, grey, subdued, sweeping the streets, collecting rubbish, clearing rubble from bombed buildings. He had walked by them, taking in some of that, and yet not seeing at all. He had let them step aside with bowed heads, to allow him to pass. He had asked no questions, but there was nothing normal about these people. He had not seen them because no one saw them. They were invisible.

'It's how it is.' The man shrugged. 'Is there news of the Fraulein?'

'No good news. You know they'll execute her.'

The Pole nodded.

'I know she didn't do it,' said Stefan.

The man shook his head.

'Were you here that night?'

Fear returned to the man's face, but finally he nodded again.

'Did you see Hauptmann Rilling?'

'No. I—'

Stefan could see that wasn't the end of it, but he moved on.

'Did you hear the gunshot?'

'I don't know. The S-Bahn is always – and there were bombs . . .'

'No bombs that night, not according to Kripo,' said Stefan.

'I heard nothing. That's the truth.'

'It's not me who needs help, it's Zandra.'

The Pole looked away, out through the window.

'Did you see her come home?'

'No.' He was still looking away.

It sounded convincing, but Stefan felt there was more.

'You saw no one else?'

The Pole looked round to Stefan again. 'If I tell you—'

'Whatever I do with it, I won't say where I got it.'

'There was the boy – that's all I saw.'

'A boy?'

'I say a boy, I don't mean that. A young man. I know he came to the apartment. I was cleaning the stairs. And when he knocked, I think it was Hauptmann Rilling who let him in – I didn't see him, but I heard his voice.'

'You knew the captain? You knew his voice?'

'I knew he came to see Fraulein Purcell.'

'And this other man – the boy?'

'I have seen him, but not here, not at the apartment,' said the Pole slowly, hesitating again. 'I think . . . Rudi, that's what they call him. But it's all I know.'

'It's not, is it? I know it's not.'

'I work from just past here to the Zoo Station, and I sweep along by the entrance to the Zoo, into Hardenberger-Platz. He is . . . the boy, Rudi . . . there is a street – behind the station – where men go. I sweep there, when I finish at the end of the day. A place they go . . . to pay . . . for sex with other men . . . It's not somewhere you talk about at all . . . in the day it's fine . . . but once it's dark . . .'

'And Rudi goes to this place?'

'I work there every day – and I see the same men. You recognise people. I'm not saying I ever saw Herr Rilling there, but I think that maybe. . . '

'Maybe?' laughed Stefan. 'So, was our friend Rudi a buyer or a seller?'

The night was black. There was a half-moon, but low cloud hung over the city, and it was growing darker as Stefan walked from Carmerstrasse to the Zoo Station in the blackout. He crossed from Steinplatz into the wide boulevard of Hardenbergstrasse, aiming for the low bridge that carried the railway lines into the station. Hardenbergstrasse was busy, the traffic driving on pale blackout lamps or no lights at all. Stefan followed the flow of Berliners under the bridge to the station where most of them turned in for the U-Bahn and S-Bahn trains. As he walked beside the railings of the Berlin Zoo, past the entrance, he met the railway lines coming out at the other end of the station, heading north across the River Spree. Quite suddenly he was alone. He had left the station behind. That had been easy enough to find, but now he was following the Pole's directions. Ahead of him there was a narrow road, little more than an alley, leading towards the river. The gardens of the zoo were on one side; on the other, above him, the railway. There were trees on either side; it was darker here. There was a brief flash of electricity as an S-Bahn train rattled past. He saw a figure under a tree, further down the alley. He walked on.

Stefan Gillespie was aware that he was not alone. He could not see anyone, but he felt the presence of others. Then, as he walked, there was a flash of light to his right. A man lit a cigarette, letting the match light his face. He smiled at Stefan, and then the match went out. Stefan could see several tiny points of light now, at intervals along the road: cigarettes. He passed one man and then another; he could just make them out, standing under trees or leaning against the zoo railings. He knew how carefully he was being watched. Then another match was struck, although the man whose face it lit up already had a burning cigarette between his lips. He let the match keep burning, and smiled.

'Looks like no bombs tonight, sweetheart,' said the man. He was young, barely out of his teens. He pursed his lips and moved out from the shadows.

'Still early,' said Stefan.

'Unless you brought one with you?' The young man laughed, and then he let the match drop to the ground as it burnt out. 'So, what way do you like it?'

'I'm looking for Rudi,' said Stefan.

'I see, a fussy one. You might just have to make do with me.'

'You know who I'm talking about, then?'

'Does it matter? Do you want a fuck or a conversation?'

'I want some information.'

'What are you doing, running your own vice squad? You're not Kripo.'

'I'm the next best thing,' Stefan replied.

'I think you maybe need to fuck off, darling, if you're not here to do business. You wouldn't be very wise coming down here on your own and upsetting the boys, unless you like having the shit kicked out of you. Some do, I know. Get lost, eh? Before I tell my friends there's a jerk looking for trouble.'

'I didn't bring a bomb, just this,' said Stefan, taking out the Walther PPK.

'I see, sweetheart. Well, it's not big, but it's a nice one.'

'Tell me about Rudi.'

'Why? If you've got friends at the Alex, his life's an open book.'

'I'd like you to tell me.'

'Well, it takes all sorts. I wouldn't go to these lengths – not for that.'

'For what?'

'We all sell ourselves, but some come cheaper than others.'

'He's an informer.'

'We all are, one way or another. You know that. To survive you either fuck an SS man or you're a pet Kripo nark. But there are people you can trust to keep their mouths shut – sometimes, at least. You wouldn't trust Rudi if his lips were sewn up and he was drowned in the Spree. He'd still come up singing.'

'I see. He sounds like the man for me. Where would I find him?'

'Sure you haven't got anything better than a bullet for me, sweetheart?'

Stefan took a banknote from his pocket. The man looked at it.

'That would buy you a hand job on a bad night. Ratting costs more.'

19

Die Drei Bären

The next morning, Stefan Gillespie left the Hotel am Zoo and returned to the Zoo Station. He took the S-Bahn to Westend. The male prostitute had told him he was likely to find Rudi Trunz on his allotment there. When he reached the Westend Kleingärten, a woman who sat in a hut at the entrance gave him directions. The allotments spread out along orderly avenues, each identified by a name and number. Rudi's was among the best tended in a line of well-tended gardens. It was very early, and he saw no one as he walked through the plots of flowers and vegetables, and neatly painted huts. The reason he was there didn't seem to fit any of this. But as he entered Rudi's bright hut, it fitted too well.

He assumed the man who was tied to a heavy wooden chair in the middle of the room was the man he was looking for. He was the right age, and underneath the blood that had dried on his face, he was probably good-looking. His hands were tied behind his back. His feet were strapped to the chair legs with belts. A rope was pulled tight round his waist, holding him in the chair.

He lifted his head as Stefan came in. He opened his mouth. Most of his front teeth were missing. He tried to speak, but only a hoarse whisper came.

Coming closer, Stefan could hear that he was saying, 'Water.'

Stefan looked round the small room. He saw bottles of water on the table. He fetched one and opened it, and poured some between the bloodied, bruised lips. He let it dribble and then put the bottle down. He went to the back of the chair and untied the knots that held Rudi's hands. As he did there was a cry.

'Elbow – Jesus – it's broken – it's— For fuck's sake, Jesus, it hurts.'

Stefan bent down to undo the belt holding Rudi's feet.

'I'd better get you some help.'

Through the pain, Rudi Trunz made a noise that was almost a laugh.

'Don't fret, it's on its way. They left me last night, but they'll be back.'

'What happened?'

'Gestapo, Kripo – what's the difference?'

'I can get you to a hospital – there must be—'

'What are you, a comedian? I thought you were Kripo.'

'All I wanted to do was talk to you.'

'Help yourself. I'll talk. About anything. Any answer you like.'

'If you can get—'

'There's nowhere to go, Herr whoever-you-are. They left me here to be picked up when they're ready. I can hardly run, can I? I think my foot's broken too. And there's nowhere to go. Whatever you're doing, you'd better piss off.'

'My name's Stefan Gillespie. I am an Irish policeman.'

'Well, there's a novelty. I didn't know we had any.'

'You know who Zandra Purcell is?'

'I should do – my God, I should!'

'And Johannes Rilling?'

'Are you an Irishman or an idiot? Or is it the same thing?'

'I am trying to help Zandra. I know she didn't kill . . . your friend.'

'I shouldn't think there's anyone in Berlin who doesn't know that. Not that it's going to stop them cutting her head off. But we've all got problems.'

Stefan waited. Rudi Trunz closed his eyes, wincing with pain.

'Do you know who did kill him?'

'Why would I tell you if I did?'

'Why not?'

'You've got a point,' said Rudi. 'What does it fucking matter now?'

'I know you were there that night, at the apartment.'

The other man looked hard at Stefan, then shook his head.

'What did you come to the party as, a real policeman?'

'I am trying to find a way to save her.'

'Wow, sincerity! We don't see a lot of that—'

'You didn't shoot him, did you?'

'I might have done if I'd known the shit he'd land me in.'

'The police were there, before Zandra got back,' said Stefan.

'Yes, they followed me there. I led them to him. You get the picture. I'd given them information about him before. Not the way he thought. I'd never said – about the fucking diary – until they made me. They didn't find out from me, but they knew . . . I never told them anything at first. I should have. Fuck, I should have. He hid the thing here! But all I told them, whatever Hannes believed, was what I had to – about him and me – about sex – you don't have a choice – we all have to. They picked me up that day, after he'd been here – they didn't know he'd got this fucking book from here – but they knew he had it with him. I was still trying to protect him. Can you believe that? I knew he was never going to get to his regiment – he wouldn't get out of Berlin – they'd been watching him. But they'd lost him, that afternoon. They said. And I thought I knew where he was. So I went to warn him – I thought if he got back to the war, he might be safe. I went to find him. But they followed me. Course they did.'

Rudi drank more water, painfully. He looked up at Stefan.

'You don't know what I'm fucking talking about, do you?'

'No, I don't.'

'Keep it that way. I should have left Hannes to fuck himself.'

Whatever Rudi Trunz was talking about, it didn't help Zandra Purcell. Stefan didn't know what he needed; he needed more, and he hadn't got it yet.

'So what happened at the apartment, after you got there?'

'Dremmel and Lamm came – Kripo detectives—'

'I know who they are,' said Stefan. 'Did one of them kill him?'

'They told me to fuck off. I fucked off. It's what you do. I didn't go back. I've been keeping out of the way. But they picked me up tonight. I know what happened, though. You could say they didn't shoot him, for what it's worth.'

'All right, and what is it worth?'

'They told me some of it last night. They were still pretty pissed off. They had him in the flat while they were searching it, looking for this fucking book. They thought he had it with him. They couldn't find anything. He'd got rid of it somewhere. They'd taken his gun. But when they started to interrogate him, somehow, he grabbed it back. He went in the bathroom – and—'

'Blew his head off,' said Stefan quietly.

'Faced with limited options,' said Rudi, 'that was the best one.'

'So why was it covered up? Why not just an arrest that went wrong?'

'They should have left it for the Gestapo. They were there to find this fucking diary that Hannes brought back from Poland. They screwed it up. They let him kill himself before they got him to talk. That's not the sort of fuck-up the Gestapo allow. So, the story is Kripo were never there. They never got him.'

'And his girlfriend shot him?'

'You could smile, if it wasn't going to cost the poor cow her head.'

Stefan heard a noise behind him. He turned.

'Well, Inspector, you're a very determined man.' Vordermaier walked in. 'I used to like that in a policeman. I used to be quite determined myself. I still am. I'm determined to survive. A different order of determination altogether.'

Dremmel and Lamm followed Vordermaier in.

'He needs a doctor – a hospital,' said Stefan.

The Kriminalkommissar spun round.

'You boys didn't break any of the poof's fucking bones?'

'Sorry, sir,' said Dremmel. Lamm grinned.

'You'll want promotion next! Get the bastard out of here.'

Dremmel and Lamm stepped up. Dremmel untied the rope that still held Rudi Trunz to the chair. They hoisted him up by his shoulders. He screamed.

'Your arse has earned that pink triangle, Rudi. It's had some wear, eh?'

The detectives half-carried, half-dragged him out of the hut.

Vordermaier looked at Stefan. He took out a cigar.

'He was always going to get a pink triangle, that one.'

'I don't know what that means,' replied Stefan.

'He'll be in Sachsenhausen tomorrow. You've never been in a concentration camp, I suppose. But you know what we Germans are for organisation. Well, that's all bollocks, as you might put it, but we try. Red triangles for commies and politicos, black for gyppos and asocial cunts, yellow for Yids, green for ordinary decent criminals, pink for poofs. They like pink.'

The Kriminalkommissar lit the cigar and offered Stefan one.

'No, thanks.'

'Anyway, you got the gist of events in Carmerstrasse, Stefan?'

'I've got enough.'

'For your purposes.'

'For my purposes, yes, I'd like to think so.'

'I did know you'd be here. You wouldn't ever want to trust one of those queers at the Zoo Station. We only tolerate degenerates as long as they're useful.'

'So, what happens next, Diedrich?'

'There is a certain amount of, well, embarrassment,' said Vordermaier.

'I'm sure Herr Warnock can do something with that. If it gets embarrassing in Wilhelmstrasse, when he gives them my version of events, I'd say your Foreign Ministry wouldn't be beyond dropping a hint to the Gestapo about the way you blew the opportunity to get whatever it was Hauptmann Rilling had. I haven't got the faintest idea what it was, but it seems it mattered a bit. Covering up losing it mattered so much you had to finger someone for that.'

'You're beginning to understand us very well, Stefan. Risky business.'

'You've got enough on your plate without knocking me off.'

'I trust you didn't think I was threatening you, Stefan?'

'I certainly hope not, Diedrich. It would hardly be diplomatic.'

'Not at all. But there's been a development in the case. Your job's done.'

'In what way?'

'We found out who really shot Hauptmann Rilling.'

Stefan gazed at Vordermaier, who was smiling now.

'You may not know, but there was a Polish guest-worker, a street sweeper, doing illegal work at 2 Carmerstrasse. He was sleeping in the cellar, or with the rubbish bins, when he should have been back at his labour camp. There's a reason for keeping them in camps. They can be devious, especially the Poles. People had been helping the bastard out, feeling sorry for him, and what did they get for it? He was breaking into the flats, stealing food, money, you name it. He thought Fraulein Purcell's flat was empty. He came in off the fire escape.'

The Kriminalkommissar shrugged. He already knew what Stefan knew.

'The gallant captain was there. Caught him red-handed. He went for his pistol, as any soldier would, but the Pole got there first – shot him. A sad end for a bearer of an Iron Cross Second Class. So, we got to the bottom of it in the end. The Pole confessed. Fraulein Purcell has already been released. No stain on her character, as they say. I'm sure your ambassador will be delighted with it.'

'You know that's all bollocks,' said Stefan.

'It's the only bollocks I can offer, for Fraulein Purcell's life.'

'And the Pole?'

'There was a special session of the People's Court this morning. He will have been guillotined at the Moabit – about half an hour ago, give or take.'

'Did he have a name?' asked Stefan.

'Who?' said Vordermaier, not connecting the question.

'The Pole.'

'I'm sure he did,' replied the Kriminalkommissar.

Stefan Gillespie walked back through the bright rows of allotments. People were working, planting, pruning, digging up vegetables; others were talking, laughing; children played. As he left the Kleingärten, the little gardens, there was gramophone music coming through the window of one of the huts. He recognised the song. A woman's voice. He had heard it all over Berlin, in cafés, in the bar at the hotel, even playing in an office at police headquarters.

From today I see the world
In such a rosy light,
Happy people everywhere,
Not one sad face in sight –
I've got you and you've got me,

And never mind the weather,
We'll turn sadness into joy,
Just because we're together.

Stefan Gillespie sat in the bar at the Hotel am Zoo and wished that he could have shaken the dust of Berlin from his shoes there and then. He would be there another two nights before getting the train that would take him to Sweden and, eventually, home. But there was nothing more he wanted from the city, except to be away from it. He had done what he needed to do for Zandra Purcell. It had come at a price that didn't surprise him. It had been decided, somewhere in the Reich Main Security Office, that someone would have to die to maintain the fiction that Hauptmann Johannes Rilling was a German hero, cruelly and arbitrarily cut down. In a continent full of cruel and arbitrary cutting-down, it shouldn't have mattered much who died, let alone why. It was nothing to do with Stefan, but he had become part of it. He had pushed some of the pieces.

The image of the dead Pole, climbing into Zandra's wrecked apartment to look for food, kept coming into his head. If it hadn't been for the Pole he would not have found a way to save Zandra. She would be there now, back at the flat, with its broken furniture and its bloodstained bathroom, and the bed untouched since the police pulled Johannes Rilling out of it. In the bathroom there would still be parts of his head on the floor and walls. He didn't know what friends the Irishwoman had. He suspected there weren't many. He knew enough to be sure that a lot of them, at least the German ones, would not want to go near her – not till the smell of the Reich Main Security Office and the Moabit had gone.

Stefan found Zandra Purcell in the bedroom of her flat. She was sitting on the edge of the bed, staring at the pillows that had been supporting Johannes Rilling when she found him.

The front door had been open. She didn't turn her head as he came into the room. He knew she had been sitting there for a long time.

'I'm going to eat,' said Stefan. 'Why don't you come with me?'

She looked round very slowly.

'They killed someone else, the Polish man who used to—'

'I know who he was,' said Stefan.

She stood up, looking round the room, out to the hall.

'I don't know where to start. I don't know what to do with the place.'

'Do it in the morning. Do it when the sun's shining.'

They sat at a table at the back of the Three Bears. There were only a few customers, all at the front. They spoke in a kind of whisper, leaning close to each other in the semi-darkness. The head waiter assumed they were lovers. He had put them somewhere they could be alone. He could not know that their intimacy came from a very different place.

Zandra Purcell had nothing to say about the Moabit Prison, or about what had almost happened to her. She had shut that away, for now at least. For a time she talked about Johannes Rilling, and how much she had cherished his friendship. He had been a friend not only to her but to her son Andreas. And Andreas had loved him too. It was what had happened to Johannes that seemed to be digging into her most. She wanted to talk about it, about why he died. There had been no room for grief till now. It mattered to her, and Stefan felt he had to tell her how her friend had really died.

'All I know,' said Stefan, 'is that he had something they wanted.'

'I know,' said Zandra quietly.

'And you know what it was?'

She nodded.

Stefan said no more, but she still needed to talk about it, about Johannes.

'I know some of it. He told me once, when he was drunk. It was the only time. He never said it again. He didn't want me to know. He told me to forget it – whatever he said – it was the drink talking – and it was dangerous to know.'

'Is that what they really wanted from you?' asked Stefan.

'I don't think so. They asked me about it, but I didn't say anything. I said I didn't know what they were talking about. I don't know if they believed me, or if . . . if I was there for another reason, and it didn't matter.' She closed her eyes. 'If I'd said I knew anything – I'm not sure I would have got out of there.'

'Whatever it is, they haven't got it, I know that much, Zandra.'

'Good. I hope Johannes did what he wanted to do.'

'And what was that?'

The waiter arrived with a bottle of wine. They had finished the first and barely noticed. Stefan looked up and nodded. The waiter opened the bottle.

When he had gone, Zandra waited, and then began again.

'It's a book. A notebook, and some photographs, and maybe a few other things. It was something Johannes found when he was in Poland. A man he knew, an SS man, was killed there. There was something about it – Johannes didn't say it – even when he was drunk. He said the man was shot by the Poles, but I don't think that was the truth. Johannes had to go out and bring in the body. And there was a book – the man's notebook. It was a report, about all the people they were killing in Poland. I don't mean soldiers. Ordinary people, thousands and thousands – tens of thousands – that's what Johannes said.'

'You wouldn't read it in the papers at home,' said Stefan, 'but it doesn't take much imagination to think that's how they'd deal with any opposition.'

'It was more than that. Johannes said what was going on . . . I don't know . . . When he stopped, he wouldn't say any more. There were a lot of Jews, of course, and communists and socialists, but people you wouldn't even think – teachers and doctors and priests – just people, everybody, anybody sometimes. And the book was a report – not about who they were killing, just how many, and how they killed them, and how fast. He said it was like a book of accounts.'

'And what did he do with this book? What did he want it for?'

'He kept it – and it was like an obsession – I think it was always in his head. I think he put more together – he found out more. That night he said it wasn't only about what happened in Poland – for a few weeks last year – it was about doing it all over Europe – the same thing – everywhere they went, every country – and it wouldn't stop with thousands or tens of thousands – it would—'

She stopped and shrugged. Stefan poured some more wine.

'That's it, except that he felt he had to get the book to someone who would do something – he said if the world knew – it wouldn't happen. So, I guess he hid it when he was in Belgium and France. And when he was back here, he decided he had to get it out of Germany. But they knew by then. They knew what he had, I mean. The Gestapo, whoever it was. He did know that.'

'Did he say where he wanted this book to go?'

'The Church. He was very devout.' She laughed. 'Never off his knees, as my mother would have said. He believed if the Catholic Church knew about it . . .'

'And he thought that would be enough to stop it?' said Stefan. 'That's a lot of faith.'

'Yes.' She shook her head.

'And did he get it out?'

'I don't know.'

'I wonder,' said Stefan.

'You think he did?'

'I'd say the day he died, he was giving the people watching him the runaround, Zandra. I think he planted the idea that somehow, wherever this book was, or whoever was going to get it out of Germany for him – that there was some Irish connection – I think he had them chasing their tails, literally.'

'How do you mean?'

'I don't know what else he did that day, but he visited several people he had no real reason to visit, to no apparent end. But always an Irish connection. I'd say always people who might have contacts outside Germany. And he kept losing the policemen tailing him. Then they'd pick him up again – or he let them pick him up. But they were watching people who knew nothing at all.'

'But they did follow him to my flat?'

'No, they followed— It doesn't matter. You can only have so much luck. And that's when his ran out. But I doubt he was ever going to get out of Berlin.'

'I think he still felt safe here, despite everything,' said Zandra. 'But nowhere is safe, is it?'

There were tears in her eyes for the first time, though she wasn't really crying. She was still and composed. And she had said all she wanted to say.

Zandra Purcell didn't look very strong, sitting there across the table. Yet Stefan knew how strong she was. What Johannes Rilling had told her once, and all the rest she had put together just by knowing him, was everything Kripo, the Gestapo and the whole Reich Main Security Office wanted to discover. But she knew the world she lived in too. She recognised that knowing it and telling it would not help her. It would put an end to any chance she had of leaving the Moabit Prison. There were not many who wouldn't have told everything they knew in the hope that it might save them. But she was right. It wouldn't have saved her. It might have meant a bullet rather than the guillotine. And when there was almost nothing to save her, she knew that silence was all there was. And she kept her silence.

The second bottle of wine was empty. And there was no more to say. Stefan ordered two brandies and suddenly, at the same time, they started to talk about the ordinary things people talk about. That was the life Zandra needed to hear in her head again. They talked about Ireland, and their childhoods, and their jobs, and their children, and the people they had loved, and the ordinary hopes they both still had for the future, which she had even after everything that had happened. And they found things to laugh about, even if in her laughter, and in the gaps between her words, there were silent tears never too far away.

Neither of them could have said when it became clear Zandra would not go back to her apartment that night. They did not discuss what would happen, even as they left the Three Bears and walked through the darkness of a blacked-out Kurfürstendamm to the Hotel am Zoo. They did not touch until they reached Stefan's room. Then they barely spoke, before they were in each other's arms.

20

Der Stettiner Bahnhof

The next morning, when Stefan woke, he saw Zandra silhouetted in the light that was seeping round the edge of the heavy curtains. Her back was to him, and she was pulling on her skirt and her jacket. She only saw him as she moved round, and he sat up in bed. He smiled, but before he could say anything, she walked to the bed and bent over him. She put her finger to his lips to stop him.

'I know there's nothing to say, Stefan. This is enough.'

She took her finger away and leant forward to kiss him gently.

'If we say anything, we'll just say nothing, or we'll lie. Don't.'

She got up and took her coat from a chair. And then she was gone.

Stefan lay back on the pillow, looking up at the ceiling, hearing the morning traffic on Kurfürstendamm. The word 'Shit!' formed on his lips, but he wasn't sure why. The truth was, she was right. There was nothing to say. It wasn't that it had meant nothing, but somehow, whatever it was, it stood outside him. It was this time and this place, and left there, it was a small point of light, and nothing more. He wasn't sure what was worse: the fact that in terms of everything that he cared about in his life, it didn't matter, or that in a small, tender way, it did.

Stefan Gillespie spent one more day in Berlin. He saw William Warnock at the embassy in Drakestrasse one last time. He received a number of verbal reports that Warnock wanted taken back to Joseph Walshe at the Department of External Affairs, and he told the ambassador what he assumed he would want to know about Zandra Purcell's release from the Moabit Prison. He was right to judge that Warnock wouldn't want to know much, though the chargé d'affaires was well aware there was more. The measured memos Warnock sent to Dublin did not reflect his knowledge of the cesspit the city he still loved had become. It occurred to the ambassador, more frequently than he would have liked now, that a diplomat was not so much someone who knew whether to wear morning dress or evening dress in a slaughterhouse, as someone who always knew where to find a good dry-cleaner's the following day. The words he asked Stefan to carry home presented a bleaker picture now, not only of German reality, but of his own isolation. There were times, such as his visit to the People's Court to see Zandra Purcell arraigned, when the stench was unavoidable, but that was a truth he did not often confront. His job could only be done by avoiding that confrontation.

As Stefan packed his case in the room at the Hotel am Zoo, the telephone rang. The receptionist told him there was a man to see him. Stefan listened uneasily. The last visitors had been Diedrich Vordermaier's lackeys. But what else could there be to say? Surely it was over now. The receptionist gave a name that didn't mean anything to Stefan; it didn't even sound like anything.

'Herr Rien? Prinsch Irien?'

'What?'

Another voice replaced the receptionist's. A man, speaking in Irish.

'Proinsias Ó Riain. You never did call back!'

'I didn't think you'd want me to,' Stefan replied in Irish.

'I didn't.'

'That makes sense, then.'

'You're leaving today?'

'You're well informed.'

'There's not many of us. It's an Irish village. Fancy a walk?'

'I've a train to catch.'

'I know. I'll walk you to the station. I need the exercise.'

Ten minutes later Stefan Gillespie and Frank Ryan were walking towards the Tiergarten, on their way to the Stettiner Bahnhof, and to the train for Sweden.

'I don't think I'm being watched today,' said Ryan lightly.

'Are you usually?'

'They keep an eye on me. All in their own inimitable fashion.'

'Don't the Abwehr look after you?'

'You thought I'd end up here, didn't you, when we were in Spain.'

'Didn't you?'

'I suppose I hoped . . .' Frank Ryan let the sentence end. 'Did you see María when you went back to Salamanca? I know she died. I don't know how.'

'She was already dead. I'm sorry.'

'Because of me. I do know that.'

'I don't know, Frank. Because of a lot of things.'

The two men walked on in silence for several minutes. María Fernández Duarte had been Frank Ryan's lover when he fought for the Spanish Republic as a brigadier in the International Brigades. When he was captured and imprisoned by the Spanish Nationalists, María's love, and her refusal to abandon him in the hell of the prison at Burgos, had been part of what kept him alive. She visited him as often as she was allowed. She put her own life, and the life of her friends, at risk in a failed attempt to help him escape. She stood by him at every step, until German Military Intelligence came to see him as a man who might help Germany's war in some small way, whether he wanted to or not. The events that had taken Frank Ryan out of Spain were largely beyond his control. They had brought him to Berlin. They had nothing to do with María, but she had been there, and Stefan, who had played a part in those events, had met her in Spain. He knew that once Ryan was released, Franco's death squads had come for their revenge. The little protection María had, as the lover of a man who counted, in some small way, beyond the borders of Spain, had been lost.

'She paid a high price for me to sit and rot here, wouldn't you say?'

'I didn't see so much of Spain,' said Stefan, 'but it's not a world away from here, is it? People die because there's no shortage of people to kill them.'

Ryan said nothing. He crossed himself and they walked on in silence.

'Do they know I'm here?' Ryan asked eventually. 'In Dublin?'

'Yes.'

'I think Warnock has an idea, so they must,' said Ryan. 'I've never seen him. I'm not supposed to have contact with anyone they don't trust. Helmut Clissman, Francis Stuart, some others. Do they know about Seán Russell?'

'They know he was with you when you left Spain.'

'Seán's dead.'

'I don't think they know that. What about the IRA?'

'I'd say they know,' said Ryan. He hesitated a moment. 'The Abwehr lads have dropped a few agents into Ireland. They'll have told the IRA by now.'

Stefan knew Frank Ryan could have said more, though he had no idea what. And Ryan could have done. He could have said that Seán Russell died in a German U-boat off the coast of Ireland, and that he had been with him, waiting to land.

He could have said that, after Russell's death, the Germans didn't trust him enough to let him ashore in Ireland by himself. But he said nothing. The pain of not reaching home was his own matter. Like the pain of María's death. Berlin was his penance, for how long he did not know. For now, he risked enough.

'So are we here for a chat, Frank?' asked Stefan. 'I don't mind if we are.'

'I want people to know, that's all. I'm here advising the Abwehr on what they're doing in Ireland. I'm not going to go into all that. I can't. I'll say what I think I can say. What I should say. Maybe what needs saying. I don't know. I'm living under a false name – not much of one. Frank Richards, Jesus! The idea is that the lads over at the Reich Main Security Office, the SD and the SS and the fucking Gestapo, don't know who I am. They do. Of course they do. And if I wasn't being protected by Admiral Canaris and his boys, I'd be in a fucking concentration camp now. There's not a lot of retired International Brigades men wandering round Berlin. So they watch me from time to time. And the Abwehr watch me as well. Mostly I'm left alone. Because I'm fucking useless to them.'

'No chance of getting out?'

'Only on their terms.' Ryan was obviously evasive for the first time.

'Do you want me to tell anyone in Dublin their terms?'

'Look, there's a group of people in the Abwehr's Irish section who want to make things as easy as they can for Ireland. That doesn't mean they don't want to use us against the English, but they'd like to see Ireland left alone, when it's over. If Britain is invaded, they want to make sure we're out of it. All it takes is for Ireland to step back when the time comes – step back and not stand in the way if the Germans need to use the South – to get to the North. To step back if there's war in the North, and the IRA are taking on the British. That's about it. People like Helmut Clissman have sold that idea to the Abwehr.'

'Dev and the IRA hold hands – and it'll all be roses? Is that the message you want me to take back to Dev? Should I sing a chorus of "We're All Off to Dublin in the Green" as well? I'd say they've had that message already, Frank.'

'I don't believe it either,' said Ryan. 'And I don't see Dev as a Quisling.'

'Have you told them that?'

'Yes.'

'And is that it?'

'There's another version, Stefan. Another plan for Ireland. I know because it's what Helmut and the Irish section are trying to fight. In the other version, the only view of Ireland is it's there to be fucked. When England is invaded the German Army in the south-west keeps on till it gets to Wales and the Irish Sea. And they keep going. They don't wait for Dev or the IRA or anybody to put out the welcome mat. They invade. They destroy the Irish Army in a few days. They take out anybody who matters and probably shoot them. Dev would finally make peace with the IRA general staff – they'd all be in front of the same firing squad. Then the SS would come in to clean the place up. Fuck neutrality. And in that version, if Britain becomes a fully-fledged Quisling state, they'd be as happy to give Ireland back to them as leave it to rot. If you were here, and you knew people who wanted to stop that, what would you do?'

They walked on again, now in the busy streets near the Stettiner Station.

'They probably know all that, Stefan. If they don't, they might as well.'

'Do you want absolution now?' Stefan smiled.

'Don't make it too harsh, a Athair! My sins are mostly sins of omission. I do and say as little as I can. And I'm listened to, not trusted. A lot of the time I lie.'

When Stefan Gillespie boarded the train for Sassnitz it was, like the train he had travelled on from Paris to Berlin, full of soldiers, now going back to their units, changing en route for Denmark. He had a window seat in a compartment full of officers, which would empty out as he neared the Baltic coast. It would be another long journey; he had been told to expect the delays that now accompanied all train travel. As the train stood in the Stettiner Bahnhof, Stefan was in the corridor, looking out at the platform. It was full of women and children, waving goodbye to husbands and lovers and brothers and fathers. All along the train men leant out of the windows, reaching for a last kiss. The thin figure of Frank Ryan, a hand-rolled cigarette between his lips, out and not relit, as so often, was not a part of it. As Stefan watched him, he seemed the only unmoving figure on a platform full of energy and noise, statue-still, isolated from everything around him. But nothing was what it seemed. Frank Ryan had told him what he wanted to tell him, what he wanted to get back to Dublin. He had told him what he thought was useful to tell him. Stefan knew he had still chosen what to say and what not to. Sins of omission or lies? He kept watching Frank Ryan as the train pulled away. And then he was gone. So was Berlin.

Two days later Stefan Gillespie was in Stockholm, and on neutral ground once more. He had travelled to Sassnitz on the Baltic, and from there took the train ferry that crossed to Trelleborg in Sweden. When he arrived in Stockholm he went to the British embassy, carrying a letter from William Warnock. The embassy already knew he was coming, as Warnock had got a message through via the Swedish embassy in Berlin. There was a plane ticket for the BOAC flight that still flew from Stockholm to Leuchars in Scotland. At the British embassy Stefan was interviewed by an elderly consular official who asked barely any questions. The man held a naval rank, and Stefan recognised him as an Intelligence officer. The Englishman recognised him for what he was too, an Irish Special Branch officer who, for some reason, was masquerading as an Irish diplomatic courier. As they were both in the same line of business, more or less, the Intelligence office did not expect to get any real replies to his questions about Berlin. He got none. The next day Stefan was sitting with a dozen other passengers in a Lockheed 14, as it took off from Stockholm's Bromma Airport. The crew wore BOAC uniforms, but they were all RAF personnel. Stefan, like all the other passengers, had been advised that they flew at their own risk. The pilot warned them once more, as they took off. No one seemed bothered by the prospect of several hours flying through enemy territory. No one travelled this route unless it was about the war, or making money out of the war. No passengers spoke about their reasons for being there.

'Next stop Scotland. We don't see many German fighters up here, and we do keep out of their way if they're about. We haven't lost a plane yet, but if you can keep your fingers crossed for the next couple of hours! Good weather at least.'

Three hours later, Stefan Gillespie had landed in Scotland, at the RAF base at Leuchars, near Dundee. He was taken aside and interviewed again, this time by two men he assumed were Special Branch officers. They also knew that they would get no answers to their questions, beside the barest details of Stefan's route, and the repeated statement that he was travelling as a diplomatic courier for the Irish government, but they felt obliged to make more effort than the Intelligence officer in Stockholm. They would have liked to find a reason to do more, but only because their posting, stuck in the Kingdom of Fife, gave them nothing to do from one month's end to the next. He was something exotic, at least, even if there was nothing to get from him. They abandoned the attempt at interrogation eventually and gave Stefan a lift to the railway station, where he took the next train to Edinburgh, en route for England and Wales and the ferry home from Holyhead. It was in Edinburgh, with his next connection cancelled until the following morning, and a night in the station waiting room ahead of him, that he stood next to a train for London King's Cross, and realised how much he needed to see Kate O'Donnell. And he could. There was no one to stop him getting the train. No one knew how long it would take him to get to Dublin. Why would anyone care how he got there? He hesitated, though, till the doors had slammed and there was steam hissing from the engine at the front. Then he ran forward, wrenched open a carriage door, and flung himself inside.

Part Three

The Book Of The Dead

Mr Sean MacEntee, Minister of Industry and Commerce, speaking at the Local Security Force Rally held in Sandymount on Sunday, said that it was only by being alert and vigilant that they could hope to ride out the bloody storm which raged in Europe. When they asked the people to be loyal to authority, they were asking them to be loyal to themselves. They were ringed about by the tide of war. It jeopardised their trade, and the lives of those engaged in that trade, and it even encroached upon their shores. If they did not walk warily in the midst of the surrounding belligerency, they might find themselves, at the end of the war, without trade, without friends and without freedom. The unity brought into being by a common sense of peril, manifested by nearly every element of the community, must be maintained, and the authority of those, no matter who they might be, who were called to the Government of this country must be upheld.

Irish Times

21

Parco Adriano

Rome

It had not been easy for Sister Mary Joseph to get to Rome. She had not lied to the Mother Superior but she had leant heavily on the arthritis that had been spreading through her body, slowly and intimately, for the last five years. It did not yet prevent her from doing the work she loved – the only thing she really loved – which was caring for the children and teaching them, but it was true that the time would come when it would, and perhaps it was not so far away. The doctor had told her that the disease was accelerating. There would be pain that could be managed but not stopped. She would find her hands harder to use, and her legs were already stiff and clumsy in a way that angered her rather than made her feel sorry for herself. In a few years – four, five, however long it was – she would find it difficult to move easily, and when that time came, she knew the children would go to one of the younger nuns. She would still be there. She would still do what she could. But it would change. The special place she had in the children's hearts would be a smaller one, as the children grew and went away, and new ones came. It was a time she dreaded, when all she would have was prayer. She had never much liked prayer, and though she had never spoken the words, in her heart she believed it was not the prayers that had mattered in her years at the convent but the children she had loved and nurtured there.

Sister Mary's desire to go on a special pilgrimage to Rome had surprised the Reverend Mother. But the nun was getting older, and the Mother Superior thought it was no bad thing that she was thinking about her soul a little more.

The pilgrimage was as close to a lie as the Irish nun had told in thirty years, but this was the only way she could carry out the charge Johannes Rilling had laid on her. And it was like that. It was as if he had laid his hands on her, and had made her believe in him. He had trusted her out of nowhere. He had explained only part of what he knew. He had asked her to help him out of faith. She didn't know why she accepted almost instantly; yet she did. It wasn't in her nature, and yet she had no doubt. She believed that somewhere, the hand of God was in her decision. But she also believed Hauptmann Rilling was right. Even behind the walls of the convent her sense of smell was keen enough to know that what he said was not impossible. Whatever made him ask her, and whatever made her accept, required little explanation. What mattered to her was that Johannes Rilling believed in what he was doing; he believed he had a duty as a Catholic to act.

Now she sat in a room in the offices of the Vatican Secretariat of State. She had waited two days to see someone, in response to the letter she had delivered when she arrived in Rome. The letter was Johannes Rilling's. It spoke in veiled terms of the importance of what Sister Mary Joseph carried with her, and it spoke of Rilling's own sense of conflict in making the decision to ignore his duties as a German soldier because he had a greater duty: a duty to his faith.

The man who had read the letter, Monsignor Erik Fränkel, a Vatican undersecretary of state, found the German captain's soul-searching a little irritating. It was the stuff of the confessional. But he recognised the force of what Rilling was saying, even though the letter only hinted at what it was he had asked the nun to bring to the Vatican. He already knew what it was about. Reports and rumours had come in from all over Europe, especially from the east. What found its way into the Secretariat was often as veiled as Johannes Rilling's letter, but the drift was always the same.

The monsignor had been in two minds about seeing the nun at all, but in the end the strength of Rilling's words made him agree to meet her, and to take whatever it was she had brought from Berlin. It was best that he saw her, rather than someone else. He couldn't know how persistent she would be. The management of what was happening in the war across Europe was no easy matter. It was part of his job to ensure that all the information that came into the Secretariat, from all over the continent, was used to protect the Church. And sometimes that protection involved making sure that some information went no further than his office, or if it did, it descended into the endless underground corridors where what was no longer required was filed away. There was certain information that no one wanted to rise any higher than Monsignor Fränkel's office, up the ladder that eventually ascended to the Holy Father. His job was to ensure that the intelligence he sent to his superiors was the right intelligence. There were things that could not be changed, however much they were to be lamented, and when it was all over, as it would be soon – soon, at least, in the Church's eternal calendar – the Church had to remain untouched and uninvolved. The Holy Father's business was to pray for peace. There could be no criticism of any faction, and that included sitting in judgement on any of the enormities that were the natural consequence of war and human fallibility. Here and there, quiet diplomacy might express concern, but nothing could be allowed to antagonise the victors or to let the Church be tainted by the squalor of war.

'I can only look at this, Sister, and see what it is. I have read the letter.'

They spoke in German; Sister Mary Joseph spoke no Italian; the undersecretary of state spoke no English. He was Swiss; he was also German.

'I am only his messenger, Monsignor Fränkel. He's dead now.'

'I understand that.'

'He believed there were . . . there were terrible things coming.'

'War is a terrible thing, Sister.'

'He didn't mean war. He meant . . . It's what he saw in Poland, and what the book . . . I haven't looked. I only know what he told me. And he said very little, really . . . I knew what he was talking about, though, that's what so surprised me . . . I know so little of what's happening outside the convent, even in Berlin . . . and yet I could see . . . I could see, in his face . . . and the photographs, I did see—'

She stopped, looking down and shaking her head.

'I do understand. I was in the first war. I have seen what men can do.'

'It isn't just that . . . that's what Herr Rilling believed . . . that's why he wanted this to come to you . . . the Church can stop it. That's what he said—'

'The Holy Father prays every day for peace, Sister.'

Sister Mary Joseph knew a pious platitude when she heard one. She still carried enough of Ireland with her for that. She looked hard at the man sitting opposite her. He was round and comfortable. Out of clerical garb he was a middle-aged German with the twang of Switzerland in his voice, and behind his intelligent eyes was the kind of soft, cosy complacency Germans call *gemütlich*. He was smiling, and he was looking through her. She felt a word that had not entered her head for three decades forming on her lips; the word was gobshite.

'I will look at all this, and I assure you that Hauptmann Rilling's concerns will be properly examined. I appreciate what you have done, in the belief that you were helping a troubled man. And what man would not be troubled by the slaughter of his fellow man? But I think you need to return to your convent and forget about it. Direct your prayers, as the Holy Father does, to the end of all this, and the coming of peace. And speak to no one about all this. Well-meaning as your intentions are, I think you have already trespassed beyond the confines of your order and your vows. Prayer and humility will reinvigorate your spirit.'

It was an hour later that Monsignor Fränkel walked through St Peter's Square and out of the Vatican. He walked the length of the Via della Conciliazione, to the gardens of the Parco Adriano, below the Castel Sant'Angelo. He stopped at a bench where a young man sat reading a newspaper. He sat down next to him.

'You know the best thing for us, Herr Berninger?'

The man folded the newspaper, and smiled at the priest. Udo Berninger was the head of the German tourist agency in Rome. It was a job that left him with a lot of spare time in the middle of a war. However, his real occupation, which was as an officer of the Sicherheitsdienst's Ausland-SD, the Reich Main Security Office's foreign Intelligence section, kept him very busy indeed.

'And what would that be, Monsignor?'

'If you keep the more sordid aspects of your Thousand-Year Reich to yourselves. I do my best to ignore it, because to do otherwise will not serve the interests of the Holy See, but that doesn't mean I want my nose rubbed in your shit.'

'We're only at this a little while, Monsignor. You've had almost two thousand years to bring keeping your shit out of the public eye to perfection.'

'The amount of information I get now, about fucking concentration camps and death squads and civilian killings, is growing all the time, not to mention the fact that you can't even do us the courtesy of sparing priests.'

'I take no pleasure in it, I assure you. Once the war is over, I don't think we'll tolerate Germany being run by thugs for very long. But until then I'm afraid the SS and the rest of them, well, they are the people the Führer trusts.'

'And they're out of control,' said Fränkel.

'Out of control, in control – it won't be for ever.'

'Someone should stop it, Herr Berninger.'

'I don't know what you mean.'

'No, I don't know what I mean either. Please, help us keep it that way.'

Monsignor Fränkel opened a briefcase and took out a folder.

'This is what I telephoned you about, Berninger. It came to me this morning. Normally these things can be filed away where they can do no harm. Most of the time I'm only dealing with rumours anyway. Though I wish there weren't quite so many. This is rather more dangerous. It was brought to me by a Holy Mother nun, from the convent in Berlin. It was given to her by a German soldier, a Hauptmann Rilling. Dead, I believe. The nun seemed to think she was carrying out some sacred trust, but it's one I don't want within the walls of the Vatican, not even buried in the archives. So I'm giving your shit back to you.'

Udo Berninger took the folder and opened it. He took out the book that Johannes Rilling had brought back from Poland. There was a collection of a dozen photographs and pages of Rilling's own notes in a tiny, cramped hand.

'You'd think at the very least you could prevent your soldiers taking photographs of each other lining up men, women and children to be shot. What the fuck do they do with them, send them home? "Wish you were here!"'

'I'm afraid they do.' Berninger smiled.

'This book lists a series of mass shootings in Poland. It goes into great detail about quantities, and it seems preoccupied with the speed at which death can be delivered, and the numbers that can be dealt with. From what this man Rilling says, it was put together by some SS officer, or whatever particular branch of thuggery is appropriate. You have too many for the uninitiated to appreciate the distinctions. The man was killed, and Rilling got hold of the book. His interpretation of what's in it is that it is some exercise in drawing up schemes to kill people – a lot more people, in circumstances that have nothing to do with even the broadest interpretation of war. Your SS man does some sums and despairs – despair is actually the word he uses – of what's going to happen in the future unless more efficient methods of killing en masse are put in place. And Hauptmann Rilling, having got all this in his head, opened his ears and listened, hard. What he heard was more, more of the rumours I am hearing.'

'Fama, malum qua non aliud velocius ullum.' Berninger shrugged.

'Rumour may be swift enough, my friend,' said the monsignor, 'but even the swiftest rumour can be denied. The book is not a rumour. Take it away.'

The German put the book back in the folder, and stood up.

'Thank you, Monsignor Fränkel, if there's—'

'No, Herr Berninger, don't thank me. I don't think there's enough holy water in the Vatican to wash away the filth, if I have to bear your thanks too.'

22

The Blue Anchor

London

There was a certain nervousness about Stefan Gillespie as he came up from the Underground at Hammersmith Broadway and walked down Queen Caroline Street towards the river and Hammersmith Bridge, to the house in Chancellors Street that Kate shared with two other women. He had been there only once before. The decision to change trains at Edinburgh had not been without its problems, as he had a ticket to Holyhead rather than King's Cross, but in the end he got where he wanted to go. The railways seemed to be caught up in a kind of amiable chaos that meant a garbled explanation about a couple of spare days and a girlfriend in London eventually smoothed the way. The train was full of soldiers on leave, just as the train through Germany had been, and the guard assumed that Stefan must be one of them. Unexpected changes of orders and the confusion caused by the abrupt granting of leave, or its equally abrupt cancellation, were the stuff of every railway platform and every train journey in Britain. The dates on military travel warrants never meant much, and unlike Germany, the trains had not been taken over so relentlessly by the forces of war that, if you could squeeze yourself on to a train as a civilian, with some sort of ticket, even a wrong one, you didn't still have a good chance of staying on it.

It wasn't a comfortable journey in any sense. Having made the decision to see Kate, he wasn't sure what it was he wanted. To see her. That was all. And yet it wasn't. He needed to reassure himself that what had happened in Berlin changed nothing, nothing about them. It didn't, but since she would never know, it was only about Stefan comforting himself. With time, the night with Zandra Purcell would be little more than a memory, and yet for a moment it had been more. It had been the cry of life in the face of death, in a dying city. It meant more than he was easy with it meaning. But now, only days after sleeping with Zandra, his silence would feel like something else: a kind of lie.

He had no time to send a telegram to Kate; he hadn't even thought about it. But it was almost eight o'clock. She ought to be home. If she wasn't she soon would be. It was a bright evening still. It would stay light late with double summer time still in force. And suddenly he was glad he was in London. He had done the right thing. They could go down to the river and have a drink in one of the pubs. He would tell her something about where he had been. The secrecy that had attended his outward journey wasn't needed on his return. It would surprise her. Yet talking about Berlin wasn't really what he wanted to do at all, for reasons quite apart from Zandra Purcell. He realised he wanted to forget it.

He arrived at the house in Chancellors Street and walked up the front steps. The door was answered by Kate's friend, Helen. He had met her for no more than a minute, when he had arrived at the house with Kate before, and she was coming out. She didn't know him immediately, and when she understood who he was she seemed put out, nervous. Whatever it was, Stefan felt awkward, and it was clear Helen did too. She told him that Kate wasn't home yet. She didn't know when she would be; probably soon, but she couldn't be very sure.

Stefan assumed he would be asked in to wait for Kate, but after several minutes he was still standing on the doorstep, and the two of them were saying nothing. He smiled. She was trying to. She didn't find it easy. He felt he couldn't demand to come in. He thought if he said something, she would ask.

'I suppose I could walk down to the Blue Anchor and wait . . . and you can tell her where I am . . . when she gets in. You don't think she'll be long . . .'

The answer was not the one he expected.

'That's probably a good idea . . . she'll come and find you . . . I'll tell her.'

It was clear by that point that all Kate's friend wanted to do was shut the door. Stefan decided it was best to let her do it. He shrugged and walked away.

He strolled slowly back towards the river. He turned and paused as he reached the steps that would take him under Hammersmith Bridge to Lower Mall and the Blue Anchor. He looked out at the river, and took a cigarette and lit it. He glanced back up Queen Caroline Street. He didn't see Kate immediately, because all he registered was a man and a woman, a couple, approaching Crisp Road. And when he did see, within seconds, that the woman was Kate, he was startled. She was walking slowly, talking to a man in an RAF uniform who had his arm through hers. Stefan's first reaction was simply to be puzzled; but as he walked forward, his second was to stop. Kate was absorbed in conversation; she was laughing. As they walked into Crisp Road he waited, not because he was waiting for anything. He simply didn't know what to do.

He dropped the cigarette he had lit and then walked back the way he'd come. All the complicated and confusing things inside his head had been pushed out; his heart was beating fast. He was thinking with his body, not his mind. Kate and the man were turning into Chancellors Street ahead of him. He walked faster. As he stood at the corner of the small street of flat-fronted houses, Kate was halfway down it, standing at the bottom of the steps that led up to the front door. Her back was to him. The man in the RAF uniform was looking down at Kate. He bent and kissed her. It lasted only a couple of seconds, before she turned and walked quickly up the steps. But Stefan was already heading back to the river, walking faster, lighting another cigarette as he went. What was in his head was shit. The kind of shit that left no room for thinking. Even now he knew that wasn't made better by all the shit he had brought with him. He wanted a drink.

The small bar of the Blue Anchor, looking across the Thames, spilled out, as it always did, on to the pavement of Lower Mall. The drinkers were a mix of civilians and soldiers and airmen. The noise was cheerful and loud. Stefan Gillespie stood at the bar, hemmed in by a group of men in RAF uniforms. He was nursing a pint of Guinness. There was a part of him that wondered if the easiest thing was to walk away. It had been a stupid decision to come at all, and the knowledge that it was a decision born of guilt, almost entirely guilt, made what he had seen harder. The thought, surrounded by a kind of self-righteousness now, that what had happened in Berlin meant nothing, while this was betrayal, only made him feel more like walking away. He looked round to see Kate beside him. She was smiling, but she was flustered. She was a little breathless. He knew she had run from the house.

'Stefan, why didn't you say something? Why didn't you send a telegram?'

'It was a spur-of-the-moment thing,' he said lightly.

'Where were you? Where have you come from, then?'

'It's probably better not said in here.'

She laughed. 'Should I have guessed that?'

'I will tell you, Kate—'

The barman called out to her over the hubbub.

'Gin and tonic, Kate?'

'Please, Ted!'

One of the RAF men glanced round.

'Kate, I didn't see you. How are you?'

'Grand, thank you, Rob.'

'Helen here?'

'She's at the house.'

'Can I get you—'

'It's fine – I'm fine.'

The man smiled. He nodded amiably at Stefan and turned away.

'When did you get here, Stefan?'

'Not long. I would have waited but Helen was . . . guarding the pass . . .'

There was a moment of awkwardness. He could see it.

'Just back from work?' he asked.

'Yes. Look, let's have a drink and go back to the house. I'll cook.'

Kate took the gin and tonic from the barman. Stefan paid.

'Let's go outside, Stefan.'

They walked out on to Lower Mall to join the other drinkers there.

'You can stay, Stefan?'

'Yes. I will have to get to Holyhead tomorrow night.'

There was silence for a moment. Stefan was looking at Kate quizzically.

'So, good day, Kate?'

'Well, nothing special. Not till now.' She smiled; his words sounded odd.

'You haven't been out?'

'Just into town.'

'I did see you, Kate.'

'What do you mean?'

'You know what I mean. Feller in tow and a kiss goodbye.'

Kate said nothing for several seconds. She breathed hard.

'I'm sorry. I don't know why I didn't say it, Stefan. I didn't want to—'

'You didn't want to tell me? Well, I can understand that.'

'I didn't want to spoil things. And you don't understand.'

'No?'

'I went to the pictures, Stefan, that's all. It was a foursome that Helen pestered me into. There's a feller she likes. She wanted a bit of moral support.'

'She was at the bloody house, Kate!' Stefan's voice was louder.

'Jimmy's leave was cancelled. I wanted to get a message to Tony, that's the boy you saw – just walking me home, for God's sake. I tried to get hold of him to say I wasn't going, but I couldn't. I had to go. It was just a film, Stefan. I didn't intend to go on my own. I didn't want to go at all. It just happened.'

'Tony had other ideas, though, I could see that.'

'Please, Stefan. He kissed me goodbye. It didn't mean anything.'

'Not even to him?'

'Stefan, please . . . people are . . . looking . . .'

People were looking round; people who knew Kate. Stefan's voice was louder now. Kate's agitation wasn't hard to see. She was uncomfortable, upset.

'That's the trouble with being a fucking detective, isn't it, Kate?'

'We don't need to argue about this. He's just a boy I know, from a gang of airmen who drink in here sometimes. They're friends. Helen pushed me to—'

'That why she was so scared I might come into the house?'

'For God's sake, Stefan, we've got a night together. I'm sorry I didn't say anything. I should have done. There was no reason not to. It just seemed—'

'You didn't just ignore it, Kate, you lied.'

Even as Stefan said it, he wanted to stop. He had no right to say it. He was the one who was going to lie. Whatever conversation they had that night, whatever he said about Berlin, he was still going to lie about Zandra Purcell.

'Yes, I did. I have no idea why. I didn't want to have to explain. Because there's nothing to explain. Nothing happened. Nothing was going to happen. But I didn't want to spend the few hours we've got talking about something that doesn't fucking matter. I didn't want to . . . Jesus, you see, now . . . you've got me bloody crying. Did you have to spy on me, Stefan? That's what it feels like—'

'I just fucking saw you, Kate, that's all.'

'Then why didn't you just walk up to me and kiss me?'

'Is that what you'd have wanted?'

'Yes, it bloody is. I talked about you all the way home, you know that?'

A group of men in RAF uniforms had moved closer. One of them was looking at Kate, watching her with a mix of puzzlement and protectiveness.

'You all right, Kate?'

'Yes, thanks, I'm fine.'

'If this chap's bothering you—'

'Of course he's not bothering me, don't be silly, this is Stefan, my—'

Another airman stepped closer to Stefan, cutting off Kate's words.

'Kate's a friend of ours, old son. Maybe take it easy, eh?'

Stefan could smell the whiskey on the man's breath.

'What?'

'You heard me.' The man's face was very close to Stefan's.

'I did hear. And now I have, maybe you'd piss off,' replied Stefan.

'You don't understand,' said Kate gently. 'There's no problem at all. It's nothing to do with anyone else. Please, boys, will you just leave us be—'

'I'm keeping an eye on you, old son, got it?' continued the man.

'Billy, you heard Kate,' said one of the other RAF men. 'Not our biz.'

'Isn't it?' said Billy, his eyes still fixed on Stefan.

'I know you're English, Billy,' said Stefan. 'I should make some allowance, but you've got a fucking problem with minding your own business.'

'Stefan, let's just go home, shall we?' Kate took his arm.

'You're a bit out of place here, mate,' continued Billy.

'You mean if I'd come as an arsehole, then I'd fit in?'

'You fucking Irish bastard – where the hell do you think you are?'

'David,' said Kate, looking at one of the other men, 'this is Stefan. You know who he is. I've talked about him enough. Billy's drunk. Just do something!'

The man Kate had spoken to stepped forward. He took Billy's arm.

'Come on, Billy. You've got the wrong end of the stick.'

But whatever end of the stick Billy had, he wasn't letting go.

'Oh, the fucking Irish policeman. There's a turn up for the books. There's Irishmen in our squadron, real Irishmen. We don't think much of you shitehawk Irish, sitting across the water on your arses, waiting for the Jerries to turn up, so you can watch us get fucked. That's your business, eh? That's the craic, as you say. You're a bunch of cowards, got it? I'd say Kate could do better than that—'

'You're right,' said Stefan, laughing. 'She could get someone like you!'

The man called Billy lashed out with his fist. It was unexpected, but only caught Stefan a glancing blow on the cheek. He didn't wait for another one. He slammed his own fist into Billy, and the man collapsed on to the pavement.

'Stefan, Mother of God!' shouted Kate.

Stefan suddenly found two RAF men were holding him, one on each side.

They were simply trying to stop things going any further, but Stefan thought he was in for a beating now. He tried to struggle, and a third airman grabbed hold of him. Two more held Billy back, as he got to his feet. Then Kate, misreading the signs in the same way Stefan had, threw herself at the men holding him.

'Let him go, you bastards! Let him fucking go!'

There was the shrill sound of a police whistle. The crowd around the fight broke open, and a constable walked through the gap. Everything was still again.

'What's all this?'

'A misunderstanding, George,' said the man Kate had called David.

There was a ripple of laughter. The three airmen released Stefan's arms.

'Now let's go home,' said Kate firmly.

'He didn't mean it. He's pissed. I'm sorry,' said David to Stefan.

Stefan shrugged. He didn't want to say any more. He bent down to pick up his suitcase. It had been kicked across Lower Mall and it had burst open.

'Give him a hand,' said someone.

Two RAF men bent down to help him.

'Can I buy you a drink?' said David. 'I do know who you are.'

'No thank you,' said Kate, still furious. 'I've had enough shite for one evening. Let's go home, Stefan Gillespie, if you've had enough shite, that is?'

'I'd say I have, Kate,' Stefan said with a grin.

'And so have I,' said the constable, looking hard at the airmen.

'What the fuck is this?'

One of the RAF men who was picking up Stefan's belongings walked towards the policeman, staring down at a piece of paper he had just picked up.

'What's what?' asked the constable.

'It's got a fucking swastika on it, George.'

The policeman looked at the piece of paper, then at Stefan.

'Is this your name on here – Gillespie, Stefan Gillespie?'

'I suppose it will be,' said Stefan, standing up with the suitcase now.

'Can you explain what this is, Mr Gillespie?'

'It's a travel pass, Constable. A train ticket.'

'Hammersmith via Berlin?' said the policeman.

'No, Hammersmith via Berlin and Stockholm.'

There was complete silence outside the Blue Anchor.

'Jesus wept,' said Kate, looking at Stefan in disbelief.

He nodded. 'It never was going to turn into a good night, was it?'

23

The Royal Over-Seas League

Half an hour later Stefan Gillespie was sitting on a hard, wooden bed, in a cell underneath Hammersmith police station. Apart from the routine procedure of the custody sergeant cataloguing his belongings, and the removal of his belt and shoe laces in the interests of preventing any attempt at suicide, no one had spoken to him. The station superintendent had arrived in the cells as he was being locked up. He peered in at Stefan momentarily from the cell doorway.

'Is he drunk?' he asked the custody sergeant.

'No, sir. He's a policeman. Irish Special Branch.'

'Yes. Haven't we got enough of those wankers without importing them?'

The sergeant nodded, but managed to find a friendly wink for Stefan.

'He's not for us, anyway. They'll be here for him later.'

The door was shut and locked. A faint glow from a bulb in the ceiling lit the cell. Stefan lay back on the hard boards of the bed. It wasn't his finest hour.

Two hours had gone before the custody sergeant returned and opened the door.

'He's here,' was all he said.

Upstairs, in the sergeant's office, a slight, pale man, barely in his mid-twenties, was waiting for him. He had blond hair that was too long and too well cut for either a policeman or a soldier, and he wore a moustache so thin that it only seemed to accentuate how young he was. He already had Stefan's suitcase and the small attaché case that he had carried all through Europe, in his role as an Irish diplomatic courier. He held up the case with an apologetic shrug.

'I'm afraid they've been through your diplomatic bag, old man.'

'I'll make sure the High Commissioner complains.'

'Well, it's nothing the Jerries won't have done, is it?'

'They didn't. Well, not as far as I know.'

'Funny bastards, aren't they?' said the man. 'They'd put a blow torch to your private parts as soon as look at you, but they won't open a diplomatic bag.'

He stretched out his hand. 'Ellison.'

They shook hands.

'No third degree, I hope?'

'Not even a cup of tea,' said Stefan.

'Well, there are things we draw the line at when it comes to spies.'

Ellison led the way out to the station's front desk.

Kate O'Donnell was sitting on a bench by the door to Brook Green. She got up and came towards him. She was anxious and concerned, but still slightly unsure about how he was going to react to her after what had just happened.

'Are you all right, Stefan?'

'As cells go it wasn't bad. Brand new almost. Didn't even smell of piss.'

She moved close and took his hand.

'Stefan, I'm sorry things got a bit . . .'

'I don't know, meeting your friends is turning into a bit of an adventure.'

She smiled. 'It does seem that way.'

'At least they didn't beat me up in Dún Laoghaire. Maybe if we'd stayed?'

She started to laugh. He leant forward and kissed her gently on the lips.

She looked into his eyes. 'You do believe me, Stefan, about the rest?'

He nodded, but not easily; again he knew the only lies were his.

'You're Miss O'Donnell,' said Ellison pleasantly.

'Yes, I am.'

'I'm afraid we have to get on.'

'When will I see you, Stefan?'

Stefan shrugged and looked at Ellison, who merely returned the shrug.

Kate held herself against Stefan. She looked up and kissed him. She didn't understand what had happened. There had been no explanation of where Stefan had come from, or why he had German papers, or what any of it meant. But for now, that wasn't in her mind. She wanted to put what was wrong, right.

'Cheer up, Miss O'Donnell,' said Ellison, 'they'll never know what to make of you in the Blue Anchor now. You'll be the toast of Hammersmith. It's not every woman who can say she's got a German spy for a boyfriend, is it?'

It was dark now, but there was a half-moon and the streets were clear and sharp, even in the blackout. The car pulled away from Hammersmith police station towards Shepherd's Bush. Stefan glanced back. He could still see Kate, standing at the kerb, watching the car. And then she was gone. He turned to Ellison.

'So what are you? You don't look like Special Branch.'

'MI5.'

'Military Intelligence.'

'That's the ticket.'

'So, it could be a long night.'

'I don't know, old man. I rather think that's what my section chief had in mind. But you're hands off. He had to cancel the sandwiches. He's not happy.'

Stefan had been sitting on his own in a room overlooking St James's Street for almost an hour. He knew where he was. The drive from West London had taken them through Knightsbridge and Hyde Park Corner and into Piccadilly. They were all places he knew. Ellison had turned into St James's, just after the Ritz, and stopped at a building close to the Piccadilly end of the street. A woman had taken him to a room on the first floor, furnished with a desk and chairs, and little more. She had brought him a cup of tea and a plate of shortbread biscuits. The furniture was not what you'd find in the cellars of Dublin Castle, but take away the walnut veneer and the Regency stripe on the chair, and it was an interrogation room, although no one had asked him to explain himself yet.

When the door finally opened, the man who walked in was someone he knew, but not someone he expected to find in an MI5 office in London. Colonel Liam Archer was the head of Irish Military Intelligence. Stefan had met him once, just before his journey to Portugal and Spain. Now Colonel Archer was dressed in civilian clothes, but he had no jacket. He was in shirtsleeves and braces. A half-smoked cigarette was stuck between his lips. It was obvious he had not just arrived to see Stefan; in some way, somewhere, he was working in the building.

Stefan stood up.

'You're a fucking embarrassment, aren't you, Inspector?'

'It wasn't intentional, sir.'

'That's always the best kind of cock-up.'

'I'm sorry, sir.' Stefan wasn't sure whether an apology was right.

'Well, at least they'd ask a question here before they'd hang a feller for a spy. But walking round London with German travel papers, looking for a fight, you probably deserve it. At least they knew something about you when the police called in. They knew you'd come in from Stockholm. I suppose the fact you're here at all means you must have been a bit more circumspect in Berlin.'

Stefan could only smile; he wasn't sure circumspect exactly had it right.

'So,' said Archer, 'whose eejit idea was it to send you to Germany, and have you stop off here on the way home? That's another embarrassment. I knew nothing about it, not till a couple of hours ago. That makes me look an arse!'

'It was Mr Walshe, sir.'

'If Joe was in it, so was Dev. You'd think they'd have enough to do.'

'Mr Walshe wanted me—'

Liam Archer shook his head. It meant shut up.

'No one authorised you to make a trip to London and start a fight.'

'No, sir, that was . . . entirely my own idea.'

'We won't want to say any more in this room, Gillespie, or in this building. You can work that out, I know. There'll be no shortage of people to debrief you – but it'll be in Dublin. MI5 would love to talk to anyone who's back from a jaunt to Berlin, but I've persuaded them that our relationship matters more than a few traveller's tales. They'll get what I decide they get. I assume if Joe didn't want me to know, he didn't want anyone else to know.'

'Yes, sir.'

'They do want some bits and pieces, especially the military travel passes and the train tickets, and there's some restaurant and hotel bills. They like all that.'

'What happens now, sir?'

'They'll get you a room round the corner so. It's too late to leave. You'll stay the night in London, and then you head back to Holyhead first thing.'

'I was hoping—'

Colonel Archer's frown did not look promising.

'I did come to London to see someone . . .'

'I think we all know that now, Inspector. Half of West London does.'

Stefan gave a slight smile.

'Eat, drink, sleep and leave, Gillespie. And be grateful you can. Your personal affairs will have to wait for another day. I'll see you in Dublin so.'

Stefan sat on a sofa in the reception area of the MI5 building. There was nothing remotely secretive about the place, at least as far as St James's Street went. There was a uniformed commissionaire on the door; a woman sat at a desk. It looked like any office, though its twenty-four-hour opening hours were unusual. At one stage a uniformed policeman came into the building and went into a room at the side, where Stefan glimpsed more men in uniforms. A man in civilian clothes followed him, minutes later, and Stefan did see the bulge of a shoulder holster under his jacket. The man nodded to him briefly. He had no reason to, but Stefan read the unspoken gesture of recognition. The man would be Metropolitan Police Special Branch. The building was guarded; but no more so than Iveagh House, and a lot less than many Irish government buildings.

As Stefan waited for the details of where he was staying, a man walked in and spoke to the receptionist. He made a joke that Stefan didn't hear, and then walked over and sat in an armchair across the reception area. Stefan looked up idly, and the man smiled, stretching back and yawing. His face was slightly flushed. That, with the way he moved, the way he sat, said he'd been drinking.

'How's it going?' said the man.

'Not so bad.'

'If it's not so bad, it could be worse, I always say.'

The man laughed, more loudly than the remark called for.

Stefan was looking hard at the man now. He knew him, and for a few seconds he was trying to place him. He knew, as a policeman often knows, that he knew him as a face. It wasn't someone he'd met. He knew he had seen him, watched him, looked at his photograph. He remembered him in that way. The place was wrong. The man didn't fit. He just needed to find where the fit was.

'Been in the Ritz. I've had better meals in a pie-and-mash shop. It's getting sticky there, if you believe it. If you can't get a decent steak for a quid under the table there, the country's in a bigger bloody mess than I thought!'

Stefan heard the Welsh accent under something more English. He saw the man at the Curragh, through a crowd of people, arguing with Simon McCall, the dead horse trainer from Dunlavin. He saw him in the Shelbourne Hotel, again with Simon McCall, talking to the German press attaché. He hadn't thought about any of that since leaving Dublin. But this was the Welshman he had wanted to question, Owain Jones, German agent and IRA contact. And now he was sitting in an MI5 building in London, half cut, as if he owned the place.

'You're Irish?' the Welshman said abruptly.

'I am.'

'G2?'

'Special Branch.'

'I've a funny story about that . . .' Jones chuckled, then seemed to forget what he'd meant to say. He stretched lazily. 'But you'll know Gerry de Paor?'

'I know Geróid, of course I do.'

'He's a good man,' said Owain Jones expansively. 'Solid.'

'I'd say he is,' replied Stefan, recalling the Shelbourne Hotel and the sudden departure that meant Owain Jones could not be questioned about the deaths in Dunlavin and his connection with La Mancha. The sudden departure de Paor knew nothing about, though he was the first to get to the Shelbourne.

'You staying?' asked the Welshman.

'Yes, I'm waiting to see if they've got me a room, somewhere near.'

'Royal Over-Seas League?'

'That's it.'

'Not up to much as a hotel. It's a club, you see. But not a bad bar.'

'I'll remember that.'

'I'm there tonight myself. See you for a drink, perhaps?'

'Good idea,' said Stefan. 'I wouldn't mind one.'

'I wouldn't mind several,' laughed Jones.

Stefan nodded. That much was obvious.

'Mr Gillespie!' It was the voice of the receptionist. Stefan got up.

'Get me one in, old boy!' the Welshman called after him.

Stefan turned and smiled. He was going to get a few in for Owain Jones. He already knew him. He was a piss artist with a big mouth. He hardly needed to open that mouth without advertising the essential qualities of his character. Henry Casey, the man who was sitting in a cell in Mountjoy Prison, probably waiting to be hanged by now, had not entered Stefan Gillespie's head in weeks. But he was there now, an unsettling reminder of what he had felt when Terry Gregory sent him to look into the murder in Dunlavin; not because anyone in Special Branch cared how the McCall family died, but because there was a German radio transmitter in the kitchen of the burnt-out shell of La Mancha.

That was done now. There had been no shortage of evidence to say Henry Casey was a murderer, and the confusion and contradiction in his story only hammered that home. But Stefan had come away from that with a gnawing doubt about Casey's guilt. Where everything fitted, there was something that didn't. Owain Jones would not be difficult to talk to. Whatever he was doing in the MI5 offices, he thought Stefan Gillespie was doing the same thing, in one way or another. He owed Casey something. He owed his doubts something. Perhaps, with the smell of Berlin and the Polizeipräsidium still in his nostrils, he felt he owed something to himself, too. He was a policeman, of sorts.

The Royal Over-Seas League was an old house in Park Place, a cul-de-sac off St James's. It was a club that mainly catered for travellers from the British Empire and its colonies. It was much more of a hotel than the other clubs that lined St James's, but it had the same quiet, discreet atmosphere. Its position at the end of a small street that led nowhere, and the high, solid gates that closed off the approach to it at night, made it a useful place for MI5 and various other agencies of the government to put overnight visitors. But like the MI5 building further up St James's, there was no special attention given to securing the place, and although rooms had been requisitioned in the club, members came and went as well, along with people parked there by the various agencies of government that operated in and around Piccadilly and Mayfair.

Stefan was in a room at the back of the Royal Over-Seas League, looking down to the club's small garden and Green Park beyond. He could see the trees of the park clearly in the moonlight. He wasn't sorry to have found something to think about other than the mess he'd made of things with Kate. It was a mess they would resolve, he knew that. Perhaps it was resolved already. And once the mess in his own head had been forgotten, everything would return to normal.

When he got to the bar, Owain Jones was already there, leaning against it, talking to the barman with the peculiar intimacy drinkers keep for people they barely know except across a bar. The Welshman turned with a broad smile. There was no one else in. It was an intimate space; more sitting room than bar.

'What'll it be, Stefan?'

As they hadn't introduced themselves, it was clear Jones had got the information himself. It seemed a good idea to take the same approach now.

'A glass of beer for me, Owain.'

'And something to go with it?'

'Maybe later,' said Stefan.

'Bollocks, as the Irish have it,' laughed the Welshman. He picked up a bottle of whiskey from the bar. It was Jameson's, and it was three-quarters full.

'Looks good,' said Stefan.

'And does you good! Max says they're bombing over in the docks tonight.'

The barman nodded, handing Stefan a glass of beer.

'With luck we should be all right over this side. But it's anyone's guess . . .'

Jones walked across to some French windows.

'Turn the light off, Max, we'll sit in the garden.'

'It's closed up for the winter now, Mr Jones,' said the barman.

'Not to me, old son, you know that.'

'No, Mr Jones.' The barman shrugged. Stefan saw the contempt in it.

The barman reached round and flicked a switch. The room was in darkness. Owain Jones pulled back the blackout curtains and opened a door. He carried his drink, and two glasses, and the bottle of whiskey. He walked out to a set of steps. Stefan followed him and the barman shut the door behind them.

'You can talk out here,' said Jones, moving down the steps.

Stefan came down after him.

There was a small square garden stretching back behind the

house, and ending in a set of railings that looked into Green Park. There were people walking along the path between the garden and the park. It wasn't late. Owain Jones sat down on a wooden bench. Stefan pulled up a wrought-iron chair.

'You hear it?' said the Welshman.

Stefan hadn't noticed it straight away, but now he could hear the deep rhythm of explosions. They sounded a long way off, but they still shook the air.

'That's a long way up the Thames,' said Jones. 'Tilbury, maybe.'

Stefan said nothing, listening. He had heard the sound in Germany.

'Get some fucking whiskey down you, old man!'

The Welshman poured two very large glasses of Jameson. And as they drank their way down the bottle, Stefan would find no difficulty, in the darkness, in disposing of most of it in the flower bed he was sitting next to.

'Here's to war!' said Jones, raising his glass and grinning.

Owain Jones was not a man who had any reservations about hogging a conversation, and the more he drank, the more the complacent and self-satisfied sound of his own voice entertained him. For the most part all that was necessary was for Stefan to listen and agree. And once the Welshman had remembered his funny story about Special Branch in Dublin, a new friendship born over a bottle was fully established. The story was about the day some of Stefan Gillespie's oppos had pitched up at the Shelbourne to bring Jones in for questioning about the murder of a man he had been working with, and how G2 had tipped him off and got him out of the country before the Guards embarrassed themselves. The Welshman still thought this was funny, though he did add a serious reflection on the deaths at La Mancha. 'Strange chap, Simon, but what a nasty business, poor old bugger. And the rest of them. Nutty as a fruitcake, the brother and sister.' But with that brief caveat, the egg on the face of Special Branch was capital!

Although the Welshman didn't tell Stefan Gillespie he was a double agent, every sentence was full of winks and nudges that said he was. Having accepted that Stefan knew something about what was going on at La Mancha, he had no problem referring to it as if it was all his own creation. Establishing a string of safe houses for German agents in Ireland, smuggling equipment, arms, explosives, money and information back and forth between Britain and Ireland, and trying to pull the IRA into a conspiracy of Celtic nations that didn't even exist. Some of it Stefan did know; some of it he had worked out. What he had not known was that everything Owain Jones was involved in was an open book to the people who employed him in British Intelligence, and that G2 was a part of that. The Welshman was clearly disappointed that the whole thing had virtually fallen apart. He never did get all the information about the IRA's safe house. His way in failed, with the demise of Simon McCall, and although he didn't say so, it seemed likely the IRA had shut down whatever contacts Jones had as soon as the deaths in Dunlavin became part of a Garda investigation.

Stefan soon realised that the Welshman had two preoccupations. The first was being on the right side, whichever way the war went. He made no bones about claiming he was in a position to do just that. His arse, as he put it several times, was covered. He seemed to feel that since Stefan was Irish, he would have the same approach to the war. After all, as he said, again several times, wasn't Ireland playing a blinder when it came to playing both sides against the middle? The second preoccupation was making money. He didn't say he was being paid by both sides, but he glowed with self-satisfaction each time he came near to saying it and ostentatiously pulled back. But he had other ways of making money, and what he did gave him plenty of opportunity to peel a few notes off the bottom of the bank roll. There were various terms the Welshman had for doing that, but what Stefan read into them was that they were all euphemisms for blackmail. In some way Jones had made money out of his connection with Simon McCall. He said it. But by the time Stefan got him to this stage, the whiskey bottle was almost empty; Jones, who had been drinking all afternoon, was slurring his words and talking himself into blind alleys.

'Got to make what you can. Everyone does. Use it, Stefan, old man!'

Stefan nodded, as if what the Welshman was saying mattered.

'Use it. The fucking war. Get what you can, before the other buggers—'

'You got a bit in Ireland,' said Stefan, steering him back.

'A bit, a little bit more than a bit. A bit—'

The Welshman stopped suddenly; he had forgotten what he was saying.

'Is that bloody whiskey done?'

'There's a drop,' said Stefan, pouring more into Jones's glass.

'Need another, eh?'

'You made a bit in Ireland anyway,' Stefan said again.

'Doddle. Fucking doddle. Wasn't easy with old Simon, though.'

'No?'

'Man of high principle!' Jones giggled. 'I got him there, though. And once I got him there. Well, if he did it once. I had the bastard cornered! Should have got more. Should have got the old boy running faster. Wouldn't. In the end—'

'Clever enough, though, Owain,' said Stefan, pouring the last dregs out.

'Clever, I'll say. He thought he was doing it for Ireland! I think he wasn't far behind his brother and sister on the nutcase front. Money for the Boys, eh!'

'So how did it work?' asked Stefan.

'What?' replied the Welshman blankly.

'The diddle – old Simon McCall.'

'What do you want to fucking know for?' said Jones abruptly.

'Looking for tips,' grinned Stefan.

The Welshman drained his glass and roared with laughter.

'It got blown out in the end, Stefan.'

'Yes?'

'Couldn't blame the old fool really. I might have pushed him too hard. No one would suspect a Turf Club steward, but you can only get so much mileage out of any scam. Not that the Turf Club would have twigged. But the bookies smelt it. I hadn't put that one in. They've got the noses.' Owain Jones shook his head slowly, almost sadly. Then he sniggered and started laughing.

'That was a show, though. Better than a heavyweight bout. Knocked the shit—'

Jones broke off, peering down at his empty glass.

'What happened?' Stefan risked another direct question.

'The racecourse. The Battle of the Curragh. You must know about that!'

'Jesus, course I do! So what's that got to do with you, Owain?'

'I was finished in Ireland, but you might say that was my swansong!'

The Welshman stood up shakily, giggling to himself.

'I need another drink. Where's that fucker Max? Let's get a bottle—'

Owain Jones took two steps forward and collapsed.

Stefan got up and walked to the flower bed, where the crumpled shape of Owain Jones lay, unmoving. He bent down. The Welshman had passed out. As Stefan walked up the steps to the bar of the Royal Over-Seas League and knocked at the French window, he realised London was silent. At some point during their conversation, the bombs had stopped falling. He hadn't noticed.

The French window opened, and Stefan walked back into the dark bar. The barman pulled the door shut and closed the heavy curtains. He went back to the bar and switched on the light. Stefan asked him for a whiskey to take up to his room. Now the job was done, such as it was, he could afford to have a drink.

'Mr Jones is still in the garden.'

The barman nodded; he seemed unsurprised.

'I mean he's horizontal in the garden, in a flower bed.'

The barman handed him the whiskey and grinned.

'He often is, sir. I won't leave him if there's any bombing. Goodnight.'

24

Zehlendorf

Berlin

The Gestapo came very early to the Convent of the Holy Mother in Charlottenburg. It was not light. Coming early was the business they were in, but on this occasion there was no one to catch unawares, no one to surprise, no one to intimidate. Normally there was no secret about who was taken away in the early hours of the morning; that was never what it was about. But on this particular morning discretion did matter. The job was a necessary one, for Germany and for what it meant to be German, in a nation whose strength was in pure blood, healthy blood. But there were things even the most dedicated Party members found difficult. It was better that as few people as possible knew. There were natural feelings of compassion and kindness that in ordinary times were to be applauded, but these were not ordinary times. A new world was being created, and old sentimentalities had to be pushed aside. Not everyone could do that. The demands that were made on the few involved a kind of heroism, a kind of steel, that the world had not seen before, and it was all the more profound because it would go unrecorded even in the annals of the Thousand-Year Reich.

A black car and a small bus with blacked-out windows pulled into the yard at the back of the convent. Two plain-clothed

Gestapo men were in the car, along with Kriminalkommissar Vordermaier from the Kriminalpolizei. The operation that was underway needed more men than the Gestapo and the SS could provide. In the bus were two uniformed policemen and two SS officers. They were all armed, though the handguns they carried were kept respectfully out of sight.

The Gestapo men had not considered that the convent would be awake at five in the morning, but it was. The Sisters of the Holy Mother were in the chapel. Lauds, the morning office, was being said, as it was said every day. And as the caretaker came to call the Mother Superior, the chanting of the Canticle of Zachary hid his whispers. 'Et tu puer, propheta Altissimi, vocaberis praeibis enim ante faciem Domini parare vias eius.' And thou, child, shalt be called the prophet of the Highest: for thou shalt go before the face of the Lord to prepare his ways.

Mother Cecilia left quietly. She took only Sister Mary Joseph with her, to prepare the children, and left instructions that the nuns remain in the chapel until she returned. She knew, of course. She had already heard the rumours, and more than rumours. The Convent of the Holy Mother wasn't the first. She had been told there was nothing that could be done, in words that made no comment on what was happening. And when the children had gone, she would only say, repeating what was not entirely a lie, that the state had made a new provision. No one in the convent would ever ask her what that was.

There were eight children who left the convent that morning, still barely awake, dressed without washing, some still clutching blankets and toys. Their belongings would follow. The Gestapo officer who ticked them off on his list as they entered the bus was awkward and impatient. He wanted it done quickly.

Sister Mary Joseph helped the children on to the bus. Andreas Purcell and the other two Down Syndrome children, Claudia Krannich who was six and Eckart Fäustel, Andreas's best friend, who was ten. Seven-year-old Johannes Richter and his sister Dorothea, eight; they had both survived polio but he could only walk with a leg iron and she had lost the use of her legs entirely; there was no room for her wheelchair, and one of the policeman carried her on to the bus. No one had ever found out what was wrong with Frieda Schumann, but at nine she would allow no one except Sister Mary Joseph to touch her, and had never spoken. Gerald Mohr was five and had been blind since birth; his cleft palate meant that only the other children and a few of the nuns could understand him. Christa Niehoff, at eleven, was the oldest. Cerebral palsy made it impossible for her to walk some days, but as her wheelchair would not fit on the bus either, she walked on with two sticks.

The children were confused and upset, but it had all happened so quickly that the idea that they were leaving their home had not sunk in. Only Christa sensed that this was strange, more than strange. She refused the help of Mother Cecilia, who stepped forward, reluctantly, because no one else had. Christa shook her head and pushed herself up on to the bus.

'I'll go with them, Mother,' said Mary Joseph quietly.

'I think it's better if you stay, Sister.'

'No, Mother. I'm sure it isn't better.'

The two women looked at each other. It was the Reverend Mother who was helpless. It wasn't that she felt no pain. She was struggling to fight back tears. But she had a responsibility that made pain an irrelevance. She had a duty of care for the convent and its sisters above all, as well as a duty of obedience. She had been told to cooperate. Silence in the face of evil was not an easy burden, but when the Church itself had to be protected, all burdens must be borne. She had to accept that; she could do nothing else. If there were other responsibilities, and other duties, she would face them alone, in her prayers.

'Go with them on the bus, then. And you must take a taxi back.'

'Yes, I will. Bless me, Mother.' Sister Mary Joseph bent her head.

Mother Cecilia raised her hand. It was a gesture she would make to any sister leaving the convent, even for the shortest of times, but the words didn't come straightaway. She could feel herself trembling, and for a moment she wanted to bow her head herself. She felt she was the one who needed blessing.

'Benedicat tibi Deus.' She made the sign of the cross. 'A taxi, Mary!'

Sister Mary Joseph walked to the bus. She smiled at a Gestapo officer.

'I shall be coming too.'

'Are you Sister Mary Joseph Aherne?'

'I am.' She smiled, hearing his German pronunciation of her Irish surname. It was a long time since she had heard it. Entering a convent, you left everything behind, even your name. Now it seemed not quite a part of her.

'Good. That's done, then. Your name's here too. Please get in.'

She looked at him, surprised, and then, suddenly, not. She nodded.

'Almost done!' The Gestapo officer addressed his colleague and Kriminalkommissar Vordermaier. 'You two go on in the car. I'll be on the bus.'

'Will do!' The second Gestapo man turned away. Vordermaier followed him. He had done nothing since entering the convent but smoke a small cigar.

The first Gestapo officer ticked off the last name on his list. Minutes later the back gates of the convent closed; the bus pulled away. The Reverend Mother made to cross herself. It was a gesture she made dozens of times a day; she had done so all her life. It was the first time she had stopped herself. She turned and walked through the dark yard, into the cloisters, back to the chapel.

Zandra Purcell stood at the black door to the Convent of the Holy Mother for almost ten minutes before anyone came. It was already dark when she got there, and the blackout made it darker still. The streets were silent, wet after the light drizzle she had walked through from the S-Bahn station, unaware that it had drenched her to the skin. The little light there was, as the moon appeared and disappeared through low cloud, gave the streets a clean, black sheen. The walls of the convent stretched out on either side of the door. No light shone from the high windows. She pulled the rod that sounded the bell, over and over again; she hammered with her fists; she called and shouted. Eventually, the small wooden window behind the iron grille at the centre of the door opened. She could not see the face of the nun who had opened it, only the white of the coif that surrounded it. The nun did not move closer to the grille as she spoke. She seemed to want to stay in the inner blackness that hid her features. Zandra didn't recognise her voice, but the nun would know her. They all knew her.

'I have to see Andreas. I have to see my son.'

'The convent is closed.'

'I have to see him. I heard something. I heard—'

'No one can enter now. I'm sorry. You should go home.'

'I have to see him. I have to know he's all right. Please, Sister.'

'The children have gone.'

The words were very simple. Zandra stared.

'This is a house of prayer now.'

'What do you mean, the children have gone? How can they go? This is their home – my son's home, since he was tiny. What are you talking about?'

'I'm sorry. The authorities—'

The nun's voice stopped abruptly. She could find no words.

'Where is Andreas? You know who I am – open the door!'

'The Reverend Mother has instructed us all—'

'Fuck the Reverend Mother, let me talk to her!'

'We are an order of prayer only now. I can't say any more.'
The wooden window closed. And there was silence again.

It was a long time before Zandra Purcell turned away from the door to the Convent of the Holy Mother. She couldn't know how long herself. Half an hour, an hour, more? She pulled the bell again, over and over, all that time. She hammered on the old wood with her fists, until both her hands were bleeding; and when they were, she still pounded on the door. She shouted and screamed until her voice was hoarse and her throat ached, and as her shouts dried up and faded away, the only word she could still find to say was her son's name 'Andreas'. It was a plea and a hopeless prayer, and even that became, finally, no more than a whisper, a breath on her lips she could barely hear herself. But if anyone heard her, no one came. A few people passed by, on the other side of the street. She didn't see them, and they moved deeper into the shadows as they saw her and heard her, and walked quickly past. No one needed to understand what anyone else's troubles were to know that keeping yourself to yourself was, in every area of life in Berlin, the only sensible course. It was probably true that hardly anyone knew what had happened at the convent that day, but nobody wanted to. Truth was not in high demand. It was common knowledge that the Gestapo had been there that afternoon. It was truth enough.

The sirens were sounding even before Zandra walked away from the convent. She would come back. In the morning, she would come back. She would not take no for an answer. She would force her way in, somehow. They would tell her what had happened. They would tell her where Andreas was. There were a lot of words like that in her head. The same words, turning inside her, endlessly, emptily. But they were only words. She knew, without needing to be told, that she would never see Andreas again. It wasn't that she could even begin, yet, to imagine what had happened. She had no idea, and she couldn't even start to give shape to one. But she felt his absence – unclear what it meant, yet with a certainty that she could not deny. In the morning the light would begin to give form to what she would not be able to speak. Her dead friend would be there. Her dead friend's words. The book Johannes had brought back from Poland. There would be a connection to make. And she would make it. And when she had, she would know why she could never see her son again. And then she would have to choose to shut that away in the deepest recesses of her mind, and to carry on with the lies she would need to embrace if she was to stay alive.

For now, she walked. She simply walked. Neither fast nor slow, and with no sense of where she was going. The sirens had stopped, though she hadn't noticed. High overhead there were planes flying; she didn't hear them. The first explosion was some way off, closer to Berlin. The second was much nearer, and it lit up the street behind her. Ahead there were searchlights, spiking up into the night sky. She didn't see. There was the irregular pop of anti-aircraft fire.

As she turned into a wide boulevard there were people rushing past, racing into the concrete shelter that stood at the entrance to a children's playground. A woman shouted at her, pointing to the shelter. Zandra walked on. She wasn't unaware of the noise around her, but it seemed unimportant. When an explosion in a parallel street sent shards of glass and splintered timber hurtling in front of her, she didn't stop. She was walking towards the S-Bahn station; her instincts were taking her home the way she had come. There would be no trains, of course, and the station was lit by a fire blazing up in front of her. It was brighter, much brighter; there were other fires further away, to her left, right, all around. The sound of more bombs exploding came from further ahead, closer into the city centre. The clouds had cleared; the moon was white. High above her, small black crosses, blacker than the night itself, were caught momentarily in the beams of the searchlights. There was the rattle of the ack-ack again, and the firework-blaze of tracer bullets. What she saw she took no account of. Still she kept walking – past the station. What she heard around her seemed far away. There was something clearer in her head. Her bloodied fingers moved rhythmically, playing the notes of his song. The song she had played him on the saxophone as a baby. The song he loved. All she heard were the words inside her head, and Andreas's laughing voice singing.

Oh, when the stars begin to fall,
Oh, when the stars begin to fall,
I want to be in that number
When the saints go marching in.
Oh, when the saints go marching in,
Oh, when the saints go marching in,
I want to be in that number,
When the saints go marching in.

The children had spent the afternoon in a room in an empty hospital in the south-west of the city, close to the Teltowkanal. The building had once been a hospital for the mentally ill, but it had been closed for over ten years. It had, from the outside, the appearance of a small fortress. There were ornamental turrets and the walls contained few windows. The windows there were, were barred. The corridors and the wards contained almost nothing. In the room where the children were, there were several bed frames, and a heap of broken papier mâché furniture, which still smelt of urine a decade on. They were not directly under guard, but at the end of the corridor a medical orderly, wearing an overcoat over a dirty, white nurse's smock, sat with two SS men. The orderly had several boxes of files in front of him, though the box was never opened. He sat all day with the SS men, drinking beer and smoking, and when Sister Mary wanted to take one of the children to the toilet, he stood at the door and waited for her to come out. Intermittently, through the day, Sister Mary heard voices in the corridor outside and she saw, shuttling back and forward to the toilet, that the other rooms were filling up with people. There were more children, like her children, and there were others: old, in wheelchairs, on crutches. In the room next door, as she passed by on yet another toilet trip, she saw four men and women, staring vacantly out through the open door. Like Andreas Purcell they had Down Syndrome. As she passed the door a woman in an SS uniform came out and pulled it shut. She smiled at the nun, and walked ahead of her to the table, where one of the SS men took a bottle of beer from a crate on the floor and opened it. The woman sat down, yawning, and drank from the bottle.

By the time it was dark, there were fifty or sixty people in the rooms on either side of the corridor. All of them had been brought from some kind of hospital or sanatorium or care home or mental institution. This was the collecting point. The policeman who had sat in front of Sister Mary Joseph on the journey from the convent had explained that vulnerable people were being evacuated from Berlin to the south of the country. There would be more buses, when the operation was complete. When she asked him his name, he had been reluctant to give it. She thought he wasn't Gestapo; even inside the convent walls the nuns shared the instincts of Germans everywhere. She didn't ask again, but as he saw the last of the children off the bus at Zehlendorf, she had thanked him and her words left his unknown name hanging like a question on the end of her sentence, and he had answered: 'Kriminalkommissar Vordermaier.' Then he had turned away, almost irritably, as if he regretted saying it.

There had been no food all day. Bottles of water had arrived eventually after an hour of pestering and pleading by Sister Mary Joseph and a male nurse who had arrived with a group of men and women suffering from dementia. The children were tired, hungry and beginning to get tearful and fractious. The buses that would take them south were still coming, they were told. They would leave that night, though it would be later now. The sound of bombs was quite distant when it started. It was far enough away, at least, that the children were not disturbed. Even after only a few weeks, people had learnt quite fine judgements about how close the explosions were, and how ready they needed to be to go to the shelters. But shortly after the bombing started, the medical orderly walked down the corridor, opening all the doors and summoning everyone out. They were all to go down to the cellars for safety. It was an abrupt request that sounded like a command, and as Sister Mary Joseph ushered the children out, joining all the people from the other rooms, she saw that there were more SS men now, and there were several more orderlies and nurses.

The nun saw the man who had argued and complained with her until they managed to get some water. He was hugging several old men and women, who seemed to have no idea where they were or what was happening. Some seemed happily indifferent; some were confused, distressed. He was saying goodbye.

'I have to go back to the hospital. Don't worry. I'm sorry—'

The man seemed to be having difficulty saying anything, and he turned away from his charges very suddenly and started to walk away. Sister Mary Joseph smiled. He stopped, looking at her, and shook his head. She could see there were tears in his eyes. She stepped towards him. He just walked away.

The medical orderly who had sat at the end of the corridor all day was ticking off something on a clipboard as the other nurses and the SS men began to usher everyone towards a dark staircase at the other end of the corridor.

'Sister, you'll have to leave now,' said the orderly.

'Leave?'

'The children will travel on alone. We have our own nurses.'

'I have no intention of leaving the children.'

'It isn't your decision, Sister.'

A man stepped forward, in a dark leather overcoat.

'The sister stays with them. That decision was made higher up.'

The orderly shrugged and walked on.

'Thank you,' said Sister Mary Joseph. She recognised the Gestapo man.

'My orders,' he said. 'I hope you enjoyed your trip to Rome.'

He walked away. She looked after him, puzzled. The journey to Rome had been no secret, but why a Gestapo officer had something to say about it, out of nowhere, during an operation to evacuate the sick and the vulnerable from Berlin, was strange. But as she moved to the staircase, down to the cellars of the hospital, with the children round her, she held the crucifix that hung from her waist. She was praying. She was praying before she knew she was doing it.

Outside the hospital, in a closed yard, six heavy army trucks were backed up hard against the hospital's back wall. Their engines were running. They had been for a long time. From each exhaust a pipe ran to three small windows, just above ground level. The windows were no more than two feet square, and each opened into one of the cellars. Two pipes ran into each window, and they had been packed round with rags, so that none of the exhaust fumes could escape.

Sister Mary Joseph sat in the darkness, with her children round her, holding all of them as far as she could. With her, too, were the older men and women with Down Syndrome. She knew what was happening now, and she knew she could do nothing, except try to keep them as calm and still as possible, until it was over. She prayed quietly, and her voice did calm them. The children were exhausted, but they knew what it was, already, to hide in the dark air-raid shelter across the road from the convent. She could feel that some of them were drifting away into sleep. She could feel it in herself. She said their names to herself, several times, gently, tenderly, as if they were a prayer in themselves, but loud enough that those still conscious could hear them. Claudia Krannich, Eckart Fäustel, Johannes Richter, Dorothea Richter, Gerard Mohr, Christa Niehoff, Andreas Purcell. As she said the names, some special memory of each of them was in her head, so much so that more than once she smiled. She tried to hold them tighter, but she was growing weaker; she could feel herself beginning to fall. She spoke the words of the Nunc Dimittis, in English, as she had once known it, a long time ago. There was a memory of Ireland; a green patch of grass that lay just beyond the door of the farm kitchen she had spent her childhood in, and the keen, sweet smell of the grass. Now Thou dost dismiss Thy servant, O Lord, according to Thy word in peace; Because my eyes have seen Thy salvation, which Thou hast prepared before the face of all peoples: A light to the revelation of the Gentiles, and the glory of Thy people Israel.

Kriminalkommissar Vordermaier stopped as he was driving home from the Alex in the early hours of the morning. He simply wanted to stand and smoke a cigar in the night air for a moment, on his own. He had stopped by the side of the River Spree, and as he stood there, enough moonlight filtered through the drifting clouds to make the grubby water sparkle into something else. But it wasn't something else. Like everything else, it was exactly what it was, and you wouldn't have wanted to get too much of that shitty river into your stomach.

The day had been shit. But then a lot of days were now. It wasn't that Vordermaier found the things he had to do so very difficult. It was just a question of doing them; getting on and doing them. The way everyone else did. But he missed being a policeman. He did think about that. It was a long time since he had been a policeman. The word meant something to him. It wasn't about justice or truth. It was about work. There were no grand words he associated with it. It had been an honest job, in the same way his father's job as a carpenter had been an honest job. Now it was a different thing. It didn't really have a name, and the idea of honesty wasn't any part of it. He sometimes thought he should be more troubled by what he had to do, but he told himself there were reasons for it. Other people knew the reasons; at least they said they did. But if he did ever get as far as thinking about that, he didn't believe reasons had much to do with it. What you did was only what you were expected to do.

As he stood looking out over the dirty river, his hand was in his pocket. He felt the hard, cold metal of his Kripo badge. He had found himself holding it a lot recently, just holding it when he stuffed his hand into his pocket. He took it out now and looked at it. The small brass oval that simply had the word 'Kriminalpolizei' embossed on the front. It was too dull to catch the moonlight.

He looked up. The bombing had stopped two hours earlier. It had been light. But on the horizon, looking back towards the city centre, he could see the glow of several burning buildings. A long time ago, he had liked what he did. Now he didn't; that was how life was. Once he loved his wife; with a passion he had never forgotten. It was a memory that surfaced sometimes, usually when he was on his own, drinking. It had nothing to do with her any more. They inhabited the same apartment; they didn't live with each other. They slept in the same bed; not in the same place. They didn't argue; they didn't do anything. They had said nothing that mattered to each other in ten years. Their children were somewhere else: a solider, a nurse in Dresden. He hardly saw them. Most days it was all Vordermaier could do to speak to his wife; for her, his presence in the flat only drove her out. The job was all he had, and yet it was nothing now. So what? The badge had been something once. It didn't matter that it was nothing now. Who cared? He didn't need it. No one asked anyone who worked for the Reich Main Security Office for identification. They knew. They could smell it. It was irrelevant which branch you worked for. It was all the same. He stepped forward and dropped the badge into the dark water below.

25
Dublin Castle

Dublin

Stefan Gillespie had spent two days at Iveagh House, in the long and repetitive debriefing that followed his return to Ireland. He had been questioned meticulously by Joseph Walshe, whose questions were also the questions of the Taoiseach, Éamon de Valera, by Colonel Archer of G2, and, on the second day, by Superintendent Gregory as well. There was no attempt to divide up the information Stefan had brought back from Berlin between the various interested parties; everyone could know everything. Much of it was of no real importance, however important it had been in Berlin. The death of an unknown German captain and the near execution of an equally unknown Irish saxophone player concerned no one. Walshe was grateful that Zandra Purcell had been released and was safe, and that however messy the circumstances, Stefan Gillespie had enabled William Warnock to perform his consular duties. But his relief was less about a woman he knew nothing of than it was about the diplomatic consequences that would have followed the execution of an Irish citizen in Germany. The circumstances surrounding the murder Zandra was accused of didn't concern anyone. Whatever was in the book Johannes Rilling had died for, the details of what he thought he saw on Germany's horizon interested no one.

However, what Stefan brought back in terms of information about the other members of Berlin's Irish community was clearly important to Walshe, to Archer and even to Terry Gregory. Francis Stuart was quickly consigned to the file that Stefan thought was probably labelled 'Eejits Abroad', though he had a feeling that Walshe would have few qualms about what the British might do to Stuart if the war turned in a different direction, Irish citizen or not. The news of Seán Russell's death was greeted with little satisfaction, even though he could have presented a far greater threat to the state than the IRA leaders who had now taken his place permanently. Stefan was sure that Colonel Archer, at least, had already known Russell was dead, and also knew more about how he had died than he was prepared to say. There was a greater degree of sympathy for Frank Ryan than Stefan might have expected. But it was clear that it didn't extend to any attempt to bring him home. If he was harmless in Berlin, he might be far from harmless as a rallying point for the IRA at home. Walshe was particularly keen that between External Affairs in Dublin and Warnock in Berlin, some way should be found to screw the ex-ambassador, Charles Bewley, and persuade the Germans that whatever he had to offer, it was not worth risking Ireland's relationship with Germany. Ireland didn't have many cards, but they were stacked against Bewley. Walshe clearly found it difficult to talk about the man without anger. The news that Bewley probably had a Vice Squad file in the offices of the Kriminalpolizei left Walshe with food for thought.

The only question that arose from all the talking was how much to tell the British. That was what was being discussed between Walshe, Archer and Gregory, when Stefan Gillespie left Iveagh House for the last time. If Stefan harboured any doubts about the intimacy of the relationship between Irish Intelligence and British Intelligence, after his stay in London, he heard enough now to make him realise how much further it went. It was the one thing that made Dev's rigorous pursuit of neutrality a kind of performance. Even as Winston Churchill railed against Irish betrayal and de Valera held his hands up in horror at Britain's bullying and cajoling, the British and Irish worked together. It would never be about Ireland declaring war on Germany, but it was still far more than the Germans could be allowed to know. It made neutrality not simply more one-sided than it appeared, it made it a quiet and understated lie.

On the second day, Geróid de Paor was at Iveagh House with Liam Archer, and as Stefan left, so did de Paor. They walked into Stephen's Green.

'You had quite a time in London,' said the G2 man, laughing.

'It wasn't the only funny thing that happened to me,' said Stefan.

'I'd love to have seen you in that cell!'

'I bumped into someone,' Stefan continued.

Commandant de Paor nodded idly, taking out a cigarette.

'Last time we talked about him, he was staying over there—'

'Over where?'

'The Shelbourne. Our friend Owain Jones, the Welshman.'

'I see,' said de Paor quietly.

'You tipped the bastard off, didn't you?'

'I didn't make the phone call,' said de Paor.

'But you wanted him out of Ireland before he talked to me.'

'He was an embarrassment at that stage. MI5 use him as a double agent. He's worth something in that regard. The Germans really think he's their man.'

'I gathered that.'

'But he fucked up here. He did get into the IRA's safe-house system, just about. What they've set up for German agents here. That wasn't so hard, because of his credentials. He is a German agent. He has got access to radio equipment, codes, and he's the point of contact for their agents when they drop them in Britain. That's why they don't last long. But the man's a gobshite.'

'I gathered that, too.'

'He's lucky the IRA didn't get on to him. MI5 set up this fictional Celtic-fringe thing. Welsh, Irish, Breton, Scots, probably even the fucking Cornish and the Manx, all taking on the British Empire. It might be the sort of thing you'd hear Francis Stuart broadcast from Berlin, but no one in the IRA is that daft.'

'And what about Simon McCall and La Mancha?'

'That's as far as he got. Smuggling in a radio and waiting to see if he'd get on to the rest of the safe houses along the way. But after what happened at La Mancha, the only thing to do was to get him out and tell MI5 to keep him out.'

'And the rest?'

'Rest of what?'

'Dessie MacMahon's got good contacts with Dublin bookies.'

'Get him to give me a tip,' laughed the commandant.

'Well, he saw this feller yesterday, and he put a few things I heard from Owain Jones to him. About some heavy losses and some bets being hedged, and a bust-up at the Curragh that I'm sure you remember well enough. I was there.'

'I know,' replied de Paor.

'All those bets, all that hedging, all that fighting between the bookies on the Northside and the Southside, it was all about Owain Jones. They don't know that, but they know someone in the Turf Club was involved in nobbling runners, and my guess is it was Simon McCall. Somehow Jones persuaded him to feed some dope to a few horses, so the favourites dropped down the field. I don't know how he did it. Probably told McCall the money was going to help free Ireland. Money for the Boys! And if Jones couldn't keep that story up, it was too late. On top of everything else I'd say he was blackmailing McCall. One more thing to add to the shite in the old feller's life. All he had left was racing. And he'd fucked that up, too. He was a member of the Turf Club, respected, liked. It was one place he mattered. If it got out, if any of it got out . . .'

'You might not be far from the truth, Stefan.'

'Thanks for that, anyway.'

'But what's it supposed to mean? I lied about Jones. That was my job.'

'Remember the horse?' said Stefan.

Geróid de Paor frowned. He didn't know what Stefan meant.

'La Mancha, the dead horse.'

'I remember the smell.'

'It always bothered me. Why would Henry Casey kill the horse?'

'Spite, stupidity, who knows?'

'He didn't.'

'He didn't kill the horse?'

'No, Simon McCall killed La Mancha.'

'That's the La Mancha he loved more than anything?'

'That's right.'

'Is this still about Owain Jones?'

'No, this is about a man whose life is so fucked that when the only thing that gives him any self-respect is taken away from him, he decides he's had enough. He's failed at everything he's touched. He's been stuck with his mad brother and sister all his life. He's close to bankrupt. Then he's finished in racing if the truth comes out. Maybe he's got gaol waiting. That's what the Battle of Curragh was to him. Doped horses and hedged bets. And I'd say with everything in the papers, and court cases coming, he thought he'd be exposed.'

'I don't know about any of that, Stefan. It was a bookies' brawl.'

'You won't hear it. Bookies' brawl is where it ends. That's what Dessie heard yesterday. A couple of people have been locked up over the fight, but no one's ever going to hear about a Turf Club steward who helped nobble horses.'

'Maybe. You could say, what would be the point?' said de Paor.

'You could say, what if all that flipped Simon McCall and made him top himself? Where would he start? Not with himself. He'd start with the horse. It wouldn't have been around for long. He wouldn't have left it.'

'And then he killed his brother and his sister, Stefan? Oh, and his niece? Is that for the same reason? Or is there another one for that. Nuts, perhaps?'

'Nuts could come into it.' Stefan smiled. 'But as far as the brother and sister went, yes, the same reason. I don't know about Alice. That was different.'

'It was. He beat her to death.'

'Don't you think some of this needs saying, Geróid?'

'I thought this case was over and done with. Casey's been convicted.'

'I was never sure he did it. But I couldn't see any other way to explain it.'

'Well, you've found one. Good luck with it.'

'Is that it?' said Stefan.

'What do you want me to say?' replied de Paor.

'You were involved, Geróid.'

'I'm not involved. I was never involved. But from where I was sitting the killer was Henry Casey. It's what the investigation said. It's what a jury said.'

'And if they'd listened to the rest?'

'You mean IRA safe houses, German spies, a double agent over from England, doping horses and cashing in, and a bookies' war? I can't imagine it would make the slightest bit of difference to the verdict the jury came up with. Henry Casey was lying through his teeth from the beginning. You know that.'

'I know. But if that was just about getting what he could before—'

'Have you tried this on Inspector Harrington? It was his case.'

'He thinks what you think. I wonder, though, if he'd spoken to Jones . . .' Stefan took out a cigarette. He stopped to light it as they emerged from Stephen's Green, just down from the Shelbourne Hotel. De Paor stopped too.

'We weren't only there for the radio. We were there to make sure nothing came out of La Mancha that said anything about how closely you're working with British Intelligence. We were there to protect their man too, weren't we? The man's a double agent, after all. He did fuck up here, and he's not far off a crook over there, I'd say. But he matters, doesn't he? So if any of that, any of Owain Jones's shite and blackmail and cons, had anything to do with what happened to the McCalls, if it pushed Simon over the edge, it can never be said.'

De Paor watched Stefan for a moment. He shook his head.

'I think you're wrong, and I know you're right.'

'What does that mean?'

'It means you're wrong about the murders. It's not that complicated. I've talked to Harrington, too. I've seen enough of Henry Casey. He did it. And you're right nothing else that happened at La Mancha ever happened, not as far as the Guards are concerned, not even as far as we're concerned. Owain Jones was never there. He was never anywhere. We do not even know who he is.'

Stefan Gillespie had come back to Ireland after the night he spent drinking with Owain Jones in London in the belief that there might be something he could do to stop Henry Casey hanging. The information Dessie MacMahon had got out of one of the bookies involved in the Battle of the Curragh had made sense of the Welshman's words. And there were other people who knew something. He remembered the conversation with General Trevor in Kiltegan. He knew that Simon McCall had done something. It was inevitable that other people in the Turf Club knew. But none of it meant anything. None of it would be said. And on the other side, in terms of Owain Jones, none of it could be said. It was doubtful, he knew, that even if all the things that had turned Simon McCall's fragile world upside down, and had finally shattered it, were spoken at an appeal, it would change anything. The idea that a man would kill his brother and sister because he was committing suicide himself would make no sense to anyone. And there was still Alice McCall, beaten and killed. He didn't understand that himself. If there was another story to be told about La Mancha, that still didn't fit. And what else was there? The horse. The horse that had been shot the day before the four McCalls died. Stefan did not believe Casey shot the horse. He had no doubt only McCall himself could have done it. The rest followed. But it only followed in Stefan's head. Henry Casey had been sentenced to death. There was nothing to do. Nothing anyone could do now.

As Stefan stepped through the Palace Street Gate into Dublin Castle and walked down towards the Police Yard, he knew he had little choice but to forget Henry Casey and the deaths at La Mancha. He had spoken about his concerns to Inspector Harrington in Naas, and he had tried to talk to Superintendent Gregory. Harrington had no doubts about the case he'd put together, and since Stefan couldn't tell him most of what he knew, he wasn't about to find any now. Terry Gregory had no interest in the case. He listened, but when Stefan finished he offered him the truth, even more bluntly than Geróid de Paor had done.

'If the fucker's innocent, it's tough shite. Tell him there's a war on.'

It was as those words echoed in Stefan Gillespie's head, and he was walking through the archway into the Police Yard, that a roar of noise filled the air around him. He felt the shock wave. There was glass and wood flying around him as he flung himself to the ground. But it was too late. A piece of shattered wood, thrown up by the force of the explosion, smashed into his head.

26

Neary's

The bomb at Dublin Castle had caused no fatalities, and not even any serious injuries. It had gone off in the records office, which was empty at the time, and it had done more damage to paper than people. Several windows had been blown out, and the damage had extended to the entrance hall. The detectives' room, Terry Gregory's office and the other offices across the hallway from the records office were virtually untouched. A day later the smell of smoke hung over the building, but there had been no fire. Most Special Branch men were back at work. There was a broken arm and a fractured rib keeping two officers who had been in the corridor outside the records office in hospital, and there were several men at home with wounds that had mostly come from flying glass.

Stefan Gillespie and Dessie MacMahon had returned to work the same day. Stefan had a bruise down one side of his face, and his scalp was peppered with small abrasions where splinters of glass and wood had been removed. Work continued, and the work, inevitably, was yet another trawl through the ranks of Republicans not yet interned at the Curragh Camp, but who soon would be.

The IRA had issued a statement to say that the bomb was

in retaliation for the two Volunteers who had been executed in Mountjoy. The statement appeared in no newspapers. Apart from senior Gardaí and government ministers, hardly anyone saw it. The report of the bombing was no more than a few lines in the *Irish Times*, which gave no details and offered no comment. It was treated as a matter of almost no consequence, though Terry Gregory and every man in Special Branch knew that if the bag containing the bomb had been left in the detectives' room, rather than the records office, the results would have been very different. It was clear to every man in the Police Yard that the ease with which the bomb had been brought into Special Branch meant only one thing. It had been brought by a Guard or someone else at the Castle. That was the best interpretation. What was barely voiced, despite the shock, was that one of their own could have done it.

In the detectives' room two builders were replacing the window by the door to the hallway that had been blown out in the blast. Terry Gregory was in his office with Danny Skehan, going through the lists of Republicans and IRA sympathisers who had been brought in that morning. It was a futile exercise as far as the bomb was concerned. These were people who knew nothing.

Stefan Gillespie and Dessie MacMahon had come into the office after spending an hour interrogating a publican who knew nothing, a butcher who knew nothing, a tailor who knew nothing and a librarian who knew nothing.

Dessie took out a Sweet Afton and lit it.

'I'd say the Boys planted the bomb so they could bore us to death.'

Stefan shrugged. What they were doing had nothing to do with investigating the bombing. It was about intimidation. The IRA had scored a hit, however empty the result. Now the Guards had to show it changed nothing.

Danny Skehan came out of Gregory's office, heading for the door.

'Don't bring us any more, Danny!' groaned Dessie.

'Ah, come on, Dessie, you know you love it!'

As Chief Inspector Skehan left, the superintendent walked out of his office, heading towards the door to the entrance hall too. He called Stefan.

'You can come with me, Gillespie.'

Stefan followed Gregory across the entrance hall to the records office. Here the signs of the blast were everywhere. The blackened walls and the piles of paper and files, scorched but still intact. The records officer was on his knees there, gathering up paperwork and trying to put it in some sort of order.

'Are you getting there, Conor?'

'I am, sir.'

'Check it all, see it's all there.'

'I will do my best, sir.'

'Check it and check it again. I want to know if anything's gone.'

'I'm not sure yet, sir. I think maybe a few things.'

'I think so too. If not, why leave the fucking thing here? If you wanted stuff out, and you didn't want anyone to know, blow the place to pieces and no one would be any the wiser. Only it was a fucking IRA bomb. A piece of shite.'

'Is that what it was about?' asked Stefan.

'I don't know what it was about. I don't know if this was what was meant to happen or if it was a mistake, a cock-up. But I do know how it happened.'

There was real anger in Terry Gregory's voice.

'As for why in here: maybe the fucker couldn't quite do it.'

Gregory said the last words very quietly.

'I want to smoke, Gillespie. Come on.'

Stefan followed Superintendent Gregory out of the records office into the Police Yard and through the archway into the Castle grounds. They walked in silence for some minutes before Gregory stopped to light a cigarette.

'I fucked up, Stevie. I fucked up.'

Stefan didn't reply.

'You're on this now. No one else. You understand?'

'Not yet, sir.' Stefan smiled.

'You and me. You're still an outsider. I like to keep you that way.'

They walked on.

'I gave the fucker too much room. Why the hell he used it to do this, fuck only knows. One of the things you can do, when you're on the inside, working for the other side, is just try to sit it out. You give a bit of information here, you take a bit there. You hold something back, you let something out. You give them what you need to give. Never too much. Enough to keep you on the tightrope. It's not easy, but he was doing all right. He was clever enough to keep me looking at all sorts of other people – not at him. But there's always a stupid mistake. It's always like that. It was the diplomatic bag that put me on to him.'

Stefan's eyes were fixed on Gregory.

'You know who I'm talking about?'

'I don't know if I do, sir.'

'It's Danny Skehan.'

Stefan's instinctive response was to shake his head.

'I've known the Boys had a man in the Branch for a year. Danny would have been a long way down my list. He kept it that way. Maybe there were other things. Maybe I'd seen something. But Danny went with the British diplomatic bag every time. And the one time he found a reason not to go, the Boys came in with the Thompsons. Why didn't he stick with it? Maybe if he had, they'd have got the fucking thing. Maybe if he had no one would have been shot. Maybe if he had, no dead Guard, no IRA men hanged in Mountjoy.'

'And the bomb?' said Stefan, still not quite believing all this.

'If he'd played it the way I thought he would, he could have run a long time. Once I knew the IRA man, it had its uses. But I can't let this go, can I?'

'Does he know you're on to him?'

'He'll have a good idea. His gut will tell him.'

'What happens now?'

'Danny has good friends. I can't know how good. So I've taken a course I don't much like. Telling the other bastards about the shite on your shoes is never very comfortable. But I need Danny watched, and not by people he knows. I had to talk to Colonel Archer. De Paor's put some of his fellers on to it. I need to know what he's going to do. I think he's taken files out of the records office. I don't know what that means, but I've known Danny a long time. If the writing's on the wall he won't stay to read it.'

'And what do I do, sir?'

'You liaise with de Paor. It won't be long before Danny spots the G2 men, but maybe long enough to get an idea what he's going to do, who he's taking orders from. The bomb wasn't his decision, I know that. But once he knows he's being watched, riding it out won't be an option. No one was killed, but even if I can't get proof he planted the bomb, he'll end up in Mountjoy or the Curragh. And that'd be his best result, though. If the Boys want to show us they can, Dev'll want to show them they can't. He'll want a hanging for this.'

That evening Stefan Gillespie met Geróid de Paor in the upstairs bar at Neary's in Chatham Street. It was a quiet night; the upstairs bar was closed. They would not be disturbed. They knew Stefan in Neary's; they knew how to keep quiet.

'We lost him,' said de Paor, 'not much point pretending otherwise.'

'I don't think that's going to surprise Terry Gregory, Geróid.'

'No.'

'How long did you get? What did you get?'

'I'd say he wasn't on to us till this afternoon. He spent half the morning in Doheny and Nesbitt. He was talking to people in there, but whether any of them mattered, I don't know. It's not an IRA pub, but you'd get all sorts in there. He did use the phone several times. Three times. Each time he called the German embassy. Mostly he was drinking. A lot of the time he was on his own. But at three o'clock he walked down to Merrion Square. He sat there for half an hour. Then he was joined by Dr Petersen, our friendly German press attaché.'

'And what happened?'

'Apparently, Dr Petersen was very pissed off. He stayed not much more than five minutes. My lieutenant says it wasn't hard to work out what was going on. Petersen told Skehan to fuck off, three or four times, then told him to fuck off again, in case he hadn't got the message, and then he left. Skehan went back to Doheny and Nesbitt and had a few more drinks. He made one phone call. It was to the North. We have the number. You'll want to find out who that was.'

He handed Stefan a piece of paper.

'Where is he now?'

'I think shortly after that he spotted one of my men. I did ring the changes, but I'd say we only got as far as we did because his mind was on other things. I had three men on him, but he gave them the runaround, without a lot of difficulty, via three pubs. I was there myself when we lost him. So, *mea culpa*. But it's blown. Terry needs to bring him in. The man's played out, isn't he?'

When de Paor had gone, Stefan used the telephone in Neary's to call Gregory.

'Geróid's right,' said the superintendent, 'the game's over. He's not going to lead us anywhere we can't go ourselves. And I'd say he's sniffing for a way out. The Germans won't help him with it. You'd think he'd know that. Petersen's been slapped down by his ambassador, very hard. I think his days of playing with the Boys are over. The call to Belfast means he's going around Dublin, I'd guess. They might help him, but by tomorrow he's a liability here.'

'Are you going to pick him up?'

'I can make a guess where he'll be. If he thinks he's shaken off G2, he still can't go home. He can't go anywhere he'll be seen. He knows I'm coming. He's got a bolt hole, a safe house on the corner of Haymarket and Burgess Lane, just off Arran Quay. If he's not there, then I don't know. Eight Haymarket.'

'And he thinks that's still safe?'

'Chances are. I'm the only one who knows.'

Stefan didn't ask how he knew. If the IRA had someone in Special Branch, he knew already that Gregory had someone high up in the IRA.

'Go there now and see if there are any signs of life. If he's there, wait. I'm on my way. If he leaves, follow. You can do better than G2, can't you?'

Stefan left Neary's and walked down Grafton Street to Trinity and the Liffey beyond. He crossed at O'Connell Bridge and walked along the Quays until he reached Burgess Lane. He had not seen the man who was waiting outside Neary's, across the road, on the corner of Balfe Street. He had no reason to think anyone was following him. All the following should have been going the other way. But Danny Skehan didn't see it that way. He did know the game was over, but if he was going to get out, he needed to know what was happening. He needed to work out what Terry Gregory was going to do, so that he could do something unexpected. There was panic in him now, but he still felt there was time for him to find his way out. If he was watching them, he had a chance. Finding help wasn't easy. He wasn't sure who he could trust. He knew Gregory had a man in the IRA. He didn't know where he stood. He was no longer useful. They might decide to help him run or write him off as a sacrifice.

As he followed Stefan Gillespie over O'Connell Bridge, on to the Quays, Danny Skehan suddenly knew where Stefan was going. It wasn't a guess. He simply knew. The safe house was no longer safe. But that was where he had money. That was where he had weapons and ammunition if he needed them. That was where there were false papers and a false passport. If no one was going to help him get out of Ireland, the house held the only things that would. He turned off the Quays as he passed the Four Courts. Stefan was still ahead of him, walking by the side of the Liffey. He ran through the streets that would take him to Smithfield and Haymarket. He had to get to the house before Stefan. He had to get what he needed and get away. Now. If Stefan Gillespie knew about the house, that could only be because Terry Gregory knew too. For the first time he felt he was on his own. Where the fuck he would go, what the fuck he would do, he didn't know. But if he was going to get away, this was it.

Stefan Gillespie turned into Burgess Lane, a short, narrow alleyway that led to Haymarket from the river. The safe house at 8 Haymarket was a disused shop. It had been a grain merchant's. He could see it as he walked slowly along the lane; he could see the corner of a shop window ahead. He was walking past a high wall and the high wooden gates that led into the yard at the back of the shop. The wall was draped with weeds and ivy. There was no lighting in Burgess Lane, but there was a glow of light ahead in Haymarket. All Stefan needed to do was see if there were any signs of life in the shop, or the rooms above. Whether there were or weren't he could only find somewhere across the street to give him cover, and wait for Superintendent Gregory. He did notice that one of the double gates into the shop's backyard was slightly ajar. He did stop. There was nothing to see, nothing to hear. This was a dead place, an empty place. But as he walked forward the gate opened wider. He saw the shadow for only an instant before a pistol butt crashed on to the side of his head, in almost exactly the same place as part of a window frame had smashed into it on the previous day.

27
Haymarket

Danny Skehan dragged Stefan Gillespie along the lane, into the doorway of the shop. Stefan was unconscious; blood oozed from his mouth and the side of his face, where the pistol butt had smashed into him. Skehan unlocked the door and pulled him inside. He took a pair of handcuffs from his pocket, lifted the pliant wrists, and snapped the bracelets shut. It wouldn't be long before Stefan came round. He half-pushed, half-slid the body along the shop floor in the darkness, cursing under his breath. A fucking bomb. What was the point? He'd told them. He'd argued. But in the end he obeyed the order. This was the result. You couldn't do something like that without leaving your scent in the air. The fuckers wanted to push, and this was what they got for it. Did they believe all that bollocks? The Germans are coming. This is our time! Let's get Dev's lackeys on the run! The bomb was a mistake; he had told the bastards.

Pulling the dead weight through to the back of the shop, Danny Skehan pushed Stefan up against a wall, sitting him up. He switched on a dim overhead light. The room was long and narrow, piled with empty boxes and crates. Unsold piles of the Republican newspaper *An Phoblacht*, still tied up, were stacked along the wall. There were blankets and pillows on the floor, along with empty food tins and beer bottles. There were dead cigarette ends everywhere. Skehan reached up to a shelf where there were a few unopened beer bottles. He took one down and knocked the top off on the side of a packing case. He drank most of the contents, and then let the rest dribble down on to Stefan's face, standing over him. Stefan shifted. He opened his eyes, and as he did he screwed his face up in pain. He moved his hands and felt the cuffs.

'How long's Terry been on to me? Is it just since the bomb?'

'How the fuck do I know? He told me to come here, to check the place.'

'All I'm trying to do is get out of this, Stevie,' said Skehan.

'It's a bit late for that.'

'Take your jacket off and drop it on the floor, Danny. Kick it to me.'

The voice came from the back of the storeroom. Danny Skehan turned slowly. He was less surprised than he might have been. Terry Gregory had stepped out from behind a row of high shelves, in the shadows of the room.

Gregory's Webley left Skehan no choice. He pulled off the jacket.

'If you go for the gun, you won't have time to reach it.'

Skehan nodded, kicking the jacket across the floor. There was no sense that he was about to try anything. It was over, that was clearer than anything.

Terry Gregory crouched down to pick up the jacket. Neither his eyes nor the Webley shifted their focus. He put Danny Skehan's gun into his pocket.

'You made a pig's ear of that, Inspector.' He glanced at Stefan.

'I did, sir.'

'This is a man who fooled me, Stevie. You'd want to treat him with a bit of respect.' Gregory's next words were directed at Skehan. 'If you wanted to get out, you shouldn't have come back here. But you'd left all your paperwork so.'

The superintendent moved sideways, to a small table. There were papers and files heaped on it, beside the dirty mug and beer bottles. He shook his head.

'Did you think because the bomb went off in the records office I wouldn't notice you'd cleared these out? Is this what you were trying to interest Mr Petersen in? You think he'd be in the business of getting a man like you out of the country? They can't get their own agents in without getting caught.'

'It was worth a try. Wherever the Boys put me, the chances are you'd find me. I thought I could get out, really get out. But you're right about that. He didn't want to know. I thought I could be useful. I thought if I could bring him something he wanted. I hoped there'd be a way to get out of being locked up.'

'Stick to your own, Danny. Not that the Boys can do much for you.'

'No, not now.'

'I think Mr Petersen's going to cut down on his jollies with the Boys. That was what the diplomatic bag was about, eh? Not much use to the IRA general staff, but German Intelligence wanted to get their hands on it. What might that have told them? All sorts of shenanigans. They might have believed there was someone in the IRA who wasn't a gobshite, a piss-artist or an arsehole. No luck. But you can take these things too far, even in Holy Ireland. I'd say it's been indicated to the German ambassador, politely, that Mr Petersen's a bit of an embarrassment on the neutrality front. He'll be back to telling us Germany's peaceful intentions and complaining to the *Irish Times*.'

'You're well informed, Terry, but times change. They can still change.'

'Then you'll get an Iron Cross and I'll end up interned in the Curragh.'

'It's not about Germany, you know that, Terry.'

'Do I? You'd know better than me. I just have a job to do.'

'Jesus—' A spasm of pain went through Stefan's jaw.

'Look up,' said Gregory.

Stefan turned his face up slowly. It hurt.

'I hope you didn't break his fucking jaw, Danny.'

'He'll be grand,' said Skehan, grinning.

'Fuck you!' grunted Stefan.

'Open your mouth again,' said Superintendent Gregory.

Stefan opened his mouth and Gregory peered down.

'You knocked a fucking tooth out, Danny.'

'Sorry, Stevie.'

'It's no problem, Danny, no problem at all! Ah!'

For a moment longer the superintendent and the chief inspector looked down at Stefan Gillespie, both smiling, as if they were sharing a joke. Then Terry Gregory stepped across to the table. He pulled out a chair and sat down.

'It's a waste, Danny, a shocking waste, after all that good work. It's in our natures, isn't it? Do you ever wonder that? It doesn't matter what we do, how well we do, there's always that Irish moment when we fuck it all up.'

'I should have known you wouldn't send him here on his own.'

'You should have known a lot of things. I thought you did.'

Danny Skehan moved closer to a chair.

'Will I sit down?'

'You may. Take the weight off your feet. You've had a day of it.'

'I've maybe had enough of it so.'

Skehan sat down, across the table from the superintendent.

'Will I get out a fag, Terry?'

Gregory nodded, and as Skehan pulled a pack of Woodbines from his pocket, he put the Webley down on the table. He took a box of matches from his coat and pushed it across the table. Skehan lit a cigarette and held out the pack.

'I will, Danny, thanks.'

The superintendent took a cigarette and lit it. There was a kind of weariness about the man opposite him that was genuine enough now; a kind of relief, alongside the feelings of failure and anger; relief that it was over, that all the lying that was the purpose of his life, that had consumed him, was done.

'Why? Jesus, Danny, why the fuck – what was it for? The bomb?'

Skehan shrugged.

'Weren't you more useful in Dublin Castle than where you'll go now?'

'It wasn't what I wanted,' said Skehan quietly.

'Orders, then.' Gregory smiled. 'A soldier's life, eh?'

'Making a point,' said Skehan.

'Not much of one, eh? And was the diplomatic bag orders, too?'

'There was no reason for anyone to end up dead, Terry. They put a boy in there to drive the car. If it had been down to Johnny Costello, he'd have run—'

'I've every sympathy. What could your man do except kill someone?'

Skehan said nothing. He stubbed out his cigarette and lit another.

'You should have stuck with it, Danny.'

'Stuck with what?'

'You did escort duty on the British bag for two months. You knew it like clockwork and that was information the Boys needed when the time came. It was too cute, Danny, swapping with Dessie MacMahon the day of the snatch. You had that wrong. You thought if you were there, I'd be looking at you sideways. But it was the other way round altogether. When something goes wrong, you don't look at what's the same, you look at what isn't. And the fucking dentist! At least you could have done it for real. Jesus Christ, I'm insulted a man who pulled the wool over my eyes for so long couldn't do better. Or was the lad not the only one who panicked? Did you decide it'd be too uncomfortable if your comrades had to shoot it out? You might have been obliged to shoot one of the bastards. Beating the shite out of them's one thing. That was good, though, the beatings. I have to hand it to you there.'

'Was that all it was, then?' asked Skehan.

'No, not all. It's like any bad smell. Once you get it in your nostrils, you can't get it out. But I thought I'd leave you where you were and see where it led. Sometimes that's a handy thing. The bomb was a surprise, though. Jesus!'

Skehan shrugged; there was nothing he could add.

'You didn't want to do it. You knew it was stupid.'

Skehan shrugged again.

'Is that why you put it where you did?'

'I don't know, Terry. I didn't know what to do with it.'

'If you were going to do it, you should have done it. You could have taken me out and a good few more. I know that. Should I be thanking you?'

'I didn't want to do it. Isn't that enough?'

'So what was the point?'

'To show the country Dev and his cronies can't get away with hanging Volunteers. To show there'll always be a price to pay. To show no one's safe.'

'You know, when Michael Collins had men in Dublin Castle, he kept them there. When he wanted to dispose of British Special Branch men, he used what he had from the Castle to do it, but he left his informers where they were.'

'I did what I was told to do.'

'That's a very soldierly response, Danny. But who told you?'

'You can work that out, I'm sure.'

'As a matter of fact, I can. I can work quite a bit out for myself. There's a bit of a scrap going on at the top now, isn't there? I'd hesitate to say your general staff are at each other's throats, but stranger things have happened.'

'If you know all that, why ask me?'

'It's the Boys in the North, isn't that right? Not happy with the way your chief of staff is running things down here. Because he's doing fuck all. So much fuck all, that you could be tempted to believe fuck all is a plan. But your friends in the North want attacks on the British Army there, and they want Dev taken on down here. Because when the Germans finish off the English, they don't much like the idea of a cunt like Dev being left in charge. They don't like all this neutral bollocks either. There's a fucking war on, and you need to be fighting it. We know who our friends are so, and the word is they are on their way.'

'You always did tell a good tale, Terry. But I'm out of it now.'

'You are so. And I'm sorry.'

'Mountjoy or the Curragh. It could be worse.'

'There is that. I'm not sure some of your comrades are going to take too kindly to the idea that you pulled your punches on the bomb to save your skin.'

'I can live with that. I told them it was a mistake.'

'The question is not what you can live with, Danny, it's what I can.'

'I'll leave you to worry about that.'

'Problem is, I don't know what you know. That's why I wanted to keep you around. I wanted to know what you'd got. I wasn't ready to let you go.'

Terry Gregory brought out a packet of cigarettes. He took one himself and offered one to Danny Skehan. He lit his and then bent to light Skehan's.

'They had you inside. But do you know who I've got inside?'

'Inside where?'

'The IRA general staff.'

'Bollocks, Terry!' Skehan laughed.

'You think I'm joking? Or do you want me to think you think that? I slipped up with you, Danny. I admit it. And I am fucked off. But fair play to you. I know how good you are now. You'll have plenty in your head that you've kept to yourself. There's a lot you won't have told them, whoever you think you're working for. We all protect ourselves. We all need something to give when things get tough. Sometimes we need to prove our worth. Or prove we're not playing both sides. Because sometimes we have to play both sides. But here's the thing, Danny. I don't know what you're carrying away with you.'

Superintendent Gregory looked at the files and papers on the table.

'You knew you were finished, and your first thought was to see what more you could get. Caution to the wind, eh? But how long is that list of names in your head? One day it might be the IRA deciding there's some on that list that need trimming off. One day it might be the feller the Germans give my office to. Comeuppance, that's the stuff to feed the troops. Mother of God, I could even be on the list myself! You see, you never retire in this job, not if you're in it the way we are. Trouble is, you're a victim of your own success.'

The atmosphere had changed in the room. Gregory's tone had altered. The expression on his face was the same. It had remained the same throughout, almost kindly in its understanding. But Skehan had detected the change, and it was the tension that suddenly returned to his body, which had been relaxed through most of this, that alerted Stefan Gillespie. Only then did he feel that Gregory's mood was different too. What had seemed almost idle felt pointed. And yet, if anything, the tone of the superintendent's voice was lighter now.

'And there's the other thing. It's not only the Boys who can feel a little discombobulated by fellers getting away with things. I don't even know what you have got away with. But I do have you down for at least one dead Guard, Jack Daly. There might be others. And I can't have lads walking around like I'm the kind of eejit who'd let any fucker set off a bomb in Special Branch.'

Terry Gregory reached forward and picked up the Webley.

'A spell in Mountjoy won't cut it for me, Danny. I'm sorry.'

Skehan suddenly moved. He pushed the table at Gregory, sending him and the chair he was in flying. At the same time he wrenched a small drawer out of the table, diving to the floor as Terry Gregory fell. And as the superintendent began to stand up, slowly, almost hesitantly, Skehan was already on his feet, and he held a revolver. He raised it and fired. Nothing happened. He pulled the trigger again. There was another click; an empty chamber. Then a shot fired, and a second followed immediately. Danny Skehan collapsed. He was dead. The shots came from Gregory's Webley. The superintendent walked forward and gazed down at Skehan. He didn't need to check he was dead. He squatted down and picked up the dead man's revolver. He broke it. He took six bullets out of his pocket and slotted them into the chamber. He said nothing. When he had finished, he turned round and fired a single shot across the room. He bent over and put the gun gently beside Danny Skehan's body.

As he stood up, he seemed suddenly aware of Stefan again.

'I better get you an ambulance. You'll need patching up.'

'You knew the gun was in the drawer. You emptied it.'

'I knew he'd come here. I came first. Danny was always careful.'

'You might as well have shot him – I mean, just shot him.'

'If he hadn't gone for the gun, I would have done.'

'He knew that.'

'He did. And now you do too. But it looks better this way.'

'So what the fuck am I supposed to say?'

'You lie, Stevie. You know how to do that, don't you? You can find enough truth to make a thorough report. Death deserves a bit of thoroughness. But the real truth is no one needs the truth. So it doesn't matter. No one gives a fuck, apart from his wife and his kids, and his dear old sainted mammy. I knew Danny a long time. Did I ever tell you I was his best man? But times change.'

Terry Gregory turned away. He looked down at the dead man again, for a long moment. Stefan thought his lips were moving. It could have been a prayer; it could have been nothing. Then the superintendent walked out. Stefan pushed back against the wall, grimacing as the pain in his hip bit harder. He looked across the room, past the overturned table and the chairs, at Danny Skehan and the revolver beside him. He knew Terry Gregory was right. He knew that no one would want to hear the truth of what had happened. He knew he would lie.

28
Moatamoy

When Stefan Gillespie left the flat on Wellington Quay, on his way home to Baltinglass for the weekend, he looked in at Paddy Geary's tobacconist's next door, to collect his post. There was a letter box in the door that led up to the three floors of rooms the tobacconist let out, but the postman always left the letters for Paddy's tenants in the shop. Paddy felt it was safer that way; it meant nothing could go astray, especially for a tenant like Stefan, who wasn't always there. It was part of the service. It also meant that the round and red-faced tobacconist could keep an eye on his tenants' comings and goings; that was part of the service, too. On this morning, as on most mornings, Paddy Geary was leaning in the doorway of his shop, looking out across the Liffey and up and down the Quays. It was how he spent most of his days, idly greeting people he knew and didn't know, and occasionally exchanging news and gossip. Having scanned the newspapers when they were delivered in the early hours of every morning, Paddy was as happy to pass on the headlines as he was to sell a paper.

'Lot of bombs on London last night.'

Stefan nodded, following Paddy Geary into the shop.

'They say there's so many bodies, they have to get rid of them at night, so no one sees. They take them up the Thames on barges and dump them at sea.'

Paddy crossed himself.

'Where was that, Paddy, *Irish Times* or the *Indo*?'

'You won't see that in a paper, Stevie. A feller told me.'

'Did he so?'

'He did. He's a brother who's a fireman in London, and he knows the feller who sails one of the barges. Thousands of the poor fuckers. Piled high.'

The tobacconist shook his head grimly and handed Stefan a letter.

'She wants to get out of there. You want to tell her.'

Stefan gave a questioning look. Paddy pointed at the letter.

'Your woman.'

Stefan smiled. Paddy always knew who wrote to his tenants.

'I'll tell her.'

'You should. It'll get worse before it gets better.'

On the train to Baltinglass, Stefan opened the letter from Kate. He had shoved away recent events as far as he could. Shoving things away was all he could do. Most Special Branch detectives called it, 'not talking shop'. It was an easy way to describe lying. And the only answer to that, such as it was, was for Stefan to put the same barricades up inside himself that he put up between himself and the people he cared about. He couldn't change where he was. He couldn't even walk away. For now, all he wanted to do was to be home again. To be away from Dublin. To be away from the clutter of deceit that was still piling up inside him. It wasn't all his, of course, but some of it was, and it all sat in the same untidy heap in his head, so that what was his and what wasn't didn't seem to signify. The weight of it was there. The debris was there. It wasn't only him. Everyone was after carrying the debris of something around with them. There was bomb damage whether bombs were dropping or not. A lie about one act of betrayal was no different to a lie about another, whether it happened in Dublin Castle or a hotel room in Berlin. But the smell of Berlin was still in his head. It made it no easier for him to face himself now, and to rid himself of that smell. Even the one moment of light he found there had been in an act of betrayal: when he and Zandra Purcell reached out and touched one another, only, truthfully, because they needed to push aside the dark. It was no more than that; yet that wasn't nothing. But maybe Berlin was just how the world smelt now, all of it, London, too, Dublin, everywhere, anywhere. And there was nothing anyone could do about it. Now it made him want to taste clean air. It made him want the small patch of green fields and scruffy woodland that lay below the three mountains he had grown up with: Keadeen, Kilranelagh, Baltinglass Hill.

He sat with the letter in his hand for several minutes before he read it. It was a letter; she wasn't there. But he still felt the awkwardness he hadn't yet got rid of. It was as if she was sitting opposite him, and all he could think about, as he looked into her eyes, was the lie he was telling her, by not telling her the truth.

The letter was not what he expected, and yet, perhaps it was. As he read it he knew there was something inevitable about his lies, the lies she knew were part of his job, the lie she knew nothing about, compelling her to tell the truth.

Dear Stefan,

I started writing a letter that said all the usual guff, then I felt I had to say more. Because things aren't right. I don't know why. My grandmother always said she was never convinced absence did make the heart grow fonder, though she never told us why! A family secret there, I'll bet! But I'm not sure it is only absence with us. I'm not sure it's even us. I was very uncomfortable last time I was home, not over a stupid row with someone with too much drink taken, but because, well, I suppose, even after a few months, I have become a part of this, here, being here in London. It's not that I feel I belong here. I don't think I do. I get very bloody Irish about a lot of things, whatever that means! But I do feel out of place at home suddenly. Still, home isn't what I am thinking about.

It seems, in the little time we get together now, we're not close, in a way I can't pin down. I love you. I know I love you, but sometimes, when I'm with you, there is another kind of absence. Maybe it's just that nothing about your life is open or feels real. That's how it seems. I don't want to know what you do all day, but every conversation is about avoiding it, knowing your mind is still stuck in it half the time. It's hard talking to you. If I'm not talking about what I'm doing, it's as if we're making small talk out of nothing, about nothing. Once I thought, I've had easier conversations with a stranger, down the Underground, during an air raid! Well, not quite, but not far off. You can be very far away, Stefan, and more when we're together than when we're writing to each other.

However much I love you, sometimes it's easier being with other people, talking about what we're all doing. No great emotions, just, I don't know, fun. It sounds awful, but it's not about how much I care. The mess in London, never mind the fight – and I am 'Kate with a German spy for a boyfriend', a permanent joke now! – I mean the man I went to the pictures with. I explained it didn't mean anything. I know he had a crush on me, but he was young, almost a boy. Just part of a gang of friends. He was nice, and it was no more than a pub chat or a movie. He kissed me. It lasted a couple of seconds. Yes, I let it last for those couple of seconds.

Should I have pushed him off, slapped his face? I didn't want him to kiss me. I stopped him. It didn't matter. Perhaps it mattered to him. He was killed a few days later. His plane was shot up over

Germany. When it landed he was dead. Helen and I went down to Worthing for his funeral.

I shouldn't say this, but I will. In the church, looking at his coffin, what went through my mind was: would it have mattered? If something had happened? It wouldn't have changed anything I felt about you. If we married and had a house full of kids and grew old and crotchety together, and lived a long, ordinary, happy life, would it have mattered? It's not that I wanted to. It never crossed my mind. But he's dead, and I could have let him kiss me a bit longer without turning my life on end, or changing my love for you. A woman can't say that! And because such a thing would never find its way into your head, it says something terrible about me. I don't know why I told you. I wanted to say something real.

I know I love you. I think you love me. But there's a distance between us that I don't understand. There's something that holds you back with me, still, wherever it comes from. That's the only way I can put it. I don't know where you are, inside. I don't know if you do. The life you're leading isn't you, I know that. It won't let you be you. I don't know what all that means, but we need to find out what we want, both of us, and somehow there's a whole war in the way, in Ireland as well as here. Maybe it won't let either of us be ourselves. Let's not expect too much of each other, Stefan. We are apart. That's one true thing. We have to see where that leads. I don't know what I'm saying. I do love you very much.

Stefan Gillespie walked from the station in Baltinglass, through the town and out through the townlands of Newtownsaunders and Woodfield Glen, and up to the farm below Kilranelagh. In Baltinglass the brief words he exchanged with people he met were about families, and the price of cattle and sheep, and last month's funerals, and the weather, and the new butcher's shop Mr Patterson had just opened, with barely a nod to the war. It was there, somewhere, but no one felt it was a more important thing to talk about than the ordinary stuff of life. He didn't know where the letter from Kate left them, only that what was wrong was in him, not in her. Yet she was right, too, that what was wrong was a part of what was going on all round them. It wasn't any different for millions of people, whether they were fighting a war or not. The war was there. Terry Gregory had said as much, months before, when he told Stefan that if he didn't like working in Special Branch, he'd better find a way of liking it. There was no option to walk away. The bollocks of war was a game for everyone, even in a neutral country. The only rule was that you couldn't leave the field until you were carried off. And Stefan had seen a few carried off in the last month. There was no more an exit for him than there was for a soldier in any of the armies throwing themselves at each other all across the world. It was the shite you were in, and it was the shite you had to stay in, until it was all over. That was where Stefan was; in a different way it was where Kate was too. She was right. They had to see where it took them; when the time came, where it left them. There wasn't an answer, except to hold on to each other, in whatever way helped them survive. It wasn't much, but it was something. And as Stefan walked up the hill towards the farm, with the high ditches on both sides of the road, and the gates looking into the fields he had known all his life, and the woods below, on either side, he breathed in something of the air of who he still was. He knew they would try to hold on. And it had to be enough for now. It was all they could do.

The atmosphere at Kilranelagh was more sombre than Stefan had expected. He didn't know why, though he could see it came mostly from Tom. Something was upsetting him, and no one was keen to talk about it. It was only when he asked about Tess, the sheepdog, and he saw the quiet smile from his father and the tears now welling up in his son's eyes, that he understood what was wrong. The new puppy, Jumble, had been shut away. Stefan had heard her whining as he walked through the farmyard. It was not often that the dogs were shut away.

'Is she not good, then?' he said.

'I'm glad you're here,' replied his father. 'She'd want it to be you.'

Tom moved close to his father, and Stefan put his arm round him.

'Opa said we should wait for you,' he said through his tears.

'It's her time,' said Helena quietly, not turning from the stove.

In the corner of the barn, where Tess had slept all her life, she lay stretched out, breathing slowly, with a low rasp in her throat. Her eyes were half closed, but as Stefan knelt down beside her she opened them. Her tail lifted and fell several times, and then stopped. Her eyes closed again. She seemed to give a long sigh.

'I'd have had to do it, if you hadn't come today. She's had enough.'

Stefan nodded as David Gillespie spoke, stroking Tess's head slowly.

'Dogs always have one person, just one,' said David.

Stefan put his arms under Tess and picked her up. She had never been heavy. She wasn't big even as collies went, but he felt the lightness now; she was only bones. He carried her out into the yard and through to the field beyond the pigsty. He laid her down, and as he bent over her, he leant his cheek against her muzzle for a moment, breathing in the familiar animal smell of her. Then he got up and took the rifle his father was carrying. He put the barrel to her head.

A little later, Stefan and Tom walked down through the farm to the mound at the western boundary that was called, for reasons no one quite knew, Moatamoy. A thousand years ago it had been the motte of a settlement of Normans – the fortified hill they retreated to when the Irish came down from the mountains in a less than friendly mood. Now it was covered in trees and scrubby vegetation: hazel, blackthorn, brambles, gorse. It rose high over the steep, narrow valley that formed the western edge of the townland that made up most of the farm, and it had a long view down to Woodfield Glen and the outskirts of Baltinglass. When work was done on the farm, and there was still a long summer evening ahead, it was the place Stefan walked to, and Tess would always come. There was nothing very much to see; the view was unspectacular. It was simply where the farm ended. A place to sit for a while before turning back home. And Stefan had sat on the top of Moatamoy with Tess more times than he could remember. She was twelve, and though he had been away much of that time, as he was now, she was always there when he came back. She was almost the first thing he saw when he walked into the farmyard, hurling herself at him across the cobbles in a frenzy of excitement. She was part of what made home; that within minutes of being back, it was as if you had never been away.

Stefan had dug a hole at the top of the mound, where he used to sit with Tess. Tom had helped him dig it. And now she lay there, below them, and they shovelled the earth over her, saying nothing. Tom's tears had stopped. They had been as much for his father as for Tess, and he had soon felt what his father and his grandfather and his grandmother felt. A friend had gone. There was nothing sentimental in acknowledging that. She was gone and Kilranelagh had been her place too. Stefan said a prayer, because Tom expected a prayer, but the words that came into his head, and made him smile, were not a prayer, but something else altogether. 'What larks, Pip!' And finally, when it was done, father and son walked through the fields, back towards Kilranelagh, and started to laugh again.

For Stefan, there was something about what had happened that made him easier with himself. He felt it now; another, cleaner breath of air. Putting Tess down and burying her was the most honest thing he had done in a long time.

Afterword

Henry Aloysius Casey (43), of Dunlavin, Co. Wicklow, was hanged in Mountjoy Prison, Dublin, on 3 November, for the murder of Simon McCall, Patrick McCall, Anne McCall and Alice McCall, at La Mancha, Gormanstown, Co. Kildare. Pierrepoint was the executioner. Dr Louis A. Byrne, sitting with a jury, held an inquest in the prison mortuary. A verdict was returned in accordance with the evidence of Dr B. J. Hackett, Mountjoy Prison, who said that death was instantaneous.

Irish Times

29

The Hanging Cell

Dublin, November 1940

Albert Pierrepoint took a taxi into Dublin from the harbour at Dún Laoghaire and asked it to stop outside the Rotunda Hospital. He then walked, by a slow and circuitous route that took in O'Connell Street and Abbey Street, and a number of side streets, to Capel Street, where he was staying in a small, private hotel. As usual, it was a hotel he had never used before, and would not use again. He had travelled from England overnight, under an alias provided by the British government, as he always did on his occasional visits to Ireland. He had asked for no one to meet him, and he never availed himself of the Special Branch protection that was offered to him. Bluntly, he did not trust the Irish police and their connections with those who might have a particular interest in killing him. He preferred to trust his security to his anonymity, as he did in Britain. He spent most of the day in his room, apart from a walk across the river to eat a late lunch at Bewley's Café, which he liked because it was always busy, and no one stopped to take any notice of who came and went. That evening he took a taxi to the Mater Hospital and he walked from there to Mountjoy Prison, where he was expected. He encountered only three senior prison guards as he was taken to meet the governor. That was the way he asked for it to be. The conversation with the governor was short and avoided pleasantries, before he was escorted to the room next to the condemned cell, where a hidden opening allowed him to see the man he was to hang. He needed to judge his height and weight, so that he could make his calculations regarding the drop. He preferred his own eyesight to the Home Office charts that provided this information, and somewhere in his head, he felt that it was only right that there was a personal, if unseen, moment of contact between the hangman and the man to be hanged. It was, in an odd way, a matter of respect. He was in the gaol no more than fifty minutes, most of which was spent on his own, checking and testing the gallows for the next day. When he was satisfied, he left and returned to his hotel, walking all the way into Dublin. He had no doubts about the job he did; it was a necessary one and he did it with a professional regard that was entirely directed towards the men he hanged. However, he did prefer to avoid contact or communication with people when he was about to perform an execution, and not simply because of the anonymity he fostered so carefully. As far as possible, he tried to keep conversation to a minimum. The business of hanging was between only two people. He was very conscious of that. There were few things more intimate, though it lasted so short a time.

The next morning, just before five o'clock, a taxi arrived at the hotel in Capel Street to take him back to the Mater Hospital; from there he walked to Mountjoy again. He was at the gallows, in the hanging cell, when Henry Casey arrived. Casey said nothing and looked at no one, except for barely a second, as the hood was put over his head, when his eyes met Albert Pierrepoint's. Most men, in Pierrepoint's experience, went to their deaths quietly. There were those who screamed, and cried, and struggled, but most maintained a stoical, or at least still, demeanour, which had never ceased to surprise him; it was something between dignified acceptance and a silence born of drained emotion and numbing confusion. Fear was there, but it was rarely the thing that showed.

The walk to the gallows and the speed of the hanging left almost no space. By six o'clock Henry Casey was dead. A car took Albert Pierrepoint back to Dún Laoghaire. Shortly afterwards he left Ireland.

30

Dunlavin Green

West Wicklow, September 1940

In the church of St Nicholas of Myra in Dunlavin, Simon McCall knelt in the enclosed darkness of the confessional, his hands clasped in front of him in a position of prayer that he had not adopted since his childhood. He was a regular visitor to confession; he had been all his life; yet until recently he had treated it in a way that was more relaxed. It wasn't that he was unserious. When things were wrong, as they very often had been, the Church was a place of refuge, a place not to confront what was wrong but to find the hope that was in the Mass. His sins had never been great ones. The burdens he carried, in the shape of his brother and sister, he carried generously and for the most part cheerfully. Those burdens had shaped his life, certainly, and they had closed it in; without them he might have lived a different life. Sometimes he imagined what that life would have been. There was a wife, who had a name, though there had never been a woman, even in his youth, to inspire the imaginary spouse. At one time there had been imaginary children. Two boys and a girl, just as once they had been two boys and a girl – Simon, Patrick and Annie – before anyone knew that anything was wrong. The imaginary children had names once. They came to him as he spoke through the latticed grille to the parish priest. He was aware that he wasn't listening to the priest, and that his own words were coming out by rote. He was thinking about a place he had never been, a beach in Cornwall he had read about in a story. He had once imagined a holiday there, with the wife and the children he didn't have. The children were playing on the beach, and he felt sorry, not because they weren't real, but because it was as if they were, and he had lost touch with them.

'Are you all right, Simon?' said Father Clinton. It was six weeks since Simon McCall had been to confession. The priest was conscious something wasn't right. McCall was always talkative once the preliminaries were over and a few venial sins disposed of.

'No bother, Father.'

'And Annie and Patrick?'

'Ah, you know how it is.'

'And Alice?' Father Clinton asked the question, as ever, with no indication that he knew who she was, though he was well aware she was Annie McCall's daughter. He never put her in the same sentence as his other enquiries.

'She's grand.'

'Did you have a good day at the Curragh?'

There was no answer. It was odd. Horses were what the old man liked to talk about, and even in the confessional he normally had something to say: a story to tell, a race to describe, even a tip to give. Now he said nothing at all.

'I was going to go myself, but I'd a funeral up in Donard.'

'You didn't miss a lot, Father.'

The priest could feel that this was the end of the conversation.

'I heard about the fighting, and decent people afraid for their lives!'

But even what was the talk of the whole country got no response.

'I may call in one evening, Simon. It's a while since I was there.'

Simon McCall's next words were the words that would conclude his confession; the act of contrition the priest had not yet asked him to speak.

'O my God, I am heartily sorry for having offended Thee. I detest all my sins because I dread the loss of heaven and the pains of hell, but most of all because they offend Thee, my God, who art all good and deserving of all my love. I firmly resolve, with the help of Thy grace, to do penance. Amen.'

There were words missing; McCall made no promise to amend his life. It was nothing Father Clinton noticed. He was slightly irritated, when he always gave Simon so much time, that he seemed to be rushing to get away.

Words of absolution and forgiveness followed, as the confession ended.

'Passio Domini nostri Jesu Christi, merita Beatae Mariae Virginis . . .' May the Passion of our Lord Jesus Christ, and the merits of the Blessed Virgin Mary and all the saints, the good thou hast done and the ill thou hast endured, profit thee unto the remission of sin, increase in grace, and reward in eternity.

Simon McCall left the church, conscious that he had said nothing that mattered. He didn't know why he had gone. Since he had said nothing, since he had spoken none of his sins, since he had not confessed what he was about to do, all the forgiveness he carried away was worthless. To say nothing that was in your heart in the confessional was not merely to avoid the truth, it was to lie, and to lie while partaking of a sacrament. To have gone was worse than not going. Yet it was all he had left, the hope that God would hear the lie and understand the truth. He tried to give shape to that thought as he walked across Dunlavin Green to Kevin Deale's taxi, which had brought him from La Mancha.

He sat in the back of the taxi and said as little as he could. He looked back at the Green. He looked out at the wide street and the familiar shops and pubs. He looked at the courthouse and the last houses in the town. The place had never meant very much to him, but it had meant something. That was true of most things in his life. Now he simply registered that he would not see it again. He heard none of the driver's complaints about the shortage of tea at Molyneux's and the hoarding of petrol in Dublin; he heard nothing of fighter losses over Britain and the bombs falling in Berlin; or the next race meeting at Listowel, where Kevin's cousin had a horse running the following week; or the German forces massing on the other side of the English Channel and the parachutists to be landed in the Phoenix Park at night, who might be German or might be English, but would be coming any time; or the news that half of London was now living in the Underground.

He entered La Mancha through the back door, passing the archway to the stable yard. The horse had gone. That was done. Now the rest had to be done.

When Simon McCall got to the back door, he was startled to find it unlocked. He had locked everything as he left. He was sure. At least he thought he had. But the doors were rarely locked at La Mancha, even at night; it wasn't easy to think, let alone remember. His heart was beating faster as he approached the kitchen. If someone was in the house, if Henry had come. He had told him to take the weekend off. And Alice had gone to Dublin to stay with her friend. She would not come back until Monday, and then it would all be done. There was no one else who could be there. But as he opened the door to the kitchen, it was Alice. She had come back. He stared at her, uncomprehending. She had just come in; she still wore her coat. She was anxious.

'I came back, sir. I had to come back.'

'I said . . . I said you could have till Monday—'

'You can't leave them, Mr McCall!'

'What?' He looked at her in bewilderment. 'What are you talking about?'

'They've been sick for days. It's not right. We have to do something.'

'They're in bed, Alice. It's a bug. They have a bug—'

'I've been upstairs. I can't wake them up properly. They open their eyes but . . . I asked you to call the doctor, sir. You said you would if they got worse.'

'I will call the doctor. I'll go in tomorrow. First thing.'

'No, Mr McCall. I'll go now. I don't know what's happening!'

'They're ill, that's all, Alice.'

'They're dying, can't you see?'

She was crying. He said nothing.

'This isn't right. You know it isn't. I have to go, now!'

He stood between her and the door.

'It's too late, Alice.'

'What do you mean, too late?'

'I can't explain, I can't . . . Jesus, why did you come back?'

'What have you done to them?' She spoke quietly, looking at him hard. She had no comprehension of what was happening, but she realised this wasn't about some sickness or some accident. He knew. And she had been sent away because of it. He knew they were dying. She could see it in his face. He knew.

'I'm going for the doctor. Please, let me go.'

He didn't move. He shook his head, sobbing.

'It will be over soon. It will be, Alice—'

'This is madness, Mr McCall. I have to get them some help!'

She turned towards the door to the hall, but before she could reach it he grabbed her from behind, pulling her back. She tried to push him off, but he had his arm round her neck. She tried to hit out, but he held her tighter. Whether it was anger or despair, he had found an unexpected strength. She was struggling to break away. She tried to turn, to hit him, but as she did she fell. Then they were on the floor, her arms were flailing. Desperately she hit back, then he pushed her hard. She fell again, knocking over the fire irons on the hearth of the kitchen fire. He stood over her, gasping for breath. His face was bloody where her nails had scratched him. He was crying incoherently.

'Too late . . . you can't . . . I can't tell you . . . but this is . . . it has to . . .'

She was backing away, half-crawling, half-sliding. Her hand touched something. It was a heavy poker. She held it behind her. He moved towards her.

'You have to know . . . it is for the best, Alice. I won't hurt you—'

She stepped forward suddenly and struck out with the poker.

'You're mad, you're fucking mad!'

He saw the blow coming. It was too slow, too weak. His hand shot up and grabbed her wrist. He wrenched the poker out of her hand. She screamed at him.

'Get out of my way! Let me go!'

She gathered her strength and charged towards him.

'You can't go!' he screamed. 'You can't!'

And now he was the one who hit out with the poker. He struck her head hard, and she fell, back towards the fireplace, knocking over a scuttle and a footstool and a newspaper rack, and hitting the stone hearth with her head.

She didn't move.

He stepped forward and looked down at her. He was shaking.

'Alice, will you listen while I tell you . . .'

The words were quiet, almost tender.

'It has to be this way, Alice. It is the only way.'

He bent down beside her. He saw immediately that she was dead. He saw the blood on her temple, and he saw the blood on the sharp corner of the hearth. He had returned to La Mancha, believing it was all over, that beside what he had to do, nothing worse could happen. He had believed that all the unpalatable things that filled up his life could be left behind; all the old burdens, all the new failures and mistakes that made continuing impossible. The end had come, and the end would be manageable, because there was no hope to abandon. Yet there had been a hope. One small hope to leave behind, spoken to no one. Alice didn't know her ordinary life was that hope. And now he had destroyed it.

As he looked down at her, he felt he should have known. There was a price; he should have known it would be high. Yet there was no other way. He was finished. There were truths that would come out, once it started, that would destroy him. There could be prison. The house would go. And how would Annie and Patrick live? An asylum at best; locked away. He had carried them through life; he had no choice but to carry them beyond it. And what else would come out? The truth about Alice? The father who had been Annie's brother, Patrick. He had protected them; he had made them forget it. But he never had.

It was still a sin beyond sinning. And God's judgement wasn't like other judgement. There was no legislation for it; no time or place. And it had started. It had come now, even before they were dead. Because Alice was dead. She was to be all that was left of them; left to lead the life of ordinary fulfilments the three of them had been denied. She was young enough to find it. He had tried to ensure she could. He had left her what there was to have out of La Mancha. It would have been something, enough; enough to leave La Mancha behind.

He let her head lie back on the carpet, and stroked her hair. He didn't know if she ever understood who he was, that he was her uncle, that Annie had been her mother. People knew; but it was never spoken of at the house. Such secrets were kept in plain sight. She addressed him as Mr McCall to the last.

He took an envelope from his pocket. He shook the arsenic on to his hand and funnelled it into his mouth. A glass of water pushed the poison down. Annie and Patrick were in bed. They had been barely conscious when he went into Dunlavin earlier; they would be weaker now. He didn't know how long it would be before the poison killed him, but he had time. He had given only small amounts to the other two, hoping they would seem to die naturally, but it had taken too long. He knew that with what he had taken, it would be short. He started up the stairs, last to bed, as he always was. He would smother his brother and sister first, then change into his pyjamas and go to bed himself. He had thought of it as going to sleep for a long time. They were all going to sleep.

Notes and Acknowledgements

The real La Mancha murders took place in Ireland in 1926, at a house in Malahide, north of Dublin, not in West Wicklow, in circumstances close to the version told in this story. Six people died in Malahide: two brothers and two sisters of the McDonnell family, and their two servants. Henry McCabe, their gardener, was hanged for the crime, which contained the same elements of madness, isolation, violence and arsenic, and an attempt to destroy evidence by burning the house. No one ever doubted McCabe's guilt, but the deaths remain peculiarly unlike other murders; there is still an ill-fit between the nature of the killings and what we know of the mind of the supposed killer. None of that says that McCabe wasn't guilty, but there is something uniquely haunting and unexplained about what happened. My main source was Kenneth Deale's *Memorable Irish Trials*. The Battle of the Curragh actually took place at Baldoyle Racecourse (no longer in existence) in 1942, when Southside and Northside gangs from Dublin fought a proxy battle on behalf of several disgruntled bookies. The double agent, Owain Jones, is loosely based on Arthur Owens, who did great service to the British war effort, despite being as two-faced, unreliable and unscrupulous as his fictional counterpart, and quite as much of a drunk. It was only the threat of hanging as a German spy that kept him onside. Zandra Purcell is inspired by Zandra Mitchell, an Irish saxophone player who led her own all-girl band, the Queens of Jazz, in Weimar Berlin, and did manage to survive the war in the city. Charlie's Orchestra did broadcast parodies of popular songs and jazz standards from Germany. Francis Stuart, Charles Bewley and Frank Ryan were Irishmen living in Berlin through much of the war, more or less in the roles they have in this book; Bewley eventually fell out of favour with the Reich Propaganda Ministry and moved to Rome. Helmut Clissman was a German Hibernophile who probably did help maintain the 'softer' Abwehr and Foreign Ministry approach to Ireland, against the harsher intentions of Nazi-dominated agencies. Throughout this period William Warnock's dispatches from the Berlin legation were constrained by knowledge that Irish codes were being read by both belligerents. The IRA attempt to snatch the British diplomatic bag and the bomb at Dublin Castle are real events, though aspects of both incidents have been conflated. I should mention the following books, which gave me a very particular insight into life in the Third Reich during the war. Bryan Mark Rigg's *Hitler's Jewish Soldiers* catalogues in meticulous detail the way some Jews and *Mischlinge* survived (and didn't survive) inside the German military. *War, Pacification, and Mass Murder, 1939: The Einsatzgruppen in Poland* by Matthäus, Böhler and Mallman is in part a collection of contemporary documents recounting the activities of the death squads that followed the German Army into Poland in 1939 – these include some of the 'trophy' photos German police and soldiers took. There are clear signs here that this was a lot more than a series of one-off containment operations. It was already evolving; its purpose was as much about finding out how to kill large numbers of civilians as eliminating influential Poles. As always, in walking the streets of Emergency Dublin with Stefan Gillespie, I have two incomparable guides: *Thoms Directory* and the *Irish Times* archive.

For more information about the real history behind *The City of Lies*, go to:

michaelrussellforgottencities.com